THE REDOUBTABLE PALI AVRAMAPUL

THE REDOUBTABLE PALI AVRAMAPUL

VICTORIA GODDARD

Copyright © 2022 by Victoria Goddard

All rights reserved.

No part of this book may be reproduced in any form or by any electronic or mechanical means, including information storage and retrieval systems, without written permission from the author, except for the use of brief quotations in a book review.

For my sisters, Nichola and Kate

CHAPTER ONE
FACULTY MEETINGS

The Senior Common Room of Freeman College at the University of Stoneybridge in Chare smelled of dust and chalk and old, dry sherry, the sort of fug that got into the back of one's throat and coated one's tongue. A fly buzzed against the window behind the Dean, who was speaking.

Pali Avramapul of the Red Company, one of the most notorious folk heroes and wanted criminals in the entirety of the former Empire of Astandalas, and current tenured Professor of Late Astandalan History, eyed the fly meditatively. Her hand twitched.

Around the long oval table were two dozen men and women, each of them dressed in the brilliantly coloured antique formal garb of a Scholar of their colleges. Maroon and mauve, royal blue and imperial purple, green and grey, silver and white, orange and bronze, and Pali's own sable lined with scarlet.

As each of the Scholars shifted minutely, the rustling of the stiff brocades and heavy wools formed a soft, sleepy susurrus under the Dean's drone. Pali sat with strictly upright posture, irritated with the too-tall seats. Freeman was a men's college, and the chairs had not been intended for someone of her diminutive height.

Her pen scratched across her notebook, making desultory notes about the likelihood of even lower student enrollment this coming term as a consequence of the troubles in the northeast of the continent.

Pali enjoyed teaching, and enjoyed the relentless pursuit of understanding even more, but dear gods of her far-distant desert, there were aspects of being a faculty member that drove her up the wall. When there were rumours of war no more than the next country over—

She stifled a sigh. There had long been restlessness to the south, in the dozens of squabbling baronies and free cities and petty kingdoms between the southern border of Chare, the river Ouzen, and the mountain country that had never quite been conquered by Astandalas in the years before its cataclysmic collapse. Pali could have gone seeking adventure any day she pleased.

She hadn't yet pleased. She enjoyed her place, her scholarship, her students, her life.

Mostly.

It was earliest spring. The snow geese had started to pass overhead on their way to the mysterious north. Pali could never quite find it in herself to be happy when the wind was full of their cries.

Was happy the word? She pondered, doodling a little sketch of a goose on the edge of her page. There was a word in her own language, *dzēren*, which meant happy, and also joyful, and also joyous, and also ... It was hard to translate. It had connotations of tranquility, of calm, of peace.

Brimful was the best literal translation Pali had ever come up with. Brimful of joy, of happiness, of burgeoning peace, like a goblet of water overflowing, a spring rising up into an oasis. Something restorative, reflective, gentle. Quiet.

Pali looked up at the Dean, who had just begun to turn his head towards her, and met his gaze frankly, attentively, alertly. He nodded, cleared his throat with a long ratcheting sort of a cough, groped for water from his glass, and then continued on.

Her tenure at Stoneybridge was the closest Pali had ever come to dzēren, to the *brimful*. Certainly she had never managed it at home. She had never been gentle. It was, she thought, boring. Life was so much better with someone to fight. Here there were her colleagues to debate, her students to instruct, her own opinions and hypotheses to test and reshape and defend.

That was joy. There were few things Pali loved more than a just fight.

Her right-hand neighbour reached to the water carafe set before them. Professor Vane's bright mauve sleeve was astonishing every time Pali glimpsed it, her pale-skinned hand a seeming afterthought. Pali admired her friend's finely buffed nails, one of the other professor's little vanities. Professor Vane poured herself water, the soft *glug-glug-glug* making Professor Hillcrest, across the table, startle awake from his near-doze. He caught the motion, frowned drowsily at the water, and settled again.

Professor Vane slid a piece of paper towards Pali as she returned the carafe to its trivet. It was a movement well-rehearsed and better-practiced. The Faculty of History of the University of Stoneybridge conducted what everyone but for the Dean considered an excessive frequency and duration of faculty meetings.

Pali's eyes dropped down to the paper.

No spitballing

She never had been very good at keeping her expression blank. She ducked her head to examine the nib of her new fountain pen, a present from her favourite student upon his graduation the previous spring, and made a note in the book she ostensibly used for Faculty Meeting notes. She was not the recording secretary, but everyone knew if you wanted the salient points, you went to Professor Black. It was always good practice, she felt, to notice things.

For instance: Professor Vane was bored, and Professor Black, otherwise known as Pali Avramapul, was about to crawl out of her skin in frustration.

She wanted—oh, she wanted to have an *adventure*.

The geese were crying in the dark before dawn, when she walked through the chill air to the stables. Pali could hardly bear this *quiet*.

She would never be *brimful*, not of peace.

She made a note about reduced funding, again, for out-of-country symposia, and scrawled a response to her neighbour.

Not even the fly?

Professor Vane, who had exchanged notes with Pali for the past five years of their shared tenure at the university, considered this sally before making her reply.

Can you hit it?

Pali considered the distance, the half-slumbering audience, the Dean, and her own openly acknowledged skills.

It was known that she fenced at a salle in the town three or four days a week, and that she kept a riding horse at a stable at the edge of the university campus, which she rode daily. She occasionally assisted the university falconer with his birds, which few were permitted to do, and at the cut-throat interfaculty competitions held every third Friday she was noted for her skill at darts, though it was also maintained by some of her colleagues that this was because she tended to drink less than the rest of them.

She and Professor Vane went on long rambles once or twice a week, depending on how their lectures and tutorials overlapped, and they often stopped in at any of the many taverns or public houses around Stoneybridge for a meal and a drink. Professor Vane inevitably started talking with the other patrons about their local ghost stories or religious customs, and Pali would invariably get bored and drift off to whatever game was on offer. Quoits, shuffleboard, boules, darts, even marbles. Anything with a frisson of competition.

Pali made another note in her book, this time about the potential hires happening in Kitteredge. One of her current students might do well there as a lecturer.

Assuming the young man managed to stop drinking his evenings away and actually finish his degree.

A drink tonight says no, wrote Professor Vane.

Pali felt her lips curl into a small smile. She put her left hand into the inner pocket of her academic gown, where she tended to stash small items she found out-and-about. Interesting stones, pieces of broken pottery, intriguing seeds.

Three apparently ordinary dried beans and a feather, white with a black tip, from oh, long ago. She stroked the feather with one finger, delicately, remembering receiving it. Three feathers had she been given, by a being out of a legend not a one of these historians would ever have heard tell.

Three feathers, three wishes, and three quests.

Two feathers had she made use of, two wishes had she made and been granted, and two quests had she fulfilled.

Pali had never quite found a third wish worth the wishing; and she had never quite decided that that third quest, for dzēren, for that brimful of quiet, reflective joy, was what she wanted.

She did not wish for an end to these faculty meetings. They were a part of the small annoyances that were halfway to being a small pleasure, for she *did* enjoy the society afterwards, the drinks with Professor Vane or the entire faculty depending on the week.

And besides, very soon she would be leaving.

She let the beans fall back down into her pocket, clacking softly against the marble she'd found on her walk to the stables this morning, a small milky-glass bauble. She rolled the cool, hard, roundness between her fingers, enjoying its texture, then reluctantly let it drop as well. She didn't want to break either the marble or the window.

Deep in her other pocket was a chestnut, left there from the autumn. It rattled slightly in her fingers, the inner nut dried out. She might have to have a word with the charwoman who saw to her rooms and clothes for not turning out her pockets.

The Dean droned on about new upper university regulations, which they'd all heard about last month and would probably hear about next month as well. Pali did not bother writing anything down. She tilted her head slightly as the fly landed on the upper right window pane, three inches above the Dean's shoulder.

He paused to shuffle his papers, and as his head was momentarily downturned Pali flicked her wrist. The chestnut sailed across the table, arced over the head of the Professor of Pre-Astandalan Alinorel History, and nailed the fly with a sharp *thwap*.

The three people who had been looking in the correct direction to witness this gave astonished and impressed looks at Pali's spot. The Dean lifted his eyes from his papers with a befuddled glance over his shoulder. "Was there something?" he asked doubtfully.

"Probably the students outside," Professor Vane said blandly. She was much better at keeping her face straight than Pali ever had been.

"Yes, yes," the Dean said, frowning down at his papers again. He leaned forward to peer at Pali, who thought he really had no excuse for not replacing his spectacles if they were failing him so badly.

"Professor Black," he said gravely.

Pali ensured her expression was as solemn as she could manage, which wasn't very. "Yes, Dean?"

"I believe you are leaving us very soon."

That caused an uproar amongst those still awake, who roused the rest, who demanded to know what had caused all the excitement. Through it all Pali sat calmly, smiling slightly. Professor Vane, who knew what this was about, wrote, *What a pack of hyaenas*.

"Now, now," the Dean said, eventually managing to corral his unruly faculty. "Let us not act like undergraduates."

Perish the thought, wrote Professor Vane.

"Professor Black is not leaving the university *permanently*," he assured them all seriously.

Alas. But where would she go?

She might not have found that brimming cup here, but she *was* content. Even happy. She had learned there were pleasures in the ordinary, the common, the familiar.

When she had been younger, she would have gone wandering at even the first inkling of boredom. She would have gone questing for wrongs to right, injustices to mend, just battles to fight.

There were plenty of all three in the halls of Stoneybridge. When the geese called she reminded herself that her pen and tongue were weapons, too, as sharp and as effective as her great-grandmother's sword (with which her great-grandmother had cut down the sun) or the dagger Masseo had once made for her out of a fallen star.

"Where is she going, then?" the Professor of Pre-Astandalan Alinorel History asked. He looked a little sour, possibly from the scare the chestnut going past his ear had given him, as usually he and Pali got on quite well.

"We should all congratulate Professor Black," the Dean continued imperturbably, "for she has received an invitation to travel to Zunidh in the company of the Last Emperor's ambassador and undertake some research in the Imperial Archives in Solaara."

There was envy on the faces of those who were only hearing this for the first time, but they all applauded her politely enough. Pali gave a brief scholar's bow, trying not to laugh when she saw Professor Vane had written *Like they couldn't write for an invitation if they wanted too*, followed by *Celebratory drinks in the Lower Quad?*

"As the passage between worlds is only open on specific dates, Professor Black will be leaving Stoneybridge shortly to meet the Ambassador in Yrchester, that they can make their way to the passage together in good time."

And with that he started handing out reassignments of her students and classes with the brisk decisiveness that never failed to surprise those who slept through half his speeches.

∽

Stoneybridge was arranged in colleges, eleven of them huddled together on the north side of the river, and three at a more distant remove. Professor Vane belonged to Sisterlen, and Professor Black to St Erlingale's. Sisterlen was in the main cluster, while St Erlingale's, which had once been a monastery, was the farthest out of town.

That was one of the reasons why Pali had chosen it, when she was offered a place in the Faculty of History and half a dozen of the colleges had vied for her seat. She had brought an already-shining scholarly reputation with her, created by her own intelligence and the idiosyncratic methods derived from her cultural background, her widespread travels, and the alchemical researches of Pharia and the natural philosophy-inflected studies in the history of medicine that Ayasha had pursued. Not that Pali told anyone that members of the Red Company had been her inspiration.

She also brought with her an endowment for a new research chair, presented to her by a very rich merchant philanthropist who had a few secrets of his own, and so the competition had been fierce. As a result, Pali had ended up with a fine suite of rooms on the ground floor of St Erlingale's.

She thought she looked very fine in her black robes lined with scarlet silk, as well. Scarlet was the colour of the Red Company, after all. It was a reminder to her never to let herself become *too* comfortable. One never knew when the fates would suddenly issue a challenge, and Pali would be called to take up her great-grandmother's sword and set forth on adventure once more.

She might not *wish* for that—for wishes were dangerous things when they might come true—but she could hope for it.

Yearn, even, though she would never say that out loud.

She accompanied Professor Vane to her rooms in Sisterlen after the faculty meeting, where her friend took off her heavy formal robes with a relieved sigh. Professor Vane was in her forties, with rosy pale skin, constellations of brown freckles, and curly brown hair she wore down in the Taran fashion.

"I'll just change my dress," Professor Vane said, and disappeared through one of the doors in the room. Pali leaned against the desk in the sitting room, surveying the room idly. She had spent many happy hours in here, drinking and conversing on all sorts of topics, from the highest scholarship to the most mundane.

Professor Vane's rooms were cluttered and homely, full of books and papers and pretty clothes. She had a kind of passion for owls, and the room was full of owl-shaped ornaments: clay and wood sculptures, a few paintings, a round stained glass sun-catcher in the window, even a tapestry. The room smelled a bit of the perfume the professor wore, a bit of the long branches of forced cherry-blossoms in a pretty vase shaped like an owl, and a bit more like the calico cat currently asleep on the chair.

They were friends, passing notes like students in their faculty meetings, meeting up two or three times a week for drinks or afternoon-long rambles in the countryside, sharing books and opinions. The somewhat absurd formality of Stoneybridge kept them to their titles and surnames. *Professor Vane* and *Professor Black*, never Elena or—

Professor Vane came out, now in a gown of finely striped green muslin, and pulled the common Scholar's black robes over her in lieu of a coat. She added a scarf, striped in Sisterlen mauve and white, and the black kid gloves Pali had given her last Winterturn. She stroked the cat down its spine; it yawned and rolled over, eyes slitted with pleasure as it folded its paws in the air and let her rub its belly gently.

"There we are," Professor Vane said, smiling brightly. "All set."

Pali returned the smile, if a little less brightly, and held the door open. It was a good friendship she had with Professor Vane, she told herself, pushing away the pang of longing for Jullanar, her first and greatest friend. It might not be *brimful*, but it was good, and with that Pali had learned to be content.

Happy, she reminded herself. She was happy.

CHAPTER TWO
THE SIRUYAL

Pali was to meet the Zuni ambassador at the crossroads town of Yrchester in Middle Fiellan. She pondered the map.

The Craslins were a tall mountain range that ran northeast to southwest. Chare, the Lesser Arcady, and Lind were all on the eastern side. The mountains curved around in the northeast to form the northern rim of Orio Bay, with Orio City and the university of Tara tucked into the far end of the Tarvenol peninsula.

The main highway from Chare led up the coast to Orio City, which had once been the capital of the Imperial Province of Northwest Oriole and was still the largest city in this half of the continent. Smaller roads led up into Lind, and eventually met up with the main east-west highway.

The shorter route led across the Craslins by the southern pass into south Fiellan, and then up the old north-south highway to Yrchester. The only difficulty with that route was that it was a much higher pass and would be impassible with snow for several more months.

Pali's favourite student, who had graduated the previous spring, lived in southern Fiellan. He had written to her several times over the winter to inform her of increasingly intriguing developments in his region.

Pali had noted the signs of powerful wild magic gathering around him. She was not at all surprised to hear that he was at the epicentre of some sort of nexus of oddities. She had spent time with a powerful wild mage before, and she remembered the chaos of serendipities and inexplicable events that trailed in one's wake. An untrained one would surely be even worse than—her old friend.

The sensible thing to do would be to take the stagecoach up the inland route through Lind, and cross the mountains at the northern pass, and thence drop safely down to Yrchester. There were pirates and mountain brigands alike raiding the coastal road. The mercenaries and old soldiers who normally guarded merchants and travellers going to the conflicted lands south of Chare and West Erlingale were finding work on the traditionally safe northern routes.

Not that Pali needed a *guard*. Or was particularly sensible.

And then again—she had promised herself that she would take seriously any invitations to adventure the world offered.

Well. To be truthful she had once promised Jullanar she would *not* follow *every* impossible quest that landed in front of her.

She had been very good, all these years.

Surely she was due for an adventure. Jullanar would understand that there came a time when the impossible was the only appropriate course of action.

~

Half term came upon her with a flurry of tearful students and studiously casual colleagues. Pali consoled them both as best she could, which wasn't very, and packed and repacked her bags more times than she had ever been used to.

It had been a long time since she'd last set out.

But that wasn't the difficulty she faced, in fact. Professor Vane came to visit her one afternoon, the day before Pali had decided to leave, having promised to take Pali out for supper after she'd finished packing.

"I am surprised," her friend said, "to find you still unready."

Pali glared at the piles of offending belongings. The problem was that she knew what she should take for an *adventure*. Going as a Scholar was throwing her entirely off-kilter.

"It's been a long time since I last travelled so far," she said, and was chagrinned to realize it was true. She hadn't been farther than up the coast to Orio City since—well, since the Fall of Astandalas, and that was a dozen years and a distressing, unchronological, period of magical upheaval ago.

Professor Vane perched herself on the arm of one of the uncomfortable chairs, the only unoccupied space. She looked around the room, gaze arresting on the carpet which usually hung on the wall and was currently draped on the back of the other chair. "What have you decided on so far?"

Pali pointed to the neat pile on top of the chest. Her robes and sash and veils, which looked enough like her ordinary garments to be unremarkable; her sword; a pot and bowl and spoon. Her oiled cloak, an extra dagger. A small box of salt. Two shifts, an extra set of the snug wraps she used instead of Charese-style stays when she wasn't wearing Charese dress, two extra loincloths. Her good comb and brush, and a small bag of other toiletries and hair accessories.

She did not include the carpet. Professor Vane would not expect her to take one with her; and Pali was not prepared to explain it was a magical flying carpet, famous in song and story.

Professor Vane regarded the collection with astonishment. "What about a book?"

Pali nodded sharply. "Good point." She set out a new notebook, her fountain pen and a bottle of good ink, and a new history of the Ouranatha by a scholar she respected—and then nodded in satisfaction. "I knew I was missing something. It's hard, not going on horseback. Though of course the horse's tack takes up room, in that case."

"What clothes are you taking?" Professor Vane asked.

"That's all I need."

"What about formal occasions?"

"I'll braid my hair differently."

The other professor laughed, though Pali was quite serious. "Surely you should have some sort of formal robe? Are you not going for research? You must uphold the honour of Stoneybridge, if not St Erlingale's!"

"True." Pali considered, and fetched out her good Scholar's robe and a blue dress of some sort of crêpy material that folded without undue wrinkles and would look well enough with her breast band and shift. "There."

"Shoes?"

Pali had a secret love of shoes she had only discovered after her time with the company. "I thought I might get a new pair there," she said. "Something fashionable in Solaara. My boots and slippers will do for the rest."

She fetched the slippers—tooled leather with removable felt liners, sturdy soles, and a light and flexible design, good enough for fencing or dancing as well as warm for cold nights at home. "And a couple of pairs of socks," she finished, adding them and a pair of leggings. "I'll wear my gloves, hat, and scarf to start with. That should do. Thank you, Professor Vane, those were good suggestions."

"When I went home for last Winterturn, I took a full trunk and three bags."

Pali smiled at her. She'd never travelled with anything so much as that. On her journey from Arkthorpe to take up the position at Stoneybridge, she'd had one trunk and her one bag. Even then, the trunk had been mostly empty, but as she'd commissioned it she hadn't wanted to leave it behind. "You probably had gifts."

"Will you not be taking anything?"

"For whom? Emperor Artorin?" Pali laughed at the thought. She had spent the past fifteen years (and the Interim after the Fall) studying the last emperor of Astandalas. She would say, if a little reluctantly, that she *admired* him—she might be a folk hero and infamous criminal, but she could respect his efforts to reduce the corruption she and the Red Company had decried—but despite the years of studying his reign she was hardly going to bring him *presents*.

She knew too much about his character to not be baffled by the vast eccentricities at play within it. She had wondered whether it was some hereditary madness, before the news had begun to trickle back from Zunidh over the past three or four years and she had learned he had a gift of wild magic. Hiding that must have taken its toll, and probably accounted for at least a portion of his black depressions.

There were questions even that theory had been unable to answer, however. Some of his decisions were unfathomably strange for a man in his position.

"I might see if I can get an audience," she said, imagining the joy of presenting those pointed, poniard questions to the man himself. She could hold him accountable for some of his disastrous decisions, couldn't she?

Indeed, who else *could*? Or *would*? Domina Black of Stoneybridge, highly regarded historian of his reign, might think of the hard questions; Pali Avramapul of the Red Company *certainly* dared to ask them.

She felt a warm glow at the mere thought.

"Hmm. Did you say the ambassador had arranged this? You might give him a token of your appreciation. You could give him your last monograph and perhaps some Charese specialty."

"Saffron," Pali decided, for the traditional tokens of her appreciation—which involved stabbing some enemy—were probably inappropriate for the ambassador. She added two copies of her monograph—one could be a guesting-gift for her student—and made a mental note to acquire some of the spice from the merchant in town before she left.

With the contents decided, she packed quickly.

"You're so efficient," Professor Vane marvelled, as Pali turned her pile into a stack of "things to be worn" and "in my bag."

Pali had designed her bag herself to be both practical and elegant when she had been home with her sister and trying so hard to be content with her place in her clan. To be brimful with the pleasure and peace of being at home, in her own culture.

That she kept making prototypes of travelling bags that would be *particularly* useful for someone not travelling with camels and horses and wagons had perhaps been a sign that she would not stay. No one else had seemed surprised when she told Arzu that she thought she would take her leave again.

The bag was caramel-brown leather, soft and supple, tooled with the designs familiar from her childhood. The lining was woven—her sister's work, of course, bright and lovely under her hands, keeping her belongings safe and clean, unmarred by insects or dust or thieves.

Of course, anyone who stole something from Pali Avramapul would regret it. Deeply.

Arzu did not have such grand magic as—certain other mages of Pali's acquaintance had possessed, and she had not been able to make the bag more than unusually roomy. Pali fit her clothes and books in one side, her cooking gear and some long-lasting foods in the other, and still had room for a bottle of wine and another of water.

And the flying carpet.

Not that Pali told Professor Vane any of that.

∼

The morning before she left, Pali woke even earlier than was her wont. She lay in her bed, listening to the wind rattling the latches on her windows. Familiar sounds, after nine years in these rooms.

She rose, restless, knowing it was too early to collect her hired horse from the livery stable, and after pacing about her rooms, checking her gear for the hundredth time, she lifted up her great-grandmother's sword.

The handle settled easily, familiarly, into her hand. The curved blade was foreign in this world of straight lines and straight swords, of straight-edged buildings and straight roads. And it was famous—

famous from a dozen songs. She drew the blade and kissed the thousand-folded steel. The sword nicked a drop of blood from her lower lip, and she smiled at this silent promise.

It had been too long since she had performed the shēhen.

She set her feet in the first position, not perpendicular as in most of the Astandalan forms, but staggered in parallel. Her weight over her knees. Her left hand found the dagger without effort; her right hand the sword.

This was what the Warriors of the Mountain called the Song of the Siruyal.

Pali had always thought of the Siruyal, the resplendent magical bird of her clan's legends, as purely mythological. That was until she had seen it, she and her friends of the Red Company, when they had been sent across the Holy Desert to parley with the Wind Lords at the navel of the world.

Or—no. She had seen it before then.

Not on her first adventure, when she and Arzu had gone to rescue Sardeet from the Blue Wind. Nor on her second, when she had taken the bones of the Blue Wind's first six wives home to their kin. Nor on her third, when she and Arzu had gone to visit Sardeet in the city by the sea, and climbed up a magic vine into a cloud-country that she now knew had been at the edge of Fairyland.

On her fourth adventure, when Arzu had settled in with her newborn son and Sardeet had married her third husband, both of them happy, secure, satisfied with something Pali had never even known how to want (*brimful*, came the faint thought), Pali had taken her great-grandmother's sword and her veils and her horse and ridden off after the wind.

The Siruyal had a wingspan of thirty paces, the tales went.

(She slid her sword through the air, as softly, as sweetly, as inexorably as the shadow crossing the sand.)

The Siruyal had talons made of electrum, shining like lightning, sharper than the bite of the scorpion-men who guarded the Underworld.

(Her dagger darted forward, in and out of the crescent of her blade. She had fought the Scorpion-Men, with a chunk of fool's gold her only weapon, when she and her sister Arzu had followed the road East to rescue Sardeet from the god who had stolen her away.)

The Siruyal had a beak curved like a rainbow and a tongue the blue of the sky, and it sang a song like rain falling, a song that like the rain brought flowers in its wake.

(Her feet tapped lightly as the first drops of rain, as a cricket, as the sand grains leaping across the surface of the dunes. Her blade sang in her hand, an eerie wail as it cut the cold humid air, the cry of a falcon high as a star in the sky.)

The Siruyal brought destruction with one wing, and new life with the other.

(Pali's hands had known both justice and mercy, and the death that was both, and that other death that was neither.)

The Siruyal had milky-blind eyes, with which it could see into the very heart and soul of the one before it. Be careful, the stories said, for if you met the Siruyal and it judged you unworthy, it would lift you high in the sky and drop you.

(Pali had met the Siruyal. She had found it grounded, drinking from an oasis, its lighting talons deep in the earth, its singing tongue silenced, its wings furled. She had been hunting, had an arrow strung to her bow.

She had looked full into its eyes. She had been lifted up, high above the desert, with her great-grandmother's sword in her hand; and she had been lifted even higher, to the ridges of the mountains that had no roots and peaks that held up the sky, and the Siruyal had given her three feathers and three wishes and three quests.

The first, for glory.

The second, for knowledge.

The third, for dzēren, that brimming promise, which she had always pretended to herself was joy, for she had never wanted peace.

Stepping foot on that high mountain, she had followed the Siruyal's whispered directions until she had found herself in another world, where all had been strange and uncertain until she found the first friends of her heart.)

She spun into the second set of the Shēhen, the Song of the Siruyal taken at double speed, each step and each movement of her hand precise, clear-edged as if it had been months, not years, since she had last performed it.

She had always thought she'd found glory, and knowledge, and joy in the space of time encompassed by those three wishes, those three feathers. But yet—

Had not the first portion of her life, from meeting the Siruyal until the dissolution of the Red Company, been her quest for glory?

And the second portion, in the universities of Alinor, her quest for knowledge?

Joy had never been an object she had *sought*. It had come with the sword in her hand and the horse between her thighs, her friends at her side and the wind blowing before her. It had come too with the hunting out of secrets and the orderly arrangement of thoughts, the precise choice of words, the arguments lined up on the battlefield of scholarship.

But that was not dzēren, not the brimming peace.

And yet—her hands dipped, the dagger and the scimitar, her feet tap-tapping on the stone floor, on the rugs before the fire, the scent of the desert in her nose, her mind stilling at the centre of the whirling motion, the Song of the Siruyal that brought flowers in the wake of the rain—what would it mean to seek that?

∽

Pali rode out of spring and back into winter as she headed north and west. She arrived at the inn at the lower end of the pass in the late afternoon of a cold, clear day. Snow still lay in the shadowed edges of fields, and there was frost in the air.

It was early when Pali took the candle the innkeeper offered her and clambered up to bed. She was a little sore after three days in the saddle, and felt chagrinned at the realization she was so unaccustomed to what had once been her life.

She had been at Stoneybridge nine years, the longest by far ever settled into one place. There had been a year before Stoneybridge teaching at Kermon, and two years at Tara attaining her second degree. Three years at Arkthorpe before that; she had been there for the Fall.

Before then she'd not stayed a year in one place since her adolescence.

The room was fair-sized, with a rather impressive canopied bed piled high with blankets, a stand with a washbasin and ewer of water, a fireplace, a bench. She'd neglected to ask for a full bath, but there was a shallow tub in front of the fire waiting for her, and two buckets —one with cool water and one empty—and a kettle at the edge of the fire.

She performed her ablutions gratefully, albeit quickly—her breath was steaming in the air. She was glad it was not the depth of winter, when there would likely have been ice on the windows, this far into the alpine country.

Then she dressed in leggings and shift before getting into the bed, where she was pleased to discover the innkeeper's chambermaid had put in a warming pan. Pali made a mental note to leave a good tip in the morning.

She left the curtains open as she brushed out her hair. It would have been easier to sit on the bench to brush it out, of course, but there was something so cozy about sitting with her feet on the felt covering of the warming pan as her hair crackled with static electricity and clung to her hands.

Eventually she braided it back again, blew out the candle, and fell asleep.

∾

She woke when the moon rose and shone full in her face.

It was a full moon, Pali saw when she rose. She intended to close the curtains at the window and then those around the bed, but when she stood, hissing at the cold floor underfoot, she could not help but be captivated by the view.

The window looked northwest, up the pass into the mountains. Under the moon the mountains gleamed bone-white with shadows that almost seemed to glisten with their depths. The sky was clear, and on another night the stars would have been brilliant, but now were faded to pinpricks by the moonlight.

Pali had fought the moon, that time the Red Company had travelled to the country of Night, and Pali had found that the celestial orb had a form almost as petty as any human woman.

But tonight she could forget that.

She shuffled the rug from beside the bed over to the window and leaned against the sill, yearning to go explore those strange, dreamlike landscapes she could see before her.

The yearning was familiar; the same wistfulness she felt when the geese called, or the wind blew with a hint of *somewhere else* caught in its wings, or the river-barges sounded out their deep horns as they set off downriver to the sea.

Each time Pali would look up at the birds, or scent the wind, or turn her head towards the barges, and then she would tell herself *Not yet, not yet, this is not for you.*

The moon was calling her tonight. That cold beautiful smile, which Pali had once punched. She clenched her fist with satisfied reminiscence.

For a moment Pali thought, as she had thought these many years since the dissolution of the company, *Not yet, not yet, this is not for you.*

And then with a curious shock, and a feeling that took root in her heart and blossomed into a fierce smile, she realized this *was*—at last! at last!—for her.

CHAPTER THREE
THE HIGH PASS

She had already paid the innkeeper for the horse's stabling, so she left coins for the room and a tip for the chambermaid, took a deep draught of water from the ewer, and then fiddled with the catch on the window until it creaked open with a gust of cold air.

The glory of the evening caught in her throat, her eyes, ice crystals dancing in the moonlight.

Pali flung out the carpet with the snap and twist that caused the magic to waken. It hovered just below her waist, the scent of her sister's jasmine and neroli perfume, the scent of the desert, the scent of magic, full in her nose, her mouth, her heart.

The last time she had flown it had been her journey home from that last, unsuccessful quest, when she had flown seven days and seven nights into the Sea of Stars, and a year and a day back.

She stroked the carpet, as if it were a horse, and like a horse it shuddered and leaned into her hand, quivering with eagerness for the flight before it.

Down below there was a cry and a shout of laughter, as someone in the taproom cried out a joke.

They did not know—could not know—that only a floor above

them there was a song, a hero out of legend, a moment of magic such as had hardly ever been seen, this side of the mountains and this side of the Fall of Astandalas.

She flung her bag over her shoulder on the strap made for the purpose and slid onto the carpet, her sword angled out flat against the weave, and laid her palms on the symbols that would guide and direct her flight.

With a sinuous ripple, firm and supportive against her crossed legs, the carpet rose and passed through the window. Pali caught the window as she went and shut it behind her, the latch falling into place with a quiet, assured, *snick*.

It was not particularly late. Lights still shone in many of the houses in the little village where she'd found the inn. There were fewer as she followed the valley into the mountains, as woodsmen were like farmers, and went to bed with the sun.

The road was easily visible in the moonlight. Pali guided the carpet to sweep up at about the height she was accustomed to from horseback. The woods were dark, black and grey, the snow a strange luminous colour somewhere between blue and white.

She reached the end of the cleared road, where the snow was still banked several feet high. Pali paused there, feeling the cold wind off the mountain against her face, aware she was at a threshold.

And then she laughed to herself, tapped the carpet with a firm hand, and lifted up into the untrod lands.

∽

The mountains shouldered up around her. They were thickly forested, though Pali was not good enough with trees to recognize the types, not in the dark, in the winter.

The air was cold in her nose, against her cheeks, in her eyes. The path ahead was clear: one valley led deep into the mountains. Three peaks stood close together, the Three Brothers looking down upon the pass. There had been a story in the taproom that evening about giants and ancient, long-vanished gods that Professor Vane would undoubtedly have found fascinating.

The moon rode high, a full circle, white mottled with a grey nearly silver. The sky around was bleached-black, the stars faint pinpricks. Pali lay back on the carpet and remembered other moonlit nights, and what it had been like in the Moon Lady's country, when all was black and white and silver except for what colour they brought with them.

Black were the shadows, and white the moon, and silver the snow.

Pali lay there with her clothes fluttering around her, her gloved right hand on the hilt of her great-grandmother's sword, her gloved left hand on the warm weave of the carpet. The cold air danced around her, pricking her skin, tugging at her hair, brushing all thought of past or future out of her.

She and the moon might have been two vessels mirroring each other, sailing the sky and the land below the sky, Pali the new moon with her sword its crescent edge, her eyes on the full moon who had nearly, nearly, stolen Fitzroy Angursell's heart away.

She was not usually able to think his name. She had to listen to it often enough, on the mouths of undergraduates drunk with their own daring, singing his songs and reciting his poems and pretending themselves into adventures that they never understood. Pali wanted to shake them into recklessness sometimes, those young men and women who studied in the quadrangles and common rooms of Stoneybridge, tell them that the adventures were *there*, that they need only leave the trodden path and they would find them.

But she said nothing, for Domina Black of Stoneybridge did not speak of her past.

∽

Eventually she grew cold, and sat up.

The valley was narrowing. The trees were thicker, and she

thought she might be following a frozen river-bed rather than the road proper. She had ridden this pass once before, taking the road into Lind for a conference in Markfen. That had been a late summer's trip, and she had been unable to bear the thought of the heat along the coast.

To speak the truth, she had wanted even a mere inkling of an adventure. She'd ended up travelling with colleagues. A book had come out of the journey, and tenure for one of her colleagues, but nothing grander.

The valley twisted and narrowed into a gorge. Up here there were no permanent human inhabitants. She had passed the last of the woodsmen's cabins. There might be the odd hunter who ventured up in the winter, but the landscape was treacherous enough without several feet of snow cloaking all the sinkholes and streams riddling the stone. In the summer there would be herders and hunters, quarriers and foragers.

Now Pali had the valley to herself. The wild things were quiet: no birds rose up at her passage, no deer or wolves or wolverines ran through the deep snow.

At the top of the valley was a headwall with a waterfall, the water frozen into fantastic pillars and curlicues. Pali slowed the carpet as she zigzagged up the face, looking at the ice glittering in the moonlight. There were pale rainbows within the crystals, lavender and the eerie green of the aurora borealis.

There was a music there, too: the faint susurrus of water rushing behind the ice, herald of a spring that felt far away this cold winter's night.

Pali rose like the sap, angling away from the earth, back and forth across the frozen waterfall, the breath of the ice a benediction on her face.

At the top of the ridge she looked first back to the east. The moon was nearly overhead, Pali's shadow a puddle of ink boring a hole into the ice.

To the east the valley was a white spill between the dark grey masses of the woods. Far down below were the few golden lights from the last village; she could not see farther out into the plains. For all she could see, past the village was the grey emptiness of the sea or the desert.

Pali turned her back on the civilized lands of Chare and looked up into the Craslins. The Linder range went north; the Craslins headed south, petering out into the hills encircling what had once been the kingdom of Morrowlea on the shores of a lake long since lost to changing weather and land use.

(There had been freshwater sea serpents in that ancient lake, according the earliest histories of what this part of Oriole had been like before the coming of the Empire. The serpents had not been large—perhaps hardly longer than two horses—but they had been, so the stories went, especially wise, and known to grant wishes. Pali had been interested, of course she had been, for she had once been granted those three wishes by a legend of her own people. But whatever other records or knowledge there might yet remain of those ancient sea serpents was held in books that had never been translated into Shaian, or perhaps in libraries that never been conquered by the empire.)

On the other side of the three-way crossroads at the pass was the road that led down west and north into southern Fiellan. To the west and south was a mystery: land that had never been fully conquered by Astandalas, never brought within the magic binding the empire, but yet encircled and enclosed by lands and peoples that were.

Pali turned her attention inland. The gorge opened up into a flat-bottomed valley she vaguely recalled was a lake in the summer. There were two valleys coming down into it, one leading south and the other north.

Tempting as the southern mystery was—and it was—Pali had only ten days before she was due to meet the Zuni ambassador in Yrchester. While it was certainly more than possible to have an adventure in less than a week—she could recall some, subsequently renowned in song and story, that had taken less than a day—she was not in the mood for a solitary winter's exploration.

The moon was high and there was a three-way crossroads ahead, and the snow sleek and silver below her.

The carpet was nearly as alive to her touch, her mood, as a living horse. For all that it had hung quietly, quiescent, on a wall for the past fifteen years, before that Pali *had* flown it seven days and seven nights into (and a year and an endless day back out of) the Sea of Stars above the Abyss, where things and ideas took on shapes and voices and sometimes even souls of their own.

"Away then, lovely one," she said to the carpet, and gave it the equivalent of free rein.

It leapt forward, swooping down so that its dangling tassels scored faint lines in the snow, kicking up a wake of powdery crystals behind her to hang in the air and twinkle like fairy dust. Pali laughed aloud, her voice chiming silver against the white stones, the silver snow, the black sky, the moon high above, impersonal and yet, Pali knew, quite possibly watching.

Up in a wave upon a wave of the air, catching some invisible current, intangible but for the way the fabric shaped itself against the air. The trees sighed and shivered with their passing, the pines' boughs singing over the rush of the air in her ears.

Pali sat cross-legged, her boot-heels under each knee, her hands resting in her lap, the hilt of the sword in her hand, her sash comforting at her waist. The veils across her face should have felt odd, unfamiliar, foreign; they did not.

She could have been any age. When she was not yet twenty she had ridden far to the north, to the land of those who lived under the Crown of Heaven, taking the bones of the Blue Wind's first wife back to her people. She had arrived at the edge of the northern spring, when snow lay in dirty skeins and the tundra was blossoming, insects in clouds around her like a coming sandstorm. The ground had been so wet, she remembered, moss squelching in the narrow rim between sky and permafrost.

That had been an alien land, as featureless to her eyes as the sandy desert was to a stranger's. Yet the tundra had its ways and its secrets, open as it seemed; and the blood of that people ran in Pali's own veins, for her great-grandmother, coming down from cutting down the false sun out of the sky, had met her great-grandfather coming up with the lantern holding the true sun in in his hands.

Pali stroked the hilt of her sword, her great-grandmother's sword, as the carpet wove through a thicket of twisted evergreens, leaped over a field of boulders, huge and mutely significant in their stark shadows and white caps of snow, and came suddenly up to a steep clamber.

The carpet did not zigzag up this cliff: it turned vertically, and Pali had to bite her lip and trust her sister's work, her sister's wisdom, her sister's skill—

She did not fall, not though the carpet tilted so the blood rushed into her head as she tried not to clench her jaw.

She did not fall.

The carpet flung itself over the top of that headwall into a cirque, like someone had taken a scoop out of the mountain—Pali was sure she had not seen this when she had ridden up through the alpine summer, the sound of cowbells never far away—there were yodellers in these mountains, calling from field to field at the waning of the day.

She did not have long to wonder if she had mistaken her way, or allowed the carpet to take the wrong fork, for suddenly they were skimming the edge of the cirque, like a spoon around the curve of a bowl, and the carpet took the shoulder of the mountain at a vast and impossible speed, and there before her was spread a vast and impossible world.

The Moon's Country had been full of flowers: white lilies and asphodels, huge clouds of starry virgin's bower, carpets of lily-of-the-valley, white bluebells. All white flowers, in a land whose springy turf must have been green in the daylight, but which Pali always remembered as the dim grey of twilight, when the fireflies hung their tiny lanterns in the thorn brakes along the road that dreaming poets had built.

Here the mountains raised high white peaks, white snow and whiter stone against the bleached-black sky, all their edges etched with black ink.

(She had looked down into the Abyss. It had been an endless fall of stars until even they were swallowed in a velvety darkness. She had never previously understood why someone might find it appealing; after that journey, that flight out, that flight back, she had known why it was feared.)

Below her the snow was pristine, ripples and knife-edged drifts shaped by the endless mountain wind. The carpet played with the snow cast up by the wind, dancing with its own shadow. There were hardly any trees up here, and what there were were all wiry and twisted things huddling in the lees of great rocks or rough-edged stream beds.

Many of the trees had ribbons tied to their branches, pale and glimmering in the moonlight, strips of shadows on the snow. One of the trees had bells hung on it, long strands of silver-chiming bells of the sort they used for horse-harnesses in Lind.

The wide heath of the saddle between the three mountains crested and then sank down into a shallow bowl with the crossroads at its heart.

Pali noted the wooden refuge on the farther side of the crossroads standing stone. That marked the path down into Fiellan, she knew; the Linder road went north and east from here.

The carpet carried Pali nearly due north towards the standing stone, a grey megalith of a stone that was not the native limestone of these mountains. It stood nearly foursquare, roughly shaped to the four directions despite there having always been only three roads meeting here.

There was no one and nothing in sight but for the moon full overhead and the standing stone and the dark rectangular bulk of the refuge ahead of her. When Pali reached the standing stone she drew the carpet to a halt.

The wind had dropped. With herself still, her breath was the loudest sound. She breathed shallowly, meditatively, controlling her heart and her attention.

She had been to such places before, on less significant moments than midnight under a full moon.

There was nothing to meet her.

No wind blew from Faerie. No ghost rose from the crossroads. No stranger knight came thundering up with his visor down and lance readied.

She was disappointed.

Disappointed: and then angry, for this was not the heart of Astandalas in the days of its glory (its bloated and decadent end), when adventure had to be prodded out of it like someone winkling a snake out of its hole.

She only had ten days, and even with the carpet it would probably take a full day to get to Yrchester—

Nine days was plenty long enough for an adventure. And was she not, after all, Pali Avramapul?

Pali smiled, and stood up, balancing at first awkwardly—she had not stood upon the carpet often, though she had practiced, of course she had practiced, just in case.

She balanced her weight, and felt the carpet firm and responsive beneath her feet through the soles of her boots. Her boots were well made, leather moulded to her feet by long use in the fencing salle.

One breath, two. The carpet shifted as she shifted her weight, lifting up, ducking down, feinting left, feinting right.

Pali drew her great-grandmother's sword with the stately hiss that had never failed to bring joy to her heart. She drew it when a moment was significant. Never in jest, or idleness.

"A first quest, for glory," she said, looking down the northern road into Lind.

She drew her dagger from her sash with her left hand. It was a solid weight in her hand, the leather hilt easily held even with her gloved hand, the folded steel catching the moonlight. Masseo had made her that dagger with iron ore he had smelted from a fallen star.

"A second quest, for knowledge," she said, whirling the carpet around the standing stone so she faced the road back to Chare. The snow stretched out across the high moorland of the pass, shaped only by the wind save for those places here and there where the carpet had trailed its tassels onto the surface, marking the powder with a touch as delicate as an owl's wings.

Pali bent her knees, barely thought her direction, and the carpet continued the circuit until she faced the unknown and untrodden road down to Fiellan.

She raised her hands, crescent sword and star-iron dagger, high up to the wind, the sky, the mountains. "And the third quest, for ... dzēren."

Dzēren. A cup brimful of peace, joy, quietude, plenitude. She had never sought it, never wanted it, and yet—

And yet that was the third quest, the one left undone, never undertaken.

There was no one there to meet her, but the wind blowing ice crystals into her eyes, tugging at her veils.

Pali bared her teeth to the wind, the moon sailing high above, the stars in their multitudes and the snow immeasurably beautiful below them, and she moved from opening stance to the movements of the *shēhen* the Warriors of the Mountains had called the Great Challenge.

Under her feet the flying carpet her sister had woven moved like a well-trained horse, at once ground and mount for her motions, the fabric supporting her like an extension of her own will.

Once around the standing stone; twice; a third time.

Pali moved, her sword-hand singing, her dagger-hand percussion, her feet dancing, the wind her dancing-partner. A night wind, a mountain wind, an icy winter wind for all that it bore the faint promise of spring in the fragrance of distant flowers.

The moon crested the zenith, and there before her were three figures.

Pali stopped, sword and dagger in the fifth position, the Guard.

Three hooded robes hung in the air before her. Their hems did not touch the snow, and no feet descended below the cloth; their hoods did not cover their faces, but faces there were not.

One the gleaming white of the snow all around them.

One the shining black of the vault of the heavens between the stars.

One silver as the stars, the ice crystals, the moon's secret hollows.

Pali smiled, and lifted her sword and dagger once more to the opening of the Great Challenge.

"Do you come to meet me?" she asked, her voice low and rich.

The three figures looked at each other, shadow-blank in the hollows of their hoods. When they spoke their voices came in eerie unison.

"Do you not fear us?"

Pali smiled again, and shifted her feet into the proper opening. The carpet was eager as her finest horse would have been before a battle.

"If you are men or the ghosts of men, what have I to fear? If you are demons or of the fairy folk, I have fought worse. If you are gods—" She could do nothing more than spread her sword and dagger wide, her smile sharp as the wind for all they could not see it below her veils. "I have slain gods before."

They were silent. Only the wind whistled around them, the snow hissing like sand.

Finally they said, "And if we are none of those?"

"If you are the Fates or the Sovereigns of Time or the messengers of the Silent Ones," Pali replied, "then I salute you."

And so she did, for she had never been stingy in courtesy.

One heartbeat, two, three; and for a moment Pali could smell both charnel-house reek and the flowery scent she knew from the further reaches of the Sea of Stars, when she had flown seven days and seven nights after Fitzroy Angursell before turning back to the mortal lands.

For a moment she could almost see visages in the mist within their hoods. Stars glimmered there, eyes deep and mournful, deep as the Abyss falling away from the light.

"We shall not fight you tonight," they said at last, and disappeared as silently as they had come.

Pali sheathed her sword in some disappointment, but the air seemed to require something more of her, after her challenge had met such an initially promising response as that, and so she removed her glove to prick her thumb with the point of her star-iron dagger.

Masseo had made that dagger, and she knew the runes etched on the blade, hidden under the wire-bound hilt.

She then lifted the knife high and plunged it deep into the standing stone.

"When it is time for the challenge to be met," she said to the wind, the snow, the stars, the moon, the mountains, the mysteries, "you will know how to find me."

CHAPTER FOUR
MOONSET

The moon fell away from her zenith as Pali sat back down on the carpet, tucked her hands under her arms in a futile attempt to warm them, and proceeded at a much more decorous pace towards Fiellan.

The refuge was dark, snow blown up against its door. She considered halting for the rest of the night, but she was still awake and elated from the challenge and its answer, and she did not fancy the cold morning wakening.

From the maps she knew the main route bore south to descend by an easy gradient into the upper valley of the Coombe, and that there was a steeper path, unsuitable even for mules, that led down more directly west. She picked the most likely of the shallow valleys leading away from the refuge, the one where the wind was at the side of her face, and followed it down.

Down a vale: up a hump to a saddle; and there in front of her was a wide dark valley. The moon shone down on dim grey fields and wide silver rivers. There were no human-made lights visible from this height, this side of midnight.

She let the carpet set the pace, swift and steady: faster than a horse could gallop, fast as the wild geese soaring on the wind.

The snow was greyer on this side, less gleamingly resplendent. The air was warmer as well: after the carpet went over a headwall and started a steep descent into a thickly wooded valley it was clear she had left winter behind and was once more descending into spring.

By the time she had reached the valley floor and was following a swiftly flowing river, young and noisy with snowmelt, she was warm enough to remove her gloves and warm oiled cape.

The river entered a woodland: the air was rich and redolent of leafmould and new growth, the shy scent of primroses. Pali guided the carpet towards the bank when she saw an open glade.

The first place had a patch of nettles springing up in all its springtime vigour. Pali wished she had left her gloves on after she set her hand directly on the stinging leaves, but the sudden transition to warmth had made her sleepy, and she only muttered a mild curse and flopped back onto the carpet.

A path led up from the nettles. The carpet followed it, at something much closer to walking speed. The path was wide enough for her passage, which was silent enough to startle the small creatures of the night when her shadow passed over them.

The second glade was marked by a spring trickling over a stone basin next to some sort of dark building. Pali drew the carpet to a halt and slid down, stiff after sitting still so long. She removed her face-veils and drank deeply from the spring before trying the door of the building.

It opened; was empty, though it smelled good—sweet rushes and other strewing herbs on the floor, Pali recognized. Good beeswax, and was that honey? And perhaps incense?

A friendly sort of place, she decided, and laid down the carpet before setting out her bedroll and promptly falling fast asleep.

In the morning she woke to a loud conversation being had by a group of small songbirds very enthusiastic about the dawn.

Pali usually woke with the dawn, but she also usually went to bed far before moonset. She yawned and sat up, running her fingers through her hair. She hadn't undone the braid before laying down, and it was frizzled and knotted with sleep. So were her shoulders, knotted that was; her thoughts felt frizzled.

Whom, she wondered, had she challenged at the mountain crossroads?

She looked around the building. It was a tiny chapel, dedicated to the Lady worshipped by most of the northerners of the continent. The Lady of Summer and Winter, something like that. Pali recognized this by the mosaic depicting a woman wearing green and white, blue water streaming from her hands, on the wall behind a stone altar.

Withered leaves and new candles sat on the altar and in niches around the room. Strewing herbs were on the floor, scenting the air sweetly. Pali had dreamed of pleasant things, though the dreams were melting away into the pale light coming in through the one window opening.

She fetched out her hairbrush and began to unravel the knots in her hair as she surveyed the chapel.

There was a sizable community of the Lady's worshippers in Chare, and indeed if she recalled correctly her own college's monastic foundation belonged to that religion, but otherwise Pali had had nothing to do with them.

One of her requirements in taking her endowed chair to St Erlingale's had been the assurance that she might worship her own deities and keep her own holy days, and after some discussion about the dates and frequency of said holidays—Pali had not initially intended them as days off, but once she realized what *holiday* meant in Chare she was quick to establish a framework that seemed suitably religious —she had gladly ignored any invitations 'to chapel'.

Not that they were pressing. While things had grown perhaps

more religious after the Fall of the Empire, Northwest Oriole had been an imperial province too long, with too many soldiers drawn from and retiring to its population, to be anything but thoroughly ecumenical.

Or so Pali thought was the term the college authorities had used. She had smiled one of her Warrior of the Mountains smiles at them, and they had stuttered to a halt and assured her they respected her traditions.

There were gods amongst her people, of course, but unless one was called to their service, one usually did not bother them, nor they human beings.

Pali pondered this habitual thought, which wasn't quite *true*, really. Her own younger sister Sardeet had been so beautiful she'd been stolen away by the Blue Wind, one of the lesser gods.

A lesser god in truth. Immortal—but not unkillable.

Pali could not suppress her smug smile, and let her hair hang down freely as she packed up her bag. There had been water outside the night before. She would wash her face and drink her fill, eat some of the dried sausage and bread she'd brought from Chare, and see what she could find out in Ragnor Bella about Mr. Perry Dart, lately of Stoneybridge. She had no idea of his family situation, and decided it would behoove her to find a room in the hotel and invite him to call upon his old tutor.

She smiled as her black hair swung in front of her face. She pushed it back. It was laced with silver, but she'd had laugh-lines around her eyes since her thirties, and no one looking at her would believe her *antique*.

No matter how much that cranky bastard at the Kitteredge library claimed anything over fifty counted as such.

∼

After the brilliant cold moonlight of the night before, the walk from the little chapel was homely and springlike. Pali followed the path that went uphill, away from the river. This led through a woodland running largely to evergreen hollies and some sort of small twisty tree with wicked blood-red thorns.

Underfoot were primroses, mostly the familiar pale yellow but there were also patches of a soft, pleasant faded-lavender. Snowdrops were mixed in, their strappy leaves a much more solid green. Otherwise it was all the manifold browns and greys of fallen leaves, and the scent of earth waking up.

It was a faintly cloudy day, the sky a milky grey. The air was warm, mild; clement, she might say. The wind was soft and curious on her face, barely ruffling her sleeves and the hems of her robes. She wore her sky-blue sash, the sword at her waist, though she had left off the face-veils.

One of the cultural habits she had come to find pleasing, if initially perplexing, about the people of northeastern Northwest Oriole was their propensity for walking tours. Half the faculty of the universities around Stoneybridge spent their afternoons tromping the hills and fields surrounding the town. Ostensibly this was to facilitate creative and critical thought, and certainly it provided a certain degree of physical activity for an otherwise sedentary group of people.

Professor Vane was one of the more enthusiastic proponents of the activity. She and Pali had formed the habit of going for a long ramble once or twice a week. Pali was therefore quite in the habit of walking in the countryside.

Her friend would like this country for a ramble, Pali mused—so long as there was a good pub at the end of it!

At the top of the hill the path from the chapel met a lane. There was a stone marking the path, but no indication of what lay in either direction. Leftward led south and east, back towards the pass she had crossed in the night. That meant right should lead her to the barony seat.

Accordingly she turned that way. The road was muddy, but the verge was grassy and proved firm underfoot. Pali walked with an easy, swinging stride, accustoming herself to the weight and length of the sword at her side, her bag over her shoulder. How long had it been since she walked thus, facing adventure?

It was a quiet, decorous sort of adventure she was facing, admittedly. Visiting a favourite former student, catching a stagecoach north, crossing a friendly border—even a border between worlds—in the company of an ambassador, researching in a great library archive.

She probably should not be dressed quite so clearly like Pali Avramapul of the Red Company, who still had a considerable price on her head.

Pali lifted her head as a shadow flashed across the path. A small falcon, a merlin perhaps, darting out from the covert into the wider heathland now opening up before her. In the distance blue smoke rose from a misty valley hidden behind low hills to the west.

Ragnor Bella, she presumed, and strode faster. *Her* joy had always been tinged with danger.

∼

She came in past a small public house called the Ragglebridge, presumably from the nearby bridge over a river next to it. There were two men fishing on the bridge proper. She nodded at them as they turned to watch her approach.

"Good morning, ma'am," one said, touching his cap politely.

Pali smiled at this evidence that she did not look quite so ferociously academic as had become usual. "Good morning, good sirs." She glanced politely at their rods. "A good day to be standing; is it a good morning to be fishing?"

"Not bad, eh," the same man said, his eyes crinkling with good humour.

Pali enjoyed fishing, though she had always concentrated on the useful aspects—catching supper for the ten members of the Red Company had never been easy—and she noted that the man's rod had a reel type with which she was unfamiliar. A few questions elicited the shyly proud declaration that this was his own invention, and a few more showed her how it worked to reel the line in and release it out when he cast.

"Forgive me," the fisherman said eventually, "but you surprise me."

Pali laughed. "How so?"

"You look like one as might have come down the highway in the old days," he said, with a serious sort of expression.

"I might have."

"It's rare for such as you to come by nowadays."

Pali smiled at him. "Rare? But not, I take it, unheard of?"

"There have been strange things afoot this year-tide," the fisherman said. His silent companion, who had fished steadily through their conversation, though Pali was sure he was listening intently, nodded sharply enough to make his cap bounce. He settled it with gnarled, well-used hands. Pali regarded them thoughtfully. The man could probably pack a serious punch, with knuckles like that to suggest he knew well the art of fisticuffs.

"But belike you know about them already."

What had they always said? *The world is full of invitations.*

Were these for her? *Could* they be?

Perhaps, Pali acknowledged. They could be. She could turn aside from her course, not go to Zunidh, not do that research in the Imperial Archives, not write that monograph, not seek that audience with the Last Emperor.

There was a danger there, that someone might recognize her—there were those in the Last Emperor's court who had met the Red Company, or might have, in their younger days.

But over all, it was a quiet sort of adventure, a scholarly one. Respectable, even. Reputable.

She was Pali Avramapul, who had challenged the empty crossroads and the three mysterious hooded figures who had come to meet her, only to retreat from her challenge—

They *had* retreated.

She could follow their clues, their hints, their mysterious identities, find out what secrets they held and what those might portend, this side of the mountain pass or the other ...

But then again, did she *want* to delve deeply into whatever mysteries this small, quiet town held?

And then again, Perry Dart lived here, with his secret, surreptitious magic, which had trembled about him like a brewing storm. Still far off in the distance, barely the hint of the air pressure changing, a front moving in. Those who had come to the crossroads might well have come expecting *him*.

"Perry Dart was my student at Stoneybridge," she said therefore, and saw the fisherman's shoulders relax and his expression settle into satisfaction for guessing correctly. "I was hoping I might be able to call upon him as I travelled north."

"Dart Hall's six miles out t'other side of town," the fisherman said. "He's often in town, however—his friend's at the bookstore off the market square. Opposite the bakery. Follow the main road, there, and Master Jemis will be able to tell you if young Peregrine's to town today or no."

Pali had already regretted bringing only the history to read, which was so boring she was embarrassed for the author, and thought a bookstore opposite a bakery a fine prospect indeed.

～

Ragnor Bella was a pretty town, even in the slightly mucky end of winter. The yards she could see were still bedraggled, and few of them had the neat rows of vegetables and fruits that graced almost every available space in Charese towns, but there were pots of spring bulbs and flowers—more primroses, along with sprightly violas in purple, white, and yellow, and tiny narcissus in yellow and white.

Pali was quite pleased she was able to name so many of the flowers. That was another thing she had learned from Professor Vane, who invariably pointed out the flora as they passed it on their walks.

The buildings themselves were largely brick or plastered timber-frame, pleasing and homely rather than spectacular or graceful.

Jullanar was from Fiellan, from the north, Pali remembered suddenly as she went past a more classical facade that appeared to belong to the primary hotel of the town. That was where Domina Black of Stoneybridge would be expected to stay, no doubt. Pali eyed it as she passed. It might be more comfortable than one of the smaller inns, but would it be more *interesting*?

She pondered the rival merits of a hot bath versus good conversation as she passed out of the square in front of the 'Ragnor Arms' and went along what appeared to be a short high street, containing as it did butcher, fishmonger, milliner, and two haberdashers facing each other across the narrow street. Both haberdashers bore the same surname, and Pali was briefly amused wondering about the rivalry implicit in their existence.

The market square was generous in size, and contained a fountain, some sort of market cross—they were fairly common in Lind as well, so Pali knew that the tall stone pillar marked the symbolic centre of the town and fulfilled a role for certain ancient legal and cultural traditions—and a statue of one of the emperors.

All the emperors had looked much the same, given a natural variation in age and girth. They had run to tall, with a beaky nose—aquiline, according to the ardent imperialists—and good skulls, well displayed by the custom of shaving the head. This particular emperor appeared to be Artorin Damara, by the cut of his dress and the rod in his right hand. The Last Emperor was usually depicted holding the pentahedron that had long been a symbol of the emperors in his left hand, and the rod in his right.

Why that had been chosen as Artorin Damara's symbol was one of Pali's questions for the Archives. She suspected it was because he was of the lineage of Damar, not Yr, and the rod had some significance for the early empire, but beyond that it had generally been dismissed as insignificant.

She cast a wry, dismissive glance at the stone visage looming over her. She'd be back to thinking about him soon enough, no doubt, but some rural town's indifferent sculpture was no concern of hers. She'd never seen Artorin Damara close-to, and did not know how accurate this depiction was. It could have been any man in the imperial family: it could have been a thinner version of the Emperor Eritanyr, or of his son Shallyr Silvertongue, whom she *had* met, or ... or anyone.

She watched a couple of women walk across the square, a bevy of small children squealing around them. They were headed for the bakery.

The bookstore first it was.

Pali walked unhurriedly around the perimeter of the square, glancing into the shop windows as she passed them. The day's white light reflected against the glass, showing her herself more than the goods for sale. With her sword hidden in her over-robe she looked a touch foreign, but not exactly the infamous Pali Avramapul. She supposed she was being sensible.

The grocer had stands of flowers outside his door, more violets and narcissi and pots of pink and white cyclamen. Pali moved to go around a boy walking a small white dog, which was interested in her shoes and sniffed energetically as the boy futilely tried to call it off.

Pali patted the dog, let it smell her hand, exchanged a few polite nothingnesses with the boy, who was curious about her sash, and found herself right at the bookstore.

It had a good window, with an orange cat draped across a cushion, and stacks of books arranged decoratively. Someone had made a little scene out of cut paper, depicting a man in a blue tunic fighting a splendid green dragon in front of some sort of pavilion. Pali chuckled at the sight, and ducked inside.

A bell over the door made a pleasant tinkle as she entered. The store was warmly welcoming, with a wood stove burning merrily despite the mild day, a copper kettle gleaming on its surface. Pali stood a moment by the door, taking in the space.

A young man stood behind the counter, writing something with a lovely fountain pen.

Perry Dart's friend, she guessed, finding him familiar. Had not Mr. Dart introduced his friend, when they met by chance walking down the street? He had been an earnest and bright-eyed young man —almost too bright-eyed—who had chattered excitedly about poetry.

He had reminded her of another earnest, bright-eyed young man who chattered about poetry, and she had barely been able to be more than briskly polite.

Mr. Greenwing, then. A famous name, for those who studied the history she did. If she remembered, he was talented in the martial arts that had made his father renowned. She could only presume it was better to disregard the half of what the *New Salon* said of him; though if he *had* slain a dragon she would be very interested in hearing more about the deed,

He glanced up with a warm smile. "Good morning! Can I help you, ma'am?"

She glanced again around the room. The cat purring in the window. The books stacked neatly, their covers bright cloth or gleaming leather, the scent rich and familiar, fond.

"I am looking for something more interesting to read than the book I had brought with me," she said. "I presume I have come to the right place."

"It is a place of many adventures," Mr. Greenwing replied grandly, with an extravagant gesture. "Is there one in particular you are seeking?"

Some mischief—she would swear in court it was mischief—made her open her mouth and ask, "Anything by Fitzroy Angursell?"

"Depends on whether you think *The Correspondence of Love and the Soul* is his work or not. Certainly it has never been attributed to him," Mr. Greenwing replied promptly, in a feat of sophistry Pali could only admire. "Should you be interested in seeing it?"

"I am unfamiliar with the book," she replied.

The young man grinned. "Most people are. One moment—it's in the back room."

He ducked out from behind the counter and crossed behind a

bookcase that extended out into the room and apparently hid another door. Pali drifted into the room, glancing at titles as she passed them, until she could see behind the bookcase. An open door led into another book-lined chamber, the 'back room' presumably, and another door was closed.

Pali had never let propriety prevent her from heeding the invitations sent by the world.

Mr. Greenwing was apparently engrossed in seeking out the book. She set her hand to the closed door handle.

It turned easily under her hand. The door nearly fell open.

Another woman stood on the other side, equally startled by the unexpectedly open door, as familiar as Pali's own reflection.

"Jullanar!" said Pali.

And—"Pali!" said Jullanar of the Sea, falling into her arms. "Oh, *Pali!*"

CHAPTER FIVE
THE BOOKSELLERS OF RAGNOR BELLA

Pali enveloped her friend's soft bulk, the floral fragrance of her hair, and felt as if some internal dislocation had wrenched unexpectedly back into place. She tightened her arms.

Jullanar was trembling against her, the rhythm of tears or laughter or perhaps a combination of both. Pali felt both emotions rising, and did not know what to do with them—had she ever known what to do with them?—even for Jullanar she had been slow to utter the quieter, kinder emotions—and squeezed harder before stepping back to observe Jullanar.

Yes. Jullanar. It *was* Jullanar.

She looked amazingly the same, for the twenty-five years since they had seen each other last. A little rounder, a little softer, her hair a little greyer. Pali had always thought Jullanar's hair was the colour of a desert partridge, all shades of fawn and sand and those odd hues between umber and grey.

She still had her freckles. She still had that soft heart, that soft look in her eyes, belying the courage and strength that was at her core.

Oh, it *was* Jullanar. Pali did not feel the shock of their first meeting, but an upwelling, an overflowing—a *brimming* of happiness.

"You look just the same," Jullanar said, surveying Pali. They smiled at each other, Jullanar's hand on Pali's elbow, Pali's free hand waving oddly in the air until she tucked it down by her side.

Pali huffed and regathered herself. "So do you."

"Oh, a little older, a little wiser ... perhaps a little less respectable.."

"But here," Pali said, despite herself. "You're here."

"And so are you," Jullanar replied, her eyes crinkling as she laughed.

Pali swallowed at the beloved sound, immediately familiar. Homely. Home.

"*What* a surprise! Come, Pali, we must—we must catch up." She turned into the hall behind her, frowned, and turned back to enter into the main room of the bookstore. "Mr. Greenwing, are you there?"

Pali had entirely forgotten the young man, and bit her lip in minor consternation. Jullanar saw this and grinned mischievously at her, an expression that was so familiar it stabbed right to Pali's heart.

"Don't worry," Jullanar said, turning to her young employee. She was beaming with such fondness that Pali could only surmise the young man was a dear student or protégé of some form. "Mr. Greenwing studied puzzle poetry. He figured it out by Winterturn, after starting working for me in ... when was it, Mr. Greenwing? End of September, wasn't it?"

"Yes, Mrs. Etaris," the young man in question said, grinning sheepishly at Pali as she caught him staring in wonder.

"You translated the Gainsgooding conspirators for Mr. Dart's book," Pali said, nodding as the names came together in her mind. "An excellent translation, and superb riddling."

"Thank you," he replied, with an expression to suggest he would treasure her praise. Pali could not help but inwardly preen at this response.

She raised it in her undergraduates, of course—she worked hard to do so—but this was because *Pali Avramapul* said so. And it had been far too long since she'd had occasion to admit her true thoughts at all.

"Have you read their new book?" Jullanar enquired, frowning slightly.

"Oh yes, Mr. Dart was my student—I teach at Stoneybridge," Pali explained.

Mr. Greenwing gaped at her before catching himself again. "You're *Domina Black?*"

～

Few moments in Pali's life had ever been so fated as that first encounter with Jullanar, with Fitzroy, with Damian. It was no exaggeration to say the entire course of the Nine Worlds had shifted because of that meeting.

"You are magnificent! We should get married," Fitzroy had cried, from his perch on the balcony overlooking the yard where Pali had just duelled and defeated Damian Raskae.

"How do I know you are magnificent enough for me?" Pali had retorted, narrowing her eyes as she looked up at that strange figure, all black skin and startling clothes—had he already been wearing the sky-blue and scarlet he had come to love, or was that later memory overlaying that first meeting?—and the magic coruscating around him, crackling in the air like an incipient thunderstorm.

He had been magnificent already, to tell the truth, but she had met gods before, and knew they asked for things mortals did not always know they gave.

Pali was not her sister Sardeet, stolen away by the Blue Wind to become his bride.

Pali was the one who had widowed her.

"I am the poet Fitzroy Angursell!" he had cried back down, his face ringing with joy, with certainty, with glory. His hands outstretched in benediction, the gleam in his eyes visible even from a storey below.

Pali had only crossed the boundary between worlds a week or two before. She had been lifted up by the Siruyal, granted three feathers and three wishes and three quests. She had used one of the wishes to grant her knowledge of the languages of the first three people she met. He was the second, after the swordsman she had just defeated. Pali had understood his words, if not the verve with which he cried them, or the emotion in them, or that answering in her own heart.

She had always chosen adventure, when the world held out its invitations.

But she would not succumb to some mischievous god, some trickster come mumming a human being.

"Ask me again when you are famous," she had replied, her tongue caustic, for even then she had never been good at bowing before power.

He had only laughed, joy in his eyes, in his voice, in his whole being. And Pali had known, as she had always known such things, that she was as caught by his look, his laugh, his rich voice, as her sister Sardeet had been by the Blue Wind.

But looking away, refusing to bow, refusing to succumb—she would be no mortal bride taken by a divine lover—Pali would not be *ravished*—she had looked at Damian, the blond swordsman who had pushed her to her own limits, until she surpassed even her own estimation of her skill, and overmatched him.

He was frowning, his grey eyes blank, his face like one of the marble sculptures Pali's father made, fine-featured and still.

One challenge met and won; a second met and parried.

Between the swordsman and the poet came forth a human woman, ordinary—so very ordinary—if foreign, even alien, to Pali's eyes. Wearing an incongruous dress, holding a sword in a shaking but not entirely incompetent hand, her hair escaping its confines.

Pali remembered thinking that she should show this young

woman how to braid her hair so it would not interfere with her fighting.

"You *are* magnificent," Jullanar had said, smiling at her not with awe and amazement, but with what seemed almost conspiratorial pleasure. Pali had smiled back, suddenly uncertain, glad of her veils. Her sword in her hand, in case this was some sneak attack.

"You have bested Damian at the sword," Jullanar had said, gesturing at the blond, "and Fitzroy with words."

Her smile grew, something longing, yearning in it, the desire for—was it for *friendship*? Pali had not been able to parse the emotion, had been so surprised by the words, by the approach, by this incongruous young woman in the rough and bandit-overrun inn.

"I cannot offer you such a challenge to your skill myself, but I can offer you an invitation to a great adventure."

"What adventure?" Pali had asked, suspicious but also intrigued. She assisted women who did not have the skill at sword she had earned; she did not usually have such skill at words as this stranger had suggested of her.

"We three seek to stop an invading army," Jullanar had stated baldly. "Will you help us?"

And Pali had laughed at the ridiculousness of that offer; laughed, and gone with them, for the coruscating magic of Fitzroy and the solemn skill of Damian and the laughing, yearning desire of Jullanar for a friend.

For Pali had been lonely then, too, and not known it.

Now, thirty—almost *forty*—years on from that meeting, she followed Jullanar up the narrow stairs that had been hidden behind the door by which her friend at entered. There was another door there, a back door to the store, heavy cloaks hung on a rack on the wall.

Upstairs was a small, cozy flat. Jullanar opened the door to reveal a wood stove like the one below, burning low but cheerily, the embers a warm red. She nodded and swiftly moved to add a few logs from the basket set behind the stove.

"There we are," she said. "Mr. Greenwing is a dear. This is his flat—perk of his job. Though really it was to my benefit, he cleaned it out for me. Do sit down, Pali, I'll find his kettle. He's a fairly good baker, you know. Went to Morrowlea—though perhaps you knew that?"

"I believe I was told that, yes," Pali replied. She looked around the room curiously. The stove; two cushioned chairs positioned near it, as if Mr. Greenwing often had a friend over to chat. Two wooden chairs were pulled in to a small table near the corner he apparently used as his kitchen. There was a counter, a tall cupboard built into the corner, several shelves holding mismatched plates and drinking vessels along with a splendid green-and-white jade crock that was probably worth the entire rest of the room's contents.

She closed the door behind her, and discovered it had hidden her view of a bookcase full of untidy volumes—she recognized the new binding of the book Mr. Dart had just had published about the Gainsgooding conspiracy—and on the wall above, a fantastically elaborate gold pectoral showing the sun-in-glory of Astandalas.

She had never seen one in person before, but there were drawings in books. "The Heart of Glory, awarded to Major Jack Greenwing for holding the Border at Orkaty," she murmured aloud, moving over to examine it more closely.

"Isn't it splendid?" Jullanar replied. "Jack is a good man. His late wife Olive was a friend of mine. Jemis takes after both of them. Brave as anything, smart as a whip, and a little ... fey."

Pali considered the look in the young man's eyes, the gleam of mischief and the limning of something *other*. "Has he been to Fairyland?"

"He has fairy blood, apparently, but no; he died and came back to life."

Pali blinked. After a moment she recalled some hysterical essays in the *New Salon*, and some sort of buzz going on with the worshippers of the Lady about a new saint and what it might portend. "How dramatic of him," she observed, and flung herself down into one of the seats.

Jullanar burst out laughing. "Oh, Pali!"

"What?" Pali raised her eyebrows at her. "It's not as if *we* didn't get up to absurdly dramatic things when we were his age. Not that particular one, it's true, but," she shrugged as magnificently as she could. "It's good for the younger generations to find their own paths to greatness."

Jullanar was by now laughing so hard she could barely fill the kettle from the ewer she'd taken from the sideboard. Pali watched, but after a moment Jullanar succeeded and set the kettle on the fire. She promptly returned to the counter to mop up the spilled water, which was so very Jullanar, and then opened a pretty metal tin that appeared to contain some form of butter cookies.

Pali generally preferred a heartier breakfast, but it was her own fault to have chosen the bookstore over the bakery, and this *was* the southern Charese style: very strong coffee and some sort of sweet pastry.

"So, Stoneybridge," Jullanar said, settling into the chair opposite her.

"And Ragnor Bella," Pali replied, letting the name sing on her tongue. "How did you come to be here?"

"What happened to you?" Jullanar said at the same time.

"You first."

"No—I'm sure yours is more interesting."

This had always been Jullanar's way. Pali remembered far too many occasions when Jullanar had dismissed her own experience and ideas, her own emotions and abilities.

She remembered also that Jullanar was not especially amenable to being pushed, not at the beginning of a conversation. It would be only later on, once she was more comfortable with the moment, that she would be able to speak forth quieter truths.

But they were not twenty or twenty-five or even thirty now, and Pali had learned a few things herself. She smiled at her friend. "Let us take turns. After the Silver Forest, I found myself in far northwestern Dair, on Zunidh."

She waited expectantly. After a moment Jullanar ducked her head, her cheeks rosy. "I found myself in a temperate rainforest, which I eventually learned was the other side of the Mountains of Desire, in far Eastern Oriole."

Pali nodded attentively. Jullanar fussed a moment with the stove, putting another log on the fire and moving the kettle around so it sat on top of the hottest part. Pali preferred an open fire for its ambience and the friendly, familiar scent of the smoke, but it had to be said that the Alinorel iron stoves were much more efficient. The more recent style—used both downstairs and up here—had glass frontages, so one could still see the fire and be warmed by its merry flames. The closed ones had always seemed oddly unfriendly to her.

"I made my way back to the Silver Forest," Pali murmured, watching the flames dance.

"I ... made my way to Galderon."

"By the time I had crossed Zunidh, our trail was long cold. And of course we'd all been translated with magic, not our own feet."

"Except for Fitzroy," Jullanar said.

Pali nodded. "Except for him."

Jullanar waited, but it was her turn, not Pali's, and Pali was used to waiting out recalcitrant or reluctant students until they finally managed to put thought into speech. Jullanar smiled in wry defeat.

"I snuck back into the university and helped them ready their emissaries for going to Astandalas for the parley with the new emperor."

Now it was Pali's turn to shift and hesitate, but this was not so bad, was it?

"I followed his trail," she said quietly.

Jullanar regarded her sharply, but although she opened her mouth, she said nothing. The kettle was coming to the boil, and she got up and fussed with an old stoneware teapot and richly fragrant tea.

"Mr. Greenwing does himself well," Pali observed of the tea.

"He inherited a fortune from his stepfather at the Winterturn Assizes. He's also the Viscount St-Noire ... he's a good lad. The tea came from a little spot of blackmail."

"Very good," Pali replied dryly.

"It was a difficult year before he came home from university," Jullanar admitted. "I was struggling ... anyway, we're not there yet, are we?"

"No," Pali replied softly. "Not yet."

Jullanar left the tea steeping but did not return to her seat. She leaned over Jemis Greenwing's kitchen table, forearms resting on the flat surface, and regarded Pali intently. "You followed his trail ... where? How?"

"You must have heard the stories."

Jullanar scoffed. "Fantastic stories about his horse flying through the sky, magic thundering around him, cracking like lightning, as if he were a storm god. I always wondered, you know."

Pali could barely keep from laughing; it was a feeling too near tears for her liking. She frowned at the biscuit on her plate, at the fire in front of her.

"When I was first become a woman," she said slowly, "I went out into the desert, as was the custom of my people, to see what I might see. It was a kind of ... vision quest."

Jullanar cocked her head, visibly struck. "I remember you telling me ... you saw all sorts of things, you said. Those huge trees in ... where was it? That island on Colhélhé with all the houses built into the trees."

"Sardeet saw us ... him. Saw that grey horse, the thunder about him, as he rode helter-skelter through the sky."

"And what did you find?"

What, indeed.

Pali frowned until the stinging in her eyes abated.

"I followed his trail, the stories of the horse running through the sky, the black-skinned wizard in sky-blue and scarlet, the magic foaming about him. Across Ysthar; across Zunidh; across Voonra; across Alinor; across Colhélhé. All the way to the Long Edge."

"That tower," Jullanar breathed.

Memories were crowding close for both of them. Pali shivered and drew her chair closer to the stove. Jullanar poured the tea, which apparently was the sort to be taken with milk, for she offered Pali some.

Pali sipped the tea before adding her habitual milk and half a teaspoon of honey. It was a robust black tea, the flavours softened by her additions. A little bitterness, a little sweetness, mostly ... reviving.

A cup, brimming, brimful ... Now that she had been reminded, *let* herself be reminded, of that unfinished, not-yet-undertaken quest (that quest whose reminder she kept in her pocket, a handful of beans and a feather—)—now she found its traces everywhere. She could track this quarry to its heart, if she chose. If she chose.

Jullanar stirred her tea methodically before bringing it back to her own chair. She sat down and then pushed her feet up against Pali's, as they had on ... oh, so many occasions, sitting beside their campfire. "I stayed at Galderon until the embassy came back. Successfully, to everyone's surprise."

That was one of the wildly unbelievable decisions Artorin Damara had made. It had been so early in his reign for him to decide to grant a breakaway republic the recognition it sought. The decision might have unseated him, had there been a clear figurehead for another faction—by then his sister, the obvious alternative, had retired in her unconvincing deep mourning—and if Artorin Damara had not developed a nearly miraculous ability to play off three factions against each other.

"They opened the doors and decided to award degrees, finally." Jullanar smiled wryly. "They let me challenge for one."

"From all I could see," Pali said quietly, "he jumped his horse into the Sea of Stars on the far side of the Long Edge."

Jullanar looked up, her eyes stricken. "That tower?"

"I searched it," Pali said gently. "No one had been in there since we had."

That wizard-tower—the wizard-tower of Harbut Zalarin, Fitzroy had called it—where he had been exiled, or had gone to study ... There were so many mysteries about him, so many odd gaps in his accounts of himself, so many *clues* that never seemed to lead anywhere.

"So that was it, then?" Jullanar asked.

Pali gave her a long, flat look. "I had my sister's carpet; that's how I had reached the Long Edge. I flew seven days and seven nights into the Sea of Stars before turning back."

Jullanar closed her eyes, and then she snickered softly, and then began to laugh, and finally said: "Oh, Pali! Only you would follow him so far!"

CHAPTER SIX
THE TALE OF MRS. ETARIS

Jullanar's laughter was too close to tears. Pali stirred uncomfortably. "I didn't find him. I left him to his mystery, and went home. What about you?"

They sat there, the two old friends who had not seen each other for twenty-five years.

Jullanar said nothing, and then, finally, sighed. "Why cannot we let him go?"

"We must," said Pali, who had ruthlessly rooted out thoughts of Fitzroy Angursell until they came no more than once or twice a week.

It did not help that each successive wave of undergraduates discovered his poetry and sang his songs in the quadrangles of Stoneybridge, telling over the stories of the Red Company, taking the inspiration from their deeds that they had always tried to give.

It did not help that no one had ever found out what happened to Fitzroy Angursell, and somehow he was the one they all wanted to know about.

It did not help that Pali still wondered what she would have found, had she not turned back.

"I earned my degree—geography—and ..." Jullanar sighed. "And went home."

"To your parents?"

Jullanar nodded, her eyes on the fire.

"I went home, too," Pali said.

"To Kaphyrn?"

"Yes." Pali dipped her biscuit into the tea, a luxury that had once been commonplace. One did not do that with the outrageously expensive teas served at the high tables of Stoneybridge; not though those teas were not always of the highest quality. Some of them would have been much improved by the addition of biscuit crumbs. "It wasn't the same."

"At least you could tell your family what you'd been doing," Jullanar said, an old, soft bitterness lacing her voice. "Mine guessed—how could they not?—but they refused to admit it. My father told me outright not to describe any of my *adventures* while I was away at Galderon. My oldest sister, Maudie, was the only one who even came close to talking about it."

Pali vaguely remembered Maudie, the oldest of the five Thistlethwaite sisters and the one whom Jullanar had liked best. "Was she the artist?"

"The scholar. She's at Vaunton." Jullanar smiled, albeit a little weepily. "I went to visit her after I came back. She asked me about the friends I'd made while I was 'away', and ... oh, she said she was so proud of me, but that it was too dangerous. I didn't want to hurt my family, you know."

"I understand," Pali replied. "I didn't exactly trumpet my name when I came back into the empire."

"Why did you? If—were you looking for Sardeet?"

"Sardeet sent Arzu a letter saying she was going on an adventure all of her own, and that if I were there to read the letter I should remember that the fates had laid down many paths, and ours would cross again if I was able to let her go now."

"How very Sardeet."

Pali's heart swelled with that simple, wry, companionable statement. Because Jullanar *knew* Sardeet; loved her; was equally exasperated by her.

"I couldn't stay. It was boring," Pali admitted. "There were adventures, I suppose, but they were things I had already done."

"There's no shame in loving learning."

Pali pushed her feet against Jullanar's. "Not to you, my fair Alinorel lady!"

She could not open the box of her heart so quickly. She kept her voice light, conversational, proper. She probably did not fool Jullanar, even after so many years ... but Jullanar would understand that Pali needed some time to re-learn how to speak to her. No doubt Jullanar would, too.

"I was curious about things I could not learn there, and so in the end, I came back. First to Colhélhé and then here. I heard about the new emperor and became interested in him. I received a first degree at Arkthorpe and then another at Tara, and then I taught first at Kermon before taking up a chair at Stoneybridge."

"I visited my sisters and tried to be what they expected me to be," Jullanar said. "I had never wanted to be a scholar. I thought perhaps I might start a business of my own."

"You'd always wanted a bookstore."

"And a family." Jullanar looked down, tracing her tea cup with her fingers. "I was visiting my sister Lavinia here—she married a physician, very respectable."

"Very."

"There was this building for sale, and I thought—I had a bit of money, not much but some, from our adventures. I told my family it was my share of the moneys Emperor Artorin granted Galderon as damages ... I thought perhaps I'd buy it. Lavinia was never my favourite sister but I liked Ragnor Bella, and she was easier to get along with as an adult. I made a few other friends almost immediately ... had a couple small adventures ..."

"Sounds promising," Pali commented when she trailed off.

Jullanar smiled. "It was. Unfortunately, during the course of one of the small adventures—and it *was* small, a matter of a missing parcel—one of the grand doyennes of the town discovered I was *that* Jullanar, Jullanar of the Sea, and she ... blackmailed me."

"You let her?" Pali winced the moment she'd said the words, wishing she could retract them. She was honestly surprised that Jullanar *had*, for her friend was strong.

Surprised, not *shocked*, because she too remembered what it had been like, those golden days of the middle of Artorin Damara's reign.

In some ways their popularity had never been higher, nor the authorities' desire to see them brought low.

"I was afraid," Jullanar admitted. "I would have told her to publish and be damned, if—if there had been anyone else to stand with me. By myself? And there was my family to think of. They would have been *ruined*. How could I do that to them?"

"I'm sorry," Pali said. "I didn't mean it so sharply."

"You were always braver than me."

Pali wasn't so certain of that. She had been raised in a different culture, with far different expectations; she wasn't *afraid* of nearly so many things as Jullanar had been taught to fear. Jullanar had been taught to fear discomfort, and social opprobrium, and rumour, and the new.

And yet she had never let those fears stop her, or not for long: she always looked, and thought for herself, and decided if the cost was worth the prize. If she had decided the cost of being blackmailed was worth the prize ... well.

"What did she blackmail you into? For I see you do have a bookstore."

"And it *is* mine, yes." Jullanar blushed. "Marriage. Marriage to her son."

Pali stared at her. "She blackmailed you into marrying her son?"

Jullanar blushed even more fiercely, until she seemed nearly to be glowing scarlet, like iron ready to be forged.

Pali could only laugh, at the thought of a woman who knew

Jullanar was the infamous criminal and outlaw Jullanar of the Sea, and decided that *she* must be the one to marry her son.

Eventually she sipped her tea until she was able to speak clearly. "Was he objectionable in some way? Has it been a happy marriage?"

From the sudden stricken look on her friend's face, it had not been. "It's fine," Jullanar said quickly. "I have two children. Samantha is my daughter ... she's smart. Fearless. My son, Benjy, is smart too, though more cautious. He's to write the Entrance Exams this spring. Hopes to make the Silver List, at least."

She stopped there. Pali raised her eyebrows. "And?"

"It's not enough," Jullanar admitted. "It was better when we were first married. I had the store, and that took up most of my time ... and then when the children were young, that was plenty to occupy myself ... and then the Fall, of course ... and ... I lost, or thought I lost, some of my closest friends here ... " She trailed off. "It's good that Mr. Greenwing came to work for me this year. I was starting to feel a bit lost."

She said that with finality. Pali considered the subject, and decided not to press. It was quite remarkable that Jullanar had been that forthcoming so early in their conversation, after all, and it was probably better to let her add more in her own time.

If Pali pressed, Jullanar would logically press back, and she was not ready for that.

"Are *you* married?"

Pali stared at her. "No, of course not."

Jullanar flushed, then grinned. "I suppose not. There was always—"

"We're not talking about him," Pali interrupted sharply. Though of course that only emphasized the direction her thoughts had taken.

"Oh, indeed not. Have you heard of any of the others?"

"No."

There was a pause. Jullanar poured them each more tea. Pali added more honey to counteract the extra bitterness, and then sipped meditatively. There were probably a thousand things she should be asking Jullanar, but—oh, there was something so immensely precious at simply being able to sit with her.

"What brings you to Ragnor Bella?" Jullanar asked eventually.

"I'm on my way to Zunidh to research in the Archives. I came over the southern pass so I could stop in and see Mr. Dart on my way. I shouldn't say so but he was my favourite student."

"He's a great dear. Very clever." Jullanar fell silent then, though her lips were quirked with an impish smile.

Pali considered asking her for the secret, but before she could, her friend went on. "How did you get across the pass? Surely it was still snowed in?"

"My sister's carpet."

"You still have it—of course you do," Jullanar corrected herself immediately. "And you flew it across? Wasn't it terribly cold?"

"Perishingly."

"Pshaw! You say that as if you are above such practical constraints."

"I wore clothes my sister wove for me."

"Fair, fair," Jullanar murmured, regarding Pali's indigo robes, her black leggings, with nostalgic familiarity. "Did you meet anything at the crossroads?"

Pali huffed in annoyance. "I challenged the night, and three hooded figures came—one white, one black, one silver—but they ran away when I challenged them directly."

Jullanar bit her lip, her eyes bright. "The Dark Kings *ran away* from you?"

"It was all most unsatisfactory."

"I expect it would be."

Pali met her friend's mirthful look and could not keep her own countenance. They laughed, peals of laughter, as if they were young women discovering friendship for the first time.

For that was what it had been, Pali meeting Jullanar. The first time either of them had a real female friend outside their own families. Jullanar had had one other friend, a young lady who had stayed at Galderon through all the rebellion—Pali remembered her, golden-haired almost as Damian, pretty and cheerful to the end, a general for the rebels—

But it was Pali who had been Jullanar's friend for a decade, and Jullanar who had been the first one to teach *her* what it meant to live outside of legends. It was not because of Jullanar that Pali had been bored in her own country, her own clan; but it was because of Jullanar that she had been able to live happily as a scholar in Stoneybridge.

"Now," Pali said seriously once they had stopped laughing. "About this husband of yours. Do I need to kill him?"

It had been years since she'd last had any reason to kill someone, and truly she did not *want* to.

Not unless it was necessary, of course.

But Jullanar said it wasn't, with an expression on her face that suggested she was starting to revolve some plans in her own mind.

"So long as you know I am ready for *any* assistance you might need," Pali said solemnly.

"Far beyond the hiding of a body?"

"Pish-tush. That's an amateur's concern."

Jullanar stared at her. "Pali Avramapul, did you just say *pish-tush?*"

That was definitely Professor Vane's influence. Pali could only see one proper response, which was to invite Jullanar out to a very early lunch.

∼

"You wouldn't actually murder him, would you? In cold blood?" Jullanar asked quietly as they picked their way through a muddy side street towards what was apparently her sister's tearoom.

"It wouldn't be in cold blood if he'd hurt you," Pali pointed out.

Jullanar tilted her head, then focused forward again. Her voice was even lower. "What if I'd ... provoked it?"

"I beg your pardon? First, unless you were deliberately prodding him for a physically violent reaction, which is, I suppose, an invitation to a fight—something which is, as you know, one of my very favourite things, and not to be undertaken lightly—you're not *provoking it*. Thus, secondly, if you *had* provoked him I'm sure it would be for a reason. Thirdly, you are family."

Jullanar had spent her time with Pali and Sardeet, even in the tents of their clan, and she knew how fiercely protective they were of their own. She blushed, and nudged her elbow against Pali, and changed the subject. Pali made a mental note to return to the subject later, but let Jullanar off the hook for the present.

"My sister's children are older than mine, already grown, and Lavinia—Mrs. Landry, that is, she's *very* keen on keeping the formalities—the very thought of calling me *Jullanar* out loud! in public!—decided that I had managed to become very nearly respectable through the good management of my bookstore, and so she started a little enterprise of her own, a very genteel sort of tearoom. Not that she serves tea, but she does do a fairly nice lunch."

Pali had, with minor regret, changed into her academic robes, though she kept her sword belted at her side, and enjoyed the feeling, so very, splendidly familiar, of walking beside Jullanar.

In a stretch with no other pedestrians, Jullanar said, "Will you be so good as to ... pretend we met at Galderon?"

Pali considered this. "I will be glad to say, with utter honesty, that we met the year you were delayed from attending Galderon, and stayed friends after." At Jullanar's exasperated huff, Pali laughed. "Come now, Jullanar, if your sister knows she knows, and if she is resolute about keeping her eyes closed, that's a sufficiency of plausible deniability."

"Really."

"Would you be able to call me Ivy?"

"Why would I call you that?"

"It's ostensibly my name."

"Ivy Black?" Jullanar laughed merrily. "However did you choose that? Did you look out the window and see ivy leaves and—you did, didn't you?"

Pali elbowed her. "I was flustered. I wasn't expecting the interrogation the librarian at Arkthorpe gave me."

Jullanar hooted, then blushed pink and covered her mouth, but her eyes were shining brilliantly as she looked at Pali. "I'm sure you were flustered only because you couldn't use your proper reputation to intimidate him."

"I have found I can be intimidating without the reputation."

"I'm sure." Jullanar directed her to a house with a window bowered with climbing plants just beginning to bud. "Here we are, my dear Professor Black. Domina Black. Which do you prefer?"

"Whichever you do. I am a full professor, however."

"That'll impress Lavinia more. She's a terrible snob. And I'm Mrs. Etaris, do try to remember." Jullanar put her shoulders back and drew open the door, smiling at the thin, sharp woman who answered. "Mrs. Landry, my dear sister!"

"Sister," the woman acknowledged, pursing her lips as she regarded Pali, taking in her fine robes and the embroidered hems of her rank and field. "Is the professor with you?"

"Yes. Professor Black, my sister Mrs. Landry—Lavinia, Professor Black of Stoneybridge is a friend of mine from my Galderon years whom I'd lost touch with until this morning. We've come for a bite to eat, if you've anything ready?"

Mrs. Landry gave Pali another, sharper glance, suggesting that she was quite aware of what Jullanar had gotten up to in her 'Galderon years'. Pali gave her an equally pointed smile in return, promising dire retribution should she make any missteps, such as calling for the constabulary.

"How wonderful for you to have one of your ... old friends arrive," Mrs. Landry said finally, stepping back and letting them across her threshold. "Did you know my sister was here, Professor?"

"Alas, no, or else I should have come to visit long ago. Mr. Dart of Dartington was my student at Stoneybridge, and as I was travelling to

Yrchester I thought I would come across the mountain pass so that I might call on him along the way."

"Was the pass open?" Mrs. Landry asked, hesitating a moment in the middle of the room.

Pali cast a quick glance around, surveying the entrances and exits and the multitude of frilly furnishings. She gave Mrs. Landry a steady look. "No."

CHAPTER SEVEN
QUIET CURSES

After lunch, they returned to the bookstore. Jullanar sent Mr. Greenwing off for the afternoon. The young man promised to tell his friend Mr. Dart (spoken with as much ostentatious and good-humoured formality as Pali ever used for 'Professor Vane'; she enjoyed the mirth in Mr. Greenwing's expression as he did so) that *Professor Black* was in town for a few days.

"It'll let him get his gushing out of the way, at least," Jullanar observed after he'd left.

"I beg your pardon?"

"Both of them will undoubtedly spend the better part of an afternoon talking over all the stories of the Red Company they know, which is most of them, with a focus on you."

Pali blushed. "I'm sure they'll get over it."

"They're fine lads. Mr. Greenwing slayed a dragon last autumn, did you hear?"

Pali had heard a garbled rumour of some such, but she settled down happily with a cup of hot chocolate to listen to the stories Jullanar spun of the secrets and magical shenanigans emerging in the vicinity of the two young men.

They talked all afternoon, mostly sticking to the news of Ragnor Bella and other such ordinary, common, subjects: Pali's studies; Jullanar's children. Nothing the steady stream of customers couldn't overhear.

Later on, Pali took a room in the Ragnor Arms, as it was apparently the only hostelry in town to have the new hot water piping. Pali was willing to rusticate as necessary, and sometimes as was simply aesthetically pleasing, but when there *were* good baths—and better food—to be had, well, she was enough of a sybarite to prefer them.

Jullanar was mildly reluctant to invite Pali to her own home, at least without first determining whether her husband had invited one of *his* friends for supper, and so Pali dined alone in the hotel, reading the first few poems in *The Correspondence of Love and the Soul*. She tended to prefer reading the primary text first, and the introduction afterwards, which meant the context of the poems was decidedly puzzling but she came at them without preconceptions.

Or without preconceptions bar the belief that they could not possibly be written by Fitzroy Angursell, for though the poet's mastery was incontestable, *he* would never been so vague and elliptical, so vertiginously blurring the images. So ... sad.

They were good poems, at least. Deeply moving. The prisoner—the narrator was all-but-explicitly one—had squeezed the blood of truth from the stone of his cell.

Pali was glad when Jullanar called at the hotel, dressed in sturdy boots and a heavy cloak, ready for a twilight ramble.

The air was cool, moist, scented with the burgeoning life in the soil. Wood-doves were cooing, seemingly everywhere, as they crossed the bridge at the southern edge of town and Jullanar directed her along a wooded lane.

Pali had thought of asking more about Jullanar's family, but the air was so plangent and soft she didn't want to say anything at all.

It was good to be with Jullanar again. Pali had not thought herself lonely, but oh, she had been. How she had been.

"We will go looking for the others, won't we?" Jullanar asked, as they came around a bend and saw before them a luminous hollow where the lane dipped to meet a mossy stream. Faint wisps of mist were rising from the stream, and soft glimmering lights threaded through the trees.

"Fairy-lights," Jullanar said. "Sometimes you see the small-folk here. We're not far from the edge of the Kingdom proper."

There was a stone seat next to the stream, a few steps away from the stepping-stones that led across. Jullanar sat down, and Pali joined her, pressed close because the seat was not really quite wide enough for the both of them.

"We will seek them out, yes," Pali replied, trailing her hand through the mist, parting the vapour. The fairy-lights bobbed and glimmered around her, following the eddies and swirls of the air. "All of them."

"All of them." Jullanar paused. They had spoken of the rest, of where they might go looking, when no one had been in the store that afternoon.

Colhélhé seemed the best direction, that grand bazaar which Gadarved had loved and which was not so far from Ayasha's original home. They could seek out a way to Daun, and see if the Rose and Phoenix Inn of Ixsaa was still there, and if anyone had news of Damian and Pharia.

"We shall have to find a ship able to take us into the Sea of Stars," Jullanar said finally.

So they could go look for Fitzroy. Pali nodded, and Jullanar slung her arm about her shoulders, comfortingly snug. "Pali, it's no shame to miss him particularly."

Pali would have scoffed, but it was a place, a moment, a cross-roads of beauty, and she could only press her lips together and shake her head. "Do you think he ever meant it? Asking me to marry him— as he did?"

Pali could not quite believe she'd thought that, let alone said it out loud. But she was not so removed from her old skills as a warrior not to have assessed the hollow for danger, and there was no one bar the tiny little lights, no more sentient than a bumblebee, to hear her. And this was her first and greatest friend.

Jullanar turned her head so she could peer into Pali's face,. Her hand had tightened on Pali's shoulder. She didn't, however, say anything. She waited.

Pali could not hold her eyes for long. "Not that it matters, of course," she muttered, turning her head away. "It wasn't as if I ever—wanted to take him seriously."

"Didn't you?" Jullanar asked, very gently.

Pali moved her hands to her lap. It was comforting to wear her sash, the garments her sister had made, underneath her Scholar's robes. Perhaps that comfort, and the familiarity of Jullanar beside her, was why she could say these things.

She had never been able to say confidences inside a building, closed-off from the wind and the world. She always had that niggling suspicion that someone could be listening behind the walls.

"Perhaps once or twice," she admitted. "I thought it would be … it might be … pleasant."

"Pleasant?"

"If he were serious. But of course he wasn't."

Jullanar took a breath, but released it on a long sigh. "Pali, did you never … no, that's not the right way to say that. Have you ever been interested in someone else?"

Pali did scoff at that. "Of course not."

"He was different, then."

Pali looked back at her friend, whose expression was thoughtful in the dim light cast by the fairy-lights. Or—more than thoughtful. Speculative. Intrigued.

Restless, Pali slipped out from under Jullanar's arm and stepped to the edge of the stream. The water was dark, with the faintest of outlines on the ripples from the fairy-lights. She could see a few white bubbles breaking the surface of the shadows.

"I suppose so," she said carelessly. "He always was, wasn't he?"

∼

Pali spent the next day with Mr. Dart and his friend, walking with them to Mr. Dart's family home—a sizable and prosperous rural manor, it turned out, governed by Mr. Dart's older brother, the local Chief Magistrate and a kind, intelligent man—and being given a tour of the area. The two young men shyly asked for some stories of the Red Company, and even more shyly recounted their escapades to her.

And then they very proudly introduced her to Mr. Dart's not-even-half-grown unicorn foal.

Pali listened with great interest to the story of how Mr. Dart had come by the creature. She had read that in the old days, before the conquest by Astandalas, the magic-workers of Alinor had had familiars, intelligent magical animal companions. Mr. Dart did not name the unicorn as such, but she saw the intelligence and fondness with which it looked at him, and she could only imagine the depth of the connection growing between them.

Mr. Dart and Mr. Greenwing seemed inclined towards breaking up the old Astandalan structures and reclaiming some of the older practices. Pali spent an enjoyable few minutes, later in the day, compiling a bibliography for them to seek out and a list of scholars for them to contact.

She would have enjoyed their company more had she not *so recently* found Jullanar; she was glad when Jullanar suggested they go to visit some of her dear friends the third day of Pali's visit.

It appeared as if this part of Fiellan was similar to Stoneybridge, and everyone walked everywhere. Instead of heading north towards Dart Hall, Jullanar guided Pali south, back along the same route she had originally taken. When they came to the old imperial highway, Jullanar directed her south.

Ahead of them were the mountains, the fringe of high peaks which formed the old southern border of the Empire. There were valleys behind them, lands that only a handful of soldiers had ever seen: this part had not been contested, for there was an impassible swamp on the other side of the pass, and no one lived there.

Astandalas had encircled, but never conquered, this range. To the southwest, not far as the crow flew but months by human transport to go around, was Loe and the Seven Valleys, site of a disastrous campaign from right at the end of Artorin Damara's reign. One day Pali would come back and interview Captain Jack Greenwing, who had been intimately involved with both the good and the bad there, and she would write a monograph sorting out the sequence of events that had happened.

But not today. These few days in Ragnor Bella were an unexpected treasure found on her longer journey to Solaara.

"The Woods Noirell suffered badly in the Fall," Jullanar said as they crested a gentle rise and saw before them a close-cropped green mead, bordered by a deep and swift river. The river was bridged, and on the far side of the bridge was the first of the round gates leading to a Border between worlds and, behind the still-golden circle, a great grey wood filling the whole end of the valley and spilling up across the foothills.

"Oh yes?"

"We in Ragnor Bella were generally not ... *terribly* affected. Magic failed, of course, all the works of Astandalas, but we didn't have the horrors that occurred elsewhere. We're considered the least affected region, in fact."

"Do you have an explanation?"

"Only suppositions. Mr. Dart, the incipient wild mage. Incipient *great* mage, unless I miss my mark entirely. Mr. Greenwing has his own set of oddities, curses and fey blood and the attention of the gods. Then there's ... the fact I still have Fitzroy's bag, and who knows what all is in there."

Pali glanced quickly at her, but Jullanar was facing forward determinedly, eyes bright.

Jullanar had kept Fitzroy's bag for him, all the way from that devastating moment in the Silver Forest till now.

"At any rate," Jullanar said, gesturing at the circular gate before them, "the gates are safe to walk through. I might be a trifle wary of the last in the sequence, the one that used to cross to Ysthar, but these preparatory ones are fine."

The gate stood on the far side of a sturdy, graceful bridge. The bridge was made of the same large blocks of pale granite as the highway, carved with many runes; more would be inscribed on the iron chains that ran below the stones in the gravel road-bed. The gate itself was perhaps twenty feet in diameter, and perfectly circular.

This was the first of five gates, through which the highway passed on his way to the passage between worlds. Remnant of quite probably the greatest of all the works of the priest-wizards of Astandalas, who had caused to be joined in fixed and certain ways worlds that had previously been only tenuously connected.

Pali considered the circular arch, with its gold leaf flaking in places, bright-burnished in others, and the stream blocking easy bypass. Jullanar waited while she considered, and said nothing when Pali deliberately linked their arms together before stepping onto the bridge.

～

They had no adventures in the outer reaches of the Woods Noirell, though Pali could feel fay magic in the air and knew that if they were to stray off the path, they might stray *far* off the path. She would have stepped off the path, had she been alone and seeking adventure: it was very much the sort of place where one would find it.

Jullanar led her down the highway, not cutting any of the corners when it started to loop and bend, until they reached the village of St-Noire.

Pali remembered the village, which they had passed through a number of times on their way to or from Astandalas. She remembered the inn at its heart, the great sprawling building that could house dozens of guests and all their gear (and, this being Astandalas of the emperors, their servants). She remembered it being busy as the bees in the trees overhead.

The bees were still sleeping the end of winter away, and the trees were bare and grey. The grass of the village green was as bright an emerald as ever, and there were flowers in tubs and window-boxes.

A second glance showed the scars of need and destitution: the windows of the inn's long wings boarded up, the tubs mended with wire, the buildings needing paint or repair.

"They felt the magic of the Fall hard," Jullanar said quietly. "We didn't hear any news out of the Woods till well after the end of the Interim. And then, three and a half years ago, they fell silent again. Cursed, we found out: Mr. Greenwing broke it."

Mr. Greenwing had spoken of the curse, how he was the Viscount St-Noire and his reluctant assumption of the rank and its responsibilities, some of the things he had done so far to remedy their hideous lack. Mr. Dart had supplied a few details, explaining how his friend had personally bought all the needed food and supplies to see the village through the winter after the curse was broken.

"It was an insidious curse," Jullanar added, as they paused before the open door of the inn so Pali could examine the elaborate well-head at the edge of the green opposite. "Basil and Sara, the innkeepers, are *dear* friends of mine, and yet I didn't even *think* to come check on them. I barely thought of them at all, until the curse was broken and suddenly ..." She grimaced. "One would have thought I would have been able to break it. Assist them. Do *something*."

Pali touched her on the arm, trying to offer comfort. There were quests that were not for them.

That had been a hard lesson to learn, too.

"Who cursed them?"

"That is still uncertain, but I have my doubts about some of their ... neighbours."

She glanced at the castle on the crag above the village, and then at the soft mist rising off the impossibly green moss behind the houses. If Faërie wasn't behind those trees Pali would eat her hat.

"Some such curses are laid for specific people, you know that," Pali replied. "Come. Introduce me to your friends?"

CHAPTER EIGHT
ONE'S HEART'S DESIRE

Pali liked Basil and Sara immediately, which was rare for her. Sara was a local woman, pale and slight, her skin sallow with some chronic ailment. She was ensconced in a padded chair near one of the three fires blazing in the inn's central taproom, draped in shawls and working on ledgers with the assistance of a padded wooden lap desk.

It being midmorning, and no one now travelling through the village on the highway, there was no one else in the room. It should have felt cavernous and ill-at-ease, but the inn was an ancient building made out of many extensions and additions and strange architectural whimsies, and despite its emptiness the taproom was cosy and welcoming and full of intriguing nooks and corners.

The central space was roughly hexagonal: there were open fireplaces on three sides, the outside door visible but off to one side, the counter with its kegs of beer and mead on a fifth wall, another doorway opening up to further reaches of the inn on the sixth.

Sara looked up from her paperwork when Jullanar greeted her, and hailed them with enthusiasm.

"Please don't rise," Jullanar said, kissing Sara on the cheek and then beckoning Pali over. "Sara, I am *greatly* pleased to introduce you to my dear, dear friend, the magnificent Pali Avramapul. Pali, this is Sara White."

Pali bowed. Sara stared at her, gobsmacked, for a moment, before her face split into a wide smile. She rang the brass bell that stood on a table beside her, and as the chime faded said, "Oh, how *wonderful*! I am so pleased to meet you at last! How wonderful you came to find Jullanar! Do draw up seats, and Basil will be here in a moment—ah! There's Clio!"

Clio was a boy of about twelve, his skin almost the same brown as Pali's though with a golden undertone where hers was a touch more coppery. He had wavy black hair and his mother's pale blue eyes, and he regarded her with a combination of sulkiness and fondness Pali found immediately and irresistibly endearing.

"Darling," Sara said, "will you put the kettle on? And bring out the cake for our guests. And tell your father that Auntie Jullanar is here, whom you haven't greeted, I notice—*and* her friend."

She stopped there, a smile playing about her mouth, as Clio flushed and mumbled an apology to Jullanar before giving her a quick embrace. Jullanar ruffled his hair and he tossed his head, almost laughing, before he looked more deliberately on Pali.

Pali lifted her chin, amused, and waited to see if he knew who Jullanar was, and would guess who *she* might be.

He did: she could see him running through names in his mind, before he blurted out, "Sardeet Avramapul?"

"Close," Pali said, laughing, and bowed to him as he whispered *Pali* with veneration.

"The kettle, Clio," Sara said after he simply stared at her for another few moments, not saying anything. He yelped and dashed off, calling out "Dad! Dad! Dad!" as he ran.

"He's a dear lad," Jullanar said fondly, pulling over a wooden chair and sitting down next to her friend. "Is he still struggling with school?"

"Really?" Pali asked, who felt herself a fine judge of a student's intelligence, and had seen nothing to suggest anything otherwise in Clio. "Bored, is he?"

Sara gave her a surprised and relieved look. "Oh—you see that, do you?" She sighed. "Yes. He's struggling with the effects of the curse ... We lost three years, you know. Which was bad enough for us adults, and the young children didn't mind so much, but for the youngsters ... their friends from town are *years* older than them now. It's hard."

"It would be!"

"We might find that, you know, Pali," Jullanar said thoughtfully. "As we find our friends. I've heard that it's been much longer—or much shorter—elsewhere. Didn't you say you'd heard odd things about Zunidh? Pali's on her way there, for research," she explained to Sara.

"I've heard *all* sorts of things about Zunidh," Pali replied, settling down at a pleasant distance from the fire. Sometimes she felt a bit like Professor Vane's cat, soaking up the heat. It was a long time since the dry heat of her native desert, but she still loved it. She shrugged, phlegmatic about something they could in no way control. "I've heard everything from twenty years to a thousand. They say time fractured there, and different places run at different times."

Sara lived in a wood closely entwined with Faërie and the ancient Border with Ysthar: she nodded, unsurprised and thoughtful. "We have such stories, here in our woods, from before the coming of the Empire."

"I'm sure you do," Pali murmured, once more thinking of how Professor Vane would like this area. Here was a good pub at the end of an interesting ramble—*and* there would be all sorts of strange and idiosyncratic folkloric tales to learn.

Clio came back with a tray on which were arranged a dark fruit cake studded with almonds, a wedge of a pale orange cheese, and several cups. Behind him came a portly, jovial man, only a few inches taller than Pali, who looked almost wholly the typical innkeeper bar the fact that he wore his black hair, which was curlier than his son's, down past his shoulders.

He was holding a full copper kettle, which he set on the hook set into the hearth for the purpose. After swinging the kettle into the main heat of the fire, he folded his hands together and bowed over them to Pali.

"The famous Pali Avramapul," he said, in a pleasantly twangy accent. "I am honoured to meet you."

Sara snorted.

Basil grinned, unrepentant. "Also delighted, amazed, confounded—no, I think I mean overwhelmed—no, overjoyed—ah, it is wonderful to meet you at last! I have heard so much about you from Jullanar."

Pali was surprised into laughing, and caught Jullanar's smugly pleased smile out of the corner of her eye. Basil served out the cake and cheese, then immediately set his plate aside so he could fuss with Sara's shawls and then the kettle, when Sara murmured, "Dear, I'm fine."

The tenderness with which he touched her shoulder struck Pali hard. She coughed, and when they looked at her, smiled awkwardly and said, "Where are you from, Basil?"

"From the Vangavaye-ve," he replied, eyes crinkling. "Which is to say, the Wide Seas of Zunidh—about as far away from anywhere as you could get in the empire!"

"I've heard of the Wide Seas," Pali said cautiously.

Basil laughed. "That's very honest of you, Pali!—May I call you Pali?"

She nodded, a trifle stiffly, for it had been a long time since she'd simply let a new person call her that. "What brought you here? Merchanting?"

"Oh, no, no," Basil replied, still chuckling. "I was looking for my heart's desire—and I found it!" He turned to his wife, and to Pali's surprise kissed her full on the lips.

Sara spluttered with laughter and gave him a half-hearted push. "Basil, do attempt a small decorum! We might *feel* we know Pali from all of Jullanar's stories, but she's only just met us."

"Ah, no one who's travelled so far can be too shocked at other customs, isn't that right?" Basil regarded her expectantly. Pali nodded, for her surprise came from fifteen years in Northwest Oriole, where the customs were generally much more prudish.

"Yes," Basil said, moving to draw the kettle from the fire just as it began to emit a steady blast of steam. "I was travelling, looking for my heart's desire, and when I found her here, here I stayed."

"I see," said Pali, striving for a polite countenance, for to be honest that was the sort of mawkish sentimentality she found unbearable.

"I had thought you were a great admirer of the romantic," Sara said, cutting a doubtful glance to Jullanar. Pali did not know quite what to say to this. She loved the epic, the tragic, the splendid. But *romance?*

Jullanar said, "Pali—" and then could not finish through a great eruption of giggles. Basil prepared a pot of tea, entirely unbothered by Pali's futile efforts at equanimity or Jullanar's mirth, and eventually Jullanar managed to say, "Do tell Pali the rest of the story, Basil! She'll appreciate it better with context."

"If you insist," said Basil, obviously nothing loath. He produced a knitted tea cozy from somewhere, tucked the teapot in, and sat back down in the chair next to his wife. "If you do not know of my people, then I suppose that sounds a trifle precious, doesn't it?"

He raised his eyebrows at Pali, and Pali, who had hardly ever been able to resist a challenge, lifted her chin and said, "A trifle, yes."

"Oh, my cousin Kip would have liked you," Basil said, admiration sliding into his expression. "He wouldn't have let me get away with that, either!" He cut a few slices of cheese and layered them on his piece of cake, then took three bites to finish the wedge. "In the old stories of the Islanders, that is, the Wide Seas Islanders, my people, we say that Vonou'a, the first man, had three sons."

Pali felt her face and shoulders relax with genuine interest. She might not be quite so keen on folklore as Professor Vane, but she *loved* cosmographical myths and legends of the ancient times. There had been times—there might well be times to come—when she had used such a myth or legend of her own people as a kind of waysign indicating her own trail.

"Vonou'a, the first man, had three sons," she said, pronouncing the name carefully. "Who was their mother?"

Sara nodded sharply, and gave Pali an approving glance. Jullanar was leaning back in her chair with her own cake and cheese, eating it and watching her friends interacting with evident delight.

Basil smiled. "Their mother was a velioi, from outside the Ring—the Ring is another name for the Vangavaye-ve, on account of how the component islands are distributed, in a large circle."

Pali had never been to the Wide Seas of Zunidh, but she had seen tropical atolls on her journeys with the Red Company, and she remembered how they formed rings of islets and occasional larger islands around a sheltered lagoon. She imagined such a place, fringed with coconut palms, white sand and blue water and sun strong enough even for her. "Go on," she said.

"Vonou'a was the son of Ani—the Sea—and he sailed across the horizon in a ship of his own hand's building. On the other side of the horizon he met the first woman, Samayë, the Woman of the Dawn Wind, as she is named in our *Lays*. Samayë returned with Vonou'a and together they had three sons—and one daughter!"

He laughed, as at some private joke, and went on. "When they came of age, the three sons of Vonou'a took it into their minds to travel, as their father had before them. Before you ask, their sister Anyë stayed and became the first weaver, and we honour her greatly."

Pali sat back, satisfied that the first women had not been forgotten. She was perhaps a trifle impressed that Basil knew their names; so often only the men were recalled.

"We say that the first son went to find new islands, and the second went to find his heart's desire, and the third went to sit at the feet of the Sun."

Pali felt a cold thrill run down her back.

Jullanar laughed and patted her on the knee. "I thought that would be the one you found most interesting."

"Don't you?" Pali enquired, a little absently, for she was matching these three quests to those three she had been offered by the Siruyal. Hers had been for glory, and knowledge, and dzēren, that brimming joy.

"I had a twin brother," Basil said, smiling with a great love, a great sorrow at the back of his words. "We had an older sister, as it happens, though she was no weaver! But she did prefer to stay home. Dimiter, Kip, and I, though ... we always used to call ourselves the three sons of Vonou'a. I was the middle son—middle children are best, don't you think, Pali?"

"Of course," Pali replied immediately, knowing Jullanar had told him she herself was the second of three daughters. Perhaps Jullanar had told him that her older sister Arzu was a weaver. Her younger sister Sardeet was, of course, renowned the empire over at least as the most beautiful woman in the Nine Worlds. "Kip was your younger brother?"

"My cousin, rather, but he was as close as a brother to me—closer than my twin, in many ways." Basil cast a sly, laughing glance at Jullanar, who wrinkled her nose at him. "Kip was ... probably quite a bit like you, Pali. One of those people who are immediately, obviously, brilliant—and restless in their brilliance. Everyone knew he was going to leave. It's in all our stories. The three sons of Vonou'a set out, for new islands, for one's heart's desire, to sit at the feet of the Sun. Kip wanted to sit at the feet of the Sun—to bring home the fire, to bring home *law*, to bring home ... Well, I think he thought of it as good government."

"And you didn't want that?" Pali asked, doubtful, for the idea, the very sound of the *words*, of 'going to sit at the feet of the Sun', was epic poetry in her heart.

Oh, she had been to the country of Night, walked the halls of the Moon's white tower, struck that cold smile from her face.

They had spent far less time in the country of Day. Pali still wondered what they might have found, had they not rushed so quickly from the meadows where the clouds grazed.

"Our heart's desire comes in many forms," Basil said, suddenly serious. He turned to Sara and took her hand in his, lifting it so he could kiss her palm. Sara shook her head but did not draw her hand away, and her face was glowing with a fierce, quiet pleasure that shone past all the strain and worry of her illness. "As soon as I walked into the inn I saw Sara—she was sitting right here, weren't you? With a stack of ledgers and your silver-tipped pen that mad poet had given your mother."

"That mad poet was Fitzroy," Jullanar pretend-whispered to Pali. "One of his more grandiose gestures."

Pali ignored this. She fixed Basil with a stern look. "How did you know she was your heart's desire? Or you, Sara, that he was yours?"

Sara blushed. "He came in behind his cousin Kip, who was fine, he looked interesting, but not *interesting*, if you know what I mean, and then there he was, and there was such a look in his eyes ..." Her voice trailed off.

"I saw her with her lap full of ledgers, and I went over to say hello while Kip was talking to old Dad White, the innkeeper, and I discovered that Sara was doing complicated math in her head and—" Basil stopped. "And I looked around this room, which was full of people, all *sorts* of people, and I felt as if I had stepped right into the *Lays*, and so I knew."

Pali had stepped into legends once or twice, and she did know.

"I see," she said, thinking of that first encounter with Damian, with Fitzroy, with Jullanar. That had been no song she knew, but yet she had known, immediately, that she had stepped into one.

"Kip was so disappointed I fell head-over-heels in love, because we were supposed to go to the Yrchester Cheese Festival, and I kept making excuses—a terribly transparent fake cold, I think it was—until finally he acknowledged what had happened."

"Kip wasn't much of a romantic," Sara said. "But oh, I did like him!"

"It's not as if he had any grounds to talk," Basil added, an old amusement lacing his voice. "He was one of those people who don't have much interest in sex, I doubt he ever initiated a courtship in his life, but the first time he saw a portrait of the Emperor Artorin he actually said 'our fates are entwined', and nothing would stop him from taking the exams and joining the bureaucratic service."

Pali registered a certain kinship to this Kip, who did not have much interest in sex and who understood the call of Fate. She also noted they were speaking of him in the past tense. "He was in Astandalas, then, during the Fall?"

A shadow crossed Basil's face. "Yes. Such a waste ... He was one of the greatest people our Islands had seen in generations. The sort of person we all thought would enter into the *Lays* in his own right ..."

The Empire of Astandalas had destroyed many great and wonderful things in its ruthless expansion, but its collapse had been cataclysmic even for those who had escaped the worst of its active influence. Even in such a small way, the loss of a single person, out of all those who had been lost in Astandalas, still hurt.

"I'm sorry," Pali said. "Are ... are any of your other family still alive?"

Basil drew a sharp breath. "I haven't heard from anyone since the Fall," he said, picking his words carefully. "But there was the curse ... and there haven't been any letters for anyone in the Woods in years and years. I asked young Jemis Greenwing to see if he could find if any had gone astray ..."

A good use for the well-meaning local viscount, Pali agreed. He seemed the sort of young man who did better with a task to work on.

"I'm heading to Zunidh tomorrow," she said. "If you'd like to send a letter with me?"

This time it was Sara who reached out for his hand, and held it gently, comfortingly. Basil's face was shadowed.

"Or perhaps," Jullanar said, "now that you know there is regular traffic across, you could send a letter to the ambassador in Nên

Corovel and ask him to pass it along. It would be a hard letter to write in an evening, and Pali's taking the stagecoach north in the morning."

"Thank you," Basil said. "If you hear anything of the Vangavayeve ..."

"I'll keep my ears open," Pali promised, pretending she didn't see Jullanar looking at her with a speculative expression. Whether Jullanar was thinking of what Pali might have experienced in the Fall, or her own distant family, or (perish the thought), her *heart's desire*, Pali did not think now was the time to talk about it.

CHAPTER NINE
SOLAARA

Twelve days later, Pali arrived in Solaara.

The time with Jullanar had passed dream-like and delightful. They had spent half the day with Basil and Sara, telling stories. Pali was glad that Jullanar had these friends, and that Basil had Jullanar, who was fascinated by his culture and had evidently proved an eager student alongside his son.

Pali could not help but contrast them with Professor Vane, who would almost certainly have been as enthusiastic about Pali's home culture as Jullanar was about Basil's. But Pali was not Jullanar, and had never known how to step out of her own reserve.

She had never quite wanted to. It was easier to hold the truth of herself deep inside, quiet as the flying carpet on the wall, always ready for the world's invitation but content, even happy, with the smaller challenges she faced.

It was a sad thought that she might have had so much *more*, had she ever crossed the mountains into South Fiellan.

Later in the afternoon, they walked slowly back to town. They reminded each other of more stories they had forgotten and places they had known, speculated at length about what might have happened to the others, and generally, Pali reflected afterwards, worked to fill in the deep well of loneliness and wistful longing.

Oh, she had missed this. She could not have built this again, could she? She and Jullanar had shared so much—

It was almost enough to keep her from going to Zunidh.

"Oh, you mustn't not go on my account," Jullanar had protested when Pali broached this. "I should love to go with you but really, I have a few things I need to take care of before leaving. My children, you know—"

Pali did not know, but she accepted the argument. Jullanar had finally decided not to introduce Pali until she had had the opportunity to talk to her children about her now-changed future.

"When you return," Jullanar went on, "what do you plan on doing? Finding the others?"

There was no real question in her voice, and no doubt in Pali's. "It seems time, don't you think?"

"Yes. You'll have to go back to Stoneybridge, I expect—unless of course you wish to make a grand and mysterious disappearance."

"It's tempting, but I would like my own horse."

"Of course," Jullanar replied solemnly. "When you have your horse, come collect me."

It would have been a tearful farewell, if Pali had ever been inclined to tears. She embraced Jullanar tightly, accepted the small parcel of ginger biscuits her friend pressed into her hands, and embarked on the stagecoach north to Yrchester.

She met the ambassador there. He was a tight-lipped aristocrat of the Astandalan type, whose performative humility Pali found irritating. But yet he accompanied her to the gate to Zunidh, and when she stepped through to the bright warmth of a moonlit summer night, she discovered he had made arrangements for her travels all the way to the capital, and she had only to accept them.

And thus:

On the Zuni side of the Border was a garrison, who received her with great courtesy and simple, wholesome food. The next morning they guided her a day's walk to the exceptionally tall tower on the side of a mountain where an actual flying ship was moored.

Pali very carefully reminded herself that she was Pali Avramapul of the Red Company, and she was not to be awestruck so easily. No doubt she was feeling slightly under the weather from a cold she'd picked up on the stagecoach.

The ship was not particularly different from any ordinary waterborne vessel, save for the impossible fact that it flew through the air. Pali was chagrinned to spend most of the trip in the cabin she had been given. It seemed a terrible waste of an opportunity, but her body refused to settle.

They arrived in Solaara in the night. She caught glimpses of the city's lights spilling out in a circle around the gleaming pearl of the palace at its centre, and then they were slowing and the sailors expertly tossing ropes to the top of another vertiginous tower.

Pali gathered her belongings together, thanked the captain for their kindness, and tried not to totter down the spiral stair.

At the bottom she discovered the ambassador had arranged things even unto her accommodations. She was too bemused by the solidity of stone beneath her feet to do more than follow the young man as he led her through quiet, magic-illuminated halls, down yet more stairs, until at last she was in the sultry heat of the capital of Zunidh.

The bicycle-drawn carriage—a rickshaw, she was told—took her away from the Palace and to a well-lit and well-appointed hotel, where Pali registered with disbelief that the ambassador had apparently paid for that, too, and went gratefully to her room.

She would think about all this in the morning, she told herself as she washed herself and flopped wearily onto the bed.

~

In the morning she had no good explanation for the ambassador's extravagance. The hotelier, when Pali asked her, confirmed that her room was booked for as long as she wanted.

"I was told a month or six weeks," the hotelier said, shrugging as if this were normal.

Pali expressed mild amazement at the ambassador's generosity.

"Oh, I expect it was the Lord Chancellor's doing," the hotelier said, clearly on firmer ground with that thought. "The Lord Emperor is a great patron of scholarship and undoubtedly the Lord Chancellor would have set policies for visiting scholars of your status, Professor."

That was marginally more explicable, and much easier to bear than such an obligation to the ambassador. Pali accepted this and set out to explore the city for a day or two, as the hotelier suggested, before heading to the Palace Archives for her research.

It was an astoundingly, almost impossibly lovely city. Pali remembered the grime and occasional squalor of Astandalas, and marvelled at how much more Artorin Damara had managed to achieve after the Fall than before.

But that was not her current research, she told herself firmly, even as she tried foods she had not tasted in decades and listened to accents she had never before heard. She bought sandals and a few trinkets to give to Jullanar and Professor Vane, and she resolutely kept her focus. She was not going to study the whole development of Zuni culture and government after the Fall. She was here to disentangle those late policy decisions of the last half-decade of Artorin Damara's reign as emperor.

Nothing more, nothing less.

Nevertheless, she might—once the Red Company was collected together again—suggest they come to Zunidh for a visit.

~

Pali's one previous experience with the Palace of Stars had been the splendid, strange occasion of That Party, and the place had changed considerably in the years since.

The gardens were better, for one thing, and the view from the windows. However incomprehensible the magic that had placed it here, the results were excellent.

The Archives were mostly housed in rooms along one side of the central block, next to—if separated from by thick walls of solid stone —the Treasury. As a respected Scholar of one of the most respected universities in the former empire, Pali was given a tour of the Archives' holdings.

She could admit that she was impressed.

Not simply by the vast quantity of materials held there—scrolls and tablets and books, and books, and books; ephemera carefully preserved; whole rooms devoted to records from various government departments—but by their organization and the number and skill of the librarians and archivists working there. *Someone* in this government cared deeply for the Archives, and funded them accordingly. Pali had been to enough university and city libraries and archives in the course of her research to know how rare that was.

The mysterious Lord Chancellor, who arranged such extravagant accommodations for visiting scholars? Or his master, the Last Emperor, who was reputed to admire scholarship?

The Chief Librarian, a dumpy brown-skinned woman with a near-fanatical gleam in her eye, told her that she was in the midst of developing a new catalogue of the holdings.

"Not to speak ill of my predecessors," the Chief Librarian said, sniffing, as they passed by a small room full of diamond-shaped shelves holding scrolls, apparently the spoils of a conquest of some Collian monastery. "But—"

Pali made an agreeing noise as the Chief Librarian told her all the many and manifold ways in which her predecessors had failed at their sacred art.

After the rooms and rooms of written material, and the offices and workshops of those who tended them (those who made glue and sewed covers; those whose magic was devoted to the subtle arts of preventing mould and rot and faded ink; those who were responsible for the unending work of cataloguing the holdings), Pali was shown to a desk in the Reading Room.

She could admit that she was *more* than impressed by the Reading Room of the Imperial Archives.

"This is new since the Fall," the Chief Librarian informed her, delighting in her response. "The Lord Chancellor went on a diplomatic mission to Voonra once, and was much struck by the famous Octagonal Library of the Queen's palace there. He thought we should have our own."

Everyone seemed to *adore* the Lord Chancellor. Pali could see why the Chief Librarian did, at any rate.

The Reading Room was built of a softly golden sandstone, with fossil leaves visible here and there; the stones had been cut and set to show the imprints off. It occupied the whole width of one of the wings of the Palace that extended from the central block ("The Collian Wing," the Chief Librarian informed her. "It was badly damaged in the Fall."), so there were windows on each side.

The Archives themselves were windowless, protecting the books from the light. Here the tall, narrow banks of windows poured sunlight into the room. The air was magically cooled to prevent overheating, so it was a pleasant temperature, with an airiness unusual to the Palace.

Along the walls below the windows were desks, each of them generously sized, each of them set inside a carved wooden frame. Those working in the carrels could see out if they so chose, but could close themselves off as well.

There were more desks in the centre of the room, organized around the central space where the Librarian on duty worked and assisted researchers in finding what they needed. Several pages or apprentices sat beside them, ready to run to the Archives to retrieve or return items.

As a Scholar there for several weeks of research, Pali was given one of the carrels along the wall. She was given a key for it, whose magic hummed pleasantly in her fingers. By the key, she knew, she was being given a privilege, and also a warning; the faint prick taking blood would close the door of the cubicle to others, and let them find her should she abuse the gift she was given. It was an elegant solution.

"Thank you," she said gravely. She had told the Chief Librarian her area of study on her arrival and application to work in the Archives, and had been shown the room in the Archives devoted to the public records of Artorin Damara's reign as Emperor. She had been given special dispensation to search directly in the records, because they were not as delicate as the older manuscripts and because of her position and reputation as a Scholar of History from Stoneybridge.

"How do I go about requesting an audience from the Lord Emperor?" she asked the Chief Librarian after she had accepted the key and was being walked back to the room where she wished to begin her researches.

The Chief Librarian pursed her lips. There was a flicker in her eyes at the question—at Pali's temerity in even asking? Pali had already noted how people spoke of the Lord Emperor, who was almost never named; back in Astandalan days people had always spoken almost familiarly of 'Emperor Artorin', but that custom had been replaced by his titles and especially that reverent *Lord Emperor*.

"You should apply through the Offices of the Lords of State," she said finally. "I'd do it now, before you start into your work. And be prepared to be summoned at *any* moment, if the Glorious One should condescend to see you."

It amused and somewhat alarmed Pali that the Chief Librarian meant that entirely seriously.

∼

One of the Archive pages guided her up to the Offices of the Lords of State. The boy—young man, really, of an age with Pali's younger undergraduates—presented her to a series of increasingly resplendent and increasingly busy bureaucrats.

She did not make it all the way to the Lord Chancellor, who was apparently attending on the Lord Emperor himself that morning, but she did make it to someone who seemed to be one of his chief lieutenants.

This was another woman. Pali was delighted at how even a spread it was across the whole of the Palace staff she had so far seen. Men, women, those who were not obviously one or the other.

They were also visibly and audibly from any number of places. Skin tones, hair styles, accents, features: all were varied. Far more so than she had seen on Alinor, or remembered (or had studied) of the imperial government proper.

This too, she was given to understand, was the doing of the present Lord Chancellor, who was himself from some remote hinterland region and who had worked hard to ensure the government was representative of the people it served.

Pali knew that very few government officials had ever even had that *thought*, let alone considered it good and deliberately worked to bring it into practice.

She presented her credentials and her request to the Undersecretary in Chief of the Offices of the Lord of State, a tall, handsome woman a bit younger than Pali, with expressive hands. Saya Kalikiri, apparently, to be greatly respected according to the page who had led her there.

Saya Kalikiri nodded agreeably. "I shall see your application goes to the Lord Chancellor, Professor Black," she said, accepting the letter Pali offered her. "The Lord Emperor is exceedingly ... busy at the moment, but he does admire and support scholarship, so I do not think it is *impossible* he would choose to make time for you. I would suggest you meet with the Master of Etiquette to go over the protocols required on encountering the Glorious One."

That was undoubtedly the greatest difference from Astandalan days, Pali thought as she agreed and followed the page through another maze of rooms, halls, and stairs until she came to the offices of a minor lordling called Lord Lior, who condescended to teach her the forms of address and courtesy proper to an informal audience with The Sun-on-Earth. People used those titles with all apparent seriousness.

No. That was not the greatest difference.

The page pointed out three different refectories as they passed, and indicated that her key to the Archives would gain her entry into them.

The greatest difference that not one person, from the page to the Chief Librarian to the Undersecretary in Chief of the Offices of the Lords of State, had shown any inclination to being bribed.

Not that she would have, if they'd tried to suggest it. But they didn't try, and once they would have.

CHAPTER TEN
AN AUDIENCE IS GRANTED

The Lord Emperor had opened nearly the entirety of the Archives to scholars. Pali had not realized, until she went to the nearest refectory and ate there, listening to conversations around her, that until that fairly recent decision only a tiny portion of the holdings had been accessible. None of the records she was examining had been available, for instance.

The food was decent, not exactly *good*—or at least Pali felt it should have more spices—but cheap and filling. The gossip around her *was* good, even if naturally mostly dedicated to people and events for which she had no context. Over the next few weeks Pali listened, and heard the recurring dramas and excitements of this part of the Palace.

The most exciting thing was the rumour—still only a rumour—that the Lord Chancellor was planning on continuing his incredible experiment in paying *everybody*.

Pali had been caught up in a juicy romantic triangle as recounted by two friends sitting behind her—all of them were there for a midmorning cup of coffee—when she heard someone on her other side announce that they'd applied for the 'stipend' for the first time.

Everyone in earshot fell silent and swivelled to look at the person. He raised his head and beamed at them. "It was *easy*," he declared rapturously.

"What are you going to do with it?" someone asked.

"How much was it, anyway?" enquired a second.

"Two hundred valiants," he answered the second person, and then grinned at the first. "I am moving out of my awful boarding house and into my *own* place, that's what I'm doing with it!"

That simple, joyous exclamation caused silence to ripple out, until Pali sat near the epicentre of a pool of starry-eyed dreamers.

"I could go home to see my parents," someone whispered, his eyes closed with longing. He had a definite non-Solaaran accent, and added, slowly, "I'm from the Cape of Snows. I haven't been back in ... years."

"I could afford more children," a woman said, her voice as stunned as if she'd been given a fortune.

"I could get a better job."

"I could save for a house."

"I could start my *own* business."

"I could work half time."

"Oh gods," someone said, nearly sobbing, "I could take a leave of absence and care for my sister without *starving*."

Pali sat there as all these bureaucrats and workers, the backbone of the Palace, exploded into excited discussion. So many dreams, suddenly viable.

She went back to her carrel and stared at the notes she was taking about policy developments in the second half of Artorin Damara's reign.

Artorin Damara had always been a patron of the arts. He had fought corruption, not very effectively but with recurrent attempts at reforming the deeply corrupt court and government he had inherited. He had stopped any number of his predecessor's expensive wars and tried to institute educational reforms and other benefits to his general populace.

He had never had the vision, or the skill, or the support, to bring something like this into existence.

People spoke of the Lord Emperor as a living god, but this was surely all his Lord Chancellor's doing.

The scholar in her wanted to turn her attention to this new development, this incredible experiment—what *would* happen to the society at large, she wondered? Would the entire system collapse?—but she had her own work, her fourth monograph on Artorin Damara's policies, and she returned dutifully to it.

He'd been a good emperor, heading slowly and circuitously towards greatness, but he was much better as lord magus, she thought, and hard on that thought came a knock on the carrel door.

"The Lord Emperor will see you now," the page said.

∽

The highest Pali had so far gone in the Palace was to the Offices of the Lords of State, which were four floors up. She had been given to understand that the Palace worked by a simple metaphorical logic: the higher and the closer to the centre, the more important.

The Lord Emperor himself was to be found, accordingly, at the top of the central tower.

Pali was guided up seven long flights from the Archives. They were not taken in one fell swoop, but rather progressed around the core of the tower, so that each flight was broken by a length of curving hallway. Each stair grew more impressive rather than less as she ascended.

At length she was taken to a hall of pristine white limestone. The coffered ceiling was sheathed in pale-gold nacre. The door facing her was pure black ebony on the left and equally pure whitewood on the right, with a sun-in-glory made of beaten gold centred perfectly between them.

The Emperor of Astandalas did not need any more indication of his power and prestige than that.

But changed as Zunidh might be since the Fall, there was enough of Astandalas lingering that he *did* have more on display. Two Imperial Guards stood at the door in full panoply: glistening white linen kilts, gold and onyx belts, gold and ebony spears. Leopard-skin pelts over their shoulders, short swords at their waists.

Pali eyed their muscles with a professional eye. Those were not simply for show.

Her guide, the page, announced her name to the guards. They stamped their spears in sharp unison, and the door between them parted down the middle of the sun and silently opened.

Inside was a small vestibule, where several pages sat, awaiting errands she supposed. Two more guards faced the entry doors, and her guide announced her again.

The new guards stamped, and the doors opened. This time one of the door-guards accompanied her across the next room to where two more Imperial Guards stood at perfect attention.

Seven doors. Seven rooms between them. Seven sets of guards.

The rooms were each of them increasingly magnificent. Their splendour lay not so much in their decoration, which was simple, but in the quality of the materials. Pali was hardly a great connoisseur of building materials, but she knew craftsmanship when she saw it. Those materials she did recognize she knew to be of astonishing rarity and richness.

The third room, to take one at random, was perfectly empty but for the two guards at attention and two seats arranged beside a fireplace. There was no wood in the hearth, but an everlasting flame twisted there, a branch of the fire-tree of the wizard Aignor. The Red Company had once spent most of a year looking for any remnant piece of it, only to find a singular twig the centrepiece of a dragon's hoard. This branch was ... left in an anteroom.

The walls in the fourth room were covered in a cladding made of golden sunbird feathers. Only actual phoenix feathers would have been more marvellous.

Pali was not easily intimidated, but by the time she had come to the seventh antechamber, and the seventh set of guards, she could count herself ... *impressed*. It was all very irritating.

The guards watched her as she paused in the seventh antechamber. This room was walled in mirrors. She glanced at the two guards. "This is the last antechamber?"

The one on her right nodded. He was alert, his muscles relaxed and ready. Pali considered him and decided that they were *real* guards. She could have taken one of them, even without any long weapon of her own, but she was sufficiently out of practice she wouldn't have wanted to assume she could take both out easily.

She shook away such bloodthirsty thoughts—she was not Pali Avramapul of the Red Company here, or Paliammë-ivanar of the Oclaresh; she was the respected and respectable scholar Domina Black, professor of Stoneybridge—and gave herself a quick, thorough overview in the mirrors.

She wore her formal academic robes, black gabardine over her crêpey blue dress. Embroidered panels along the hems of the robes showed her affiliations to Stoneybridge, St Erlingale's, and the faculty of History. She would have to tell Professor Vane it had been a good idea to bring them.

She had braided her hair back this morning, which was hardly a court style but kept her hair out of her face when she was working. It fell in a long, satisfying plait down her back, thumping lightly as she turned. She hesitated, then pulled out a couple of pins and a ribbon and tied it up in a loop around her head, out of the way. Just in case of ... *trouble*.

She was who she was, and if the Lord Emperor didn't like that— she could not help the sly smile that bloomed at the thought. Well. He didn't know whom he was dealing with, did he?

The guards watched her. The one on the right raised his eyebrows, but he said nothing, and quickly smoothed out his expression when he saw her looking at him.

Most people would be prostrate by anxiety by this point, Pali assumed, and bestowed upon him a delighted smile and a sharp, encouraging nod.

He swallowed, Adam's apple bobbing, and had to look at his fellow to gauge the timing of their spear-thumping. Pali forced herself not to grin, and instead rehearsed her questions in her mind. She would not be granted a *long* audience, that was certain.

The omnipresent Palace bells chimed some portion of an hour, and the doors opened.

∽

She walked in, chin up and back straight, posture loose, attention on the room.

There was a man sitting at a desk to her immediate right. Two more guards on the inside of the door, these ones even better muscled and far more alert than the ones in the antechambers. They bore the intensity of actual soldiers, and Pali noted them as potential threats.

The man at the desk was no physical threat, not to her, though he was not entirely lacking in strength from what she could see of him. He had good shoulders, at any rate. He had stacks of papers and pens and ink distributed around him. The Lord Emperor's secretary, presumably.

The room was nearly empty. The secretary's desk. Another desk, in intricately carved copper filigree with a sandalwood top. A pretty blue-and-white vase on a plinth. Some sort of golden cage at the far end of the room.

A long tapestry map took up most of the wall facing the guards and the entrance door: it was placed between two doors, presumably leading deeper into the rooms behind this audience chamber. The tapestry was a map of the empire at its greatest extent, from the nine circular hemispheres depicted. A third door, this one glassed, led to some sort of balcony or terrace.

On the wall opposite was a full-length state portrait of the

Emperor Artorin Damara, familiar to her from a hundred reproductions.

In the middle of the room, the Lord Emperor himself.

She swept down into the formal obeisance the Master of Etiquette had spent a good quarter-hour trying to find some reason to criticize.

"Rise, domina," the Lord Emperor said. His voice was richly resonant and perfectly, studiously neutral in intonation. His accent the purest court. Well, of course it was.

As she rose obediently, her glance snagged on a slight irregularity on the stone floor: just the barest hint of a shadow, tracing a line from the filigree desk up to the birdcage and back down past where she stood. Surely it wasn't grime, which meant it must instead be ... wear?

The stone stairs and floors of St Erlingale's old monastic cloister were worn from the steps of many monks over many centuries. How much had the Lord Emperor paced to wear down the stone like that?

Pali rose, setting herself to be polite and tactful and professional, and glanced directly at Artorin Damara for the first time. He was taller than she'd expected, was her first thought. Her second was that his face was eerily familiar, from all those portraits and etchings and engravings in university halls and in the frontispieces of books and on the hundreds or thousands of coins that had passed through her hands since he was crowned.

He was not precisely handsome, but she knew that already. He was black of skin, bald as were all male high courtiers of Astandalas, dressed in what was probably an outrageously simple garment. Face and body calm, serene, if a little gaunt, as if he'd been ill and lost weight recently.

His eyes were shadowed, since he stood against the door to the balcony, but it was clear enough he was staring directly at her, completely *shocked*.

Fuck, she thought. He'd recognized her.

CHAPTER ELEVEN
TEA WITH THE LAST EMPEROR

The Lord Emperor took a step towards her. She lifted her chin.

He stared at her. His eyes had caught the edge of the sunlight coming from the terrace, and for a moment seemed limned with gold.

She remembered another man, equally tall and black-skinned, with eyes like an eagle's, and could only think that *this* man, emperor of five worlds as he had been, was *nothing* compared to Fitzroy Angursell of the Red Company.

The Lord Emperor said, "We will continue this audience on the terrace. Bring refreshments."

And with one sharp hand gesture he spun around and stalked to the terrace, his robes flaring out behind him. The two guards left their position on the door and she tensed, but they swept past her to stand on either side of the terrace door.

Pali's heart pounded with the power in the air, gathering like an imminent thunderstorm. The guards were not there for her. Not yet. Not yet.

There were sixteen armed men between here and the door to the Palace proper. She had a penknife in her pocket and her dagger under her skirts and she could, she supposed, break that superlative vase and use the shards as a weapon.

No. She could not do that. It was too beautiful a piece of art.

If she were to be taken for being Pali Avramapul, she would be taken with her head high and her eyes unafraid.

"I believe his Radiancy desires you to follow, domina," the secretary said meaningfully. He had a faint twang edging his accent, and a nice voice. She could imagine the Lord Emperor enjoyed hearing him speak.

He had moved in the corner of her vision but she wasn't sure what he had done. He had not summoned the guards ... perhaps a servant?

Bring refreshments, the Last Emperor had said. Perhaps he wanted to ... parley.

She shook her head at the thought, but the idea of it was so bright and shining an incongruity that she could not help but smile at the secretary with all the sudden joy lifting her heart.

She left him to his bafflement and stalked to the terrace with a smile for the guards, she Pali Avramapul of the Red Company.

There were sixteen armed men between here and the door to the Palace proper. She had a penknife in her pocket and her wit and her words. And *he* was only the Last Emperor of Astandalas, after all.

She smiled at him with her best academic smile, as if he were a promising but unruly student, and had the great joy of seeing him just barely suppress a twitch.

"Your Radiancy, I understand," she said boldly. He twitched again.

They stood there for a moment, looking at each other. The air was warm but stirred by a cool, refreshing breeze; they were protected from the heat of the sun by a brightly coloured awning over the table and two chairs that sat on the terrace.

It was a friendly space. She wondered idly who usually sat with the Lord Emperor there. He had never married, had no consort or concubines according to any record or rumour she had ever found.

She'd never come across much reference to friends or confidantes. Not when he was the Emperor of Astandalas proper. It had always seemed a pity to her; she had wondered if he might have achieved more if he'd had some sort of personal support. She hoped he was better served as lord magus.

She would not look down, no matter how eerie she found those familiar—*familial*—features and that blank, indifferent expression.

He had never pretended not to be related. His nose had always given him away. Pali had looked at all those hundreds of paintings, etchings, engravings, coins, and refused to let herself wonder who Fitzroy had really been. He had reached the Long Edge of Colhélhé and, from all her skill at tracking could see, leaped straight off the land into the Sea of Stars. And—that was it.

The Lord Emperor lifted his hand and made a sliding gesture. Magic sparkled in the air in the wake of his hand, fizzed lightly against her skin. It tasted more like Astandalan magic than she was used to, now.

The Master of Etiquette had been very clear that she was *not* to initiate a conversation.

She had enough respect for Artorin Damara to grant him that courtesy. He had accomplished an impressive amount, really, with no consort or concubines, no confidantes or friends, faced so unexpectedly with a corrupt court at the decadent and bloated end of the Empire of Astandalas.

Certainly he had *tried*, which is more than could be said for any number of his predecessors.

He was still staring at her. She stared back. He did look ill. Drawn, nearly gaunt, with a fine tremor in his hands.

His gaze flicked past her; one hand moved minutely. She did not take her gaze from him, but did not jump, either, when a very superior sort of attendant came past her with a tray.

Artorin Damara moved his hand almost imperceptibly. The attendant set the tray on the table and efficiently laid out its contents: a translucent porcelain cup, its lip rimmed with gold, on a saucer. A matching plate containing some sort of biscuit. Ginger, Pali's nose identified.

There was a second cup and saucer, a second plate of biscuits, to go in front of the other chair. The porcelain was not quite so fine, and it was rimmed with silver, not gold. Pali felt her lips quirk in amusement at this visible delineation of ranks.

The Lord Emperor took his tea with milk and honey. The attendant poured it: black tea, rich and aromatic, just the merest hint of smoke. Pali's mouth began to water despite herself. She hadn't had such good black tea in *years*.

The attendant set down the teapot and moved to the stash of condiments on the tray. The Lord Emperor said, "Half a teaspoon of honey and a squeeze of lemon."

The attendant inclined his head and fixed her tea as directed. He didn't look at her but Pali wasn't sure she could have mustered words anyway. What sort of file did he have on her, to know how she took her *tea*?

The attendant took his tray and departed on silent feet. Pali stared Artorin Damara in the eyes.

It really wasn't fair he had inherited the lion eyes after all. She had thought—

"Please sit," the Lord Emperor said, gesturing her to one chair and taking his own.

Pali could be composed. She could. She sat down, back straight, skirts and robes falling properly. The tea smelled *delicious*. So did the biscuits, for that matter.

"They can't hear us," the Lord Emperor said, folding his hands loosely around his cup.

Pali glanced up at him and regretfully did not lift her own cup just yet. She did not care for the rules of etiquette that petty little man had so importantly instructed her to follow, but she *was* the guest here, and there were far older customs to follow.

She rallied her thoughts for the first question she intended to ask him, as soon as he gave her the opportunity.

"The biscuits aren't Jullanar's," he said, with just a tinge of mournfulness, "but they are nevertheless quite good."

"One would expect so, for the emperor's table," she said automatically.

He inclined his head, expression serene; but his hands closed more tightly around his cup.

Jullanar's gingersnaps.

Pali had had them hardly more than a month ago—

She looked back up at Artorin Damara, last emperor of Astandalas. He was watching her with those strange yellow-gold eyes, the only human being to sport them she had ever seen besides *one—*

All those portraits.

All those paintings, etchings, engravings, hundreds or even thousands of coins.

The lion eyes hidden by the convention that images of the emperor always had the eyes fully covered in gold leaf.

She looked at his hands, faintly trembling as he held the tea cup. At his face, drawn and tired, and so very empty of emotion: serene as in every portrait, every prayer. At his eyes, amber with the intensity of whatever emotions he was holding back.

She had never quite managed to rein in her tongue. "What," she said, "no marriage proposal?"

His expression didn't change, although his eyes sharpened, lightened, magic kindling in them.

"It seemed presumptuous," he said.

The *very* first thing he had said to her, the first time they met, was an exuberant cry of "You are magnificent! We should get married!"

("How do I know you are magnificent enough for me?" Pali had replied, the words coming from the same irreverent well as these biting retorts.

The Fitzroy she did not yet know, the man who would propose marriage to her half a dozen times a week and five times on holidays, had grinned at her, his whole body moving with his delight, lit with his amusement, his admiration, his earnest appreciation: "I am the poet Fitzroy Angursell."

"Ask me again when you're famous," she'd said, so very taken aback; and yet she'd gone with him, with them, with Jullanar and Damian and Fitzroy—)

"I thought that was the nature of the game," she replied, still trying to gather her thoughts together.

They felt fragmentary: a precious ornament shattered to reveal a far more precious item hidden below the surface.

He let himself smile, just the tiniest bit, and Pali felt her indignation rise. *This* was what had happened to Fitzroy Angursell? *This?*

She had thought long and hard about Artorin Damara. Had spent years studying his policies, the morass of his court, his decisions and his laws and his judgments. Had spent a good portion trying to work out all the other factors at work, the economic and the magical, the environmental and the social, the political and the social.

Had wondered, more than once, just how Artorin Damara had learned mercy and judgment.

She had a list of questions in her pocket, the half a dozen most important she had hoped to have answered.

What answer did she need, besides this?

Why did you side with the university of Galderon over the governor?

Why else, but for the fact that Jullanar and Ayasha had been intimately involved in sparking the rebellion; that the Red Company had snuck into the besieged university once or twice, bringing in food and medicines and magic and news; that Fitzroy Angursell had made one of his queerly solemn vows that if there was ever anything he could do to assist the rebels he would do so.

When they had managed to get an envoy to Astandalas, to the Palace of Stars, he had heard them out and he had granted them their requests.

It had been an *inconceivable* decision for any emperor, especially one still new to his throne and in a tremendously uncertain seat.

Pali stared at Fitzroy Angursell, at Artorin Damara, and was conscious of a disappointment he hadn't done *more*.

He lifted his cup to his lips and took a small, polite sip, barely wetting his lips before setting the cup down once more. His hands were visibly trembling.

Her own customs stated she could now eat and drink. Would he have remembered that?

He had remembered her preference in tea.

Pali took a sip of her tea, which was robust and excellent as she had imagined from its redolent aroma, then set her own cup down and leaned forward. "Tell me," she said, "what happened after you reached the Long Edge of Colhélhé?"

He betrayed no surprise at her question. He simply paused a moment before saying, "I was caught there by the magic of the Empire, and brought ... here."

He glanced around at the Palace, the elegant and beautiful terrace at the very centre and height of all the power of Astandalas.

Pali had never been good with the quiet and subtle games of power, whether at home in her clan or in any of the courts she had ever visited or in the halls of Stoneybridge. "And that's it? That's all you have to tell me?"

He regarded her with a polite, impersonal attentiveness. "What would you like to know?"

Why did you come down in judgment against the rebels of East Voonra when you had supported those of Galderon?

She knew that answer: remembered herself walking the burned and blighted fields that the rebels of East Voonra had torched and ruined with their creeping, poisonous magic. She remembered Fitzroy weeping for the hurt done to the land, to the air, the twisted fire that was still burning and which he had been unable to fully dowse.

Why didn't you show your magic when you were Emperor?

Because Fitzroy Angursell was a wild mage, and Artorin Damara had needed to consolidate his power and authority. He had had no allies, she had known that.

(No consorts or concubines, no confidants or friends. Just himself and all the bloated and decadent end of the Empire of Astandalas.)

"Did you miss us?" she asked, wishing the words had not come out of her mouth the moment she spoke them, but she could not retreat and apologize, not when he merely pressed his lips together for a brief moment and then said, "Of course," with no emotion at all.

How was this—*this*—Fitzroy Angursell? How was this the man who had been so brilliant and so joyous? What had happened to him?

(She knew what had happened to him. She had spent the past fifteen years meticulously analyzing it. How Artorin Damara, so uneducated in the ways of power, of courts, of authority, had gradually taken up the reins of government and learned to *be* an emperor. How he had nearly become a great one, before the end.)

"Of course," she hissed. "Of *course*. What would you have done, if any of us had come up before you?"

He just barely twitched again; his voice was level and calm; only his eyes gleamed, but with what emotion she did not know, could not recognize in the familiar-unfamiliar face. "I suppose we will never know now."

"A fine, courtly parry," she retorted, "for a fine, courtly emperor."

He inclined his head, and Pali lost what little control she'd ever managed to exert over her tongue.

"What, no bright and brilliant words from the greatest poet of an age?" she demanded. "No protestations of admiration or devotion, no words of grief or disappointment? No blazing words with which to set the firmament aflame?"

His hands clasped the teacup. His shoulders were back, his posture perfect, his face serene. Pali could not stand it.

(She would not, could not bear even the thought of deliberately smashing that blue-and-white vase in the audience room, that work of art and skill and love. But this? This—this—this *obscenity?*)

"Where were the stars when you lost yourself? At what point did you wake up to say, 'Oh, that was a dream?' When did you forget who you were?"

"What would you have me say?" he replied ... not *softly*, that was not a word anyone used for the Last Emperor of Astandalas, but ... Pali could not even articulate the adjective to herself. Quietly. Indifferently. *Politely*.

"Must I put the words in your mouth? *Yours*?"

That stung him, finally, although only to irritation: he leaned forward, and his face sharpened, focused on her. "Forgive me for my surprise," he snapped. "We are hardly used to such informality."

They both caught his unconscious use of the imperial plural at the same time. Some pained grimace flitted across his face before he caught it, stuffed it back behind the imperturbable facade.

Pali watched him gather himself, her ears ringing with that habitual pronoun. She felt blank, fury a white wind in her mind, like a sandstorm about to swallow her up. How was *this* the man she had once loved?

She had never been so disappointed in anyone or anything in her life.

"Is there anything left to you but the Lord Emperor?"

He flinched: a minute gesture, but it was there. And he hesitated, damnably, before replying.

Pali could hardly listen to the words, as slithering and supple, as meaningless, as much a courtly platitude as anything could be. What could he say that would be true, after the truth was shown in that hesitation, that moment of unspoken honesty?

"How can I believe that you ever told us the truth about anything?"

She didn't mean it. She knew with every fibre of her being that Fitzroy had been honest in his own bright-eyed, mischievous way, that his lies had never been anything more than poetic fictions.

But she said it, because this hard glittering carapace was not her friend, was not ever her friend, *could not* be the picture she took away with her. She wouldn't let it be. She had not flown seven days and seven nights into the Sea of Stars for this *disappointment*.

He did not flinch. He seemed beyond flinching, his eyes bright and flashing with anger, his body tense, but yet so terribly *still*. Where were the gestures, the vibrancy, the magic and the joy and the sheer verve of him?

"I suppose," he said evenly, with only a faint tremor in his voice, in his hands around the teacup, to show there was anything there but the Lord Emperor, the man worshipped as a god. "If you cannot believe what I once said, there is nothing I can now say to convince you."

They stared at each other. She was breathing hard, as if she fought for her life in some inglorious battle, some tedious long conflict with no end in sight. She, who took up every weapon she could raise, with her arms and with her words.

His eyes were that fiery gold she remembered from him the grip of emotion, of inspiration, of magic. The wind was swirling around them, more vigorously than when she had first come out on the balcony but not strongly enough to seem magically roused.

There was no fire to surge and spark here.

Once she had walked through a burning forest to reach the pain-maddened Fitzroy at its centre, daring the living fire of his induced madness to harm her; taking him in her arms and bearing him out again as the fire collapsed into ash behind her.

The thought of his face that time came starkly into her mind's eye: how light he had been in her arms, for he had been tall but slight, and he had been hungry, nearly starved, for a time, held captive in some crag of a castle, unable to escape the chains with which he was bound.

—She stumbled on that thought, that memory, of the screaming fire falling dead silent as she bore him out of the centre of his pain. The blasted tower he had burned to the ground, shattered without being able entirely to break free.

She knew the magical bindings placed on the Emperor of Astandalas. She had studied their effects.

She leaned forward, furious and intent, reaching out to touch his hand, hoping thereby to shock him into looking at her with his true emotions—

He recoiled. Flinched right back, his hands in his lap, all his body saying *NO*.

Pali stared at him, shocked.

"I am still me," he said, whispered really, so quietly it was nearly lost in the wind.

Pali felt her anger rush back, that he did not *shout* that claim, did not cry it in all its magnificence, that he did not crow it from the roof of his bloody palace like the Golden Cockerel of the Sun calling forth the dawn.

Her tongue lashed out, sharp as her sword: "Will you prove it, then, and come with me?"

He looked at her, and for a moment all the emotion she could want for was in his eyes, his face—just a moment, of longing and desire and hope—

And then he shut down, closed his eyes and closed his face, and he shook his head and spoke with a finality such as Pali had rarely ever heard human voice hold.

"No."

CHAPTER TWELVE
REVERBERATIONS

The audience was clearly over.

Pali rose from her chair, and the Last Emperor of Astandalas rose with her. He was courtly and courteous, walking her from the terrace into the study, all the way to the door which his two guards had smoothly outflanked them to bracket.

She walked half a step ahead of him, which was surely some unimaginable breach of protocol. He held himself still and calm, his face in the corner of her eyes as calm, as serene, as distant as the state portrait of himself on the wall.

Before she had quite reached the door he said, "I am sorry, you know."

She stopped.

His voice was perhaps shaded with the mildest form of disappointment, of regret.

She turned, and she looked around the beautiful, serene room, at the map of his fallen empire and the portrait of himself in all his youthful glory and power, at the superlative vase and the shadowed lines he had worn in the stone, and she said, "Are you?"

There was nothing he could say to that, if he were not going to say it all, and so he said nothing; not with his mouth, not with his face, not with his body, not even with the magic she remembered coruscating around him, as eager and inquisitive as he was himself.

She could not bear to look on him any longer, and so she plunged into the formal obeisance, for she could respect Artorin Damara even if she could not love him, and when he continued to say nothing, continued merely to stare at her with his golden eyes in brown shadow, she rose and turned her back on him and left.

∼

Righteous indignation carried her on its wave through the seven anterooms, past the seven sets of guards. One of the pages leapt up as she entered the last anteroom and guided her down the seven flights of stairs to land once more at the blood-locked door of her cubicle in the Reading Room.

There she stood, unable to fumble in her pocket for the key, unable to think through the keening in her mind.

The Chief Librarian, Anma—after a month they were nearly friends—bustled over, ostensibly to see if she needed help but really to hear about her audience. She took one look at Pali, tutted, and declared, "What you need is coffee, my dear," and drew her by the arm not to one of the Palace refectories but to a little chamber off the Reading Room that was clearly for the library staff.

Pali let herself be drawn, let herself be set down upon a cushioned chair, let herself be given a cup of hot, terrible coffee. After three large gulps she was able to set the brew down.

He had remembered how she liked her tea.

She was infuriated to discover she was sniffling. She did not keep so many handkerchiefs in her sleeves as Professor Vane did, but she had one, and she wiped her eyes carefully, blew her nose as discreetly as possible, and glowered at her cup.

Anma sat with her in companionable silence until Pali stopped sniffling and resumed drinking her coffee.

"He has *quite* the effect," Anma said.

Pali regarded her silently.

"The Lord Emperor," the librarian clarified. "I've had a handful of audiences with him—he's a great patron of learning, as you know—most recently when the Reading Room was finished. He comes down himself to look for books at times. His staff usually tell us in advance so we can clear the Archives, but one time he came down without warning. I was deep in the stacks organizing an obscure section and, golly, was I ever surprised when he came around a corner and nearly walked right into me."

"What did he do?" Pali asked.

She could imagine what Fitzroy might have done, unexpectedly happening across the head librarian of a great library.

She did not need to imagine. There had been such occasions. On one he had fled, pursued by the man's enchanted books. On another the librarian had been drawn with them and ended up a companion for an adventure. On a third Fitzroy had grown so intrigued by the books the librarian was shelving that the rest of them had had to come fetch him out before they missed their ship. On a fourth he had been so intrigued by the librarian he had launched himself into a full seduction—

"Oh," Anma murmured, smiling bashfully, "he condescended very politely. Asked me if I were well pleased with my job, if there was anything that I needed ... He'd remembered that I'm from Xiputl and asked whether I missed anything from home ... I was so overcome I nearly started crying right in front of him. I *did* cry when he'd gone. Such *presence*."

Pali thought of that cool, collected man upstairs, with his perfect posture and his perfectly neutral voice. Power he had; but all the *presence* was borrowed from his trappings.

Fitzroy had never needed the trappings.

"So I understand what it's like," the librarian concluded. "He sent me—well, I'm sure he just ordered someone to send me—some of the tea we have at home. We call it tea, anyway, it's not *tea* tea if you know what I mean. Not something you can buy here. It was so ... generous of him. Just as you expect."

Pali nodded mechanically.

Anma sighed. "Did he look ... well?"

That caught her out of her own funk. "I beg your pardon?"

"The Lord Emperor. Did he look well? He's recovering from a heart attack, you know."

Pali remembered, with a shock of horror, the drawn, almost gaunt skin, the tremble. "I didn't know," she said.

Her indignation was deflating, and with it her sense of righteousness. Which left ...

"Yes," Anma said. "Oh, we were all terribly concerned for a bit. The lights went out ... but they came back on again, so I was sure it couldn't be anything *that* bad. The Lord Chancellor made the announcement that the Lord Emperor had had a heart attack and was indisposed, and since then there hasn't been anything like a full court. We'd heard that he was back to light duties. That's probably why he had the time to meet with you. He *does* respect scholarship."

Pali's hands felt numb. "I see."

"Not that there's anything to complain about with the Lord Chancellor. Brilliant man, he is." Anma snickered unexpectedly. "Or nothing to complain about for the likes of *us*. The aristos and priest-wizards don't like him much."

"Oh."

It wasn't much of a query, but Anma seemed determined to burble pleasantly at her until she felt better. Pali would normally have been a bit irritated or possibly amused by her assiduousness, but in this case she felt ... grateful. Yes, grateful. She latched onto the simple, superficial emotion.

"Lord Madon is ... well, he's not *really* a lord, you see."

Anma continued on about the Lord Chancellor, but Pali barely listened past the occasional hum or other mild interjection. What did she care about the Lord Chancellor, when she had—had—

"You know," Anma said, breaking off whatever she had been

saying to regard her in alarm, "I think you perhaps should return to your hotel. You still seem *greatly* overcome."

Pali had twisted the handkerchief around her fingers. She unwound it with careful deliberation. "It was a shock," she acknowledged.

"Did you ask all your questions?" the librarian asked curiously, even as she waved at someone behind Pali's back.

"They were all answered," Pali replied.

Fifteen years of scholarship and twenty years of doubtful wondering answered in one unexpected encounter.

Fifteen years of scholarship, and she had never seen—

Anma looked behind her and nodded sharply. "There we are," she said, and took the cup from Pali's hands. "Now, dear, I've called for a chair for you. Just you go with Mirka here, and get yourself back to your hotel and have a rest. I've heard the Lord Emperor's magic can take people oddly if they weren't expecting it, and that on top of it being *him*."

"That's it exactly," Pali said, unable to bite back a choked laugh at the unexpected aptness.

"He's a great man, our lord emperor," Anma said seriously. "You go with Mirka now, Professor."

She would have to redo *all* of her monograph.

∼

Mirka took Pali first to her carrel, where she collected her papers, then through a maze of back halls to a discreet side door. A paved road led to a kind of circular court, which was surrounded by a fringe of fountain-like palms.

A small covered carriage pulled by a bicycle waited there, the bicyclist leaning up against her machine while she chatted with one of the librarians, who was standing in the court holding some sort of smoke. The bicyclist straightened when she saw Mirka and tossed her hair over her shoulders. "Hallo, Mirka."

"Calla," he replied, deepening his voice and throwing his shoulders back. Pali had watched undergraduates about their mating dances for years now and though she usually found it amusing, today found it merely wearisome. She walked straight to the steps leading up to the carriage. Rickshaw. That's what they called these.

"Professor Black is at the Swan Hotel," Mirka said.

Pali spared a thought to determine that she'd had to give her address when applying for a carrel at the Reading Room, and Anma must have pulled out her files when she set Mirka to fetch the rickshaw. There was nothing to worry about.

Solaara—Zunidh in general—was remarkably safe. There were people carrying weapons openly in Stoneybridge; there were none to be seen here.

Pali had a dagger about her person, of course, as well as her penknife.

She climbed up onto the rickshaw and set her leather carrier bag beside her.

The notes were probably not totally useless.

She leaned against the headrest. The rickshaw had a bright green cotton canopy, which cast a strange shade across her clothes. The bicyclist was dressed in matching green culottes and a white tunic with short fluttering sleeves. She wore her hair in a brightly patterned cloth wrap, yellow and green and white.

Pali hoped the coordinated ensemble meant that she owned the rickshaw herself rather than it being a uniform.

Her head was throbbing. She shouldn't have drunk all the coffee. More than half a cup was always a mistake. She concentrated on how when she got back to the hotel she would go up to her room and wash her face and follow Anma's sensible suggestion to rest on the bed.

The smoker said something cutting, and Mirka and the bicyclist stopped flirting. She hopped on her saddle, set her feet to the pedals, and after a glance back at Pali to make sure she was settled, set off down the paved road from the Palace back to the city.

Pali closed her eyes and refused to acknowledge the tears leaking from their corners.

How she had reluctantly come to respect what Artorin Damara had been able to achieve despite his isolation and ignorance when he came to the throne. In one of her papers she'd said he was *verging on greatness* in that last year of his reign.

How she had wondered where he had learned mercy.

How she had pitied him for his lack of consorts and concubines, confidantes and ... friends.

～

Once at the hotel she greeted the hotelier, who had been nothing but accommodating, and fumbled her way to her room. Once the door was shut behind her she spent a few minutes briskly setting down her notes and hanging up her outer robes before the headache grew too strong to ignore.

Her coronet of braids was unbearably tight. She yanked out the pins and let them tumble to the floor. Combed out the plait with her fingers, then grabbed the brush from the table and pulled it through her long hair.

That was usually soothing. Brushing her hair reminded her always of the good days. So many evenings around so many campfires. Brushing out her hair, or Sardeet's, or Jullanar's, or Arved's when he grew out his. Or—

Having her hair brushed by any of those friends, or by ... Fitzroy, who had always been fascinated by the texture of her hair and loved to brush and braid it for her.

She combed it, fighting with the curls the humidity of Solaara had brought out in it. She'd washed it practically every day, luxuriating in the hotel's bath, its endless hot water and the gorgeous view through wooden lattices of the hanging gardens of the hotel's atrium. It was shining clean, crackling around her.

The comb's wide teeth worked through the snags and tangles. At first she pulled hard enough to strike tears in her eyes—she told herself that was the cause—but slowly, slowly, as if untangling the knots in her hair worked for untangling those in her mind, she was able to acknowledge the tears for what they were for.

Fitzroy Angursell was not a god.

He had not ridden his horse across the sky of five worlds and into the Sea of Stars, never to be seen again by mortal eyes.

He had, instead, been hidden in plain sight.

He was Artorin Damara, hundredth and last Emperor of Astandalas, on every coin Pali had handled for half her life.

The thoughts sat there, placed next to each other, as unwilling to come together as two too-like lodestones.

Fitzroy Angursell: the shining poet, always laughing in her memory, always with magic and joy coruscating around him, more *alive* than anyone else she had ever known. Brimful, if never of peace. A person she had loved, a friend dear to her heart. She had sailed seven days and seven nights into the Sea of Stars after him, and always regretted that she had not gone farther.

Artorin Damara, whom she had spent fifteen years studying, who had paced his study enough to wear a shadow into the stone.

On her desk was that book of poems young Jemis Greenwing had given her. She set down the comb, leaving her hair to swing loose around her face, her shoulders, and picked up the book. It was a small, compact volume, barely larger than the palm of her hand, beautifully proportioned and a delight to hold.

She had ignored the introduction, as Mr. Greenwing had given her a fanciful story of how the poems had come to be published, and she did not need someone else's interpretations to colour her first readings. She turned once more to the first poem.

What had seemed beautiful but abstract—airy, blurred, a cascade of nebulous images folding into each other—leapt out in sharp, brutal reality.

Not simply golden morning turning stone to liquid light, and the shadow at the centre shimmering, shivering, as insubstantial as the shadow of a soap bubble, all liquid gold emanating from itself.

A black man, golden-eyed, radiant in the most literal sense, in a room of carved alabaster, dressed in court silks of white and gold, gold lacquer on his fingers, untouchable, more than halfway divine.

O Fitzroy, she thought, unable to read any further, and quietly set the book down so she could weep.

CHAPTER THIRTEEN
THE LORD CHANCELLOR

Pali lay on the comfortable bed, gazing at the stripes of light cast through the shutters, and wept.

She had never been comfortable weeping, hating the feel of it, the thickness in her nose, the half-liquid snot at the back of her throat, the inevitable headache. She felt little release on finishing, either.

She was conscious mostly of a sovereign disappointment: in herself, in Fitzroy, in *Artorin Damara*, in herself as a scholar, in herself as a friend, in herself as *his* friend.

She lay on the bed, tears dried on her face, reflecting on the truth of her own words. He always *was* different, wasn't he?

But not a god, after all.

A knock on the door roused her from what might have been classed as a stupor. She rose, swiping at her face, refusing to be self-conscious of her tears. She took a swift glance around, ensuring nothing untoward was visible, and answered the door.

One of the hotel staff stood there. He looked mildly apologetic at disturbing her.

"Good afternoon, professor," he said. "There are two gentlemen from the Palace here to see you—they sent a note asking if you might be willing to meet with them."

He proffered a small scroll. Pali took it, and while the man stood there awkwardly, she broke the seal and unfurled the scroll.

In an unfamiliar hand, even as an example-book, it said that the Lord Chancellor begged her indulgence for an audience.

She rolled up the missive and stood there for a moment, tapping it against her lip. That surely—

It did not mean *he* had come down after her.

Almost certainly.

"Professor?"

She refocused on the man before her. "Please tell the ones who brought this that I will see them."

"Will you come down, professor?"

She had a table and chairs in her room; not to mention all of her weapons, and it was as private as the hotel was likely to be. "No, they can come up."

She picked up her strewn papers and washed her face again, braided her hair back, and had put her sword out of sight when the knock came.

Two men stood there. Neither was *him*.

Pali told herself she was not disappointed. She had not *expected* him to come down. She gestured them in and to the seats around the small table near the balcony, watching them move. One was a soldier of some form: he was tall, moved with a straight-backed solidity, took in the exits and hiding-spots in the room with an easy sweep of his gaze, and had superbly defined muscles. He wore a kind of sleeveless tunic, of good cloth but very plain; his forearms and hands were smudged with what looked like gold-leaf.

The other man was almost familiar. Pali watched the soldier take the seat with his back to the wall, and the other man decide on the chair nearest the bed. She took the third, nearest the closet, and realized, when he had sat down, that he had been the secretary in the emperor's—in Fitzroy's—receiving room.

She looked at him again. He had changed into less formal clothes, but his white tunic was of fine cambric, and his draped wrap—she didn't know the name they called the garment here—was of very beautiful teal-blue silk.

He was otherwise very ordinary: about her own age, with grey liberally salting his black hair, his features pleasing enough to look on, his physique reasonably trim but without the other man's muscles. His skin was a sallow golden-brown, closer to Jullanar's friend Basil's than Pali's richer colouring.

She nodded at the soldier, who nodded back impassively, and focused her attention on the man she now suspected was not a mere secretary at all. "You are the Lord Chancellor, I think," she said.

He nodded, essaying a small smile. "Yes. This is Ludvic Omo, the Commander of the Imperial Guard."

She inclined her head. How curious that such a highly-ranked man—the head of all of Zunidh's armies, if she was not mistaken in the new hierarchies since the Fall—would wear such plain garments.

And how curious that the Lord Chancellor would have such a *rural* edge to his accent. It sounded a touch familiar—no doubt she'd heard others with his accent in the Palace refectories and Archives over her time there.

Pali thought of the gossip about his activities, how the librarians and lower clerks in the palace bureaucracy had admired him, and registered a faint internal resistance to falling for a pleasing accent and a charming smile.

She looked steadily at him and tried not to let her sarcasm be too obvious. "It is an honour. Your letter indicated you wished to speak to me, your excellency? Surely you might have summoned me to the palace."

"We are not here in any official capacity, Domina," he returned easily. "We are here on behalf of our lord."

Pali was sure she must be imagining the feather-light touch of warmth in his voice as he said *lord*. She thought of the impassive, distant, serene man who had once—once—been able to show such fire, such joy, such brilliance.

It was these men—not simply men like these, but these men *in particular*—who kept him hemmed into his place, that rootless star fixed and dimmed, diminished.

"And is that not an official capacity?" She took a breath. "Your excellency. It was my impression that all missives from your *lord* were official."

The Lord Chancellor's eyes flashed. The Commander spoke, his voice also rural, deep-toned and slow. "We are here as his friends, Domina."

Pali could only think of that shadow-line on the floor where he had paced up and down, up and down, trapped. "I suppose he wouldn't have deigned to come himself."

The soldier's eyebrows pulled together. "Madam, that is unworthy of you."

Pali turned her head, for he had cast an emphasis on *you*, as if he knew who she was—

"I'm not sure that's the best way to begin," the Lord Chancellor said, nearly glaring at his companion, his accent sharpening and his court poise just nearly slipping.

"It's true, though," the soldier said, unwavering, and Pali could not help it: the whole situation was so absurd, with their accents and their appearance and their positions and the whole emotional whiplash from discovering Fitzroy.

She caught herself from laughing outright, but she knew she was smiling. "I think I must believe you are here unofficially, for I have heard nothing to indicate you would ever be so gauche in your official business. So." She took a breath. "Your lord has sent you down to me, why?"

"His Radiancy thought you might have some questions. We are here to answer them."

For a moment Pali could only hold herself still in the face of the incredible absurdity of that statement.

And then it occurred to her that he must have been—*had been*—at least as surprised as she was to see her there.

But these men. *These* men. They were his chosen underlings, head respectively of the government bureaucracy and the army.

"What kind of questions? May I ask you about matters of the heart? Or am I limited to matters of state?"

The Lord Chancellor bowed, his eyes gleaming with some shade of amusement, which was a relief.

"We are instructed to answer *any* question, domina."

And what question could she ask? Did these men know who *he* was?

(Did she?)

"Do you think he *enjoys* being Lord of Zunidh?"

The Lord Chancellor met her eyes solemnly and said, "No," a beat before the Commander said, "Some parts."

Pali told herself that was a relief, though it felt like a blow.

She found herself speaking, unable to hold back her words, wishing *he* was there to hear them, to answer them, to look at her with his golden eyes and splendid voice and the smile she remembered. "It would be unbearable to think *he* hated everything."

"I think he hated everything about being Emperor," the Lord Chancellor said. This time the Commander didn't interject anything.

"You are very free with your words, sir," Pali said, almost at random, trying not to think too hard about what it meant that the Artorin Damara she had spent so long studying was that Fitzroy whom she had—whom she had never seen in any of those portraits or policies.

"He cannot come down and speak for himself, domina, and so he has sent us."

The Lord Chancellor was too sharp, too quick-witted, for her not to appreciate his phrasing, this idea that the men *he* had chosen to run his government and army would be his voices in such a situation as this.

"*Can* he not?" she asked, lightly rebarbative, not able to be anything but ironic, detached, for else she would fly at him with every weapon she had, that he should be so urbane and intelligent and admired and yet hold Fitzroy there, shut that star into some thieves' lantern of a cell. "Is it not the case that the Last Emperor of Astandalas is worshipped as a god? It is hard to believe in such *incapacity*. Tell me truly: does he not mean he *will* not?"

That was not fair. She knew that. Fitzroy would have come down for her if he could. If he could.

The Lord Chancellor stopped, his face blank, his eyes boring into hers. He stared: and Pali, staring back, could see him thinking, could see ideas come coalescing into new patterns; could see the moment he realized who she was.

She smiled, not with humour but with the intimation that perhaps he was a worthy foe, after all. Neither the Artorin Damara she had studied nor the Fitzroy whom she knew would ever have *chosen* a fool for a position such as this man held, and his rural twang of an accent suggested Fitzroy had, indeed, had choice. "Your excellency?"

He startled, and grinned at her, with such an open, shining gleam of admiration she was genuinely shocked.

"My apologies, Domina ... Black. I was reflecting."

"I do beg your pardon, your excellency?"

He was a worthy foe, parrying suspicion with humour, turning aside her glares with humble assurance, alive to the nuances of her words and the underlying resonances that she, this Domina Black of Stoneybridge, was also Pali Avramapul of the Red Company.

She knew Fitzroy would not choose a fool. She knew that.

It made it all the more harder that he would choose such a brilliant jailer for himself.

"Please, call me Cliopher. It is my fault that his Radiancy could not come down. I do use the word deliberately, I assure you. You are asking us, as he told me you asked him, whether there is anything left besides the Emperor."

He had told this man that?

Her response was a wild parry and a poor one, for all it caught his feint. "You are not giving me much reason to believe."

Believe what? That he was Fitzroy? That he was *not* Fitzroy? That he had wanted to come down? That he *could not* come down?

"Madam, he is the Lord of Rising Stars, the Last Emperor of Astandalas, the Lord of Zunidh, the Lord of Five Thousand Lands and Ten Thousand Titles."

She felt pushed to the back foot, and was irritable as a result. "I know his titles, sir."

"Do you know what they *mean*? You know—I am sure that *you* know—what power comes with them. Have you never thought of the responsibilities?"

She opened her mouth to say that she had spent the past fifteen years of her life studying the responsibilities Artorin Damara had held, those he had fulfilled and those he had—not shirked, or not exactly, but not completed—

(She had used the word *shirked* in a paper she had written about Artorin Damara's inexplicable reluctance to marry.)

The Lord Chancellor—Cliopher, what an old-fashioned Astandalan name for that rural accent, that gorgeous clothing—leaned forward, face intent, sensing her weakness and taking advantage of it. She could have admired it, had it been on any other subject.

"His Radiancy is planning on leaving on a quest to find an heir, according to the ancient traditions of the lords magi of Zunidh, a year and three months from now."

He kept talking, explaining something about ritual purifications, but Pali was sitting there, struck by the idea that Fitzroy had somehow managed to find himself a quest, a perfectly legitimate *quest*, by which he could simply avoid that knotty topic of his marriage or lack thereof, his lack of heirs of his body, and seize his own life again.

"... the Commander of the Imperial Guard, who has served his

Radiancy the longest of any in his household. When his Radiancy touched him he was given those scars."

Pali looked at the golden smudges. They did not look like scars to her; they did not seem inflamed or as if the skin had been damaged, only as if it had been gilded.

The Commander glanced away from her; she could not tell if he were proud or embarrassed of the marks. Proud, she expected. She was proud of her own scars, especially the odd white spots on her skin from when she had fought the Scorpion-Men in the dark tunnel between the world of men and that of the gods.

"Moreover," the Lord Chancellor went on, his voice settled into some oratorical mode, and Pali, listening to him describing all the things that had to happen before Fitzroy could leave, could only watch him, amazed at his confidence and competence, this brilliance that argued convincingly for keeping the star tight-shut in its lantern until another light was in place.

"I asked his Radiancy why he did not go down to you," he said.

Pali could not quite fathom anyone asking *him* a question with such a degree of impertinence—or—not impertinence; rather, such a degree of *significance*.

"And what did he say in reply?" she asked, nearly flippantly, as flippantly as Fitzroy must have answered.

"He said that if he went down now he would not come back. Domina, I would give anything to have been able to tell him to go, but I am not ready—he is not ready—the world is not ready for him to leave."

He had the rhetorical arts, Pali noted; he must be a brilliant scholar in his own way.

"Please, *please* give him the time to show you that in his heart he is ... he is still the man you once knew."

Perhaps the Lord Chancellor did not speak that hesitation; perhaps that was all in Pali's ears.

She thought of Fitzroy declaiming that she held his heart. Pali had always retorted that he gave it to anyone who smiled at him and asked for a song, and he had said, "Ah, they may have the appearance, but the beating, bloody truth is yours."

She murmured something to the Lord Chancellor even as she smiled reflexively at the memory, for she had laughed at his dramatics, his wild promises, his protestations of admiration and love. She had not precisely disbelieved them—she well knew that Fitzroy loved her as much as the others—but she could not help but find his humour broad and fine.

The Lord Chancellor sat there, his face back in its court poise, his shoulders back and his eyes level and calm. She looked at him for a long time, trying to see past her own intense disappointment that it was him sparring with her and not Fitzroy himself.

She was not, truly, entirely swayed by the argument. The government would probably be fine.

But to destroy a work of Fitzroy's, perhaps his only creative work if he were writing poetry only in secret, well, Pali had already put her hand to his heart and squeezed today.

She nodded at the Lord Chancellor, conceding this particular bout, but certain also that this was not—could not—be the last. "I can see why he chose you."

He did not say anything. The two of them sat there, watching her. The commander was deeply still. The Lord Chancellor waited.

Pali waited. She tried to outlast them, to force them to speak, to insist they respond next: but the man's bearing was a silent challenge to fight, and Pali was not accustomed to backing down.

She felt, obscurely, that her silence was a betrayal of her friendship, her old friend. He was not wholly lost—

She would not let him be lost.

"Tell him," she said at last, deliberate as three moves in a duel, "that the next time I see him I will ask him for his name."

The Lord Chancellor's whole bearing shifted. His eyes sharpened, his face flooded with intensity; he sat up, ready for the killing blow.

Oh, he knew. He *knew*.

She might have admired him, in other circumstances. Might have gladly studied his work, his government, his policies and plans. Might have been curious about what else Fitzroy might see in him.

But oh, if he knew Fitzroy was Fitzroy—if he *prevented* him from being Fitzroy—if he was sent or had come to argue Pali into obedience—

Pali let him take his victory. She let them go, the Lord Chancellor and the Commander of the Imperial Guard. She did not draw her dagger on them. Not yet. Not yet.

She had learned patience. Once Fitzroy was free would be the time to catalogue the grievances and exact her vengeance.

Let Fitzroy's jailer have this bout. She would not underestimate him next time.

~

As he was leaving, even as he stood at the threshold, the Lord Chancellor made her a kind of offer, or suggestion, to stay in Solaara longer, though even as he said it he seemed to regret his own words.

The Commander of the Guard watched her.

"Thank you," Pali said, carefully. "I owe you a debt of gratitude for the hospitality I have received so far."

"It was nothing we would not do for any other scholar of your stature," the Lord Chancellor replied, almost earnestly. "If you will not stay—"

"I have learned several things on this visit to Solaara," Pali said, "and I must go consider my course of action."

He blinked at her, and Pali refrained from smirking, pleased to have discomfited him a trifle. Yes, let him go off imagining what on earth Pali Avramapul had learned and what her course of action might be.

It would have been preposterous, to stay there while *he* was high up in that tower, pacing that shadowed line on the floor.

Better to leave, and find Jullanar, and make a plan.

A kidnapping first, and *then* vengeance. That was the proper order of such things.

CHAPTER FOURTEEN
THE SKY SHIP BACK

Pali did not stay long in Solaara, after that. She returned to the Archives and collected her papers, thanked Amna for her kindnesses, and resolutely refused to look up at the highest tower, its particoloured flag, its golden dome.

The ambassador had arranged for her to return by sky ship to the passageway to Alinor, which she had gathered was a very considerable honour; there were not enough sky ships to use for common transport.

She was glad, for the day and a half on the ship was almost bearable. It would have been hideously painful to spend the months on the sea train across the Eastern Ocean, or a trade-ship, seeing *his* portrait, hearing his name, unable to escape the thought of him.

Pali was given a berth on a ship apparently devoted to the postal service. She liked the captain and her crew, who ran a tight ship and did not mind distracting Pali with stories of passing through storms and atmospheric marvels.

They had a portrait of him hanging in the captain's room, where the officers dined.

There were not many officers: Captain Audmon, her brother the postmaster, their wizard, and the second, Saya Mwalasa. They were polite and interesting company, and Pali did her best to be polite and interesting in return.

She tried not to glare at the state portrait over the midday meal. *Now* she could see Fitzroy in it.

Now she could see Fitzroy everywhere. Everywhere she turned, every coin she picked up, every book she opened, there was his blank emperor face staring back at her, his eyes carefully covered in gold leaf but his very *ears* the ones she had once tugged, laughing about how he should wear a whole row of earrings like a pirate.

The Emperor of Astandalas wore earrings, one drop in each earlobe. In the ship's portrait they were yellow diamonds.

She had watched over the side as they crossed over the marshes— the *Fens*, she was informed—at the mouth of the river that ran down from Solaara, and then the busy port. Across the blue line of the sea train tracks, which formed some sort of reef, and then they passed over a handful of offshore islands before the sea became a flat, featureless blue.

Pali did not find the sea or sky so interesting as to stare endlessly into it, not when her thoughts were so consuming, so after discussing the ship with anyone who didn't seem to be otherwise occupied she went inside the cabin and stared at the portrait.

It wasn't a copy of the one he had hanging in his study (*why?*), but one done at some later age. He had the sort of face that had not changed much between thirty-five and fifty; once he had settled into himself as emperor, he had simply ... refined the look.

Pali drank a cup of the captain's herbal tea and glowered at the excessively beautiful clothing he was wearing.

She was still sitting there scowling when the second in command came in. Pali nodded absently as the woman collected a cup and investigated the contents of various pots to the side. She chose coffee in the end and sat down further along the table from Pali.

"You seem perturbed by the painting, Professor," Mwalasa observed.

Pali discovered she had gritted her teeth as well as scowled when she forcibly relaxed her face enough to smile at the second-in-command. "I was reflecting on the vagaries of representation."

Mwalasa frowned as she worked through this. "It is not an ill copy, I had thought."

A copy of a portrait illustrating the icon of an illusionary man.

"I met him," Pali said, her tongue running as if by itself. "I was surprised by his resemblance to—" She jerked to a halt, trying to drink her tea but discovering her cup empty with the effort. She set her cup down and frowned at it.

Mwalasa choked on a laugh. "His resemblance to his own portraits?"

"No, to Fitzroy Angursell," Pali replied, and then stopped, aghast at her indiscretion.

The second held herself still for a moment, and then laughter erupted. "I'm sorry, Professor, did you just say that you were surprised by the Lord Emperor's resemblance to *Fitzroy Angursell?*"

Pali blushed, but refused to prevaricate. Well, not any more than absolutely necessary. "I did. I am."

"Good Kihaura! This suggests you knew Fitzroy Angursell."

Mwalasa's voice was full of wonder and awe. Pali reflected irritably that it was *always* Fitzroy that people wanted to know about.

"I do—did, rather," she corrected herself hastily, but the woman's face was suffused with delight.

"And he looked—looks?—like the Glorious One."

"There was always a family resemblance," Pali said, frowning at the portrait again. Did he need to wear yellow diamonds and black onyx and lustrous pearls? Must he have that delicate tracery of gold lines painted on his skull? Did he have to smile like that, as empty as an idol?

"A—family resemblance," Mwalasa breathed. Her voice was threaded with doubt and shock and definite reluctance to believe, but also interest in this devastatingly fascinating gossip.

"It's the nose," Pali said bluntly. "They bred for it, the Imperial family."

"And so he ..."

"Look," Pali said, "I am a professor of Late Astandalan History at Stoneybridge. I was born well before Artorin Damara took the throne, and I did, yes, once unexpectedly encounter ... Fitzroy Angursell."

Once.

In a manner of speaking.

Mwalasa stopped to consider her own words. "The officers of the sky ship fleet report to the Commander of the Guard," she said after a moment.

"The Lord Emperor," Pali said, proud her voice came out very calm, "interviewed me in person, knowing my full background."

Mwalasa relaxed. "Well, in that case ... *he* is the final voice of authority, of course."

"Of course."

"And you reckon Fitzroy Angursell *looks* like him?"

Exactly like him. Exactly *unlike* him. Pali had a headache behind her temples, throbbing with the altitude and her off-kilter emotions. She glared at the portrait, the serene magnificence and the power, and finally said, "Every family has its ... black sheep, I believe is the phrase. Even that one."

"Good Kihaura," Mwalasa breathed, staring herself at the portrait. "To think I never heard rumour of that before."

"I expect you will be hearing more of the Red Company soon," Pali said, halfway between a threat and a promise, and then, when the sailor regarded her with speculation, begged her forgiveness and excused herself to return to her cabin.

What was she going to tell Jullanar?

∼

Pali rose when dawn shone full into the window of her cabin, and went out onto the deck to breathe in the high, thin, fresh air, to look at the light casting enormous shadows from the eastern mountains across the plains of the continent below her.

She stared at the sunrise, or just to the side of it, for a long time. She was thinking, perhaps, but not in words.

She thought of her sister Arzu, happily married, mother of three, leader of their clan after their mother's death.

She thought of her sister Sardeet, who had married three times before she was yet one-and-twenty. Pali had had cause to kill her first husband, and humiliate the second; the third had met with an ignominious accident nothing to do with her hand.

She leaned on the railing, staring at the mountains, their shadows, the sunlight, the fine clouds caught like streamers in the valleys.

He always was different, Fitzroy.

Her reasonable mind said that of course he was: he had been more vibrant, more lively, more mischievous, more splendid, than anyone else. No one else had been a poet like him; no one else had that high chivalry, that courage so nonchalant it could not even be called reckless, for he had not even seemed to understand that there might be such a thing as danger, or if there were that it could ever apply to *him*.

But that wasn't what Jullanar had meant, and not, perhaps, what Pali meant either.

For Fitzroy *had* been different, for her.

She scowled at the memory of him leaning over that balustrade, magic in the air around him, his hair crackling with it, his eyes brilliant, gleaming, laughing, crying out in that voice that had struck her sharp as a javelin, "You are magnificent! We should get married!"

She could never have borne the gilded cage that had entrapped him.

∾

She arrived at the mountain-side tower and descended to the little hut at its base, where a bored member of the army was waiting for news and letters. He brightened when he saw her and talked to her for a solid hour over a noontime meal before abruptly apologizing and admitting he hadn't seen anyone for a week and he was starved for conversation.

Pali had found his burble about the novels he had read (and which she had never heard of) the sort of empty discourse that could catch her surface attention and leave the rest of her to turn over the same thoughts she had been turning over since she had left the emperor.

Fitzroy.

Artorin Damara, who was Fitzroy Angursell, who was ...

Lost?

Pali thought over what he had said, what she had said, and what she could tell Jullanar of the encounter, and found herself more and more ... guilty.

She did not like feeling guilty, and she did not like that she had a day's walk to the garrison to dwell on her emotions.

The guardsman, on her questioning, told her that the Commander—Commander Omo, apparently—was well-regarded by his subordinates. He was considered a careful, cautious leader, solid and respectable. He had taken the Lord Emperor's desire for peace and not resisted it, had instead taken the armies and navies and made of them a dedicated organization for all sorts of complex and important tasks.

The Lord Chancellor had told her that the Commander was the longest-serving member of his Radiancy's household. That had not immediately registered, but as she walked down the well-marked trail towards the garrison, debating with herself whether to pull out her sister's carpet or not, she pondered it.

He, Fitzroy that is, had a household.

The Commander of the Imperial Guard was, for some reason, a part of it.

Had he promoted someone from inside his household to that extremely important position? Or had he decided to bring the commander into his control by bringing him into his household?

What did *household* mean, for the emperor—former emperor—in his palace?

Pali had never spent much time on the domestic side of Artorin Damara's affairs. The question of his marriage and heir, or rather lack of each, had been a matter of grave state consequence and therefore a topic she had studied with interest. The structure of his day-to-day life had only mattered insofar as she had been curious, always, at that absence of consorts and concubines, confidantes and friends.

Commander Omo had been quiet, but willing to speak out to her, speak over the Lord Chancellor, when it was necessary. He had worn plain clothes, not lording over her with his garments. He had certainly not been one of the highest courtiers from birth, not with that accent.

He had not been one of Artorin Damara's advisors in the days of the Empire. Pali had looked into that, and she would have remembered a commoner for his uniqueness.

She came to a cliff-edge and stopped blankly.

She did not recall the path, nor leaving it, as clearly she must have done. The guard at the sky ship tower had told her the path was unmistakable, wider than any game-trail, and indeed the first portion (when she had been paying attention) had been.

Pali sighed and took a moment to look around.

She stood on a cliff, perhaps fifty feet high, overlooking a noisy river green with silt. The mountains around her were old, rounded, their heads pale stone, their shoulders clad in heavy green forests. It was cool: she'd put on her proper indigo robes on the sky ship, and again this morning for the walk.

There were birds, and she knew vaguely she'd seen the small animals of a montane forest, rabbits, squirrels, a few whisking tails of deer.

She looked up at the sky, a clear light blue feathered over with clouds. No rain seemed imminent, which was some good news.

She turned, and there on the cliff to her side was a great cat.

Pali had seen any manner of felines, large and small, in her travels. Lions, tigers, leopards, the shy jaguars, the sprinting cheetahs, the lithe black panthers. This one was new to her.

It lay casually draped on a ledge, paws hanging off, tail curling down in a curious, gently moving curve. It was perhaps as heavy as Pali herself, and probably longer even without its tail.

Its colouring was superb: a deep, creamy grey, not exactly the colour of the stone on which it lay, with slate-grey to black rosettes of varying sizes dappled across its flank. It did not have a mane, but did have a kind of ruff, and it lifted its head and regarded her with sleepy interest in its pale blue eyes.

Pali stood still. There was no threat in the great cat, with its fur fluffed up, the long guard hairs moving silently in the gentle breeze. There was no magic here, or nothing beyond the thrill of an encounter with an other that was looking back at her.

She remembered the Siruyal, which had caught her up into another world.

This cat, this great leopard cousin with its fur like shadows on snow, its eyes as blue as Jullanar's, looked at her, slowly blinked, and bent its head to lick its paw.

Pali felt a lump in her throat, at its casual majesty, its repose.

She had visited the imperial menagerie one evening, accompanied by Amna whose daughter worked there. The daughter had let them in, guided them around, a gentle golden mage-lantern in her hands against the heavy, humid, tropical dark.

There had been a tiger, emblem of Zunidh, gold and black, with great golden eyes, pacing a brown rut into its enclosure. Amna's daughter had said sorrowfully that the tiger had been injured, lost half its teeth to a poacher's trap, and could not now survive outside of captivity.

Pali looked at this great wild creature in its freedom, and dared not articulate a challenge even to herself.

She stood there, watching it, until a bird calling tore her attention away, and when she looked back the great cat was silently, splendidly, gone.

CHAPTER FIFTEEN
A SECRET REVEALED

The night after she saw the great cat, Pali dreamed of the desert. It was not the rocky desert of her childhood, where sand dunes rose up out of black rock outcrops and fell away into shingled beaches of pebbles and rocks the size of her fist or head or horse.

It was the Holy Desert of Kaph, the heart of the world.

Pali had ridden it with her friends, when her sister's son had called for them in the warm western wind. They had ridden east, following the call of the Wind Lords, through a pass in the Black Mountains, into the apricot desert.

That was what she always remembered, afterwards. How the desert had risen up in dunes high as mountains, ruddy-gold as an apricot. The air had been scented with strange flowers whose names only Sardeet had known.

In her dream Pali was riding a black horse, with long waving banners of mane and tail. She was alone, and she rode bareback, her robes flaring out behind her, the solid black of her apprenticeship.

She rode up and down the dunes, across the apricot sand and through the plum shadows, and overhead the stars came falling down.

Falling, but never fading.

Over each crest she was sure she would see her end, but when she paused, the stars hissing softly through the air like the wind in her veils, like water-droplets hitting a hot stone, like the distant whisper of voices, all she could see was more of the great sea of sand that had once been the garden of the gods.

When she woke, her heart thundering, the tears drying on her cheeks, she yearned not for the simplicity and clarity of the desert, but for the one star that had landed in her mouth and tasted of peaches.

If that was dzēren—

It was a dream, she told herself. Nothing more.

∼

On this side, the Zuni side, the gate opened once a month or sometimes more, but to a random location within a wide radius of Yrchester on the Alinorel side.

Pali came out in a back alley.

Some ripe scumbag was leaning against the wall, slapping a dagger from hand to hand, as he watched a closed doorway opposite. Pali stepped through the arch on the Zuni side at a moonrise just after sunset, and took in the dull shadows of an overcast day in Fiellan.

The scumbag startled, dropping his dagger. It spun across the cobbles and landed nearly at Pali's feet.

She met the man's gaze readily, daring him to challenge her, and for a moment she thought he would.

But then she flipped the knife with her foot so the hilt landed neatly in her hand, and the scumbag sagged, defeated before Pali's heart had even started to beat.

She sighed and flicked the knife so it landed in the wooden frame of the door he'd been watching, then walked out even as someone inside the building exclaimed, opened the door, and began remonstrating with the scumbag who'd apparently been hired to mug him.

What a waste of a good entrance.

∽

She had hoped she might have arrived in Yrchester itself, or possibly Fiella-by-the-Sea, the duchy seat of Fiellan, but once she left the alley she quickly learned she'd come out in Kingsford, the capital of the kingdom of Rondé. She was much closer to the good roads south through Lind to Chare than she was to Ragnor Bella.

She had little interest in Kingsford, which was a dingy, depressing city even without the unrest she could sense in the air. From conversation in a coffee-house off the secondary square she learned that there were 'troubles' on the highway between Orio City and Yrchester, but that they hadn't so far spilled far from the highway or inland from the coast.

After a coffee—so much less good than what she'd had on Zunidh —and a pastry (rather better; fine pastry-making was more of a specialty of Kingsford), Pali decided she had best head straight back to Stoneybridge so she could gather her horse and tender her resignation.

The thought came as she collected her bag together and walked out into the fine mist that was blanketing Kingsford.

She turned it over in her mind, but though it was the first time she had consciously thought it, she knew it was true. She could not imagine returning to Stoneybridge, teaching the history of the latter days of Astandalas, writing papers and monographs, about *him*.

It was impossible. She could not even begin to countenance the idea.

She hired a horse from a livery stable near the central stagecoach inn, making desultory arrangements to change the horse at every coaching inn as she headed south, and rode into the afternoon with the desire to shake the very dust of Zunidh from her feet.

∽

She arrived back in Stoneybridge nearly exactly three months after she had left. The season was turning from spring into the exuberant fullness of high summer. The Charese winter was wet and cool, and later in the summer it would be sunny and dry, but for now it hung suspended between those two extremes, a rainbow of flowers caught between raincloud and sun.

Pali returned to her rooms and found them small.

She wandered around indecisively. Without her sister's carpet hanging there the wall looked plain and bare. Her furniture seemed ugly and uncomfortable; her sitting room impersonal.

At her desk, her books reproached her.

She wanted to write to Jullanar, as she had wanted to write to Jullanar since she had walked out of that room and past the seven anterooms with their seven sets of guards. And as she had every time, she refrained.

What could she possibly say in a letter that would not be better said in person?

And she would, at least, see Jullanar again soon. Very soon.

She saw Professor Vane first. Her friend arrived the morning after she had returned, bearing with her a great armful of blue delphiniums.

Pali eyed them with mild mystification. "Are those for me?"

Professor Vane laughed. "They were for me, but I could spare one—or two—or half a dozen stems." She extracted a few as she spoke, blue petals falling about her as she did, and held out the flowers to Pali.

Pali had never been someone who had fresh flowers in her rooms. They did not last, for one thing, and it never occurred to her to buy them, for another.

She took the delphiniums slowly, as if it were more weighty an action than it was. As if these flowers, brilliant-coloured, blowsy, early summer in a sky-blue spire, with bosses shaded with iridescent green or a delicate grey-lavender or a deep, ultramarine blue, were the life Pali was about to leave.

Professor Vane was saying something about putting them in water, and looking around for something that might do as a vase. Pali set the flowers down on the top of the chest bound with Masseo's lock and she said, "I found Jullanar. And Fitzroy. I'm resigning."

"Jullanar of the Sea? Fitzroy *Angursell*?" Her friend shut her mouth with a snap, and the great mass of flowers in her hands drooped down. "Professor Black—" she stopped, took several uneven breaths, and then: "Pali Avramapul?"

"Yes," she said, as if this was not still treasonous, not still astonishing. Not a *surprise*. Not a leap into a level of friendship she had never let herself make. There was some water in the ewer and she stuck the delphiniums in it, hastily, trying to control her emotions.

"Ah. Well. *Well*. Well. Would you like to tell me about it?" Professor Vane said, sitting down on one of the ugly, uncomfortable chairs. "You don't have to ... I am dreadfully curious, of course, but only if you wish to."

Her voice said how very much she hoped Pali *was* going to say something.

Pali shut the door and slid down onto the other seat, the jug still in her hands, heavy stoneware, the curves like the rounded bulk of a pear, the colour an ordinary, uninspired grey.

She had lived in these rooms for nine years, and yet ... had she ever done more than camp in them?

She was a desert nomad. They had carried their homes with them, strewn them with carpets and jewelled lanterns, never lacking in art for all their mobility. Those camps had never felt so temporary, so impermanent, so contingent.

The kettle had nearly come to a boil, so Pali got up, set the jug of flowers on the table by the wall, and took the kettle off the fire. A moment later she set aside the box of tea and instead went to the chest.

The lock moved under her hand, the old enchantments set by Masseo and Fitzroy still as elegantly effective as ever. (She could not yet think of Fitzroy. She would not think of where Masseo might be.)

She pulled out an ivory box and a silver knife. From the cupboard Mrs. Fing kept stocked for her use she brought out a round flat loaf of bread, a bottle of wine, and from the next shelf two finely blown glass goblets.

Professor Vane watched her, brow furrowed slightly.

Pali went to the ewer and poured a small bowl of water, which she placed on the table next to the other items. She did not have scented water such as would properly be used, but this would have to do.

She dipped her fingers in the water and rinsed them before offering the bowl to her friend. Professor Vane glanced at her cautiously, then imitated her.

Next Pali took the bread and tore it roughly in half. She opened the ivory box, which was full of the pale pink salt she had brought from home, so long ago, and sprinkled a few grains on each piece of bread. This she offered next, silently.

Professor Vane lifted it enquiringly to her mouth, and when Pali nodded, ate a portion. Pali followed suit, and then opened the wine and poured them each a glass. It was a fine Arcadian red, thick and aromatic. They each drank, silently, not offering the usual benedictions that were customary here. Professor Vane's eyes were wide and eager, but she held her peace.

After they had drunk, Pali closed the ivory box and set it to one side. She filled their goblets properly, and then sat back.

"I have offered you water, and salt, and bread, and wine, according to the customs of my people," she said. "These are offerings of hospitality: under my roof you are my guest, sacred to the gods."

There were other rules of hospitality, of course, but Professor Vane was widely read enough to know that there were obligations from host to guest, and guest to host.

Professor Vane nodded, smiling so brightly her face muscles must hurt, Pali thought a little grimly.

Pali set down her goblet and pulled out the copy of a state

portrait of Artorin Damara she'd occasionally had her students analyze.

Professor Vane took the painting—the copy was done on a board perhaps a foot in length, and was of reasonable execution—and stared down at it. "I don't understand. This is Artorin Damara."

"That," said Pali, staring at the fireplace, "is Fitzroy Angursell."

Professor Vane uttered a strange, high-pitched laugh, uncertain as to where exactly the joke lay.

Pali sighed and returned to a moody inspection of the portrait. "We always knew he was related. That nose was unmistakable. If you look at any sculpture or coin or portrait you can see it."

"I don't understand," Professor Vane said again. She lifted her hand to fiddle with the green ribbon tying back her hair. "Professor Black—Pali—"

"We knew he was related," Pali repeated. "We didn't know—he never told us—that he was *second in line*."

A part of her wondered about that. Why hadn't he?

("I am under an enchantment," he'd said off-handedly more than once, bright-eyed and insouciant, unable to be believed. "I cannot tell you my name.")

"I didn't know until I was granted an audience."

Not even then, a guilty voice added. She had not recognized him until they were sitting on that terrace, and he had offered her biscuits that were not Jullanar's. Only then had Pali been able to recognize him.

Professor Vane sat back with an unvoiced huff of astonishment. "No one would ever believe me if I told them."

"No one would believe *me* if I told them," Pali said. "I could shout it from the rooftops and people would merely think I'd gone mad."

"What are you going to do?"

"I can hardly teach what I've taught *now*." Not that Pali wanted to. It felt as if she'd walked through a door, unexpectedly, and that life had slammed shut behind her. "I am going to go back to Ragnor Bella and tell Jullanar, and then we will go back to Zunidh and kidnap him."

Pali nodded, satisfied with this plan, and sat back.

Professor Vane—Elena, she supposed, here in her rooms, for this conversation—conversely sat right at the edge of her seat, her back straight and her face eager. Her curls were coming loose in her excitement, the humidity causing them to spiral outwards.

Jullanar's hair used to do that, Pali remembered suddenly. She looked down, feeling the tears stinging the back of her nose. She crumpled her face, infuriated to be so emotional. She knew where Jullanar was. Jullanar was waiting for her.

She looked at Professor Vane—Elena—who did not look nearly as surprised as Pali had expected. She thought, with a twinge of healthful rage, of the insufferable Lord Chancellor and his easy recognition of her. It stung less with Elena.

"Did you already know?" Pali asked.

Elena caught her breath. "Only—only when you left—" Her words tumbled over themselves. Sometimes she stuttered when she grew excited, but Pali was used to that, and it never bothered her. When Elena was in full flood as a lecturer—Pali had crept in to her lectures once or twice, when they were on a topic of particular interest—her voice expanded out, high and passionate, steady as a metronome.

Pali lectured the way she had learned to tell stories at her mother's knee, her students clustered close and attentive. No one fell asleep in her lectures, either; or at least not twice.

"You once rescued my brother, my older brother that is—I have two, one older and one younger—well, my older brother is actually my half-brother, our father remarried ... this is too much, isn't it? I'm sorry, Professor—"

"Oh, call me Pali," Pali said crossly, quite as easily as if she'd told anyone to call her in years.

"And I'm Elena," Elena said, then flushed and stammered, "Oh, but you knew that already, of course—"

"Elena," Pali said intently, leaning forward to match her friend's anxious posture, "I'm the same person who's been passing notes with you in faculty meetings for the last five years."

"But I didn't know you were *Pali Avramapul* then," Elena pointed out. "It never occurred to me, until I saw that carpet off the wall, as if you were going to take it with you, and, and, I knew, I just *knew*, it had to be the one my brother described. He is a dyer, you know—that is, he studies the science and practice of dyes—he's in trade, of course, which all those cats at Rosemount used to think *so* despicable, but times are changing, aren't they? And I've always been proud of him—he was the one who created that splendid blue dye to replace the old jirgin blue, when we couldn't get the jirgin any more because of the Fall."

Pali reached forward to take Elena's twitching hands with her own. "Elena," she said, forcing herself to be calm and soothing, as if she were dealing with a particularly restive undergraduate, "it's fine. Yes, I am Pali Avramapul. Yes, I did many amazing things. I can tell you about some of them, if you'd like. Now—*breathe*."

Elena obeyed her, though after several breaths her shoulders and her hands both relaxed and she started to laugh and then, unexpectedly, to sob.

Pali was not entirely unfamiliar with students starting to cry on her unsympathetic shoulder, and so she busied herself by putting the kettle back on the fire, adding a couple of pieces of coal—they used a mixture of coal and wood in Stoneybridge, which she disliked but had been unable to persuade the charwoman not to lay—and generally making quiet, homely, useful sorts of noises.

Eventually Elena subsided and fished in the sleeve of her Scholar's gown for a large handkerchief. Pali had always liked that Elena kept a lady's handkerchief in her dress pocket or reticule and a seemingly inexhaustible supply of so-called men's handkerchiefs in her sleeves.

"I'm sorry to be such a ninny."

Pali nodded, accepting the apology and refusing to deny the fact that Elena was, in her opinion, being an utter ninny. She didn't deny either that this did nothing to offend her or demean Elena in her eyes, as she well recalled how Jullanar had been similarly afflicted with bouts of tears. They had never stopped Jullanar from achieving anything she wished to accomplish.

"Would you—do you—that is—"

Pali sighed, but it was with the realization that perhaps she *could* have had what Jullanar had with Basil and Sara, if Pali had been ... well. If she'd been more like Jullanar, and better able to make friends outside of fated moments and epic quests.

She knew that Jullanar would say it wasn't too late, no matter that Pali had every intention of leaving Stoneybridge within the month. Sooner, even. But—

But. She had blurted out the truth to Elena, and Elena had responded well. Pali could *feel* their friendship building, like a wind piling up a dune, grain by grain.

She smiled at her friend. "What's your brother's story?"

CHAPTER SIXTEEN
THE TALE OF HIGGINS VANE

Elena took a deep breath.

Oh, that was better, Pali thought. She'd always felt as if she were play-acting friendship, *Professor Vane* and *Professor Black*, that name that was not hers.

"He was, as I said, a dyer. At this time he was a journeyman, travelling to study under various masters. He took ship to Colhélhé ... so far, but yet it was not so far in those days, was it? Not so far as *you* have travelled."

"I am from Kaphyrn," Pali acknowledged, a world that had never been more than barest rumours to the lands of the Empire.

"And you travelled to the Moon's Country ..."

Pali did not either confirm or deny that half-voiced question. She still was rather bitter about some aspects of that journey to the Moon's country, all in all. Fitzroy hadn't needed to *flaunt* himself like that, surely.

"My brother, Higgins—"

"I'm sorry," Pali interrupted. "Your brother's name is Higgins? Higgins Vane?"

"Yes—well, it's Benneret Higgins Vane, we have middle names in my part of Lind. I'm Elena Astoria, my older brother is Benneret Higgins, my younger brother is George Jakory. Higgins was his mother's surname, but our father was also Benneret so he always went by Higgins."

"Extraordinary," Pali murmured, remembering with a shudder poor Jullanar's maiden name (barbaric conception though a *maiden name* was) of Thistlethwaite. They'd had a wonderful conversation once with Fitzroy about picking a new surname, or achieving one through her own deeds.

He'd spent weeks coming up with *Angursell*.

"Anyway, my brother Higgins was a journeyman dyer, and he went off to study under various people. He got a job as an assayer of dyestuffs with the Firlois merchant fleet. I'm not sure if you would know them—"

"I wrote a paper on the effects of Artorin Damara's trade policies using the Firlois Fleet as a case study."

Elena blushed, grinning sheepishly. "Oh, of course you did. I went to your presentation. Somehow it's as if there was a switch in my mind, and you went from *Professor Black* to *Pali Avramapul*, as if there was no overlap."

Pali paused, for that hit harder than she was sure Elena intended, before she said, "There's more overlap than some might suspect."

"The rumour is that you had a youthful career as an imperial spy."

Now, that was a pleasing idea. Pali smiled, and sat back, satisfied, with her wine. "It was quite the opposite, and therefore not so different at all. Indeed. Tell me more about your brother, Benneret Higgins Vane."

"He went with the Firlois ships from port to port, looking at the raw materials for the dyestuffs and fabrics and things, and talking to people to find out if there were new dyes or mordants or ... whatever. They were in Wallen, just at the southern edge of the Birlblui Archipelago, when ... well, when Higgins got into a bit of a spot. He fell in love with a Wallenese woman, you see, and he was all set to throw over his whole career and family and stay there."

"He wouldn't be the first one to fall in love with Birlblui," Pali observed. She recalled the islands: the verdant downs, rising up like so many whales' backs, arching into a place where the skies seemed lower and lovelier than elsewhere.

Clouds were born there, Pali remembered. There were people who lived in them: in certain lights one could see their houses, and at night their lights glimmered forth, stars caught in paper lanterns hung all about the sky.

They had spent a strange and marvellous week there, drinking the strange, fierce mead the cloud-people made from the honey their bees brought forth. If they ate anything besides honey Pali couldn't recall; but that might have been the result of a week of mead as much as the length of time and life since then.

"He always says it was very beautiful," Elena said. "He used to say that there were people who lived in the clouds ...?"

Pali nodded. Elena shook her head in amazement. "I never believed him. I looked it up, you know; I did a whole minor study of the Conquest of Colhélhé, but I couldn't find any reliable records of people who lived in the clouds above Wallen."

"I saw them, when we travelled there. The green islands—there were no trees on them, it was all grass, with sheep grazing—and above them the clouds that boiled up from a place in the centre of the archipelago, all hidden by mists and rainbows. There were permanent clouds, and you could see lights glittering in them in the night, gold and green and pink."

"Higgins said that when he was there the cloud-people let down all these lanterns ... not exactly paper lanterns, they were made of some other substance, and first they went up and then drifted down, hundred and thousands of paper lanterns, all coloured like the candles they burned inside them, pink and green and gold and a pale orange."

"We missed the lantern-fall," Pali said regretfully.

Elena cast her a startled glance. "You know, that makes me feel so much better," she admitted. "To know there are things *you* missed seeing, despite everything!"

"Even one world is too big to see everything, and though I have seen more than most, there is always more."

"Higgins said ... he's not a very emotional man, you know? He's really very conventional. Falling in love with Rosalie and quitting his job was the most extraordinary thing for him to do. We couldn't believe it, when we got the letter from him ... Neither could his superiors, as it turned out. The ship's captain said he'd leave Higgins on Wallen while he went off to the next archipelago, and would call for him when they came back. It was not quite the end of their route, you see, they were going on to ... oh, where was it?"

"Vilourin, probably," Pali suggested.

"Yes, the sounds right. Anyway, Higgins stayed with Rosalie in Wallen. They had the custom where a courting couple would live together in her parents' house for a year and a day before they married—*so* strange, don't you think?—oh, you probably don't."

Pali nodded. "There are many marriage customs in the Nine Worlds."

"So Higgins lived with Rosalie's family, and he worked for her father—he was a dye-producer himself, that's how Higgins had met Rosalie in the first place—learning about how the Wallenians made Birlu green dye. You know the colour I mean? It was the base colour for the First Army's uniforms."

It was a rich, pleasant dark green, very clear in tone. Green wasn't Pali's favourite colour but she did like that shade.

"Higgins was there for nearly a year, through the Lantern-Fall and everything, and more and more in love with Rosalie—we used to get these letters where he would tell us about the dyeing for half of it, which was frankly what he always wrote, and then he would spend half of it telling us all about Rosalie. It was very sweet."

"Mmm."

"There was one island, a little apart from the rest, which the

Wallenians said was ... not sacred, exactly, but special. Higgins said he didn't understand what they meant; he reckoned they were being very superstitious about it. The story was that you could go the island, but you couldn't light fires on it, and you couldn't take your sheep to graze there. People used to go there for picnics, at a certain stage of courting."

Pali was beginning to remember the likely incident concerning Higgins Vane. The only doubt she had was how she was sure the man's name had been something else—something rather silly-sounding—not Higgins at all. Mind you, she'd thought it was the Wallenese, not Wallenians ... It had been a long time since she'd last thought of the Birlblui archipelago and those who lived there.

"So when Higgins got to that point of his courtship, he decided he had to follow the custom—he's always been perfectly conventional, did I say? He hates to be considered *odd*. So he got together all the customary foods, and a few things from our home, or as much as he could get them in Wallen, and he got a boat and rowed over to the island to set up the picnic for Rosalie."

"I think," said Pali, with a growing sense of amusement, "that I may indeed recall the incident."

Elena paused and looked intently at her. "Do you really? Would you tell me your side?"

"I doubt it's anywhere near so exciting as what your brother tells," Pali replied.

"It was the most exciting thing ever to happen to Higgins," Elena stated baldly. "He must tell the story once a week, *still*. It's not *odd* to have a good story about the Red Company, you know. Not exactly conventional, but then I think this adventure shook loose a few inhibitions."

Pali laughed in genuine amusement. "Oh, do tell me his version."

"He is going to be *so* jealous I got to tell you," Elena murmured. "The problem with Higgins always was that he is enthusiastic, but if you take him even a little outside his normal activities he gets a bit bewildered. Putting together a picnic for his sweetheart was hardly difficult, but it wasn't the sort of thing he'd have been likely to do, let alone on a special island where you had to row out and set it all up the day before ... And we're from inland. Higgins knew how to row but he'd forgotten that weather changes quickly around the sea."

"Ah," said Pali.

"So there he was, the afternoon before his picnic, and a squall blew up and soaked him to the skin. It was summer, so it wasn't terribly cold, but Higgins was worried about getting sick, and by the time the squall passed it was nearly dark, and he decided to spend the night on the special island and go back over to Wallen for Rosalie the next morning. And so without thinking of the prohibition, he lit a fire."

"Ah," said Pali again.

She knew any number of stories about what happened when you broke that sort of prohibition. The Nine Worlds was *full* of such stories. You did not need to be in Fairyland for ancient and wild magic to occur.

"All was well at first. He found driftwood and lit his fire. He dried off and ate a bit of his extra food—Higgins is the sort of person to *always* have extra, just in case—and then what with one thing and another, he felt sleepy and fell asleep."

"It was a spectacular sunset that night," Pali remembered.

Elena drew her breath in sharply; then she smiled, almost guiltily. "I keep forgetting you were *there*."

Pali *was* there. In her mind's eye she saw the high cloud-castles of the cloud dwellers, their lights and their flowers tumbling from windowsills high above the shifting glimpses of island and sea. The cloud people were seers and mystics, who held their cloud-liquor was a way to attain the sacred. They were happy to share with anyone who made it to their high houses.

She had never liked such things. She enjoyed wine, a glass or two with friends; even a beer down in the pubs in the city. She would taste anything once. But she did not like anything that took her more than the one step away from herself that a glass or two of wine did.

She had tried the mead or whatever liqueurs the cloud-dwellers made: the one that was orange as sunset, the one that was clear as rainwater, the other one that was milky as the clouds around them, and that night, she had refused all after the polite wetting of her lips that was her duty as a guest.

She had climbed up from the room where the rest of the party was being guided in meditation by their hosts, and followed the strange winding and sloping stairs up and up the curvature of the clouds until she came to a sort of high peak.

She had sat there watching the sun set over the ocean: a sunset magnificent enough, in strange enough surroundings, to still resonate in her memory all these many years later.

Fitzroy had joined her, a bottle of ordinary wine in his hand; he'd forgotten the glasses.

They had sat beside each other, high on a cloud, looking out at the sunset painting the west in orange and red and green; the sea gold and silver and a deep, fulsome ultramarine blue. The islands, grey and green swells, like the backs of broaching whales.

The one island that *was* a breaching whale.

Elena continued on her story. "Higgins was not used to campfires. He put too much wood on—he was cold and wet at first. Made almost a bonfire."

"I saw it," Pali said. "Fitzroy and I were sitting on one of the clouds together."

Together, leaning against each other, sharing the bottle between them. Fitzroy always liked to be close, was forever touching. Pali had grown used to it, to his shoulder against hers, his hand in her hair, his chin coming over the crown of her head and his arms enfolding her shoulders. He always smelled of fire and fresh air and flowers, no matter what he'd been doing.

He'd been the one to point out the bonfire, on the furthest of the islands below them. He'd started spinning fancies about the earthbound star, the first beginnings of a poem in just the way the clouds behind them were spun out of the sea and air into their massive significance.

People knew that image. It was in one of the famous poems. "The Earthbound Star and the Cloud": a poem about impossible yearning, love reciprocated but always unfulfilled. Pali had always been impressed at how many varied poems and songs Fitzroy could draw out of one moment.

Ninety-nine sonnets from fourteen years as an emperor. If indeed he had written those poems.

Something cold burned in Pali's stomach as she remembered Fitzroy on the cloud, Artorin Damara in his palace.

"Higgins, as I said, fell asleep, and let his fire burn unattended." Elena regarded her with those eager, curious eyes. "I don't suppose you'd like to say your side?"

"What does he say?" Pali temporized.

"Higgins says the first he knew of anything was a huge surge under him, and suddenly he was flying through the air, a hundred feet up, and he could see the water boiling and splashing below him as a huge whale—an *enormous* whale, a whale the size of an island—a whale that had *been* an island—dove down under the surface. He said he was sure he was going to die, for he was so high up and he was not a very good swimmer, and the water was cold and the distance back to Wallen too far for him to swim. He fell ... until suddenly he wasn't falling any more."

She smiled expectantly at Pali.

Pali and Fitzroy had been sitting there on the cloud, which was as soft and springy as clouds looked—as they never actually *were*, outside of this sort of strange magical phenomenon—drinking the bottle of wine and talking about ... what they had talked about she could not now remember.

She remembered Fitzroy had looked at her, his golden eyes almost an ordinary light brown in the sunset, his dark skin, conversely, glittering with something that made him look like he had taken shape out of the midnight sky.

"What a splendid night for flying it would be," he had said.

Fitzroy's desire for flight was, by that point, a running joke. Pali had laughed. "Will you learn how this time?"

"I was thinking of your sister's carpet."

That was how they had reached the cloud-dwellers: on the carpets Pali's sister Arzu had woven for her and her friends when they sought to cross the Holy Desert of Kaph on that adventure that had forged them into a company of legends.

Pali never went anywhere without it; or she had not, in those days.

In her rooms at St Erlingale's she glanced at the carpet, still folded demurely on the chest, scarlet and gold in a thousand shades, the design the Tree of Knowledge surrounded by the knots of love.

Sitting there on the top of a cloud, with the sunset draining out of the sky and the stars coming out, luminous as the lanterns on the islands below them, the tiny moons of Colhélhé gleaming like the bonfire on the furthest of the islands of the archipelago, Pali had been unable to say anything other than, *Of course*.

She had untied the carpet from where it hugged her waist. She had flung it out, the scent of the desert rising up—jasmine and frankincense and the bitter myrrh her sister had used to soak some of the threads.

She and Fitzroy had clustered close, for it was not a large carpet, his arm around her shoulders. He had sung some song of his own invention, and Pali had thought—she remembered thinking—that it was a perfect moment.

Jullanar had asked how he was different. Pali had not let herself remember this moment, that perfect moment, when she had felt something stir and had—wondered—

Well. It was many years since then, and she had mourned the Fitzroy lost to the Sea of Stars. The one who was in the Palace of Stars—he was different. In a different way.

She shook her head. He *was* different now. She could remember that moment and let it be what it had been, no longer wondering what might have happened, had—well. Had Higgins Vane not interrupted them.

They had swooped and glided through the air, past the cloud-dwellers' houses, in and around the pinnacles of clouds, they had seen the bonfire flash, the whale shudder: the island dipping down, and then rising up as a powerful tail, the size of a mountain ridge, slapped the water.

And there, screaming his head off, a figure hurtling upward.

"He said," Elena said punctiliously, "that you caught him."

"He came right past us," Pali said. She sat back in her chair, tucking her feet up under her. Her hand curled around her ankle.

"He is always *so* impressed that you were there for him."

"We could hardly have missed him."

For a moment all had been confusion: the whale thrashing down, the water spraying up even to drench them: the man screaming as he reached the zenith of his arc and started hurtling down with even greater speed: Fitzroy laughing fit to fall off the carpet himself.

It had been Pali who had guided the carpet to catch first Fitzroy and then the unfortunate Higgins Vane. The young man had gibbered when the carpet bent around his weight as he plummeted upon them.

But Arzu had been—*was*, Pali reminded herself fiercely; her sister was surely still alive—both her sisters must be—a splendid weaver, and her knots had held. The carpet had bent, nearly folded itself in half, tumbled her and Fitzroy upon the other man, but it had not fallen out of the sky.

"Higgins said you were unflappable."

Pali could not help but preen at the compliment. She was honest enough to tell Elena the truth, however. "He took so long to recover himself I'd had plenty of time to regain my composure."

"Higgins said you were severely beautiful, with a flawless brow. And a tongue with which you flayed him alive. All characteristics you haven't lost, I must say."

Pali laughed. "My sister Sardeet is the beautiful one." She sipped her wine, letting the smooth rich liquor slide down her throat, warm her veins. "We took him down to Wallen. They were much perturbed with the disturbance of the resting whale."

"And then," Elena murmured, "you dropped him off in the arms of his beloved Rosalie, and flew off again into the night, never to be seen—at least by Higgins—again. He is *so* proud of the song Fitzroy Angursell wrote about him. He just always wishes his name had been mentioned."

Pali topped up their respective glasses. "All we heard was *Iggo*, and I *refused* to let Fitzroy use the rhyme he came up for that."

CHAPTER SEVENTEEN
THE CHALLENGE BELL

Pali spent several days sorting out her life in Stoneybridge.

At one level she felt she could have simply walked away, taken her horse and her saddlebags and the belongings that fit in them, left all the rest to be a mystery and a wonder and, probably, a scandal.

At other points of her life she might well have done so.

She pondered why she felt a reluctance to do so. She had a responsibility to her students, she supposed, and to her colleagues. And—the nomad in her resisted this, but it was true—she did not exactly want to abandon *all* of her belongings.

She would have, had it been necessary, in a heartbeat.

She would have grabbed her bag and her sword and gone.

But if she did not *need* to leave so quickly, if she did not *need* to dash out for a call that had never come (though now every time she turned around she saw that solemn, sober mask of Artorin Damara-who-was-Fitzroy, and cloaked as the eyes inevitably were in gold leaf she could not but see reproaches there that she had never recognized him before)—

At any rate, she did not want to lose all her belongings if she did not need to.

Most of the items she wanted to take with her had already gone to Solaara. She added in a few extra weapons and items related to her horse's tack, as well as a tent and bedroll and a few other books to read and leave along the way. Her other books and papers, trinkets and treasures, she tucked into the chest Masseo had made for her or tidied in her study.

She attempted to resign from the university. The authorities, upon being informed it was because she had learned some startling facts about Artorin Damara after an audience with him—a feat of truthful prevarication Pali thought even Fitzroy himself might have appreciated—instead granted her an indefinite unpaid leave of absence while she pondered these revelations and turned them into what the head of St Erlingale's College assured her was sure to be the defining book on the reign of the Last Emperor of Astandalas.

Pali managed to not say anything to contradict this idea.

She therefore put all the sensitive material, such as there was, into the chest with Masseo's lock, left her books and academic items where they were, and decided she would take her leave of Stoneybridge in style.

⁓

Stoneybridge had a handful of fencing schools (along with a range of other sporting and martial activities—Pali had visited the boxing and archery clubs, and practiced with the latter a couple of times a month). They were of varying styles, inclinations, and merits. Pali was a member of several but favoured a particular club for the quality of fighters there.

Most were ex-soldiers, with a few well-taught aristocrats: all were serious students of the art, and Pali enjoyed both the practice and the opportunity to teach. Sometimes she even learned a new trick or technique herself.

She had been procrastinating a touch, perhaps, unwilling to go to Jullanar without any plan beyond "Fitzroy is actually Artorin Damara, yes, really, the Last Emperor—yes, *really*—and we must go kidnap him away from his guards and bureaucrats. Especially his bureaucrats."

Especially that bureaucrat-of-bureaucrats.

Every time Pali thought of the Lord Chancellor's smug face she wanted to punch the daylights out of him. She had dreamed a most satisfying dream of pummelling him, while Fitzroy watched.

She kept repeating her plan to herself. Collect Jullanar. Return to Zunidh. Rescue Fitzroy. *Then* vengeance.

Since she had decided not to leave with only a whisper of rumour to mark her disappearance, but rather to be responsible about the matter, she had had a considerable number of letters to write and answer. Indeed, they proliferated as soon as she started to consider the matter properly.

Letters from other scholars and former students, some social and some seeking collaboration, advice, or her own thoughts on a matter. There were her handful of current students to console and congratulate on their new tutors, and the new tutors to meet with to go over the students' aptitudes, interests, and potential distractions.

There were new hopeful new students to pass on to the Rector to deal with. There was her handful of colleagues and friendly acquaintances from whom to take her leave.

"But where are you going?" was the recurrent question.

She could tell, usually, who had suspected her identity. They asked if she were meeting old friends, or her sister—she did have a sister, didn't she?, they'd enquire archly—and depending on how much Pali liked them, sometimes she said yes. She told the others she was undertaking further research into the last emperor's character.

But even with her being thorough about the matter, the first time she had ever taken such a long time about going on an adventure—she had spent far less effort the first time she had decided to leave her clan, or her world, not knowing anything of what she might find through the pass between mountains, between one sky and another, between Kaphyrn and what would turn out to be Daun—

But even with all her care, there came a point when she could not pretend to herself that she was doing anything other than delaying a trifle, procrastinating even.

And then there came a letter from Jullanar.

Pali recognized the writing immediately, no matter how long it had been since she had last seen it: it sent a jolt through her spine, a lift to her heart, a catch in her breath. She did not know it to be *Jullanar's*, though she guessed it was, for the only other person who might write her was Fitzroy, and what could he say to her after what she had said to him?

(She could not write to him. There were too many eyes who would look at a letter even from a respected Scholar of Stoneybridge before it reached the Lord Emperor's desk. Even if he had given instructions that it come to him unopened—and she could not be sure he had given such an instruction.)

She held the letter for a moment, tracing her fingertips over the familiar letters spelling out a name that felt ill-fitting and ill-conceived. She did not mind being Professor Black, had never felt it restricted her from being also Pali Avramapul—but it was wrong that Jullanar should write it so.

My dearest Professor Black—

I hope you have returned by now from your expedition to Zunidh, or will soon. I am greatly anticipating our common travels. My situation has not changed but my patience is wearing thin.

Fortunately I have been researching the marriage and divorce laws (Fiellan, especially South Fiellan, has some strange ancient customs enshrined still in Rondelan law) and have discovered a solution, which I may put into effect this Midsummer's Day.

I intend to then travel over the pass you know into Chare and will come to you in Stoneybridge. I shall await your return there if need be.

What stories we still have to learn and tell each other, my dear friend!

J. Soon-not-to-be Etaris

Pali did not need to question the Porter to know she had two days till Midsummer.

It was just before noon when she received the letter. She was packed; she needed only to saddle her horse and go.

She was already half-dressed for an afternoon at the salle. She'd decided to wear her proper robes, to go out with the questions rumbling and rumouring about her, after ringing her club's Challenge Bell and sending all the ex-soldiers and well-trained aristocrats into a tizzy of speculation and sweat.

She put on the rest of her robes, belted her sword, collected her saddlebags, and extinguished the fire before locking the door behind her.

She told the Porter she was leaving. He was a local man, grizzled and veteran of many a student's excuse, and he regarded her with a jaded eye.

"Surprised you're going out the front door, Professor."

"Seemed polite," Pali replied. "I've a note for Professor Vane over at Sisterlen, if you don't mind sending it over with someone, please."

"Could do that," he murmured as she dropped the envelope and a handful of coins into the tray on his desk.

"Have a drink or two on me," she suggested.

"I'll wish you well on your travels, Professor, that I will. Mayhap we'll hear about them before you come back, eh?"

She did not have to prevaricate, not with her sword at her waist and Fitzroy on the coins. She smiled at him, slow and sharp as a cat's steady blink. "Maybe you will."

And with that she nodded at a pair of students coming in, who looked at her with mouths agape (for it must be said that Fitzroy had described this very outfit in more than one of his more popular songs), and strode down the gravelled path towards the edge of town and the stables where she kept her horse.

～

She was pleased to encounter Elena Vane, going to town as Pali left it. The Porter at St Erlingale's had been remarkably efficient; Elena had Pali's letter in her hand.

"You're going, then," Elena said.

"Yes." Pali hesitated a moment. She'd said as much in her letter, and tried—oh, tried—to express a bit of the friendship she thought they had formed, and what they might have had. She had not thought she would see Elena so soon.

She tucked her horse's reins over her elbow, and dipped into her pockets.

She moved certain items from garment to garment, and sometimes, in slow faculty meetings, she would pull them out. Elena had always been fascinated by them.

The glass marble she'd found last winter. A small white pebble from Solaara, limestone with a perfect imprint of a curled fern frond a shadow in the stone. Two or three dried beans, red speckled with white, navy-blue, one green as a jade bead. Another pebble, this one a piece of rose quartz, wave-rounded and shiny where she had handled it over the years. A white feather tipped with jet-black, as if it had been dipped wrong-way-up in the inkwell.

She spread them out on her palm, rubbing her thumb over the rose quartz, nudging the beans away from the feather, the fern-leaf stone, the promises they held.

"I have always wondered what those are," Elena said shyly.

Pali picked up one of the beans, the green one, and handed it to her friend.

"It looks like a bean."

"It is a bean."

Elena considered it more carefully. Pali knew well there was nothing more to discover with smell or touch or sight. Even mages—even wild mages—often felt no more than the faintest echo of possibility.

Even Fitzroy had only been able to say it reminded him of something from a dream.

"It is a magic bean," Pali said gravely. "If you plant it at sunset, a bean-plant will grow with uncanny speed and uncanny might, and by morning you will find a vine that reaches up into a country on the other side of a cloud."

Elena laughed. "I am familiar with the tale of Jack and the Beanstalk. It's supposed to be a folk version of a story about the Red Company—"

She stopped. Pali smiled. "If you climb up the vine you have planted, at the top, in the land behind the cloud, you will find something it is good for you to find."

Elena regarded the bean doubtfully, and moved it to give it back. Pali gently closed Elena's fingers back around it.

"Keep it. Remember that you are only ever one night from a marvellous adventure."

The younger woman flushed. Her curly hair was escaping its ribbon, her cheeks flushed. She looked down at the other things. Her voice was a little husky with suppressed emotion. "And—the stone? The feather?"

"The stone was a gift from my sister Sardeet long ago. A piece of home, she said. She always liked pretty rocks."

Pali regarded the feather soberly, unable to suppress the shiver that ran up her back anytime she truly let herself think on it and what it portended.

"The feather is the third of three I was given by the Siruyal, a great bird, a legend, of my people, my desert. Once I met it." She paused, and stroked the feather with her index finger, the soft, smooth ridges of the barbs. "It gave me three wishes, three quests. This is the third wish."

Elena simply stared at her, mouth in a small *o*, eyes blinking rapidly.

"For the first," Pali mused, feeling her way into these memories, "I wished I could speak the languages of the first three people I met. For the second, nearly the same wish for my friends of the Red Company, before we travelled to Kaphyrn and had our adventures there."

"And you never thought of a third wish."

Pali held up the feather so it stood vertically in the air. Static electricity gathered around it, the moment before a thunderstrike.

"There have been few things I wanted I did not want to *earn*," she replied slowly. "I could have wished for my friends, to find them ... but wishes are dangerous, Elena. One must be careful they do not come too true. But the *possibility* of a wish, now, that is a fine and splendid thing."

CHAPTER EIGHTEEN
HOMEWARDS

Pali retraced her earlier journey, walking up the hills and cantering or galloping on the gentler downslopes. Her horse had had an easy life, perhaps, as Pali herself had had, but she was not entirely unfit, and certainly willing.

She rode, feeling legends gather around her, seeing stories and songs waking suddenly on the faces of those she passed. She heard snatches of their songs, of *his* songs, in the voices calling out to her, as those who had been alive in the days of Eritanyr looked past the robes in their foreign cut to her silver-threaded hair and saw she was no pretender to the name.

The road in early summer was much more pleasant than it had been in March. Her own horse under her, her robes and sash flying out behind her—oh, it was a fine and splendid ride! All she needed were her friends beside her.

And they would be there, Pali knew with a quiet, serene confidence. Jullanar was waiting for her at the other end of this very road, and Fitzroy in his tower, awaiting rescue. The rest—

Ah, the rest were all the mystery they ever had been. Yet Pali knew that as soon as the rumours started, which they surely already had, they would become a great cascading series of explosions, fireworks touching off each other in a night sky. Any of their friends would stir and gather themselves in readiness when they found the rumours did not fade, destroyed by falseness and imposters, but rather gathered strength.

Once she and Jullanar kidnapped the Last Emperor, no one would be able to doubt.

Pali did not smile so much as this, as a rule. Her face ached from smiling, as she thundered down the white roads of Chare, clattering on the cobbled streets of small towns and the odd stretch of Astandalan stone-flagged highways.

She cantered and walked, and both she and her horse grew fitter, more alive to the challenge, even in the two days it took for Pali to reach that same village at the edge of the mountains where she'd left, a legend in the moonlight.

It was the same innkeeper, and quite probably most of the same men in the bar when she entered.

She was not wearing her scholar's robes this time, but he recognized her.

"Lady," the innkeeper said, bowing.

He had not bowed to her before, though he had been respectful of her learning, her teaching of a brilliant local girl who had won a coveted scholarship to Stoneybridge.

"Innkeeper," Pali replied, nodding her head politely. "Have you a room for myself tonight, and stabling for my horse? A meal and a glass of wine would not come amiss, either."

"You honour my house," he said, snapping his fingers to call one of his servants to prepare a room for her. Pali took her own horse to the stables, grooming her carefully, thinking through what stories she might be asked, which ones she was unwilling to tell.

They wanted to know how she'd left in March with nary a footprint to show her passing. Pali told them of her enchanted carpet flight, the cadences of story falling out of her mouth as she wove a new tale.

What an extraordinary gift it was, she mused at one point as she looked at the rapt interest of her audience, that there were still *new* adventures to be had.

～

This time of year, dawn came early. Pali rose as the sky was just beginning to lighten, roused by an enthusiastic rooster in the yard below her window. She washed in the cool water left in the ewer and basin in her room, suddenly far too impatient for any delays.

The inn was sleepy, but there were a few people in the kitchen, making bread and beginning the day's work. Pali begged several rolls and cheese from them, tucking extra dried sausages into the food-pouch in her bag, before heading to the stables. As she had on her last stay, she'd made sure to pay the night before.

The innkeeper was crossing the yard as she led her horse out. "No midnight exit this time?" he said, chuckling.

Pali grinned at him. "There's a good ride ahead of us today. We're bound for Ragnor Bella."

"Plenty of odd things on that side of the mountains," the innkeeper observed as we walked beside her to the gate out of the yard.

Pali considered the handful of stories she'd already heard about Mr. Dart's time at home since graduating Stoneybridge, and could only laugh. "We've farther to travel than that."

"I look forward to hearing about it."

"I'm sure there will be a song or two in time," Pali agreed, her heart leaping again, and as the innkeeper unshipped the heavy bar holding the gate closed, she mounted her horse. His eyes glittered gratifyingly, which, as always, pleased her. She'd been able to mount a horse with one smooth leap since childhood, of course, but it never failed to impress.

He pushed open the gate. Pali turned her head when the rooster crowed again. He was standing on the roof of the stables, a living weathervane on top of the ironwork one.

"Fair weather ahead," the innkeeper murmured, nodding at the bird. He was a fine black bird, with great curving tail feathers of green and red.

Pali would never admit it, but she'd always liked roosters: they reminded her of Fitzroy.

She looked at this one and for a moment nearly wished she'd known all along. But she could not have abandoned him in that cage, if she'd known.

She raised her hand in a salute to the innkeeper, the black rooster, the sun rising behind the inn, and had barely to move her knees before her horse leapt out of the yard and moved immediately into a fine, energetic trot, tossing her head in eagerness as she caught scent of the mountain wind.

∽

Pali was careful not to exhaust her horse, but she was light and the mare gradually returning to condition, and they made good time up the valley road. Once they came to the narrower and steeper portions leading to the pass the going was slower, of course, but the road was dry and well-maintained by the locals.

There were no other travellers ahead of her this morning, nor within sight when she stopped at ridges to rest and consider the distance she had travelled. The plains of Chare were a rich patchwork of green and gold below her: the first hay was being taken off the upland pastures, while lower in elevation the winter wheat was nearly at harvest-ripe.

Up in the mountains the air was cool and clean, crisp as a fresh apple. The sky was very blue, only a few puffy white clouds here and there, and the leaves and stones seemed alert and alive. There were five or six eagles circling, stacked one above each other as they spiralled up a rising thermal.

The road made switchbacks up the shoulder of the valley where she had seen, several months ago, the fantastic ice formations of the frozen waterfall. In the summer the water was a murmurous thunder, fed by snowmelt from higher up. When the fitful wind gusted, a fine spray washed over Pali as she led the mare up the steep trail.

Pali walked steadily, grateful to Elena for all those long and vigorous rambles in the countryside around Stoneybridge. She smiled as she thought of her younger friend, her laughter and her pretty clothes and her bright wit. It was good to think that she need not lose that friendship by haring off after the rest of the Red Company.

Jullanar would like Elena, Pali considered as she came up to the saddle before the dip leading to the high pass. She looked up at the grassy slopes, the low thickets of juniper and heather. Marmots or pikas, some sort of small rodent, grazed on the slopes, and on the wind was the low, distinct tolling of the brass bells the locals used on their sheep and cattle.

Jullanar was on the other side of these mountains.

It was an extraordinary thought, one that lifted Pali's heart as much as the beauty of the day, the promise of adventure. Her friendship with Jullanar was so strong, twenty-five years out of time and yet immediately easy.

It had been like that from the very beginning, Pali reflected as she judged her horse properly rested and began again to walk. Pali had fought with Damian, never so challenged by any human opponent before, their swords electric with their respective skill and passion, each step as if they had practiced it a hundred thousand times, each strike meeting parry or reciprocal feint as if choreographed for a play.

Oh, that had been a moment where the world opened up to Pali, the skill and the strength and the beauty of two superlative fencers meeting in their prime. She had thought, in the moment when Damian's sword finally spun out of his hand, a bar of silver spinning through the lights of the hostelry, the air, the silent, expectant circle of watchers—oh, she had thought that she had met the summit of glory right then, right there.

Before she had even begun to deflate, Fitzroy had leant down from the upper balcony, magic coruscating around him, gleaming and glorious, striking her with a bolt of lightning from the top of her head to the very depths of her stomach, and cried out that strange, incredible proclamation: "You are magnificent! We should get married!"

And she, in those words that had come as if she had rehearsed them, as if this whole meeting was out of a fateful sequence, as if she were acting out the role of a legendary hero in a tale, she had called back, "And how do I know you are magnificent enough for me?"

She would not be caught by a god, ravished away by a divinity, no matter how he smiled at her.

And then she had looked down, away from Fitzroy Angursell ("Ask me again when you are famous," she had said, and he had asked her, again and again he had asked her, until she had told anyone who asked her why she had not married him that Fitzroy had never raised it again, for she had been unable to believe his endless proclamations of desire)—

Looked down, and there was that young woman, soft and homely after the hard grandeur of the god and the swordsman, coming forward with a sword held not entirely ill in her hand, but her face lit with a smile, shy and pleased.

Pali had looked at her: at her hair escaping its braids, at the fear and determination in her eyes, at her pretty clothes, and felt another jolt.

Not the lightning-bolt of Fitzroy looking at her with his eyes full of magic. No. She had looked at Jullanar and felt that sense of rightness, as of a sword sliding into its sheath, her sister tapping a line of thread into her weaving with one gentle, informed movement, a horse scenting the oasis a moment before the wind brought the scent of greenery and water to Pali's nose.

"You are magnificent," Jullanar had said, smiling at her that conspiratorial pleasure, just the same as Sardeet catching her eye when Arzu was being particularly lordly. "You have bested Damian at the sword, and Fitzroy with words."

Pali had smiled at her, and Jullanar smiled back, and if Pali had not held her sword in her hand—

She had never fallen into a stranger's arms, caught by their smile. That was the only time she had ever felt the desire.

Jullanar had smiled back, as if this were quite the same moment to her. As if she, too, felt that shock of recognition. "I cannot offer you such a challenge to your skill myself, but I can offer you an invitation to a great adventure."

Could there have been any question better primed to suggest that this moment was equally weighty? That her heart beat to the same drum as Pali's? "What adventure?" Pali had asked, and now, as she clambered up the valley, thinking wistfully of the flying carpet, her horse at her heels, she remembered how much she had hoped that Jullanar would answer that in the right way.

She had not known what *the right way* was, for this woman clearly of a far different culture to Pali's own.

But Jullanar had smiled at her, eyes crinkling up, nose wrinkling, sword forgotten. "We three seek to stop an invading army. Will you help us?"

Oh, there had been no chance, not after that.

∾

At the top of the pass Pali looked back once more on Chare, on the heat-haze cloaking the plains, and after a suitable pause for water and food, swung herself up into the saddle. The mare pranced in place, ears pricked forward towards the wind sweeping down the high moor towards them.

Far ahead of them was the standing stone where she had challenged those pusillanimous gods. Farther yet was the dark shape of the refuge, with a brilliant white-and-red spot in front of it suggesting someone was in residence.

It could be Jullanar already, Pali thought, looking at the westering sun, if her friend had made good of her plan and indeed left Ragnor Bella immediately.

Her heart leapt at the thought.

I can offer you an invitation to a great adventure.

And they were not finished yet.

CHAPTER NINETEEN
REFUGE

At the tall standing stone marking the three-way crossroads—much taller now, with the snow melted and gone, than it had seemed in the early spring—Pali caught sight of a great flash of reflected light.

It was the work of a thought to guide her horse in a tight circle around the stone, the canter smooth as in her dream of the desert, and as in a dream she simply leaned down from the saddle to scoop up the object from the ground.

She had thought it would be her dagger, left there in challenge to those three hooded figures who had refused to respond.

It was her dagger, but the handle was bound now in a net of silk threads, green and purple, white and gold, and a fine shimmering scarlet tassel.

They cantered onwards towards the refuge, the scent of woodsmoke blowing friendly and familiar in their faces, the westering sun dipping the whole pass with a honeyed light. Pali looked at the rune-inscribed blade, the edge sharp as the north wind, and felt the tingle of a challenge met and answered with mystery.

She tucked the dagger away in her sash, and turned her face and her thoughts forward. And would it be Jullanar waiting there, with a fire lit and a kettle on to boil?

Her heart was thundering, clattering in her throat, making her breathless with hope. Oh, it was not a foolish hope, not when she knew, now, that Jullanar was so close, on the other side of the pass, quite possibly the one wearing white and scarlet who had stood against the green grass and the blue sky like an illustration of their own legends.

The horse slowed to a walk, tired, and Pali dismounted, slid off her saddle, wiped off the sweat, shook off the exertion of the ride, whispered thanks to the mare for her fine work that day, and after checking there was water in the trough, she set her shoulders and her smile and tripped up the steps to knock on the door.

It was a public hut: after the polite knock she opened it, readying a polite question in case it was not Jullanar—

"Excuse me," she said, "I was hoping—"

But then she stopped, and could not prevent her hand from coming up to her mouth in shock.

For there, at a table set for four, was Jullanar—and beside her a broad-shouldered, powerful man, dark-skinned and curly-bearded, whom it took Pali a bare moment for her to recognize as *Masseo*—and—

And sitting opposite the door in robes as apricot as the desert in her dream, Fitzroy.

Fitzroy, his smile shy—*shy?*—his eyes as lambent a gold as in the portraits, but oh, so much more alive, so much more expressive—his features nowhere near as drawn and tired as they had been—his skin looking healthy—his eyes bright—

"You," she said, unable to come up with anything better.

Fitzroy.

Not Artorin Damara, Last Emperor of Astandalas, wearing a shadow into the white stone of his room. Fitzroy.

His lips twitched, his eyes crinkled, his face—oh, what expression could she call that? Hope?

"Pali," he said, his voice resonant, filling the room like the inside of a struck bell. "Would you like a cup of tea?"

The contrast between the commonplace offer and the high-handed assumptions of her previous audience were striking.

"Only if it's served in a cup from heaven," she said, because—oh, because this was Jullanar, and Masseo, and *Fitzroy*, and somehow he had come to meet her here!—and as if her words had broken the spell, Jullanar and Masseo crowded forward, and Pali embraced them.

Jullanar's soft honeysuckle-scent was familiar from the spring. Pali held her, breathing it in, letting Jullanar settle into her heart, steadying her, strengthening her, as if her mere presence was a cordial, heartening.

Masseo still smelled of his forge, iron and fire and charcoal, and threaded through the fire a warm hint of some spice, cinnamon perhaps. He was so strong, and so careful, so gentle, with his strength. When she leaned back out of his hold, Masseo lifted one gnarled finger to brush back a strand of her hair, and kissed her on the forehead.

Pali did not think Masseo had ever been so expressive before, but there was a light in his eyes, a lightness even, that she recognized as new but did not have the knowledge, yet, to understand.

She turned to Fitzroy, who was still seated, as straight-backed and regal as if the rough wooden chair were his gilded throne.

She had not been able to see it before, when she had been as shocked as he, but this time Pali could see that it was surprise that held him pinned there, in the posture he must have practiced until it was automatic as his breathing.

She smiled, giddiness tempered with the incredulity that he had somehow managed to meet her here, and gave him a far more fluid and less insincere curtsey than she had managed for Artorin Damara.

He stood up so quickly he knocked his chair over. Pali watched him come around the table, wondering if he would reach out to her—

But instead he offered her the cup, which tingled with magic in her hands when she touched it.

His eyes were brimful with magic. She could feel it running through her veins, stirring her blood and inner spirits, a breath blown on an ember to catch a flame.

She forced her eyes away, down to the cup. "It's not really—"

"He keeps telling us he's not actually a semi-apotheosized god," Masseo said.

Pali glanced at him, and caught something that almost seemed a warning.

Not actually a semi-apotheosized god.

Not actually a god? Not actually *not* a god? What did Masseo mean?

How would one apotheosize a god? The word meant to make divine a human being. Sardeet had been apotheosized, according to the traditions of their clan, when she had been stolen by the Blue Wind to be his bride.

She looked back at Fitzroy, who said, "I'm pretty certain I stole this from the Moon and dropped it into the Sea of Stars, so ... close enough?"

He smiled, one of those strange, tentative, shy smiles that looked alien on his features.

Pali did not know what to say. Should she fall down with apologies? Should she attack him with remonstrations? Should she ignore their previous meeting entirely? Should she be ferociously enraged she did not need to storm the Palace of Stars to rescue him?

Oh, she wished she'd had a chance to talk to Jullanar about this first.

"You're not helping your case any," she said, and regretted the half-accusatory words immediately.

Fitzroy held himself very still, his face calm, his eyes impossible to read, and Pali wished she knew what to say. The feather was in her pocket, throbbing with readiness. But she could not wish for such a thing.

Her guilt had simmered down with her plan to rescue him—but now that plan was all thrown out of use, and what was she to make of this? His smiles—were they forgiveness? She had not yet *earned* it.

Jullanar said, "By all the gods, and that includes you, Fitzroy! Sit *down* and let's talk this out like the adults we are."

They all turned towards her. She stood by the fire, where she'd turned when the kettle started to whistle, and gestured pointedly at the seats around the table. Fitzroy sat down, his face unfathomably serene.

Pali and Masseo took their own seats. Pali set down the silvery cup, reluctant to let her fingers leave its pleasantly bumpy surface, that tingle of magic, of mystery, of wonder.

Jullanar plumped herself down into the remaining chair, arms folded. Fitzroy tilted his head, his expression remotely intrigued. "*Do* people talk out their emotions in your experience?" he asked.

Jullanar snorted. "Don't they in yours?"

Pali considered the assembled faculty of Stoneybridge, and the less academically-inclined of her acquaintance in the town, and was unsurprised when Fitzroy simply said, "No."

Pali was fierce in pursuit of truth, unstoppable as a stooping falcon; but she did not disburden her heart of her thoughts very often, no, not at all.

Only Jullanar had drawn her out. She nearly opened her mouth —but she could not, not with this stranger who was supposed to be Fitzroy there before her.

At some point Masseo had made tea. It scented the air, with a smokey fragrance Pali breathed deeply to capture; though the merest whiff seemed to jolt straight to the back of her skull and awaken all those merry campfires of their youth.

"Fitzroy," he said, "have you ever told someone what you were truly thinking?"

"Masseo," Fitzroy replied, his tone dry, almost sardonic, "people have committed suicide because I told them what I actually thought."

Pali pursed her lips, frowning, as she dredged out a few sidelong comments from the annals of his court. She had not thought he had invited anyone to commit suicide, that hideous custom some of his forebears had followed—

"Desur of Erldan," he said, his voice rolling over the vowels as if he had long practiced them. "Goroghen the Tailor. Nina Firunzky. Lord Saiverdell. That was in the first six months, before I learned what not to say."

Pali felt some strange, impossible doubt slide away. He was not that person.

She had not *thought* he was that person. She had studied Artorin Damara's public decisions with a singular focus, worrying at inconsistencies and incongruities in the official record until she had, she had thought, come to an accurate sense of the way his mind worked. So she had thought.

She had only missed, oh, the greater half of his soul.

Masseo moved to pour the tea, and Fitzroy retreated back into his formal, official posture, his hands folded in his lap, his face imperturbable, his bearing perfect. He sat there in his beautiful apricot robes, there in that wooden refuge, there with the fire sputtering behind him, and looked every inch the Last Emperor.

She felt a disquieting sense of ... unbalance. Disequilibrium. For the rest time she wondered how he would have reacted if she *had* come to rescue him.

"You told me," Masseo said quietly, "that you'd made at least one apology. At the time I thought ... well, I thought perhaps you were joking, but you weren't, were you?"

Pali glanced under her lashes at Masseo, and—well, she could only wonder what had happened, that he was there in that refuge with Jullanar and Fitzroy. And her.

Fitzroy inclined his head, the famous nod, the assurance that he was attending to whatever supplicant knelt before him. Pali had read dozens of references to his 'splendid condescension', and had wondered—how could she not?—what it had felt like to be on the receiving end of it.

She did not feel condescended to. She felt as if she would be *heard*.

Unlike in most of those accounts, he spoke: "I dislike lying, it is true."

Fitzroy Angursell, the great poet, the liar, the conman, the renegade, the revolutionary, the fool—

The man who had said a hundred, a thousand times, that *he could not answer their questions*.

Could not. Never that he did not *want* to.

I dislike lying, it is true.

He was a poet; indisputably a great poet. He cared so much about words.

Pali hesitated, unsure what underlay this comment. "A nice evasion," she hazarded, for it was; "but what does Masseo mean?"

Fitzroy was silent. He glanced down at his own cup of tea, face remote, impossible. The door was rattling, as if the wind outside were picking up.

Masseo said, "When he first arrived—well, the first bit of privacy we had—he tried to apologize to me."

Pali glanced at the smith, and caught his sheepish smile. "For abandoning us in the Silver Forest," Masseo went on. "I told him not to be absurd, that it was hardly his *desire* that the protections rose up, but mostly ..." He paused, just a moment, and Pali caught the rueful regret in his eyes, and felt a certain ... kinship, that was it, that Masseo had also said something that had been unintentionally sharp.

"Mostly I made fun for how awkward an apology it was. I'm sorry for laughing at you, Fitzroy. I wasn't thinking how ... hard ... that must have been for you."

Fitzroy said, "It's fine."

That was not the Last Emperor speaking; but it was the Last Emperor sitting there.

"It's not fine. Fitzroy," Jullanar snapped, setting down her cup with a clatter, leaning forward to glare at him. "I've only spent half a *day* with you and already I can see—"

She stopped, and glanced at Pali.

Pali did not know what to say. She hardly knew what to think, when Fitzroy also turned to look at her, as if her face, her expression, her response held the answer to—what?

"We've all changed," he said quietly. "It's been a long time."

A thousand years, people had said in Solaara, extravagant in their hyperbole.

(He had worn a shadowy groove into that alabaster floor, pacing up and down that long, beautiful, empty room, from a desk where his bureaucrat-of-bureaucrats lord chancellor sat to that mechanical nightingale in its golden cage, past that long map showing the five worlds of the empire, which they had crossed and recrossed in their adventures.)

"Of course we've all changed," Jullanar cried, her voice lifting up over the wind. "We're also all the same *people* we were before! Pali is still Pali for all she's a great scholar now. Masseo isn't a *different* person for all he's learned how to laugh—and *you're* not a different person for all that you've forgotten how."

Pali almost gasped at how sharp that thrust had been. She was sure it had gone home—it *must* have gone home—but Fitzroy merely sat there, immutable, the gleaming, golden idol at the heart of Astandalas.

She was so *angry* at those jailers, that bureaucrat-of-bureaucrats and all those layers of guards, everyone in that whole bloody palace who had trapped Fitzroy Angursell into a prison even he could only obliquely express.

"I'm sorry," Jullanar said. She glanced at Pali, who shrugged helplessly, for Fitzroy was sitting there inscrutably, immovably; and Pali could see, suddenly, how he could have been the emperor he had become.

"I'm sorry, Fitzroy," Jullanar repeated, but Fitzroy only turned his face towards her, eyes narrowing; and then, unspeaking, he stood and strode right out of the refuge.

The door slammed shut behind him in a howling windstorm that had come, so far as Pali knew this mountain weather, out of nowhere but Fitzroy's own magic.

CHAPTER TWENTY
AURELIUS MAGNUS

"What was that," Jullanar said, almost as blankly as Fitzroy. Masseo sat back, tea in hand, and sniffed the aroma appreciatively. "The new Fitzroy. Somehow both entirely different and exactly the same."

Pali took a breath, and held her peace. He was Fitzroy. He was here. He had not needed her to rescue him, after all. He had simply needed—

She forced back the question of why, if he'd been able to follow her so soon, he had refused to come with her in the first place. Or—

Or left before, and come to find them himself.

Pali sipped her own tea, which was delicious, of course, and admired Masseo's teapot, which she thought she recognized. She looked at the smith, deliberately changing the subject. "It's good to see you, Masseo."

"And you, Pali," he replied, eyes crinkling. He wore his hair shorter than before, in close-cropped curls, but had grown a rambunctious beard. "I can't believe Fitzroy's method actually works!"

Of course they would immediately turn back to *him*.

"The coincidences," Jullanar agreed, shaking her head. "Wild mages."

"I should like to say that it was all *my* doing," Pali muttered. "I found Jullanar first, and then Fitzroy, and now you—"

"He found me!"

She waved her hand dismissively at Masseo. "As I said, I *should* like to say it was all my doing, but alas, wild magic and their coincidences ... How did you get here, Masseo?"

"I was working in my forge when my apprentice's brother showed up with his pregnant sweetheart, who happened to be a postulant nun ..."

"Oh dear."

Masseo laughed. "They're dear folks, but not the sharpest tools in the box, alas. Kenna, my apprentice, is much the cleverest—but her brother is a fine young man, and his sweetheart—his wife, now—is a lovely girl. Credulous, mind you. They showed up, full of excitement, to tell me that Aurelius Magnus had answered her prayers in person."

Pali considered. "The emperor Aurelius Magnus ... The one who wrote the Aurelian Code? Is he supposed to be a god?"

He was one of the famous emperors of Astandalas, somewhere around the fiftieth in succession. He had been a superlative general before he came into a powerful gift of magic and built the magic of the Empire of Astandalas into the form it had held until its cataclysmic destruction under Artorin Damara's reign.

Pali considered that thought, and shoved aside the guilty curiosity as to what exactly Fitzroy thought about being the emperor when Astandalas fell.

"What's the Aurelian Code?" Jullanar asked.

"The first great revision to the laws of Astandalas," Pali explained, falling easily into her teaching voice. "It laid out the policies for making war and governing conquered peoples. Aurelius Magnus wrote a book—we only have about half of it, alas, one of the later emperors reacted hard against it—where he talked about how to create a lasting peace. He was the one who created the magical Pax Astandalatis."

"He's one of the local gods where I lived," Masseo said. "He was supposed to have been stolen away by the Sun and the Moon and made into a god himself for his power and wisdom. People think he'll come back in their time of need to restore justice and good government." He paused, and grinned at them. "I should say, people *used* to think that. Now the general rumour is that he *did*."

"Fitzroy?" Jullanar said blankly.

"Fitzroy," Masseo agreed.

"Our Fitzroy is supposed to be the second coming of Aurelius Magnus."

"He is."

Pali had never heard that, but then she hadn't studied very much of what had happened *after* the Fall on Zunidh. Until very recently there had been no way to do so—her journey to visit the Archives had come as soon as practicable after the announcement that they were still in existence and open to researchers, and that the passage between Alinor and Zunidh was passible.

Jullanar seemed to think this was a delightfully funny idea, for she was laughing quietly. "Is he supposed to be the reincarnation of him, or what?"

Masseo shrugged. "Depends on who you talk to. We—the Cirithians—that's the religion in my area, I ... er, I converted, you see—"

Pali was immediately diverted. "Did you! Will you tell us about it?"

Masseo shifted position, but he was smiling bashfully. "After we split up, I ended up on Voonra, and after a while—after the Fall, that is—I found myself on Zunidh, near the Abbey of the Mountains. I was ... tired, heartsore, and went up to the Abbess to confess all my crimes. She was very kind."

"She didn't arrest you?"

"She didn't have any *proof* bar what I told her. And it was not too long after the Fall, so government was a bit ... unstable. That's what I mean, you see. I went to the Abbess, told her I would accept whatever punishment she gave me, whether that was to be hauled before the Lord Emperor ... At that point we only had rumours that he was alive, that he was starting to wrest back order, reclaim magic, reform good government."

Pali sipped at her tea, thinking of the slow improvement from the horrible period after the Fall on Alinor, when the broken magic of Astandalas had flailed and corrupted what it touched, no longer bound to its orderly, regular, *known* systems. People had mostly reacted by banning magic entirely; it was only in the past year or two that anyone had started to speak of it openly, and in Chare it was still considered a heinous offence. It was not a mystery that her student, Mr. Dart, had kept his incipient gift at wild magic well-hidden.

Not that magic ever responded well to being kept *hidden*. Look at what had happened with Artorin Dam—

She took a breath. She'd written an essay, not long ago, speculating on whether Artorin Damara's secret and suppressed magic had contributed to the Fall. She hadn't though how he might *feel* about that, and hoped, savagely, that Fitzroy hadn't read her essay.

"The Abbess is a fine wizard herself, strong and wise. She gave me a penance of anonymity, to serve a tiny village as their anonymous smith ..." Masseo smiled. "The village was the one under the shadow of the abbey. Hard to avoid their religion. Besides ... I liked its philosophy."

"And they believe in ... reincarnation?"

"They believe that Aurelius Magnus became one of the gods. Not in the way the Astandalan government had it, that every emperor was to be considered the genius-god of the empire, but that he, specifically, was great and noble enough to be apotheosized."

"You keep using that word," Pali observed.

"It's a good word."

Both Pali and Jullanar broke into surprised laughter at his brighteyed jest. Masseo had always been so quiet, so sober, so grim, even— Pali had always found his company restful, for he did not like to talk, and they would often go fishing together, or hunting or gathering wood, working silently beside each other, content in undemanding company.

She did like that he was visibly happier.

"They do believe in reincarnation, that souls are reborn. The legend about Aurelius Magnus was a little different ... One school holds that he was reborn over and over again, that each true emperor of Astandalas was his soul returning in case of need."

"And then the Fall," Jullanar murmured. Pali said nothing.

"And then the Fall," Masseo said, "and when the last emperor of Astandalas awoke—he was cast into some sort of enchanted sleep, we were told later—he was suddenly a great mage such as he had never shown hint of being before, and he rose to the challenge of the destruction of the empire with a skill and a vision such as had not been seen, in truth, for many generations."

Pali pondered what she knew of Artorin Damara, who had been sent into exile and returned untrained to become the hundredth emperor. Wild magic was not well-regarded in the empire. She had assumed he had simply not wanted the political mess that would come of announcing he was any level of wizard bar the most basic. There hadn't been a wizard-emperor of Astandalas for generations, and people had come to fear the power such would hold.

Knowing he had been Fitzroy ... well, it *had* been an unstable seat. It was possible no one would have believed him if he'd announced it; he would have been considered mad, dangerously mad, and ... She bit her lip, shifting uncomfortably as she imagined that scenario. The priest-wizards and the army had been very strong rivals at the time. Without Artorin Damara—without *Fitzroy*—deftly balancing their competing authorities, without the emperor at the centre holding the magic and the political power in something approaching equilibrium, it would have been terrible.

More terrible than the Fall—perhaps not. But for all his dislike of the Empire, Fitzroy would never have sought such destruction and death and devastation. She could never have believed that.

"I don't believe in reincarnation," she said, stalling.

"That's fair enough," Masseo replied agreeably. "I am not entirely convinced myself. Cirith—that's the religion, Cirith or the Cirithian belief system—is flexible in many of the elements. Reincarnation is one major strand."

"And so, if it's not necessary to this theory?" Jullanar asked curiously.

"The stories go—I know you've heard them, there was that play we went to see, remember? *Aurelius Magnus and the Seafarer King*."

"Fitzroy wouldn't stop laughing," Jullanar said, her tone wavering with the same doubt Pali was herself suddenly feeling. "He *said* it was wildly inaccurate ..."

They looked at each other, half-grinning at the absurdity of the idea Masseo had presented them with.

"In the stories, the legends," he went on, "Aurelius Magnus was taken up to the heavenly realms. In the one set of stories he was reincarnated into the true emperors. In the more popular version he waited there until great need called him back to life."

"The end of the empire," Jullanar murmured. "If it were fated ..."

"It certainly *felt* fated," Pali said. She set the idea in front of her mind, to take as seriously as any argument proposed by a rival academic. If Fitzroy were Aurelius Magnus—

"So you think that when he fell out of the sky and landed on top of Jullanar and Damian," she said, "that was him coming back to life after his sojourn in the Divine Realms?"

"That would explain a great deal, to be honest," Jullanar said.

Pali had met Fitzroy some handful of days after that extravagant arrival. He had been full of magic, of light, of energy, of coruscating power ...

She had thought, immediately, that he was a god.

"Hmm," she said.

Masseo laughed. "The Abbey of the Mountains was built at the place where he was said to have been taken up by the gods, so I've heard all the stories and had a lot of time to think about this."

"Did you know that he was Fitzroy?"

"No, no, not until he arrived. What happened was, Daro and his sweetheart came to tell me that she'd been praying and Aurelius Magnus himself had fallen out of the sky to answer her prayers—"

"Typical," Pali muttered.

"—And immediately suggested an anvil-marriage, which is a very old custom in those parts. I agreed, and when they said he'd come as one of their witnesses, I had barely a moment to wonder just *who* was going to arrive when I looked up and it was—him."

"Fitzroy."

"Fitzroy looking *exactly* like Aurelius Magnus in every depiction of him, yes. Well, every one that doesn't involve him in armour."

"Typical," Jullanar murmured, her eyes dancing with amusement. "Goodness, Masseo, what an entrance!"

"And off he swept me, back into adventure," Masseo said with great satisfaction, reaching out his hands to lay them on Pali's and Jullanar's.

"I'm going to have to think about this more," Pali said slowly, turning her hand under Masseo's warm, strong, callused grip, "but I must admit your reasoning is cogent."

"Cogent!" Jullanar cried. "What a word! Come now, Pali, this is so absurd and so wonderful I am inclined to believe it solely on those grounds."

"That does seem a peculiarly Fitzroy-appropriate sort of approach," Pali replied lightly, setting her guilt aside.

"Speaking of," Masseo said, "do we think he'll be rejoining us tonight?"

"Supper will be easy enough to keep," Jullanar said. "It's just a potage, nothing exciting, I'm afraid."

"I've got some sausages and cheese and things in my saddlebag," Pali said. "I'll see to my horse and bring it in, and we can have it as a snack while we wait for him. For a while," she added hastily. "No sense in starving ourselves if he's going to show up again in thirty years."

∼

She tended her horse, who was grateful for the thorough grooming. The air held that peculiar combination of summer-warmth and mountain-coolth, and she enjoyed brushing out the mare's coat and mane. The wind was high, and full of the tingle and sparkle of magic.

Familiar magic, blazing-brilliant as a bonfire, drawing all towards it for fellowship and company and that hunger for beauty that had kept Pali circling for half her life, afraid of being consumed by the flame, unable to leave its warmth.

And if, she thought, he was Aurelius Magnus, one of the greatest of the emperors?

Artorin Damara, once accustomed to his throne, had been moving towards that splendour. Even if he had not been the last, he would have been named—perhaps not in the very highest tier of great rulers, perhaps not in company with Yr the Conqueror or Zangora V or, yes, Aurelius Magnus—but certainly in the ranks of the very excellent.

And as the Lord Emperor of Zunidh after the Fall, he *was* great. She refused to believe it was *all* his Lord Chancellor's work.

She went back in, her stomach rumbling as she caught scent of Jullanar's hearty soup, and laid her own travel rations on the table for their enjoyment.

"I have been thinking," Jullanar said as Masseo came in with another armful of wood. "There are stories, you know, about the so-called Seafarer King ..."

"Oh?" Pali asked. She knew nothing about the historical figure, save that there *had* been one, a great navigator who had found the sea-routes to Colhélhé and followed a strange and cunning mystery left to Aurelius by his pre-Astandalan forbear, Harbut Zalarin the son of the Sun.

She shook her head vigorously, even as Masseo said, "Oh? He's mentioned, of course—the fire dance is one of those things that's so evocative you can't help but wonder about it! But you've heard other stories?"

Jullanar pulled a cloth out of Fitzroy's bag and spread it on the table. Pali watched her, touched by the casual familiarity of the gesture. It was Fitzroy's bag, yes—the same bag, amazingly—though he had another he'd placed on the sleeping platform next to his piles of cushions. They had always been able to reach in and pull things out, never exactly what they wanted, always something more or less related.

It had never occurred to Pali what a gesture of trust, even of intimacy, that had been. *She* wouldn't let people dig around in her packs without explicit permission. Not even Sardeet; not even Jullanar.

This was not the dish-towel Jullanar had probably intended; it was a spread of ecru lacework.

Masseo set a wooden plate on it, and Pali laid out the dried sausage.

"Basil—oh, Basil's a friend of mine." Jullanar explained to Masseo her friendship with the innkeeper, who was a Wide Seas Islander, as the Seafarers called themselves. "He's told me all sorts of things ... Including some of their traditions about the so-called Seafarer King who was *very* dear friends with Aurelius Magnus." She grinned impishly at Masseo. "Does our Fitzroy have a *very dear friend* who is a Wide Seas Islander, do you know?"

Pali could only think how her research had never thrown up anyone for Artorin Damara, no consorts or concubines, no confidantes or friends.

Oh, she hoped he had found *someone*—

"His lord chancellor, viceroy now, is from *somewhere* in the Wide Seas," Masseo said thoughtfully, and Pali's thoughts flashed to that unassuming man with the brilliant wit who had come down to see her and convinced her that Fitzroy Angursell was best left in his cage.

Aware of her own inconsistency and revelling in it, she once again swore vengeance on the jailer Fitzroy had chosen for himself.

CHAPTER TWENTY-ONE
POSSIBILITIES OF A WISH

They had eaten their snack, cleaned up the refuge and set out Pali's bedroll, chopped and stacked firewood for the next visitors, and Fitzroy had still not returned.

"What do we think?" Jullanar asked, going to the door to peer out at the night.

Pali stepped up beside her, momentarily shocked by her own unthinking willingness to lean on Jullanar's shoulder, breathe in her friend's flowery hair, feel Masseo's warmth on her other side as he came up behind them.

The night air was warm, the winds tossing magic through it at a level visible to anyone. The stars were very bright, almost as bright as they were in the Border countries where neither sun nor moon shone.

Jullanar sat down on the steps of the refuge. Pali looked at Masseo, who shrugged, and both followed suit. They might have been three students on the steps of a campus building, she thought, smiling at the idea of the three of them—the four of them—the *ten* of them—as students raising havoc.

Jullanar had been a student, and Ayasha a professor, and in

under a year the two of them had contrived to be fired, expelled, and spark a ten-year rebellion.

"Look," Masseo said suddenly, pointing off into the dark where a bobbing light, gold as sunlight, was followed by man-shaped shadow.

"Is he alone?" Jullanar said quietly.

They'd passed a quarter-hour of their wait by coming up with elaborate predictions for Fitzroy's return, and Pali was perhaps a smidgen disappointed that he did not appear to have been gone for more than the notional time span. At least, she assumed he would have grown out his hair if he'd been gone longer.

The sudden fear that he had been gone longer and yet chosen *not* to gripped her heart, and she said, "You don't think he *prefers* being bald, do you?"

"Why, Pali, do you have a preference?" Jullanar asked, her voice bright with amusement.

"I—no, of course not, he has a very regal skull," she stammered.

"Imperial, even," Masseo offered, shaking with silent laughter beside them. "Perhaps he dislikes how he was balding naturally."

The idea that Fitzroy could have such a human experience as a balding pattern he liked—or disliked—was almost impossible to hold, and Pali scowled at the shadows cast from the mage-light even as its caster came up to them.

He lifted his light, and looked up at them with his face that calm, collected emperor expression. He could have been standing in his study, in his throne room, in his portraits, in council or in judgment, in appreciation of music or art, listening to a criminal's confession or a courtier's blandishment's or a guard's reports with equal equanimity.

Jullanar elbowed Masseo, as Pali saw out of the corner of her eye. "You owe me a wheatear," she said. "He's back before dawn."

Masseo grunted, tucking his earlier mirth down to a seemlier amusement. "And you owe me a penny. He didn't bring anyone back with him."

"True," Jullanar agreed. "You didn't run across a mermaid in distress or a long-thought-dead soldier or a mysterious heir?"

Pali pursed her lips to keep from smirking at the list of her ex-student's adventures.

"No," Fitzroy replied solemnly, his voice so resonant in the quiet, not stolen by the wind but seeming to hold reverberations beyond the natural. "Just the road to Fairyland and a shepherdess with a dog by the name of Pip, I'm afraid."

"And you didn't bring them back with you?"

"No." He paused a moment, his eyes on theirs, opaque as that blasted gold leaf in his light. His voice was still as studiously neutral as any voice had ever been when he continued. "She gave me some advice about talking to you."

Advice from a shepherdess to the last emperor? Pali tried not to laugh, and as a result spoke more brusquely than she meant. "Come in, then."

They sat down around the fire, Fitzroy making a small detour to collect a blanket. He was in his socked feet, with no sign of the boots he'd been wearing before, and little bits of grass and twigs stuck to the fabric to show he'd walked back in them.

The blanket itself was quite possibly the most beautiful such throw Pali had ever seen that was not woven by her sister. It was in many red and pink stripes, and so soft and inviting Pali longed to bury her hands in its folds.

She folded her hands together instead, glad Jullanar took the teapot to pour out a fragrant mint tea. Fitzroy sat there, noticeably less splendidly formal in posture, though he still wore the blanket as if it were one of his great mantles of state, for prestige rather than for comfort.

"I'm sorry for storming off in a temper," he said, and before Pali, at least, could respond to that—for it had not been entirely clear he *had* been in a temper—he added, "I'm not accustomed to teasing, or being teased, and—" A minuscule pause, as they tried to wrap their minds around the idea of *Fitzroy Angursell* not understanding humour—before he went on, expertly modulated voice starting to fray with emotions: "And it hurt my feelings that you didn't take me seriously."

Pali wondered how he could possibly think they didn't take him *seriously*.

"Fitzroy," Jullanar said, her tone matter-of-fact, though there was a tiny overtone of amazement to it, no doubt for the reflection back on their earlier conversation, "you spent all the time I knew you joking about being under an enchantment and how you're secretly the heir of gods and myths and legendary wizards."

He shifted position, back straightening, great crimson-and-rose mantle curving around his shoulders, reflecting a ruddy glow onto his face. "Jullanar, I spent all the time you knew me under an enchantment and trying every way I could to get you to guess the truth yourself."

His voice was softly authoritative. So must he speak to his chief courtiers, Pali thought, drawing them into his confidences, his counsels. No wonder the commander and the Lord Chancellor had come to confront her, secure in his regard.

Oh, she would start to hate those men who had so lovingly kept him bound.

Masseo's face was wavering, no doubt thinking of all those stories of Aurelius Magnus, and Fitzroy suddenly turned a stern face towards him, his voice flashing like a blade revealed. "Masseo, please! I listened to you when you spoke the truth of your past—will you not extend me the same courtesy? Why is *my* heart a laughing-matter?"

Pali stared at him, all the amusement draining out of her.

Why is my *heart a laughing-matter?*

Had she ever truly believed he had a human heart?

Had she ever truly *granted* him sincerity?

"My name is Artorin Damara," he said, his voice precise, perfectly enunciated, an actor or an orator in the full flight of a speech—

And that, too, was a way to disregard his emotions, Pali realized. She swallowed, unable to move.

"I am the eldest son of the Imperial Princess Lamissa of the House of Yr and Grand Duke Mantorin Damara. I am the direct descendant of ninety-eight Emperors of Astandalas and was the hundredth and last. I am a descendent in a right line of the Sun, of Harbut Zalarin and of Aurelius Magnus. I am the Lord of Five Thousand Lands and Ten Thousand Titles. I am the present Lord Magus of Zunidh, High King of Rondé and, yes, Prince of the White Forest. And *yes*, I am Fitzroy Angursell of the Red Company, whom no one *ever* believes when he speaks the truth."

Pali wanted to protest, but too many counter-examples came to her mind, and she could only breathe shallowly, wishing otherwise.

"You always said," Jullanar began, and then tripped up on what must have been the same thought, for she went on, in a lower voice, "You always did say, didn't you?"

Fitzroy looked away, at the fire, which was pressing close to the grate in sympathetic resonance. At his look it subsided, flickering down to coals, red as his mantle. "I tried," he said, and his voice was dropping, exhausted, and Pali hated that she could not help but admire his rhetorical craft, his ability to control his voice, his *act*.

"I was exiled, enchanted. I found out my name when I was crowned emperor. Sometimes what I think is worse is that I didn't even realize I didn't have one until I was eighteen."

Pali had read all the accounts of Artorin Damara's history before his coronation. They had uniformly stated he'd been raised quietly, in the country, taught by the best tutors, before being installed in a comfortable home to study and fulfil his duties as the Marwn, that mysterious magical second heir who was not, usually, second in line to the throne.

She had always imagined him living in a country palace, surrounded by books and beauty, waited on hand and foot, isolated from the court but not, for all that, *isolated*. He had been full of odd ideas when he came to his throne, but he had not shown any hint of being ... mad.

There had been that tower on the Long Edge of Colhélhé, which he said was his.

And if he were Aurelius Magnus, reborn, what had that been like?

And if he were Aurelius Magnus, returned, was this his *true* history?

"I am beginning to understand why you have difficulties being touched," Masseo said, which seemed like a non sequitur to Pali, but perhaps she had missed another exchange or two while she was staring at Fitzroy and trying to make sense of all the ideas crashing together in her mind.

"I'm sorry." Masseo smiled gently. "I'm sorry I didn't listen before. You told me but I was so excited to see you again I paid hardly any attention." That was quite the honest truth, Pali thought, surprised, and surprised even more when Masseo grinned impishly at him, face lighting up, as he slyly added, "And I have to say you did a spectacular job of implying you were actually Aurelius Magnus come down from heaven to answer prayers!"

Pali could not help from mouthing *Aurelius Magnus* at Jullanar, shocked Masseo had come so close to asking Fitzroy outright if that were the truth. Jullanar shook her head minutely, even as Masseo continued.

"What was your apology for? The one you gave before."

Jullanar frowned at the smith. "That's rather personal, isn't it? Fitzroy, we're not trying to pry—"

Fitzroy actually snorted, and Jullanar laughed, her face twisting. "All right, yes, we are! You didn't seem at all surprised to see Pali arrive? Why not?"

"Didn't you arrange to meet her here?" he asked, glancing between Pali and Jullanar.

"No," Jullanar cried. "Unless you wrote to me? I must have missed that letter if you did!"

Pali shook her head slowly, feeling as if her mind were buzzing with exhaustion and emotion. "I received your letter of last week two days ago, saying you'd found a means to divorce your husband on the first day of midsummer, and I left yesterday. I hoped to reach Ragnor Bella before you left, but I wasn't anticipating you would have found Masseo and Fitzroy already."

She bit back any hint that she was *disappointed*; even if she could admit, privately, she *was* a bit disappointed. It would have been a grand and new adventure indeed to kidnap the lord emperor right out of the very heart of his palace.

That would have gone a long way to redeeming her hard words. As it was, she felt perpetually on the back foot, which was absurd. She should do an attack en flèche—

That was the problem, wasn't it? She shouldn't be *attacking* him at all.

Jullanar turned frowning to the two men. "I hardly found them; they came to me. I should have been more surprised but it's been a day of impossible things. How *did* you find me?"

Fitzroy said one of his glib, truthful-but-impossible-to-believe flippancies, but Masseo quelled him with a longer explanation that left Pali more confused than anything. A jungle kingdom cursed out of time before the days of the empire at all? A talking tiger? Somehow Fitzroy had had dinner with the Chancellor of Morrowlea and heard about the dragon-slaying Jemis Greenwing—

Pali drank her mint tea and wished she could hold on to that brief impulse of clear, clean empathy.

And then Jullanar said, "Wait, wait. What do you mean, you're the Lord of Zunidh?"

They all stared at her. Pali cast her mind back through the evening's conversations, sure that had been mentioned at *some* point—

"Oh," she said, flushing, "so when Masseo and I were joking earlier about ... *oh*."

Pali wondered what Jullanar thought they'd been talking about when Masseo was explaining how people thought Artorin Damara was the second coming of Aurelius Magnus, and so missed the first moment she had to say something, and Fitzroy had to say, "Didn't you tell her?"

"I didn't think it was something to write in a letter," Pali replied, scrambling to find her wits. What on earth should she, could she, *say*?

"Oh," Fitzroy said in a voice Pali had never heard from him, though his posture and expression were as perfectly composed as ever, and stared down at the table.

Pali looked at Masseo, but his expression was as alarmed and shocked as she was sure hers must be.

"What—what is that for?" she asked, demanded really, shocked by his apparent distress. She'd *wanted* to write, but every time she'd lifted her pen she could only imagine how upset he would be if it got out through a letter—"Surely you didn't want me to convey that sort of news to Jullanar in a letter that anyone could have opened? There were troubles with the post this spring."

"Troubles with everything," Jullanar muttered.

Pali had missed most of those, for good or for ill—she'd only heard rumours on her journey south to Stoneybridge. She lifted her chin at Fitzroy, furious that she'd somehow hurt him *again* by trying to do what she thought he wanted.

"Please forgive me for preferring to wait until I saw her next! We were planning on meeting up this summer and going to look for everyone, and I thought it would be better to tell her that news in person."

She had a sudden thought, that he looked forlorn—or rather *sounded*, for he still looked like the emperor—for a different reason, and swiftly added, apologetically, "I should have told *you* that I'd found her, yes, but you can't pretend that we had much opportunity for any sort of *real* conversation."

She'd been too surprised, and ... and so had he.

Fitzroy paused, as he must have learned how to pause, to hold back his first instinctive response. His words, when they came, were measured, once more that perfect, unemotional elocution. "I thought that you and Jullanar met this spring."

"Yes, right before I went to Zunidh and saw you. I only got back a fortnight ago—"

Something flickered in his eyes, a flash of a thought, and Pali suddenly realized, with a cold shock, that he'd thought she'd—what? Thought his existence as Artorin Damara *inconsequential*?

She wanted to laugh at the irony, and covered it instead with a flurry of snapped words, a feint to be sure, leading away from her weakness.

"Gods, Fitzroy, you think I'd sit on *that* news for long? I could hardly—I hardly knew what to think, and I would have ridden to Ragnor Bella immediately if I hadn't had to arrange for an indefinite leave of absence and sort out my house and things first."

She glared, defying him to think less of her for being practical for once, for not haring off with no plan. Who was she, him?

(Oh gods, she should have written to Jullanar first. She wished she'd had Jullanar's advice and now she was too muddled up to know what to even ask her friend. All she knew how to do was attack to defend against her own weaknesses.)

Fitzroy himself was staring back almost like in the old days, his chin up, his eyes blazing.

"In fact," Pali went on, "I am utterly amazed to find you so close behind me."

She wasn't going to admit to being disappointed she didn't get to kidnap an emperor. She wasn't.

She looked at Jullanar, who nodded encouragingly, her expression something like it had been when they'd been in that fairy-lit wood by the stream and she'd asked why Fitzroy had always been different.

Oh, he was, he was, and Pali still did not know how to account for it.

"I have been going over what I said to you, and I must apologize," she said, her voice wavering despite her best efforts, and she could not help it, she dropped into her mother tongue, the formal words of apology the best she could offer him, for those terrible words she'd wielded against him on that terrace when he'd seemed so entirely to have lost himself.

"I was sore shocked to encounter you, and I said things that must have hurt you deeply. Hear my sorrow, I beg you."

Fitzroy's face was solemn, his posture shifting with apparent unconsciousness to something that must have been the formal gestures and postures expected in such a moment, for Pali had read descriptions of the way he held his hands, palms up, the way he angled his head, the deliberation of his words and the weight he gave to them.

"I hear your sorrow, and I say it is a shadow cast by a swift-moving bird, here and gone."

He had remembered the right words.

The wish she'd wished on their behalf from the Siruyal, the second of her two wishes, had given him knowledge and understanding of her own language, but he had to have remembered the formulae himself.

He'd remembered how she took her tea. He remembered the exact phrase to use to accept a formal apology in a language, a culture, he could have had next to no contact with since they parted.

She held his eyes, was held by his gaze, the gold like the sun rising over the desert. Oh, he always had been different, hadn't he?

She did not know the name of what she was feeling, this lump in her throat, this sorrow in her heart, this joy in her mind, this light and this shadow—

She had the feather in her pocket. She could wish—

She could. If she knew what to wish for, and what cost it might have.

Oh, she could wish.

CHAPTER TWENTY-TWO
A GREAT AND WILD MAGE

It had been over a year on Zunidh, which turned to an utterly different time than Alinor.

Pali listened to Fitzroy's explanation, spoken with almost human nervousness, and could not hold the knowledge in her mind.

The three weeks since she had left him in that beautiful, luminous white room had been hardly enough time for his identity to sink in. He had had a year, more than a year (what had his Lord Chancellor said? *A year and three months?*) to prepare, to worry himself about what she and the rest of their friends would think of him.

A year and a quarter to listen to those accusations echo in his heart, no one to explain them to (no consorts or concubines, no confidantes or friends). Not even Fitzroy Angursell, surely, could be unmoved when one of his beloved friends condemned him for being no more than the emperor.

"Did you—did you know before you came that you would find me?"

She heard what he did not say: *Did you come for me?*

Pali could only shake her head, helpless. "No. Not at all." (How she wished she had another thing to say.) She swallowed. "I was genuinely there to do research." His expression ... oh, his face was calm, calm, calm, that Emperor face, but his eyes were shadowed, bleak ... She sought for something else to add. "I wondered if you knew it was me, and that was why you'd granted me the audience?"

She had not wondered that, or only briefly. He'd been so *shocked* to see her.

He smiled, though it did not lighten his eyes. "No, not at all. I'd read your books, and Cliopher brought up your request. I was having a difficult day," he added, his voice flattening into pure neutrality. "The cleansing rituals were very involved and tiresome."

And he had been recovering from a heart attack.

"And I came in, and I was so shocked to realize it was *you* that I said—those things," Pali said, hoping her voice, her bearing, showed forth her genuine contrition and remorse. "I truly am sorry. I shouldn't have said ..."

She couldn't say it. Not out loud, where it might re-infect Fitzroy's mind, hurt him even more. "I shouldn't have been so antagonistic. Your Lord Chancellor put me right when he came down after." A glimmer ran through his eyes at mention of the bureaucrat-of-bureaucrats. She had to pause to gather herself, keep her tone civil. "I deserved the chastening," she managed. "I have been worrying about how you might have taken it." She had to pause again, but he showed no indication he wanted to *talk out his emotions* as Jullanar had suggested. "It wasn't clear to me at the time. You seemed so ... distant."

He nodded, accepting that as a statement of fact.

Jullanar took a relieved breath and gently nudged the conversation along. "You told me you were going to do research in the Imperial Archives, Pali?"

"Yes, looking up a few things ..." She tried not to blush, but could not quite say *about Artorin Damara*, and turned instead to Masseo. "I'm a professor of Late Astandalan history at Stoneybridge, if no one mentioned." She cut a glance at Fitzroy, whose expression had lightened away from that terrible neutrality. "It's strange to think of the subject of one's books reading them!"

Fitzroy actually grinned, and this time his eyes *did* reflect his humour. "Meaning you didn't go read all the books about the Red Company in the Stoneybridge library? I read all the ones in the Archives!"

Pali laughed with the others, but she could not help but feel a twist in her heart as she thought of him reading the official accounts of their activities, the closest he could get to them.

Speaking of which ... it was a hard moment, but she could not see it getting any easier if she waited. She rallied herself but tried to keep her voice gentle. "May I ask about the touching?"

He flinched back, hands immediately in his lap, shoulders back, spine upright and nowhere near the back of the chair. "Is it that obvious?"

Jullanar said, "To be honest, yes."

And then he told them about the taboos.

Pali listened with her blood throbbing in her ears as he explained that he had once burned a woman by touching her; that those golden scars down the commander of the guard's arms had come from his touch.

That he had never had a consort or a concubine, and so ... there had been no one to touch.

"You never married," Jullanar said.

"No," he said simply, looking down at the table. "No. After the Fall, some of those taboos were relaxed." He listed a few, voice brightening even as Pali's heart seemed to contract into a harder and harder lump in her breast. No going outside? No uncooked food? No touching impure items? (From his tone, the list of *impurities* had been long.) No knives?

And he had rejoiced, it was clear he had rejoiced, in being able to go outside and not blind anyone by looking on them.

Fitzroy Angursell, who had spent the better part of a decade camping outside. Fitzroy Angursell, who loved everyone he met, who was interested in everything and everyone, who had kissed and hugged and touched with abandon, who had been as nosy as the wind and as welcoming as a campfire. Fitzroy Angursell, learning to be content with what he had.

"I have touched or been touched by six people since I became Emperor," he said, his voice extremely calm, and he looked at Pali as he had when she had thrown those words into his face and he had said *I am sorry, you know.*

Are you? she'd returned, contemptuously.

Oh, she *had* been contemptuous.

"I am trying," he said, and though his voice and face and body were still so, so controlled, his hand when he lifted it was trembling, and his eyes were burning.

Pali reached out to take his outstretched hand with both of hers, as if his hand were a new-hatched chick, and she lifted it to her lips, hoping her tears would not overflow.

"You're utterly impossible," she murmured, as he drew back his hand, because how could he sit there before them, every inch the last emperor of Astandalas, every inch Fitzroy Angursell, and begin to forgive her?

∽

He forgave her even unto giving her a hug when she went up to him, not sure what she dared to ask.

She had always thought being embraced by him was ... Nice.

She had never given it another name. Nice. It was nice.

(It was different than being embraced by Masseo or Jullanar. He had always felt like controlled power, even back when that power had been hardly more than a distant flicker of lightning, a muted rumble of thunder. Now he felt—

Nice. She told herself firmly. It felt nice to be embraced by him. She could ignore her guilt, for a moment, in his embrace.)

They ate Jullanar's pottage, with bread Fitzroy had apparently bought that morning. Jullanar said the usual prayer to the gods and Lord Emperor that had been common in imperial days.

They used to make a mocking response, Pali remembered, when it had just been them, the Red Company.

A mocking response was on her lips, but she held it back with an effort, and Fitzroy, straight-faced but with his eyes gleaming with true humour, replied with the words that must have been the official response.

We bless this food to our people's enjoyment and use, he said, the imperial plural sitting easily on his tongue, the sincerity rolling through the rote words.

A great mage's blessing was not to be dismissed, Pali knew, for all that it was not a true divine gift.

For all that it was *probably* not a true divine gift.

After supper Masseo and Fitzroy sat by the table, half-heartedly tidying it first, and Pali was drawn over to the corner by Jullanar.

"How are you doing?" Jullanar whispered.

Pali shrugged. "You?"

"It's been a mad day," Jullanar replied with a great sigh. "But I have just remembered something ... that might be important."

"Oh? How intriguing."

"Get away with you!" Jullanar bit her lip, her eyes looking across at Fitzroy, who had finally started to relax his posture and was staring off into space with an almost recognizable expression. Pensive, was it? Pali wondered.

"You remember that diamond, the Star of the North?"

That Party was burned into her mind. The glittering throne room of the Palace of Stars, the glittering courtiers, the betrothal-gifts piled on tables, the food and the music and the dizzying magic, and then— "Yes. Fitzroy stole it because ..." She furrowed her brow as she recalled his madcap hilarity, even more puzzling and extravagant than usual. "Something about how it sang to his magic."

Jullanar hissed through her teeth. "It was ... well ... we broke it. Do you think I should tell him?"

Pali remembered Fitzroy pulling the diamond out of his pocket, when they finally stopped running and were holed up in safety. They had all been wound up, exhausted but exhilarated, Fitzroy most of all.

He had pulled that huge diamond out of his pocket—the largest unflawed diamond ever found within the empire, so far as Pali had ever heard—and it had cast the firelight over all their faces. In his hand it had seemed to glow with gold fire, but she had been sure—at the time she had been sure—that it was only the circumstances making it seem that way. When he'd passed it around it had reflected the light.

Pali remembered holding it, cradling it in her two hands, staring at the firelight caught in its internal facets, and Fitzroy saying, in response to someone's question, "Oh, I think it belongs to me. Or at least with me. Isn't it a beauty?"

It belongs to me. Or at least with me.

At the time, a joke; they had laughed.

Pali thought now about That Party, and the song he had written about it, which had skewered the Imperial family with caricatures that had been almost ... kind.

The Imperial family. His family. His mother, sister, uncle, cousin. Who had looked on him and not recognized him at all. He had not even bothered with a mask beyond the sort one held in the hand. He had put back his shoulders and let his voice assume its proper accent, and though the assembled court had murmured with curiosity and wonder at who he could be, not a single one had doubted his right to be there.

They had merely gossiped at how daring he was to wear his hair *naturally*. Pali was sure she remembered that.

Masseo laughed suddenly, and she and Jullanar both startled. "Yes," Pali said quietly, urgently, as they went over.

Jullanar could not quite get out the right words, so Pali, worried now what Fitzroy was going to do, astonished at his temerity, his brazen *audacity*, managed to guide the conversation away from Fitzroy's too-successful quest to the diamond in question.

"Jullanar," Fitzroy said at last, "if you want the Diamond of Gaesion, we can look for that next. We need something to look for, anyway, and that's ... something I wanted to find."

Pali looked at Jullanar meaningfully, but Jullanar looked positively green.

"Oh?" Pali asked. "Was there a curse on the diamond?"

"Not exactly," Fitzroy replied, settling himself, and then immediately getting back up to go to his bag and bring out a bottle of wine. He fussed over the preparations sufficiently that Pali knew she'd been right to think the diamond important. Mysteriously so; but even if he were not, somehow, Aurelius Magnus, he *was* nevertheless a great and wild mage.

A great and wild mage who had been a boy, once. A lonely boy, Pali thought, listening to him describe his tutor's punishments of etiquette manuals and dead languages for when he had misbehaved.

None of this, truly, precluded him being Aurelius Magnus. She had no idea how the ancient emperor might have been raised: by tutors who taught him dead languages and etiquette was no stranger than to imagine the young Artorin Damara being so educated.

"In *The Saga of the Sons of Morning*," he said, "the poet describes the semi-legendary history of Zunidh until the early conquests of Yr and Damar. One of the stories in the third book mentions the sorcerer Ajuwar, who was called the Master of Birds."

Jullanar smiled with suspicious brightness. "Oh, I've heard of him! Wasn't he the one who put 'all the heaviness of his heart' into a stone so he would be light enough to fly? And then it turned out this made him immortal, and that was all very well at first until everyone he loved died and eventually he begged the gods to put him out of his suffering, and so they turned him into the Morning Star to warn people about overreaching themselves."

Pali focused hard on keeping her expression as unrevealing as she could manage.

They had *been* to the Divine Lands. Fitzroy had seduced the *Moon*. He had survived the Fall of Astandalas despite being at its very epicentre and by all the laws of magic the one designated to bear the weight of the catastrophe upon his shoulders. He had—

He appeared to think they were trying not to laugh, for he grinned at them and mock-applauded. "Sadly," he said, with that flippancy, that insouciance, that had always driven Pali to distraction, "when I was thirteen I didn't heed the latter part of the story, and I very much wanted to fly."

And oh by the *gods*, if he *were* Aurelius Magnus and had lived to see all his loved ones die, over and over again—

"You tried to put the heaviness of your heart into a stone?" Jullanar asked, though Pali guessed by her hesitancy that she wanted to ask—oh, how they *all* wanted to ask—if he were Aurelius Magnus. When exactly this had happened.

"I put something into the Diamond of Gaesion, the Star of the North," he correctly, with a sort of punctiliousness.

The sort of punctiliousness he had loved, a joke in itself, the idea that *he* would be so precise, so persnickety, so *exact*.

But he had been, had always loved using the precise, perfect word.

(Artorin Damara had—no. She would not think about those policies, those decisions, those proclamations she had studied and criticized. How each of them had Fitzroy's fingerprints all over, now that she knew to look.)

"You can see why I wasn't too keen on it disappearing into the Imperial Treasury as part of my sister's dowry. Admittedly, it probably would have been safer to leave it there, where I knew where it was. What was anyone going to do with it, besides put it on display, or perhaps make it the centrepiece of a crown or the like?"

He paused for breath, and Pali looked at him, his face mobile and attentive, *present*, himself.

What a *heart* he had.

"Instead, I took it with me, and I when I was thrown out of the high tower of the Moon into the Sea of Stars, if you remember that occasion, it was one of the things that I think fell out of my bag."

Pali remembered that occasion, yes. They'd stolen boats from the constellations and rowed madly after him. Ayasha, the best swimmer, had had to dive down and down to fetch him, and she with only one arm to pull him back up.

He'd been laughing when he surfaced, blowing spray like a breaching whale, Ayasha laughing with relief and exaltation, and moondust silvering him, lingering on his skin, smudging his shadows into cool, glimmering light, for days afterwards.

∼

Out of her rucksack, Jullanar pulled the broken shards of the Diamond of Gaesion, the Star of the North, the heart of Fitzroy Angursell.

There were no words to describe how beautiful and sorrowful the shards were. Pali could only remember the white and black bones of the enormous dragons whose death-throes had made the gardens of the gods into the great desert of Kaph. There had been such power, and such staggering grief, in those bones.

Fitzroy stared at the shards, which gleamed like melting ice on the scrap of cloth Jullanar had wrapped them in. He was back to drawn and distant, his eyes almost white with power. Pali could see a heat-haze rising above his skin, warping and wavering the air.

He murmured something, incomprehensibly, about his heart.

Pali tried to say something that would bring him back to them, not tip him over into whatever wild magic was calling him, not—

Not lose him to whatever he had bound in that diamond.

"Fitzroy," she said, but he was far beyond hearing her.

"I think," he said clearly, his voice ringing as if one of the bells in his palace, echoing through the white halls, "that this is why I survived the Fall of Astandalas. Myself."

Was that meant to be reassuring?

Pali could barely hold herself back from rising up and stopping him. She did not have that right. None of them had that right.

They had to let him reclaim himself.

Jullanar was saying something about the events in Ragnor Bella, and Masseo, and Fitzroy was snarking back, his voice his own (oh, it was how she remembered him, not the perfect accent of the Last Emperor but Fitzroy's happily variable voice—)—

"It wasn't nearly as hard as I expected," Jullanar was saying, her voice soft. "One tap and it just ... fell apart."

"Of course," Fitzroy said, his voice no longer neutral, but so, so quiet.

Pali stared at him, wondering just what this stone was. What it would return to him, if he reached out to take it?

He did reach out. He scooped the shards into his cupped hands, and his eyes blazed white as the sun at noon high overhead. The diamond fragments caught the fire, caught fire, and *burned*.

They watched him sit there, face turned inwards, serene as for every coin, every portrait.

"Do you think," Jullanar said, and faltered, but she had never been one to sy away from hard truths, and she cleared her throat and went on. "Do you think it will be ... *him*, still, when he ... finishes?"

"Yes," said Pali, for she would not countenance otherwise.

They sat there, watching the diamonds burn not into ash but into his hands. The magic seemed to puddle along the creases in his palms, the fortune-tellers' lifelines, and for a few moments Pali saw the white-gold glitter run along his veins, illuminating his dark skin from beneath, from within, until he shone there like the reverse of an alabaster vase.

She recalled, as from a far distance, those poems he might or might not have written, where light and shadow, stone and air, melted and flowed into each other, prisons of mind and body and spirit and soul.

Oh, she hoped he was coming free.

They watched as the diamonds slowly diminished, burned down, the lights in his veins softening, retreating, his skin once more human. His eyes were closed, but his eyes had always been uncanny.

The diamonds went out: and he opened his eyes.

He took a deep, deep breath, visibly girding himself, and Pali's heart stuttered.

But then he said, "Well, that was a bit unexpected, wasn't it?" and keeled over almost as soon as he tried to move.

∽

The next morning it turned out he had somehow learned how to turn into a crow, but Pali was more interested in the new road that had appeared out of nowhere, a fourth direction from the three-way cross.

Of course she was more interested in the new road, she told herself firmly, as he laughed at her, exhilarated with flight, his face mobile, attentive, present, *alive.*

"You are magnificent," he said, looking straight into her eyes, his full of sunlight, the lure of flight. "We should get married."

Pali opened her mouth in utter incredulity, before she caught the smile, the true smile, the *Fitzroy* smile, and so she said the words, as if they were her next lines in a play: "But how do I know you are magnificent enough for me?"

His magic moved and flexed in the air around him, around them, no weight on her but sizzling with the possibilities of—

Well. The possibilities. He was a great and wild mage. The possibilities were *endless.*

"I am the poet Fitzroy Angursell," he said as he had said then.

She could not say her next lines, for this was not, actually, a play.

But she had to say something. She swallowed.

He was the poet Fitzroy Angursell—oh, he was, he *was*—but he was also—

At the very least he was also Artorin Damara.

At the very least.

She refused to be rattled by the vastness of power stirring idly around him. She refused to be afraid that he was the immortal Aurelius Magnus, smiling down at her. She refused to wonder about that crow-shape.

"Oh, you're impossible," she said, meaning it entirely sincerely, and went inside the refuge with his merry laughter ringing around them both.

CHAPTER TWENTY-THREE
SPARRING

After breakfast, Pali groomed her horse. She came in to find Fitzroy scrawling some sort of letter. "Mustn't forget my people back home," he said vaguely, waving a page in the air to dry. "Necessary updates, confirmation I haven't died, all that. Statement I am progressing on my quest."

"Are you?"

He grinned at her. "Had a dream of someone who might do last night."

He sounded half-drunk, but Pali guessed it was the intoxication of magic, of flight, of a dream come true and a diamond heart returned to flesh.

He'd always wanted to fly. *Yearned* to. As if—

Jullanar called her, and Pali went behind the refuge to assist her with the privy door, which was stuck. While she waited for Jullanar to finish, there was a kerfuffle on the other side of the refuge: a post rider coming up the Fiellanese road, they saw when they rejoined the others, had absolutely not expected to be hailed by Fitzroy Angursell and asked to convey a letter 'to Zunidh'.

Fitzroy charmed the man into accepting the letter, and they

watched him canter away before returning inside the refuge to make sure they hadn't forgotten anything. The only one who had was Fitzroy, who had somehow missed one page of his letter when he sealed it.

"Well," he said, folding up the unsent page and putting it in his pocket, "That will add a certain piquancy of confusion. I'm sure Cliopher will realize what happened."

"I'm sure," Pali said dryly, feeling a shiver of anticipation for the conversations to come that day.

One of the things that she had always loved was sparring.

Sparring with Damian or indeed any of the others, whether individually or in small groups, always working to improve her swordplay, her skill and agility and cunning in the heat of battle.

And sparring verbally with Fitzroy had always been one of her very favourite things.

They set off to the east, to the new road that had not been there the night before. Everyone felt fresh and alert; the day was beautiful, the air perfect for a ramble.

Fitzroy was walking easily, his staff seeming more an affectation than anything necessary. Pali thought with some satisfaction that perhaps she could find a suitable staff of her own, and they could play at quarterstaves. That was a weapon she hadn't used for a while. Masseo might join them, and Jullanar ... it was a good weapon, the staff, discreet and often effective.

The turf was springy underfoot. The new road, the one that hadn't been there the day before, unspooled in a most alluring fashion, curving behind a hummock and into a long, shallow valley with a copse at the bottom that appeared to be their destination, insofar as magically emerging roads had visible destinations.

It was a good hour's walk away, Pali decided, given the speed with which they were travelling, and—given how open and safe the region was—a good opportunity to engage her second-favourite pastime.

She turned to Fitzroy, who was walking on her right, where his thumping staff would not come anywhere near her reins or bother her horse. He smiled back at her, and it was almost like the old times.

"I had a question or two for you," she began, which was the way their sparring-matches had often began, almost as formulaic, as ritual, as either her or Damian looking at the other and saying, "Might you have a moment to step aside?"

Fitzroy's smile sharpened, eyes crinkling, and Pali thought how *good* it was to see him like this, walking beside her, beside them, in the fresh air, his stride free and easy, his eyes bright. "I may have an answer," he replied, the words as rote, as familiar, as beloved.

No need to dance around with the formalities, as sparring a new partner, beginning a new debate. Not with Fitzroy. Her heart sang as she thought of her list of questions, the puzzles even knowing Artorin Damara was actually Fitzroy Angursell had been unable to solve.

"What," she said, precise as the first feint, the first thrust, "led you to that decision to continue the Seven Valleys campaign?"

He was silent a moment, his face going—not blank, not puzzled (rarely puzzled, never blank, not Fitzroy; not even now)—but rather politely attentive, pensive, as he considered her question. Pali watched him, admiring his control, this development in his ability to debate. She'd never been able to master her expressions, and had to turn that impetuosity to a virtue, as she turned her small frame into a virtue in battle.

Oh, what a splendour it was, to debate someone as intelligent as she, who knew the field at least as well as she did, but who knew parts of it far better—who had all the inside knowledge, details she could not ever have gleaned from the outside, from the official documents and unofficial accounts.

He began to answer, his voice calm, his words measured, all that brilliant fire of him focused on the clarity of his speech. Pali could not help but fall under the spell of his rhetorical command for a moment, before she internally shook herself, regrouped, and launched properly into the fight.

They descended the long valley, Pali rejoicing in the debate, the sheer *joy* of it being with Fitzroy—Fitzroy!—whose argumentative style had shifted considerably but was more effective than ever. No matter how passionate she grew, no matter what abstruse sources she found, he had a steady, polished answer for her.

Polished as a splendid sword, she thought more than once as they walked that long afternoon. Polished to keep the edges sharp, honed as keen as her own flashing daggers, silky-smooth and so effective she was more than once forced onto the back foot, off-balance until she could gather herself and find another angle with which to return the attack.

Masseo and Jullanar walked behind them, talking, their softer voices a pleasant counterpoint. Pali didn't listen to what they were saying: she could barely keep up with Fitzroy with the entirety of her attention on him.

Eventually, regretfully, they came to the copse of trees and an effervescent pool of magic. Pali let Fitzroy win the last bout—well. Not *let*. She knew the difference.

"I suppose I shall grant you the last word on that matter," she said graciously, even as her horse whickered at the magic ahead of them.

Fitzroy gave her one of his debate-calm smiles before relaxing out of his sparring posture and turning his attention to the situation in front of them. Pali imagined him sheathing his sword, shaking out his hands, taking off his helm to wipe his sweaty brow. It was all the same sort of feeling, she thought, satisfied, as she let thoughts of the knotty mess that was late Astandalan trade policy in western Voonra slide back from the forefront of her mind.

"What do we think?" Jullanar asked, regarding the deceptively pretty thicket.

Their path had been marked by white stones set at roughly ten-yard intervals. This part of the mountains was much-grazed by sheep, the flocks belonging to various shepherds who practiced transhumance from the lowlands of the three kingdoms, and so the herbage underfoot was springy and close-cropped, easy walking. There were patches of heather higher up, but the valley had been increasingly lush as they descended.

Down here the grass was full of flowers, pink and purple and white and yellow ones that Pali could hardly name. The sheep did not descend this far; quite possibly this was not a valley that was still part of Alinor.

"The Borderwood is through there," Fitzroy said, his voice nearly as abstractly polite as during their debate, though this time it was because his attention was on the magic before them.

Pali could feel the magic, though she could not herself work it nor read much more than its presence and general strength and orientation. She could tell this was powerful magic, and neutral or even friendly, but nothing more.

Alone, she might or might not have entered into it. It would depend on how much of an adventure she was seeking.

With her friends—

She stopped for a moment to savour that thought. Her friends were there, half of them. And if even Fitzroy could be found, could be pried out of his glorious palace and all the might and majesty (and, she could admit, *pace* his Lord Chancellor, the responsibilities) of his position and power ... she could rest hopeful that Sardeet had spoken the truth.

Leave me to travel alone now and our paths will cross again, Sardeet had written to her and Arzu, and Pali had reluctantly let her little sister set off on her own adventure. Every other time Pali or Arzu had been there to rescue her, but not since that day in the Silver Forest when they had been scattered.

"It is complex," Fitzroy said. His eyes were a soft, thoughtful gold. "Voonra and Faërie and I believe also ... Arvath, perhaps? That is far distant."

Fitzroy had been able to discern a border between the worlds, but he had never been able to determine with such certainty *which* world might lie on the other side. Pali was very impressed.

"It has just occurred to me," Jullanar said, her voice suddenly brightening, "that we are on an adventure and we—we need merely accept the invitation held out to us."

Fitzroy turned his head to look at Jullanar. Pali caught her breath as the sunlight illuminated his profile in the moment he smiled, catching the very shift from the Emperor on every coin to the great poet, like the sun coming out from behind a cloud.

"Let us link arms," he said, his voice low, almost sultry. Magic, Pali remembered, even as she came forward, her horse clopping easily behind her. That was magic in his voice, as the golden light in his eyes was magic.

"We do not want to lose each other again," Jullanar agreed, reaching out to Pali on one side, Fitzroy on the other.

Masseo took Fitzroy's other arm, moving the staff to his own left hand with a laugh and a comment that he had strong shoulders if Fitzroy needed the support, and then, together, they stepped into the trees.

~

The mist that rose had once been familiar.

Pali recalled so many crossings between worlds, sometimes using the magnificent gates the Astandalans had wrought, often finding their way through secret crevices that Fitzroy and Faleron and Sardeet had been able to discern. Other times locals had told them the way, legends and rumours held in hinterland villages and remote homesteads, for passes between worlds were often in distant places.

Not always. Sometimes they were to be found in one door in a house, or a gate at the bottom of a garden, or an alley if you happened to step into it on the right hour of the right day, or wearing the right colours, or saying the right words, or in any one of a hundred ways you might somehow meet the conditions to open a door and step through.

The mist of a soft place, where the Borderwood pressed close, was the most familiar.

The grey mist coiled up as they stepped four abreast between the trees. Apple trees, Pali identified, catchings sight of unripe fruit, even as she realized they were stepping back in seasons, and the green apples grew smaller and smaller and finally became instead a canopy of dappled pink-and-white.

The air was softer, perfumed with the sweet, uncomplicated scent of appleblossom. Pali's horse neighed; when she turned her head to check on the mare, she saw the black horse and gear all speckled with the flowers.

Fitzroy was walking more slowly than he had strode during their debate, his face soft, tilted as if listening. Pali looked at Jullanar, who was also looking at him, but turned to smile at Pali after a moment.

"Isn't this beautiful," Jullanar whispered gleefully.

It was. The mist lightened in colour, silvery-white rather than grey, and the apple trees steadied at full bloom. These were old trees, gnarled and mossy, but still blossoming freely. Underfoot was all green, green moss, and it was very quiet.

Pali tilted her head up. Through the branches above her were patches of a soft silvery-white sky, almost exactly the colour of the mist.

The white stones marked out a path; they followed it out of the apple grove and into a river valley, the sort the Linder folk called a dale. It was a shallow, wide vale, with green slopes broken by dark grey rocks. The air was cool, as if they still rode through high mountains. The mist swirled around the bald, rounded peaks of low mountains rising up above the dale.

They had entered by way of a side valley. The white stones went straight to the riverside—a shallow river, running noisily over stones—and there stopped at a singular standing stone of the same white stone, far taller than any of them.

Fitzroy unlinked his arms and walked up to the stone, running his fingers gently over its face. Something sparkled in the wake of his touch, running through shallow grooves carved into the stone. Spirals and lines; nothing Pali could read.

"This was a meeting place, a trading-place," Fitzroy said. "Long ago. No one has come this way for ... a long time."

He looked immensely sad. Jullanar made a soft noise. Masseo said, "Is there anyone waiting?"

Fitzroy shook his head and let his hand drop from the stone. "No. Not for us."

That had been a hard, hard lesson: that not all the invitations were for them.

"Which way do we go now?" Jullanar asked, looking from the stone up and down the valley. Pali copied her, and saw nothing much to indicate whether they ought follow the river up- or downstream. Or indeed cross the stream, climb the steep facing slope, and see what lay over the ridge. Except that that would be a considerable amount of trouble, really.

"I reckon downstream," Masseo said after due consideration.

Fitzroy turned around in a slow circle. "Voonra is that way, somewhere," he said.

Masseo looked pleased. "That way."

Pali nodded when Fitzroy looked at her, as did Jullanar, and realized after they had started walking again that it was so natural to look to him for the decision.

It had been a long time—not since she had left her clan—since Pali had so easily and willingly let another make the decision.

It was, she decided, rather nice.

～

They had joined the stream when it was still quite small—a stream rather than a river—and the valley narrow. The river wound its way downhill, plashing across rocks, never very deep. There were sedges here and there, and increasing thickets as they descended; the air grew warmer.

She did not resume sparring with Fitzroy, who appeared to be dreamily enjoying the feel of the magic of the place, and instead talked intermittently with Jullanar and Masseo, mostly about books they had been reading of late. It was only later in the afternoon, insofar as they could tell time—with no sun in the sky it was always very difficult in the Borderlands—that Fitzroy seemed to return to himself.

Jullanar teased him gently about his distractedness.

"It has been a long time since I was last outside the ... former Empire," he said, moving his hand in the air. Faint gold sparkles gathered around his fingers, trailing briefly in the air behind him, as he were smudging light behind him. "I had forgotten how ... freeing it is."

"You won't set things on fire, will you?" Jullanar asked, regarding the sparkling air with minor trepidation.

"I doubt it," he replied, still with that soft, mild tone, that faint wonder in his face. Pali thought he looked as if he were partway sozzled, though hiding it well.

"Let's camp at the next likely spot," she suggested, and when Fitzroy nodded a beat too late, took it upon herself to draw him away from his dreamy haze by asking increasingly pointed questions about his noted policy of educational reforms.

∽

They camped in an idyllic sort of glade beside the river. There was plenty of firewood, and while Fitzroy and Masseo built up the fire and set out Fitzroy's extravagant supply of extremely extravagant bedding, Pali and Jullanar cut poles and caught half a dozen fish for their supper.

The river was still shallow here, albeit much wider, and the two women had travelled several hundred yards away from the camp by the time Jullanar caught the last fish. While Pali gutted it, Jullanar coiled up her line and removed the hook for safekeeping in her sewing kit.

"Fitzroy seems less ... argumentative, don't you think?" she asked.

Pali flicked the guts into the river with a murmured thanks to the spirits that might be there. It never paid to be rude to the locals, after all. "What do you mean?"

"He was quite ... undemonstrative, I thought, debating with you."

"His style has changed, matured," Pali replied. "It's amazingly effective as a rhetorical strategy."

"Perhaps that's all it is," Jullanar murmured. "Still—be careful, won't you? He might not enjoy debating as much as you do."

"Fitzroy, not enjoy arguing with a friend?"

Jullanar paused as if struck by this thought. "True."

"He's glorious at it," Pali admitted, faintly blushing, glad she was bending down so she could string the fish together on her line. "I can barely keep up."

Jullanar laughed at her, but kindly, and bumped her shoulder as Pali stood up from washing her hands. "A point in his favour, eh?"

Which Pali really could not dignify with a response. She was glad that Jullanar asked Fitzroy to play for them that night, for it meant no one felt any need to debate, even so minor a topic as who was to do the dishes.

And oh, he could still *play*.

∼

The next few days were very similar. They walked down the valley, which seemed to keep unfolding before them, never revealing any grand views but always lovely in the details they could see. Pali talked with all her friends, of course, the way they always had, but she returned again and again to the sparring with Fitzroy.

There was something so delicious about debating with him. Even when he could not *satisfy* her thirst for justice, her cultural inflexibility, his arguments were always sound, his reasoning always precise within the constraints he'd had to work.

She stored up ideas, snippets of arguments, even occasional phrases, and began turning in her mind what kind of a magnum opus she could write about his reign, if he were willing to be a source such as this.

It would be a grand triumph for her as a scholar, but how much more so for him as an emperor, she thought, in a brief lull of an intense analysis of how he'd balanced the Ouranatha against the Army through the last third of his reign. He had started from so uncertain a footing—unknown, without allies, ignorant of most of the factions of the court—but his innate brilliance and skill at understanding *people* had meant that within fourteen years he had been superb.

He'd been verging on greatness, she'd written in her last book, unwilling to say the truth—so often bloviated and boasted by obsequious fools, but true nonetheless—that he'd been great by the middle of his reign.

Another year or two and he would have been one of the greatest of the emperors of Astandalas. She'd written that in her notes before she'd gone to that interview with him, when she was deep in the Archives reading through documents and reports and seeing just how deep the rot had gone.

There were a few times when she thought she might have come too close to a tender spot, when he would stop speaking, his face very still, and walk for a few strides.

She watched him in those moments, taking the opportunity to gather her own thoughts, marshall her own arguments. His very dispassion was such a contrast to his old way of arguing, and endlessly effective.

Even after three days, four, of hours-long debate, Pali could not always extricate herself from the traps her own emotions and logic led her into.

It was like fencing with Damian, always the minutest slip away from complete disaster. *Such* a splendid gift.

~

The fourth day, they came to another river-valley. Fitzroy turned his head to the wind that was rushing down from the distant hilltops, where the mist swirled and never quite revealed what lay behind the first rank.

Pali considered the valley. It had a wide mouth where it debouched into their dale, but its sides quickly narrowed into a near-gorge. There was a distant rumble of waterfalls, and a delicious scent of greenery. Her horse tugged at the reins, interested in what she could smell.

"Do we turn?" Pali asked, looking at Fitzroy.

His face was still in its debater's calm, polite and attentive and giving nothing whatsoever away. He blinked at her, as if he, too, had been deep in the mustered arguments of their conversation, unable to resurface quickly.

"Voonra is that way," he said with certainty.

"And if we continue downriver?" Jullanar asked.

Fitzroy turned his head, and the magic sparkled around him, soft gold, glinting in a sunlight that had never shone on these lands outside the bounds of the worlds.

"It ... continues," he said. "It is muddled. Foggy."

"Let's go to Voonra," Jullanar decided. "I haven't been there in ages."

CHAPTER TWENTY-FOUR
A NIGHTMARE

Pali recognized that Fitzroy was severely distracted by the magic flowing down the valley towards them, and did not try to engage him in further debate that day. His expression loosened as they walked, as if he were gaining energy from the magic despite the increasingly stiff uphill climb.

They made camp early, for as they climbed higher there were fewer good places. They came at last to a pleasant dell, sheltered from the wind on three sides; the stream bounded down a series of short cascades and deep, pleasing pools on the fourth. Masseo had sensibly suggested bringing wood with them from a tangle of deadfall further down, and so they built up a blaze with great pleasure.

Moss underfoot, thick cushions of bright green, patches of shaggy sphagnum in the boggier spots, even the pale-grey spongy type that Pali had learned so many years ago was the best for any sort of personal ablutions. Where had they been, where the women packed that kind of moss around their babies to act as absorbent diapers?—

"What a lovely spot this is," Jullanar said, taking off her rucksack with an appreciative groan. She stretched and stood there, hands on her hips as she regarded the group.

Pali watched her; watched Masseo, who had set his own pack down and was casting around for stones with which to build a fireplace. Watched Fitzroy, who was still holding his bag and had his eyes closed, his face lifted up to the grey clouds above them. The water rippled and sang.

There should have been mosquitos or midges, but that was the benefit of travelling with a wild mage. He hadn't even had to be reminded today to extend his rejection of insects from his personal space to include them.

"I'll get water," Pali said, setting down her own pack and taking the pot Masseo handed her with a smile.

The water was cold and chattered cheerfully over its stones. Deep brown water, green moss, white bubbles. Probably clean, but they would boil it before drinking, just in case an animal had died or defecated it in upstream.

Once Fitzroy had been able to tell—once Arved had had an amulet that could tell—but Fitzroy seemed to have forgotten how to do that sort of small, practical magic. And Arved was still living whatever life he had built for himself after their separation.

Pali returned to the glade to find that Fitzroy had drawn out his extravagant bedding and Masseo had started a fire. Fitzroy was nowhere to be seen, and Jullanar was kneeling beside her own pack, searching out food.

"He's gone to wash," Jullanar said. "Theoretically."

But there were no surprises: Fitzroy came back in a warm wool gown, which would have been almost ordinary if it hadn't fit him so well. And if he'd put on his boots—well. He was Fitzroy.

∽

Pali had managed to catch a couple of rabbits in a quiet moment while her horse grazed, and Jullanar made a kind of flatbread on an iron griddle Masseo pulled out of his rucksack. Fitzroy provided tea and sticky dates that tasted wondrously like *home* to Pali.

It was still light when they had finished eating, the misty sky dimming towards blue dusk but the shadows not yet filling their dell. Jullanar declared herself perishing for a wash, and picked her way towards a pool just out of sight. Pali went with her, more for company than any concern, and they had a pleasant half-hour of splashing each other in the cold, clear water while they attempted to wash their hair.

"It is at times like these that I really consider cutting it all off," Jullanar said as she wrung out the mass of hair over the stream. "It's enough of a hassle at home."

Pali agreed, though she quite liked the feeling of water running over her hands as she twisted the strands together. Perhaps it was her upbringing in a desert where water was a deeply precious commodity, and washing hair a ceremonious activity, undertaken with great care and circumstance.

They returned to the camp to find that Masseo was whittling and Fitzroy was writing something.

It was the first time he had done so since Pali had joined them, and it warmed her heart tremendously to see him sitting there, notebook balanced on a wider tome, ink pot in his left hand, quill in his right.

She and Jullanar settled themselves near the fire, and while Pali's hair was still wrapped in a cloth, she took her brush and began to slowly comb Jullanar's hair dry and free of tangles. Fitzroy looked up at them, and smiled slowly, almost wistfully, at them.

His bald head gleamed in the firelight. Pali missed his hair, the long heavy curls bouncing in the wind, the times when she or Sardeet or Jullanar would braid it for him. He'd had a period where he'd worn it in dozens of braids, each of them finished with a golden bead he'd plucked out of a pirate's hoard.

"What are you writing?" Jullanar asked, after they had sat in companionable quiet for a time. Fitzroy was smiling over whatever it was, so Pali had hopes it was a new poem. He hadn't offered any new songs to them, but surely at some point he would stop being so shy about it.

"A letter," he said simply.

"A long letter," Jullanar responded, her voice light. "Who is it for?"

Fitzroy looked down at the sheets beside him, which he'd weighted down with a stone. "A ... friend."

Pali had not hitherto imagined he had friends outside of *them*.

"A what?" she said, meaning it as a joke, and regretted it immediately when his face went immediately imperturbable.

"Have you not managed any friends?" Jullanar asked her with a sharp, reprimanding glance.

Pali blushed. "I'm sorry, Fitzroy," she said. "That was uncalled for."

Even if all she could think were all those pages of court gossip hidden in the form of semi-public letters home to remote principalities, those romans à clef, those satirical poems, that never once hinted at anyone the hundredth and last emperor of Astandalas could have called *a friend*.

But there had been years after the Fall, she reminded herself. Those two men had come down, the Commander of the Imperial Guard and the Lord Chancellor, sent down to *speak for him*, because he could not come down himself.

Because if he had come down then, the Lord Chancellor had said, he would not have gone back. And Pali had listened to him, let herself be moved by his sweet suasion, been *convinced* to leave Fitzroy in his cage. The thought was bitter in her mouth. She tried not to scowl as she spoke.

"Is it your ... lord chancellor? Or the commander of the guard? He said he was of your ... household."

Whatever exactly that *meant*.

Fitzroy relaxed minutely, though not to the point of letting his emotions show. "Cliopher, yes. He's the viceroy, now, I left him in charge when I left." He glanced down at his letter, and a smile tugged at the corner of his mouth despite ... everything.

"We'll leave you to your letter," Jullanar said decisively, and pulled out her crocheting.

Pali decided to sort through her belongings, for she could not think how to ask how he was able to smile at the thought of this *Cliopher*, that bureaucrat of bureaucrats, his brilliant jailer.

～

At some point late in the night, Pali woke to a strange, strangled noise.

She sat up, blinking as her eyes adjusted. The stars were bright enough to show the dark lumps of her friends, some of the pillows and cloths catching a sheen of starlight.

Fitzroy had been beside her, between her and Jullanar. He was the one making the noise, a choked, restrained sobbing.

It was a very quiet distress. Pali was not sure if Masseo, on the other side of the fire, would be able to hear it.

Jullanar did. She sat up, and moved first to stir up the coals, add another small piece of wood to catch. In the new flame Pali could see her eyes liquid in the firelight, her pale skin glimmering. Dark cloth over her shoulders, like a shawl made of shadows.

Fitzroy was dreaming, that was clear. As the firelight grew Pali could see his face, twisted with some deep grief. He was curled in around himself, knees brought up to be grasped by his arms, his shoulders shuddering. He did not look like a man in his sixties, neither an emperor nor a great and renowned mage and poet. He looked like a boy caught heartbroken.

Pali did not know what to do. She looked at Jullanar. "Should we wake him?" she whispered.

To her left, Masseo grunted and woke, shedding pillows as he flailed to sit upright. He blinked at the fire.

Fitzroy made a keening noise in the back of his throat. It was so quiet it was lost in the stream falling over the stones.

Jullanar crawled across the blankets and laid a gentle hand on his shoulder. "Wake up, Fitzroy," she said softly. "It's a nightmare. Wake up."

He did not flinch, not the way he did in his waking hours. He held terrifically still, eyes closed, throat quivering, all his muscles tense.

Pali put another piece of the wood on the fire. Jullanar glanced at her, then moved across entirely to Fitzroy's bed, sitting so that she could gather him in her arms, lay his head on her lap. He relaxed but did not quite uncurl.

"Sh, sh," she said, brushing her hand across his forehead. "Wake up, Fitzroy. You're safe. It was just a nightmare. You can wake now."

He opened his eyes: they reflected the rich golden-orange of the firelight. Either magic or tears made the light seem to gather there.

"There," Jullanar crooned. "You're awake now."

Fitzroy smiled at her; his voice was distant, sleepy. "I can't be. People only hold me in my dreams."

Jullanar's breath hitched. "What do you mean?"

He shifted position, so he was more half-reclining in her arms, looking at the fire. Pali could not see his expression clearly. His eyes caught the fire, and his voice was still distant, sleepy, but also ... wondering? Amazed?

"It's strange," he mused, "to dream of my magic like this."

"What do you mean?" Jullanar asked again.

He snuggled down into her arms. "This is ... lovely. Oh ... but you know, don't you? You and Masseo and Pali ... guarding me ..." He tilted his head at the fire. "I wonder when this is. The fire is so low ..."

"The fire?" Jullanar prompted softly.

"The fire at the heart of me."

Pali looked at the fire. It had been a fine cookfire, and a pleasant campfire to sit around, but even when it was at its brightest it was not anything like the splendour she associated with him. Now? The coals she had lit with a few stray twigs and small branches sat inside a puddle of ash, inside a ring of stones.

The fire at the heart of me.

"It won't go out," Jullanar said, her voice thick with tears.

"No," Fitzroy agreed, and from the sound of his voice he was smiling again. "No. It nearly did, you know." He laughed, a low, wry chuckle, much more something belonging to the lord magus than to their Fitzroy.

(It was not, for all that, Pali noted, an unpleasing sound. It was ... a window onto another part of him.)

"Of course you know," he said, and his hands came up to grasp Jullanar's, holding them against either side of his face. "Oh, it has been so hard."

"I know."

They sat like that for a long time. The aspens shirred and whispered above them, and the stars blazed against a black sky. The small fire cracked and snapped. Pali could not take it, and reached forward to add another branch, and then a larger log.

"Thank you," Fitzroy said, gravely.

Pali could not think of anything to say, but she licked dry lips and managed a hoarse, "You're welcome."

"I think," Fitzroy said, letting go of Jullanar's hands and tugging up a blanket, "that this must be sometime just before the Fall. It is such a small fire ... but the woods are not blasted as they were after. It is strange that there is not more fog. Usually I cannot see you at all. But then this is a dream."

"It's not a dream," Jullanar tried again.

"You're touching me," he said simply, as if this were indisputable proof.

No consorts or concubines, Pali thought numbly. A hundred servants or more, but there were those mentions of the taboos around the Emperor ... no meeting his eyes. No touching without solemn and grave ceremonies of purification first.

She had not realized that meant *no* touching. Did his attendants not touch him? How could he possibly dress in those fantastic court garments, those jewels of office, without assistance?

"I wish this were true," he said, and this time Pali was sure it was tears in his eyes, not magic. The firelight caught trails running down his cheeks. "I wish ..."

"What do you wish, Fitzroy?" Jullanar whispered.

He was silent for a long time. The fire settled into something more like a true blaze, not simply a young flame. The wind moved lightly about them, bringing a scent of water.

"Oh, better not to say. What if it came true?"

"It surely couldn't be that bad?" Jullanar said.

"I used to wish something would happen to depose me," he replied, almost cheerfully. "And look what happened there."

Jullanar, wisely, did not try to argue with that. "You think this is before the Fall," she said instead.

"Such a small fire," he murmured. "No pearls."

Whatever that meant.

"And here you are ... you and Masseo and Pali ..."

"Yes. We're here, Fitzroy."

"Holding me, *and* my name. Will it be worse in the morning to have dreamed this, I wonder?"

"Sometimes it's easier not to be reminded," she agreed lowly, her head bending over his.

His hand came up and cupped the side of her face, a black shadow against her pale skin. "Easier, but not better," he said. "Oh, Jullanar, don't cry. Don't cry."

"I miss you."

"You're here," he said, the dreaminess sharpening into urgency. "You're here."

She freed one hand to cover his. "I am."

Her voice betrayed her tears. Pali stirred uncomfortably, but there was nothing she could say. Masseo listened intently. He leaned forward and set another log on the fire.

"Shall I tell you a secret?" Fitzroy asked, the humour in his voice the blithe mischief Pali remembered—they all remembered—repeated in a soft, minor key.

"Oh ..." Jullanar said, tearfulness fading with inveterate curiosity. "You don't have to."

She obviously felt that there was a certain deceptiveness in listening to Fitzroy tell secrets, given that he still seemed convinced he was dreaming.

"Pali wrote all these books about my reign," he said confidingly. "She thought I was a *terrible* emperor at first."

That was, unfortunately, not untrue.

"In one of the books, she talked all about how I started to make good decisions and become a *good* ruler."

Around the first anniversary of his coronation, when he'd presumably reconciled himself to his throne, learned the basics of governance, found his feet. So Pali the historian had theorized.

Fitzroy's voice was bright with delight. "Here's the secret: that was when I started making decisions based on what I thought *you* would say."

Jullanar spluttered out a disbelieving laugh. "You didn't!"

"I did," he affirmed, satisfied, and slipped down until his head was once again pillowed in her lap. His voice was growing softer, sleepier. "You keep my heart safe ... I thought you could keep my people safe too ..."

He closed his eyes; the firelight winked out.

One last murmur, no louder than the stream. "Will you hold me until I must wake?"

Jullanar's face was starkly struck, but she kept her voice even. "Of course, Fitzroy. We'll keep the fire safe."

"Never ... doubted ..." His voice trailed off, and his breathing evened out. Jullanar pulled one of the blankets up and tucked it around him, over her hands.

CHAPTER TWENTY-FIVE
GATHERING STORMS

The next morning no one mentioned Fitzroy's midnight confession. He was bright and cheerful, the gravity of the previous day washed away, and Jullanar and Masseo both seemed equally glad-hearted. Pali wondered if she had dreamed it entirely.

She worried over the episode as they packed up. Fitzroy came by as she was checking her horse's saddle and gear with the additions of most of Jullanar's and Masseo's bags. He was wearing leggings this morning, chocolate-brown ones, and a dark orange sleeveless tunic over a cambric shirt in a kind of warm cream. This time he'd not neglected his footwear: he wore leather half-boots that were swooningly well cobbled.

"Do I look particularly fetching this morning?" Fitzroy asked, his mouth quirking up into a smile. "I think this gives a nice line to my legs, don't you?"

Pali blushed and averted her eyes. He had always been lanky, Fitzroy had: tall and slim, even gangly. He had filled out over the years, and though there was a softness overlaying his muscles, his figure was ... fine. It was fine.

No doubt it was the perfectly fitted clothes. He probably had a staff of exceptionally talented tailors. And cobblers.

No *probably* about that. "You have good tailors," she said, lifting her chin, meeting his gaze with a stubborn refusal to be embarrassed that she had been caught admiring his legs, the smooth line of his back.

"I do," he agreed, his eyes bright. "They were utterly scandalized when I started to describe the kinds of clothing I wanted for my quest, but rose admirably to the occasion. Or at least, so I think."

"Yes," she said. "Very admirable."

The horse moved, whuffled, her gear clinking softly. Pali cleared her throat and checked all the fastenings she had already checked. Her sword was at her hip, her daggers in her sash. Her boots were not as nice as Fitzroy's. His looked as if the leather had been distressed deliberately, made to be butter-soft and supple.

"They usually find their challenge in variations on a theme—black, white, gold, Imperial yellow," Fitzroy said, falling into step beside her as she untied the horse and moved to rejoin Jullanar and Masseo, who had lifted their rucksacks onto their shoulders. "The idea being that it never looks as if I'm wearing the same thing twice, unless it's for some sort of formal requirement."

"But you do wear the same garments."

"I wear the same ... elements, yes." He smiled at her. "I'm finding the freedom of choosing—any colour! any cut! Anything I want at all! —*hair-raisingly* extravagant."

He waggled his eyebrows at her, and Pali laughed a little at his silliness, and then they had rejoined the others and were following Fitzroy's lead as he turned his head into the wind and followed the scent or taste or whatever it was of Voonra.

Pali had responded to the custom of wearing a scholar's robe with relief that she didn't need to bother with keeping up with fashions. She liked shoes, and was glad enough to acquire new ones from time to time (and it was a small regret that they had not, so far, visited a place with a shoemaker whose wares she liked enough to buy), but she was deeply glad to have her set rotation of a handful of garments to wear under the academic robes.

Wearing her own Warrior's robes, her sister's work and therefore fabric disinclined to collect dirt or sweat or wear—Pali did need to wash them, of course, but not nearly so often as one would expect—was a great joy. It was so good not to have to worry.

Fitzroy and Masseo spent the first stage of their travels talking about the annual stipend Fitzroy had instituted. Or rather, as Fitzroy was very keen to emphasize, his Lord Chancellor-cum-Viceroy.

Pali listened with interest for a few minutes, until she remembered she despised the Lord Chancellor and had sworn vengeance on him, at which point she turned to Jullanar.

"What are you thinking?" Jullanar asked, pausing to wipe her brow. "That was a steep climb ... Not that *you* noticed!"

Pali looked back down the hill they had just climbed, and shrugged, a little sheepishly. "I go rambling ... hill-walking ... around Stoneybridge, with my friend Elena. She's a keen rambler."

Jullanar brightened, in a way Pali did not at all understand. "Your friend, Elena! Tell me about her? Where is she from? Is she a Scholar as well? What do you do, on your rambles?"

"She's from central Lind, not far from Markfen. She's an historian, yes, at Sisterlen—that's one of the Stoneybridge colleges—her area is the reign of Dangora V." Pali considered the final question as she and Jullanar set off again. It was a wide landscape, here, treeless dales and piles of stone that looked like ruined bothies. The sky was a dark grey, louring, promising rain.

"I suppose we explored—there's a great network of footpaths and lanes, connecting the farms and villages and other schools to the town. Often we'd choose a pub we'd heard had good food or ale and go there for supper. I always like walking back in the twilight, and of course it's cooler. Chare can be quite hot in the summer. Elena's very keen on rambling. It was quite the thing to do."

Jullanar was regarding her with a sparkling amusement.

"What?" Pali asked defensively.

"That sounds so ... *relaxing*," Jullanar said. "It doesn't involve any stabbing at all?"

"Don't be absurd," Pali said, and tugged the mare, who had strayed to lip at the grass. Fitzroy, alas, was still talking about his bloody viceroy, gesturing enthusiastically and emphatically and being a real danger, actually, with how he was waving his staff around.

Jullanar bumped her shoulder against Pali's. "It's wonderful," she said sincerely. "I'm glad you have a friend like that. I found it hard, at first. We'd shared so much ..."

Pali nodded stiffly, but Jullanar kept talking about the friends she had made, especially the women of her embroidery circle and more stories about Basil and Sara, whom Pali did, indeed, like. Slowly Pali felt her stiffness recede, her hackles lower, and in return she told Jullanar the tale of Higgins Vane.

"There was *some* stabbing," she made sure to add to Jullanar, at one point. "I did practice."

"Well," Jullanar said after dutifully considering this, fighting valiantly not to laugh out loud, "I would hate for you to drop such a *useful* hobby."

～

Around noon, or what seemed to be noon in this sunless Borderland, they came to the edge of the vales.

Fitzroy's route had taken them through the network of valleys, some much narrower than others, and they had gradually started going up and down the sidewalls of the vales, zigzagging their way through an increasingly folded landscape. On their way up the last, steep valley, Jullanar had begged a rest; when they reached the top they discovered they had a choice to make.

Ahead of them was a deep, dark lake, long and narrow and filling the whole length of the valley facing them. They sat on a scattering of large flat stones on the ridge, eating some of the trail bread, dried apple slices, and hard cheese Pali had brought.

There was a ghostly white boat on the shore below them. It was about fifty feet straight down, so the could see it clearly. There were no sailors or people visible, and it was not tied to any mooring post. The sail hung in tatters, and did not shift in any of the breezes we could feel.

There was a time when they would have *immediately* chosen that boat.

There was a time when Pali would have been bitterly disappointed to have to turn back, to refuse that invitation, to leave uncovered that mystery.

Fitzroy would have wanted to write the songs—she made up titles in her mind—*The Ghost Ship* or *The Dark Lake and the White Ship* or *The Voyage with the Evil Fae* or *The Journey to the Kingdom of Shadows* or *Under the Blackwater*—

"You don't want to take that, do you?" Masseo asked.

Pali had to admit she didn't really want to go any of the places that ship was likely to sail.

While she quite liked ships, boats in general, in fact—much more so than anyone knowing her inland-desert origin would suspect—she didn't think that one would hold much in the way of grain or hay for her horse, and that was unacceptable.

"I'm sure it would take us somewhere interesting," Fitzroy answered, and then pointed up the ridge, which snaked towards a thickly wooded upland. "Nevertheless, Voonra is that way."

"Excellent," Jullanar declared, not hiding her relief. "I can't say I mind having a destination. Random adventures are all very well when you don't have any other goals."

Fitzroy regarded the ghostly boat, his expression fascinated, before he shook his head. "The world is full of invitations. We can leave that one for someone else."

And so they did.

~

Pali walked beside Masseo in companionable silence. Jullanar and Fitzroy were chatting about Jullanar's children, and Pali smiled to hear Jullanar so proud and pleased to tell stories of her son, who was off to university in the autumn, and her daughter, who was an aspiring novelist.

She had never wanted children, herself, but she knew Jullanar always had, and was glad for her friend that even with the less-than-ideal husband she had that joy.

Seek joy, the Siruyal had said to her, instructed her, laid upon her as that third quest.

Joy was not quite the right translation of dzēren. *Seek peace.*

There was joy, but not peace, in this moment. She could not want *peace*, not when there was this walk with her friends in the Borderland, the forest coming closer, adventure to be had.

It was a very thick forest. A wood perilous, full of the prospect of danger. She looked on it with some enthusiasm.

They stopped before they'd quite reached its interior, in the shrubby edge between meadow and forest proper. There was a stream, and a few rocky outcroppings, grazing for the horse, and shelter for them.

"Let's camp here," Jullanar said, with a glance at Fitzroy. "I'm getting tired. I'd rather leave that wood's adventures till after I've slept."

It was early, hardly mid afternoon, so they were leisurely about the process. Masseo found some deadwood logs, their bark already peeled off, and rolled them over to act as seats. Jullanar asked them for their food supplies and considered the miscellaneity of offerings with a pleased, intrigued, creative sort of smile. Fitzroy cleared an area for the fire, then fetched a circle of largish stones to delineate the fire pit while Pali brought over everyone's items from her packs and groomed her horse.

It didn't take them long to gather tinder and kindling, even small branches, and Masseo used a cunning folding saw he pulled out of his rucksack to cut some of the dead branches from the logs he'd brought over, but they would need more for a good blaze.

"I'll get water," Masseo offered, and took the canvas buckets back along the trail they'd already made.

"Pali and I can collect some wood," Fitzroy offered, smiling at her. "If you don't mind, that is."

"Of course not," Pali replied, and they made a few short forays along the edge of the forest to bring a goodly pile of wood to their site.

It was obvious that none of them had been much accustomed to camping of late, Pali mused, thinking about their careful articulation and offering of suggestions. She had been out-and-about the most, she reckoned, but she camped on her own, as a rule; and even she had been revelling in the money and respectability to stay in inns.

Fitzroy, obviously, hadn't been doing anything remotely resembling camping.

Pali looked at him as he wandered around peering at trees and shrubs, stopping to examine a flower or a leaf or an insect, and staring transfixed at a grey squirrel eating a pinecone for a solid three minutes.

He didn't seem to be bothered by getting debris on his clothes. She supposed that for him it literally didn't matter how expensive the materials were. There would always be more.

He looked down at her before she'd quite looked away, and smiled ruefully as he brushed at a smear of punky wood on his tunic. "Conju would be quite disappointed in me, I fear," he said, and then grinned. "Oh, it's good not to worry!"

Pali felt a certain degree of whiplash. "About your clothes?"

"It's wonderful to wear things that are *not* insanely delicate," he replied enthusiastically, bounding over to her. "Look at this, it's what? Wool?" He tugged at the hem, turning it up so she could see the fabric. "No silk, no lace, no gold embroidery, no jewels, no ahalo cloth, no plaques of gold ... It's so *practical*."

The whisper-soft wool was nicer cloth than Pali had ever possessed outside of the garments made by Arzu.

"Comparatively," she temporized.

"It's been a long time since I was in the same *category* to be compared to anyone," he murmured, bending for a stick she'd already rejected as being too damp. He added it to his armful, and she bit her tongue. "One more trip after this one, do you think?"

She nodded, and they walked back to the campsite, where Jullanar was making some kind of bread and Masseo had lit the fire.

"If you see any interestingly gnarled pieces," Masseo said, picking up a stick with a curious burl along its length, "would you bring them back for me? I'd like to try whittling them."

That was the sort of miniature quest Fitzroy adored—Pali did not articulate how much *she* liked being given such a task—and they made a bit of a competition over looking for interesting gnarls.

This took them further into the forest than they'd so far gone, but Pali could still see the light filtering through the edge trees, and she and Fitzroy stayed well within sight of each other. She watched Fitzroy investigating stumps and deadfall, half-forgetting to do much wood-gathering of her own as questions and half-finished thoughts buzzed in her mind.

What had he *done* as emperor, that he had not lost this?

She considered the idea that it was that burning diamond that had returned this to him, but she did not think that was true, not with what Masseo had said of their journey so far. Fitzroy was two weeks out of the Palace. He was tentative and hesitant about certain activities and behaviours that were, apparently, foreign to his experience there; but he was still Fitzroy, the quicksilver mind and great spirit unquenched by his learned serenity.

They came to the edge of a shallow ravine, and she said, "Perhaps we should turn back."

Fitzroy had slithered down already, and he looked up at her with a nearly pleading expression. "There are blackberries, Pali. Blackberries!"

The Borderland had its own seasons. If it were autumn here in this forest, when it had been something like late spring or early summer in the wide vales—well, that was nothing to be concerned over.

She followed him down, catching herself on the brushwood. Neither of them had brought a container, so she looked around for some makeshift alternative. There was a large birch tree further into the ravine, with its bark peeling off in wide strips, white on the outside, a tender fawn-pink in the interior. She pulled off a few pieces, awed by the delicate patterns of layers and hidden scars, and then spent a few minutes more practically fashioning two dishes by folding the bark about itself.

Fitzroy had a handful of berries, which he was eating singularly. He seemed so focused that Pali did not like to interrupt him, and instead filled her birchbark dishes with enough berries to share.

When she had finished Fitzroy was leaning against a stone, staring at his fingers. His expression was so blank Pali felt her fury at what had happened to him surge up.

"Come," she said briskly. "I've enough for us all to have for dessert. Let's get back to the camp."

His expression remained studiously neutral, but at least he was no longer frozen. He looked at the bank, and then grimaced, almost carefully. "I'm not sure I can climb that, to be honest."

It was steep, but not high, but Pali was holding the berries and she did not fancy trying to push Fitzroy up there. "Very well," she said, trying to keep her tone from being condescending. "Let us find an easier way. Unless you want to turn into a crow?"

"Can you carry all the berries if I do?"

She would have liked to say *yes*, merely to spite his expression, but the bank was too steep for her to clamber up without either hand. They cast around for a few minutes before finding what seemed to be a game-trail leading back up. It slanted back along the top of the ravine, winding between the thickets and trees growing there, and

Fitzroy took it with a pleased expression. Pali felt vaguely uneasy; there was a heavy, greasy feeling in the air.

She was walking with one of the greatest magic-workers in the Nine Worlds. She was Pali Avramapul of the Red Company. They would be fine.

She did not like how vague and distant Fitzroy's expression was.

"Shall we continue our debate?" she asked, determined to keep him focused and *present*. "I had a few questions—" Something flashed in his eyes, and she almost continued regardless before remembering he was not one of her students or colleagues. She attempted an apologetic smile, grimacing when he gave her one of those blank, polite, looks in return. "I'm sorry. I've been choosing all our topics. You should get the fun of setting the debate too!"

He was so quiet for a moment that Pali grew uneasily aware of how quiet their surroundings were. She looked up, to see the sky a bruised-grey: thunderstorm sky. It was darkest directly ahead, but she recognized the split tree ahead of them as where they had turned to enter the ravine. They could easily reach the camp before the storm broke.

"I must admit," Fitzroy said in a strange, calm voice, "that *fun* is not the word I would choose."

She half-laughed. "What do you mean?"

He stopped walking and gave her one of his intent, emperor's gazes. She swallowed back her immediate irritation, the way her gorge rose in frustration.

"Did you really think I found that ... fun?"

It was probably just as well she was holding the birchbark dishes, as she had to keep her hands still, her fingers relaxed. "What do you mean? Of course! You always liked sparring with me."

His voice was light, unemotional, precise. "I confess I found it rather more fun when it wasn't *my* ineptitudes and idiocies I was dissecting. Pali, how could you possibly think I was *enjoying* that?"

"You didn't say you weren't," she snapped back, wrong-footed and confused. "What did you think I was doing, then?"

"When *you* spent, oh, three hours meticulously analyzing every possible angle for why I didn't marry? What am I to think but that you're punishing me."

Her heart stuttered, and her words leapt out of her in defence. "*Punishing* you? Punishing you?"

"For the crime of being *caught*, I can only assume," he spat.

She was confused, and angry at his insinuations. "Why would I think that?"

"You certainly were not very happy with the last Emperor of Astandalas!"

"Are we back to talking of ourselves in the third person, then? What was I supposed to call you, again? Glorious and Illustrious One?"

His face was so blank she almost thought she must have imagined the flash of hurt.

Pali was getting a crick in her neck, but she refused to take a step back, give in even that inch. The dark clouds were heavier, blacker, pregnant with rain. The air tasted odd. That might have been Fitzroy's magic moving around him, though otherwise she could not feel it, nor see it.

He stared down at her, his whole body tense. His face was flat, his eyes opaque bronze. She met them fearlessly, furious that he could possibly think such a thing of her. "What do you want *me* to say, Fitzroy? If you don't tell me, how am I to know which topics are taboo? Glorious One."

He flinched, and then steadied, his eyes cold, his voice like bloodied steel.

"I don't get to make those choices, Pali. I don't get to decide what topics are *too personal*, taboo." His voice flicked into sarcasm, and he smiled at her, a cold and loathsome sort of pretence that made her blood surge. "Would you not ask Jullanar first before you spent three hours interrogating her about the social and historical context of her divorce? Would you not ask Masseo first before you spent four days dissecting his greatest failures? Would you not expect me to ask you before we went through your first year of teaching, dwelling particularly on your mistakes?"

Pali opened her mouth, but he shook his head.

"No, Pali. You see, when you are the head of state the assumption is that there is no privacy. No topic is taboo. If I refuse to speak about something, that is the act of a tyrant."

Her head was buzzing like a sandstorm rising, gathering strength, stinging before it swallowed you whole. Her stomach squeezed and twisted, cold at the back of her throat.

In a sandstorm you were careful where you took shelter, for a lee might form a dune before the winds fell.

They had been caught in sandstorms, when they crossed the Desert of Kaph on behest of the Wind Lords. They had had to shelter amongst the black bones of the dead dragons, horror in the wind and in their dreams, death all around them.

She remembered that Fitzroy's music and magic had sheltered them then, and she deliberately held to that memory, and forced herself to stop, let the sandstorm part around her, pass her by.

Theoretically, the best fight was the one you did not have.

Theoretically.

If ever she quested after dzēren—well.

She did not need to undertake the quest to know that she had misstepped and needed to remedy that. She took a deep breath and made an offer in the name of peace. "It's hard to see you so changed."

He laughed bitterly, and his lip curled. "No harder than it is to see you grown so rigid and heartless."

She was not expecting the blow, and it winded her.

For a moment she stared, and then she regrouped, for she was Pali Avramapul and she let no one get away with attacking her.

"I? Heartless? *Heartless?* You bloody hypocrite of an emperor—"

"I am Fitzroy Angursell," he growled.

She flung her words at him, *rigid* as a spear. "You're not acting much like it."

"I'm trying—"

"Try harder!" Her voice dropped, sharp and true, precise as a dagger in her hand. He would remember why her retribution was feared across the Nine Worlds. "I know you haven't lost yourself. I *know* you're Fitzroy. Own yourself!"

He flinched at the crackling echo of one of the famous lines of his own *Aurora*. Pali pressed harder, forward, into his space. She was Pali Avramapul, and she never gave up.

His face was impenetrable, but he stepped back. He stepped back.

The air was cold; the sky behind his head black and bruised.

"I do apologize for being human," he said, biting off the words. "I know it's not what you wanted."

She gave him the most magnificently rebuffing sneer she could muster. "What splendid presumption! You've *never* known what I wanted."

He took a breath, as if to shout—and she could not have that, she could not *bear* that.

She took another step towards him, making him lean back, since something was impeding his free movement. But his face, his face was so calm, so serene, so much the emperor's. She could not stand it, and cast around for words, sarcastic and sharp as they were.

"Do you even know what *you* want, besides clothes you're allowed to get dirty?"

He held himself still for a moment, rallying a rebuttal, and her heart prepared to leap, for there was Fitzroy, there he was, she could see him behind that mask, that façade—and then he sagged, and all the fight drained out of him.

"I want you to see me," he said, almost pathetically. He sat down on a rock behind him, and his voice softened even further. "I want you to see me."

Not wanted. *Want.*

She did not like the simultaneously hot and cold sensation washing through her. Her hands were tingling. She wondered if she were about to be sick, and swallowed hard. Once. Twice.

But she was not fourteen or eighteen or twenty-eight or even forty. She had a sharp temper and a caustic tongue, and she had always known how to make grown men weep. She had never known how to comfort them.

She sat down on a log facing his rock, and said nothing.

All the imperial serenity had fled. He looked tired. Ill. Almost old.

She had never imagined Fitzroy Angursell becoming *old*.

"What do you want to hear?" he asked flatly. "I am not a god, Pali. I am a human being. When they bound me ... I tried."

He stared at the ground. The air gusted even more coldly around them, and the sky was a horrible yellow-green above the trees. Pali eyed it uneasily. That did not betoken good weather. At least the path they had followed out was still visible, a sandy game trail to her side.

"I tried. I tried so hard. And it made no difference. Eventually I ... I gave up. Is that what you wanted to hear? I am not perfect, Pali, I am not divine, I am a human being and I. Gave. Up."

Pali would gladly stab an enemy when he was down.

A true *enemy*, not merely a worthy foe.

But Fitzroy was not even a worthy foe. He was a man she had loved and a god she had grieved and her—her second-best friend.

He was not her enemy. She could not stab him.

A few minutes ago she might have thrown the blackberries in his face.

"I was a river," he said after a terrible silence. "Dammed against my will into a lake. I could not break the confines of my dam, and so ... and so I reconciled myself to being a lake. Eventually I learned how to be still."

His voice went even flatter, not the resonant neutrality of the emperor but the exhausted tonelessness of the lost.

"If, now that you have taken exhaustive inventory of what's left of me beyond the emperor, you are displeased by what remains, you need not feel obliged to continue to condescend to associate with me."

She jerked back, and he made a grimace that might have been a cruel smile, had he a face that could have made such an expression.

They sat there in a wretched silence, looking in different directions at the storm coming towards them, the scent of the blackberries rising up around them like the miasma of a bruise.

CHAPTER TWENTY-SIX
EBB TIDE AND FLOOD

He was not the enemy, Pali reminded herself.

That guard, that bureaucrat, the whole fucking structure of Astandalas—she breathed in through her nose. The air smelled of distant lightning and blackberries. He was not the enemy.

He was her second-best-friend. Her whole being was roiled and she would have given a great deal to have a *true* enemy to fight. She dropped her hand into her pocket, but no. She would not use the feather for that. Nothing good could come out of such a wish.

The storm crackled behind the trees, thunder rumbling through the ground beneath her feet. Finally she said, "I don't want to never talk to you again."

It was true, though she couldn't, at the moment, think why.

Fitzroy was silent for a while. "No," he said at last. She took a shuddering breath.

His voice was very neutral. They had paused to catch their breath, but the duel was not over, the conflict unresolved. But at least —at least neither of them had proved coward enough to run away.

Jullanar's face came into her mind, and Pali latched gratefully onto that lifeline. "Jullanar would be very unhappy," she ventured.

"She would," Fitzroy agreed quickly.

"Now that she's in my life again, I can't lose her."

"Nor I," he agreed.

Pali nodded, and watched lightning flicker in the belly of the storm. It was heading off towards their right, no danger to them.

He glanced sidelong at her. "Not to mention the others would never forgive us."

Pali turned her head away, just in time to see the path slither into oblivion like the tail of a disappearing snake. She exclaimed and jumped up, scattering blackberries everywhere, but it was too late: the sandy track was gone.

It took Fitzroy a moment to realize what had occurred, and she had a wild hope that it had only disappeared to her sight, and would still be accessible to his magic.

One look at his increasingly baffled face suggested otherwise. She felt a trickle of concern, and then he ... smiled.

Her heart twisted. He smiled, and when he stopped smiling his face had settled into its neutral, emperor-incognito expression, polite and courteous and so far away from Fitzroy.

She could not deny that it was easier, this way. They could set aside their quarrel in face of the immediate ... situation.

"How peculiar," he said, his eyes gleaming as he searched the magic around them. "It's ... gone."

"What is?" Pali asked sharply, her hand falling to her sword, her stance immediately shifting to that ancient, automatic readiness.

Oh, would there be someone to fight, at last?

Someone who was not her—her friend—someone whom she could legitimately *hurt*?

(Pali did not like to think she was brutal, but there were times when the opportunity to skewer an enemy with her sword was all she yearned for in life.)

"The Border just washed right over us, like ... a tide," Fitzroy said, dropping his hand from where he'd lifted it. "We're back on ... I think it's Alinor ..."

"You think?"

Pali wished her tongue had not held that sharp, sarcastic note. Why did she keep doing this?

She was not *afraid*. When had she ever been afraid of adventure?

She turned around in a slow circle. The storm clouds were still moving off to their right, down the wide valley opening out of—she turned further—out of the mountains now rising behind them.

These were true mountains, craggy and snow-capped, not the steep forested hills of the Border country they'd been traversing. The whole landscape had opened up.

"This was never part of the empire," Fitzroy whispered.

Satisfied there were no immediate threats, Pali felt able to look at him. His face was—

"What is it?" she asked, heart jumping into her throat, for he looked almost *bewildered*.

"I know Alinor," he said, as a cool wind swirled around them, bringing with it the unmistakeable scent of woodsmoke. "Alinor knows *me*. But this ... is different. It's ..." He took several deep, careful breaths. "It's the difference between the lake and the river, Pali. This is the river."

Wild Alinor. The part no one ever saw.

"If you can't go forwards, go backwards," she said, the words coming out of their old adventures, something Faleron used to say, with an insouciant cheer that drove the rest of them wild with frustration.

Fitzroy gave her a look that suggested he remembered all the frustration, and none of the cheer.

He should have chimed in with the second half of the line. ("And if you can't go sideways, it's time for a fight.") She pursed her lips, and forced herself to keep to practical matters. "There's woodsmoke on the wind," she said, pointing upwind. "There are people nearby."

"Yes," he said, and a fierce curiosity seemed to kindle in his face even as she watched, and her heart ached, for *that* was what had been missing, wasn't it? Fitzroy's impossible curiosity, his relentless thirst to meet new people and learn their ways, his joy in discovery.

"Shall we?" Pali asked lightly, and at his nod shook out the skirts of her robes and strode into the wind, Fitzroy with his longer legs keeping pace easily beside her.

For a moment her heart stirred. For a moment.

∼

They descended from one valley into a much broader and warmer vale, where they found evidence of agriculture. Grazing cattle first, dun and spotted-roan, with short curved horns and bronze bells at their necks. They were grazing intently, their udders full, though there were few calves with them.

Dairy animals, then. Pali wondered if there would be cheese nearby. Chare had a wide range of cheeses, and Pali had quite enjoyed exploring them—Elena and she had sometimes made pubs with notable cheese trays the destinations for their rambles.

She was startled by the twinge she felt thinking about her life in Stoneybridge. She had not thought there was so much she would miss.

It was natural to miss what had been her life for the past decade, she assured herself. She had not been like Fitzroy, trapped in a golden cage. She had *chosen* the academy, and enjoyed it, soporific faculty meetings and all.

Oh, it was good to be walking beside Fitzroy in the open the air. Even if the air between them was strange and strained, tense with all the unresolved words—emotions, Pali admitted grudgingly to herself—

She stalked faster. Fitzroy had such long legs, his stride was steady and sure, metronymic.

He had paced that line into the stone floor of his study. Up and down, at this very pace, no doubt, he maintained it so easily. They were following a tongue of greensward that led through out of the pastures and into a half-wild orchard, all tangles of brambles and apple trees and other fruit trees Pali could not identify easily.

I do apologize for being merely human. She bit her lip. Those words had been so raw. Too raw. Surely her comments had not implied anything more than her great respect for him?

He was a brilliant man. He knew that. He had never been shy of acknowledging his own gifts, nor admitting to his occasional deficiencies. He had been aware that he was impetuous, reckless, over-bold; that his poetry could turn a little too sharp, that he could stab far harder than he sometimes intended.

That was so easy to do, Pali acknowledged. She didn't cut anyone deeper than intended with sword or dagger; she had spent hours upon hours of practice ensuring she had that control and skill, that awareness and that ability to stop the edge or the point exactly where she intended.

Words were not so easy.

Merely human.

The sandy path had led them to this valley, then disappeared like the tail of a snake when they had made up enough to plan their return.

They came out of the orchard suddenly, at a line of beehives made of coiled straw, and while they stood there, Pali shying away a little from the insects (even as Fitzroy regarded them with his serene dispassionate interest—with his *expression* of serene dispassionate interest)—they were seen.

A woman, tall and brawny, stood not far from the hives, a hammer in one hand, a handful of iron nails in the other. Pali considered the iron nails: this was no fairy woman, then.

Probably not an enemy to fight, either.

The woman turned and crossed the close-cropped grass in front of the hives to them. While she approached Pali took in the wider surroundings.

The orchard extended in a straggling line to either side. Ahead of them was a large complex of buildings made of stone and timber-framed plaster. It was an ancient design but the buildings themselves did not look particularly old.

Pali returned her attention to the woman, who had now stopped just outside of Pali's likely sword-reach. A step-lunge might take her, she mused, before shaking her thoughts away from the question.

The woman was solidly muscular, in a way that spoke of a lifetime of activity; she balanced in a way that made Pali think she might have begun her career as a horse-fighter. She was taller than Pali, as well as more thickly-set, and had a scar down her face, making the left side of her mouth droop.

Her expression, however, was friendly, even warm.

"Good afternoon," she said, with a glance up at the sky.

She had light brown skin, sun-burnished to bronze, with freckles over her nose, and wore her hair in many long braids, black threaded with white from her age, which was not far off Pali's. She wore trousers and a smock, the trews in green cloth, the smock in an orangey-yellow.

"We don't often get strangers from this direction." She looked at their clothes. "Are you very lost?—Do you speak Shaian?" She added a few words in another language, one Pali had never heard but which sounded, to her untutored ear, something like the place-names you might hear in Lind or Rondé.

Fitzroy gave her one of his sunny smiles, one of the ones that always made Pali think he was performing himself. "We do speak Shaian! I am surprised to find you do?"

"We were trapped this side of the mountains when the Border came down," the woman said, "but we are Astandalans still. But we welcome all who come in need and peace."

She looked at Pali's hand, still on the hilt of her sword, and Pali sighed in resignation and removed it. Of course there were no enemies here, either.

~

The woman, who introduced herself as Neri, led them into the compound, which turned out to house a complex assortment of buildings within its walls. "There were troubles in the past," she said laconically as they passed through a wide arched gateway, the doors thrown open, stout bars close to hand for when they needed to be barred shut. "We started as a small farm, my brother and I, but it's grown over the years as others needed shelter."

It was now almost a walled village. There was a blacksmith, and a cooper next to him, and someone with the various parts of a wagon or cart next to the barrel-maker. There were stables on the other side of the compound, and well-tended vegetable gardens on one half of the central area. The other half seemed to serve the needs of the tradespeople, with two wells and workshops half-contained indoors, half spread out on the cobbled surface.

"You've done this in ... how long has it been for you here?"

"About twenty years," Neri replied, waving at a pair of boys who had dashed past, laughing, with a puppy barking at their heels.

"Twenty years," Fitzroy murmured, and Pali, looking at his still face, remembered the rumours she had heard on Zunidh that it had been a thousand years since the Fall for the Palace folk.

A thousand years was long enough to wear a line into the floor. What would it do to your heart? Your spirit?

Neri led them to what seemed to be the main house, which rose up three storeys. The other buildings around the perimeter were mostly one or two, the regularity of the windows above the workshops suggesting that they held dormitories or homes for the craftspeople below. All in all, nearly a hundred people must live and work there, Pali assessed.

The enclosed, bustling, productive community reminded her of the ancient descriptions of the university fiefdoms of Alinor before the Conquest. Some of the rural universities—Morrowlea was famous for it—had maintained their near self-sufficiency, while others, like Stoneybridge, acted more as landlords and paid for their scholars and libraries through their rents.

"Have you a school here?" she asked.

Both Neri and Fitzroy regarded her curiously. Neri smiled crookedly. "Are you Alinorel, then?" She went on without waiting for an answer: "We teach the children the basics, yes, and there is a small college further down the valley. Tesura, it's called."

Pali had, out of curiosity, examined the ancient Charter of the Universities, which listed all the universities and colleges known to the Alinorel of Northwest Oriole at a time before the Conquest. Some hundred of those schools had fallen under the dominion of the empire before the end—Jullanar, Pali always remembered, had briefly attended one of the last to join—but there were a good dozen that had always remained outside the empire's borders.

"One of the Lost Schools, but not forgotten on the lists," she said therefore. "It was said, long ago, to specialize in agriculture."

"It still does," Neri acknowledged after a moment. "Its experimental breeding programmes have been ... very useful."

Fitzroy did not say anything. Pali glanced at him, to see he had gone back to his emperor face, shuttered closed, and she sighed inwardly before remembering that Tesura had been in Southwest Oriole according to the ancient Charter, and this was one of the last actively expanding borders of the Empire. Even Artorin Damara—even Fitzroy—had been unable to stop those wars before the end.

Neri took them inside the main building. She showed them to a washing-up area, apologizing perfunctorily for the lack of amenities, and told them to go into the main room, where there would be food presently and she and her brother would come to speak to them and see what they might be able to do.

The washing-up area had a basin with cold water and lye soap, harsh and sharp-smelling, and a pile of well-used but clean towels. There was a small indoor privy beyond, and they took turns with both.

"It'll be easier after we've eaten," Pali said encouragingly to Fitzroy when he had finished washing his hands and was looking somehow forlornly at the towels.

He gave her one of those cool, lucid, unemotional looks, and she recalled they were quarrelling.

They went out in silence, and found that there was a table set with a jug of water and several clean glasses beside a low fire. A large golden dog lay beside the fire, short-haired and long-limbed, the breath whistling through his nose as he dreamed.

Fitzroy smiled down at the dog as he sat down. Pali hesitated, then took the seat next to him, rather than one of those opposite. She wanted the wall behind her, that was all. It was silly to let down her guard when they were in such a strange and unknown place.

When they were younger, *before*, she might have nudged Fitzroy's knee with her own.

There were a few other people in the room, half a dozen young men and women who were sitting at a long table with trestle benches that was set underneath a set of square windows. They seemed to be studying, or planning something, for they had books and papers spread out all around them. Neri had gone over to them and was speaking quietly, bent over so her hair fell down like a waterfall.

"Perhaps when my hair grows out," Fitzroy said quietly, "I could braid it like that."

Now, Pali admittedly was remembering the younger Fitzroy and his experimental hairstyles when she looked at him with a doubtful eye.

He gave her a tiny smile. "I expect Conju could assist."

Perhaps he spoke a little too loudly, for the dog lifted its head a minute degree and thumped its tail twice.

"And who," she asked, "is Conju?"

The dog sighed and rolled over, gazing up at them with soulful eyes.

Fitzroy smiled down at the dog. "His name must sound like Conju. Does it, boy?" he asked, as the dog stood, stretched, and ambled over to put his head in Fitzroy's lap. Fitzroy looked startled, as if he had not expected any such thing, and lifted his hands away.

"Conju?" Pali asked, watching as the dog rolled its eye and then wagged more definitely. She took pity on Fitzroy's discomfort and patted her knee. The dog came over to sniff her hands and accept her stroking its ears.

"Oh—he's my—my chief groom of the chamber. My primary personal attendant."

"He wouldn't be used to doing your hair," she could not quite resist pointing out, then held her breath that *that* had been another unintentional blow.

But Fitzroy was smiling down at the dog, and seemed to take it as lightly as she'd meant it. "No, but he's very resourceful."

Neri came over, followed by a tall man somewhat younger than Pali and Fitzroy, with pleasant wrinkles around his eyes. He had a whiff of fire around him, she smelled as they greeted each other politely and Neri and her friend sat down. He was a big, muscular man, barrel-chested and strong of arm, his face dominated by a long, narrow nose and grey eyes, though his mid-brown skin and tightly zig-zagging hair showed a strong ethnic Shaian background.

"Oh dear," he said, grinning when he saw how the dog was halfway clambered onto Pali's lap. "I'm sorry—he's friendly, as you can see—Ju, down." The dog wagged its tail, but didn't move. The man's voice grew sterner. "Conju, *down*."

"The dog's name is Conju?" Fitzroy asked, his face lighting with amusement.

"Fitzroy," Pali murmured, before realizing that she should perhaps not have said his name.

Neri sighed. "Yes. Now—"

But the man had tilted his head, looking at first Fitzroy and then Pali with growing astonishment.

"Fitzroy *Angursell*?" he cried, and his face wavered between wonder and anger before settling on consternation.

"What is it?" Neri asked, alarmed, as the man's expression twisted. The dog turned, whining, to him, and pressed up against his leg. "We can hardly be arrested for harbouring criminals."

"It's not that," the man said, peering at Fitzroy through his fingers, then rubbing his hands down his face and working to achieve a kind of politeness. "I'm sorry," he said abruptly. "I would offer the hospitality of our house—I *do* offer—but—no. I must ask you. *How could you be a wild mage—inside—inside—the empire?*"

His voice came out quiet and desolate, as if this were a question that had eaten away at him.

Pali stole a glance at Fitzroy, who had taken a breath, made a familiar hitch in his shoulders, just the way he did when he was about to spin an extravagant and not entirely counterfactual yarn—when he looked down at the dog and back up at the man, his posture settling to his emperor-neutrality, as he seemed to be thinking through something.

Then something seemed to fall into place, and Fitzroy said, compassion in his voice: "Are you, by any chance, Terec of Lund?"

CHAPTER TWENTY-SEVEN
RETRENCHMENT

The man—Terec, quite obviously—stiffened dramatically. Neri put her hand on his shoulder and held it tightly, obviously offering comfort.

"How—who *are* you?" Terec whispered. "How could you possibly know that?"

Fitzroy hesitated, and then he said, "I am Fitzroy Angursell. You were described to me, not long ago." He looked the man up and down, and his voice was almost gentle. "Tall, I was told, and broad-shouldered, with a long nose. Aghrib was a nickname, if I recall. An affinity to fire. And ... wild magic."

Terec breathed in deeply, shuddering with the effort of self-control. Pali watched him, unafraid of his magic, wary of Neri's shift towards a more vigilant, defensive stance.

"Who," he said flatly.

Fitzroy looked down at the dog, and his smile was kind. "The Cavalier Conju enazo Argellian an Vilius."

His voice was court-formal, court-accented, and his expression was courteous: the emperor incognito.

Neri sucked in her breath, as if Fitzroy had planted his fist in her stomach, and her free hand came up to her mouth. She bit hard on the knuckle, and blinked back bright tears.

"Oh god," Terec said, his accent picking up Fitzroy's. Pali wasn't in practice—nor had she ever been very good at them—but she knew their host's was shifting to upperclass Astandalan. "He remembered me ..."

Neri sat down hard in the remaining open seat, her expression as flatly shocked. "Of course he did," she said, her voice sounding as if she had said similar things many times. "Of course he did."

Fitzroy hesitated a moment, and then he said, even more gently, "He *does*. Conju is still alive, Terec. Neri ..." He paused while Terec sat there stock-still and Neri produced a series of near-silent gulps. "Can it be that you are *Nerisse* an Vilius? Captain an Vilius of the Seventeenth Horse?"

They had been caught on this side of the border in the Fall, Pali realized slowly, and thought that Conju had died with Astandalas.

"How?" Terec said blankly. "He was supposed to be home, Neri said. She was supposed to be home, too, but her unit was in the rear and got caught by a snowfall before they could cross the pass back into the empire. She was hoping she wouldn't miss all of them—"

And instead she had lived, and none of them. Pali knew the pattern all too well.

"He stayed late in Astandalas for a particularly important party," Fitzroy replied, "but did not attend in fact, being ill if I recall correctly, and was therefore in the Palace during the Fall. Those inside the Palace proper," he added, "survived."

"We heard that nothing survived on Ysthar," Neri said, her face set and pale, her eyes glittering. "How could—"

"It is a great mystery to everyone. The Palace, for reasons beyond understanding, ended up in Solaara on Zunidh, which is where it has stayed. Those who were within it did their best to build new lives."

"And you were one of them?" Terec asked, his voice hard-edged. "You, Fitzroy Angursell? You disappeared—oh! Before Artorin Damara came to the throne."

Fitzroy met his eyes and then spoke very deliberately. "Fitzroy Angursell disappeared *because* Artorin Damara came to the throne."

Pali glanced sharply at him, wondering if he were going to tell these random people the full and honest truth.

But then—

She stopped. She had told Elena, hadn't she? And Jullanar had told Basil and Sara. Why did she immediately feel that Fitzroy's truth was not his to give?

(Why did she want to be one of the few who knew it?)

And Conju, he had just told her, *his* Conju, was his chief personal attendant. They must have a caring relationship, at the very least, if Conju had told him stories of his lost family.

Pali sat there silently, arms loose and unthreatening, as Fitzroy regarded Terec with a kindness and compassion she did not, at first, understand in the least.

"The easy answer to your question," he said, "is that I had, and indeed still have, a unique relationship to the magic of Astandalas."

That was the sort of staggering claim he used to broadcast extravagantly, enthusiastically, with a wink in his eye and a laugh in his voice, his mouth curving suggestively, so that for a moment, just for a moment, you *believed* him, before the absurdity of the claim crashed down upon you and you could only laugh.

But—Pali had been with him when he seduced the Moon.

Masseo had watched him lift a curse that had persisted for ninety-nine generations in one glorious sweep of magic.

All three of them had witnessed him burning those diamonds into himself and opening some door that had been locked for most of his life.

She looked around the room. The dog had his head in Terec's lap, so the man could bury his hands in its soft fur and take some comfort there. The table of youths were laughing and talking, discussing whatever they were discussing. Neri was sitting there her knuckle still caught between her teeth, her face caught between doubt and hope.

"Conju is very dear to me," Fitzroy said, plainly, "and I owe it to him, if not to you, to tell you the full truth." He nodded, once, and straightened into his full emperor posture. Both Neri and Terec responded unconsciously, turning to him, their own bodies picking up the cues, so they looked the members of the Upper Ten Thousand of Astandalas they presumably were.

"My relation to the magic of Astandalas was, and is, unique, because shortly after I was born, I was assigned the position of Marwn."

"The second heir?" Neri asked doubtfully, a vague curiosity coming into her eyes.

Fitzroy inclined his head. "So it was called, when it was mentioned publicly, which it was very rarely. Very few people knew more than the barest idea, that there was a back-up heir, not ... quite in the usual line of succession. A *magical* heir."

Terec frowned. "What has that to do with you?"

"I was the Marwn. My name was taken and bound into the magic of Astandalas, set as one of its fundamental anchors. My blood was taken and spilled on the heart-stone of the Palace of Stars, to bind me and my life in service. I was raised in exile, sent into exile, supposed to live my life in exile."

He glanced at Pali, and he smiled crookedly, almost Fitzroy. Almost.

"I was as surprised as anyone to be violently summoned to Astandalas to be crowned emperor."

"I don't understand," Terec said. "You're—you said you're Fitzroy Angursell."

"I am."

"And you're also—Artorin Damara?"

"I am."

"I don't believe you," Neri said furiously. "How can you be *both*? The rebel, the renegade, the *criminal*, and also—the emperor?"

Pali sympathized. Fitzroy took a breath. "I understand your

anger," he said, and in his cool, quiet voice Pali heard the echo of the grief and fury that must have broken his heart.

(*I gave up!* he had cried, finally, when she had goaded him enough. *Is that what you wanted to hear? I am not perfect, Pali, I am not divine, I am a human being and I. Gave. Up.*)

"I was sent into exile, in a tower at the far edge of Colhélhé. A wizard's tower, full of mysterious and recondite books." He glanced at Terec. "They would have been nothing more than a scholarly pastime had I not had wild magic of my own. I did not know it then; no one knew it. But I studied, and one day I sought to put my studies into practice, and I ... could."

"What was your first magic?" Terec asked, subdued.

"I moved the majority of my enchantments to a necklace that was in the tower."

His words were simple, his voice calm. Yet Terec looked up, his eyes anguished, and met the golden eyes.

"I couldn't stay," the man whispered. "I wanted to. Oh, I wanted to."

"I know," Fitzroy answered.

"The magic wouldn't rest ... it wouldn't be *bound* under the Pax."

"I was the Marwn," Fitzroy said again, and his voice was still gentle. "My name and my blood had been bound into the very structure of the empire. I could work wild magic within its bounds, under the Pax, because at a fundamental level I *was* the empire."

Fitzroy Angursell, who had fought so hard to break it, to puncture its bloated and decadent corruption.

Artorin Damara, who had tried (Pali knew he had tried) to work with what he had inherited, to reform and reconfigure, stave off that same corruption.

Terec frowned as he worked through this.

Fitzroy let him think, let Neri consider, let Pali look at them and then at his face, still and emotionless, save for the darkness in his eyes. But not very many people met a great mage's eyes, even without the threat of blinding that had rested upon the emperor.

"I could not evade the summons," Fitzroy said, and she knew he was speaking to her as well as to these two strangers who were some kin to his attendant whom he cared for (loved, a small voice said, surely he had allowed himself to love?). "I was bound by my name and my blood to the empire. When the Ouranatha invoked the ancient magics I was ... caught."

He moved, very deliberately, to clasp his hands together on the table. Otherwise he was very still, sitting upright on the simple wooden chair.

"I was caught, and with my name and my blood they bound me to the throne of Astandalas. I was obliged to make many solemn vows I would not have chosen, perhaps, in other circumstances." He looked seriously at Neri, but once again Pali was certain his words were also for her ears. "I do not care to be forsworn, Captain an Vilius. I did not then, and I do not now. I swore to do my best for my people, and my best did I do."

"You said you had no choice," she managed, though Pali knew what it felt like to be skewered by Fitzroy full of magic.

"I could have told them the truth, and been executed or confined as a madman, or committed suicide myself," he said evenly, and he turned his brilliant eyes once more onto Terec. "I was bound, Terec, by the entire weight and might of the Empire. I was the *centre* of the Pax. No longer the anchor of the working, invisible and unknown, but instead the full flower and glory of the magic. I could not *touch* my magic as the emperor. I could not *feel* it, save for the terrible knowledge of its lack."

Pali breathed in shallowly as she took those words in.

"Not at all?" Terec asked, and the anguished empathy in his voice was like a hand on her throat, pressing down upon her windpipe.

"Not at all," Fitzroy confirmed, and the way he was sitting, the stillness and the brittle, brilliant calm, was impossible to disbelieve.

"How did you live?" Terec whispered.

Fitzroy was silent for a long moment, looking down at his hands clasped together on the table. Pali could not help but think of all the descriptions of the last emperor, the golden emperor (so often he was described that way, as a shining, distant, golden figure upon the throne, a star come to rest, to illuminate their lives; the imperial propagandists, she had thought, working hard), sitting still and serene upon his throne, solid, secure, unmoving.

Fitzroy Angursell, quicksilver in his emotions, his words, his face, his body.

(*I was a river, dammed against my will into a lake*, he had said to her. *I had to learn how to be* still.)

"I fulfilled the duties laid before me, as honourably as I could."

There were poems Fitzroy had written about the joys and responsibilities of the artist to his art. He had questioned—Pali remembered the conversations when they had discussed this—what sacrifices were acceptable.

When he was younger, he had thought any personal sacrifice worth it.

Pali remembered arguing that the art came first, that one should follow one's vocation, that one should love one's art with all one's self; and she remembered Sardeet looking at her and saying, quietly, one evening, that she thought art was not worth losing one's humanity over.

Power had never been in their discussions. They had not deigned to consider it.

She had wondered, studying Artorin Damara, at the cipher that was his background. Where had he learned mercy, she had wondered; where had he learned justice?

She had not thought that it was power, and stillness, and solitude that he had had to learn.

Terec said, "And now? After the ... the collapse?"

"The Fall, people call it," Fitzroy said, and he took a breath. "After the Fall I was ... eventually ... able to reclaim my magic."

Terec gave him a sharp glance, his brow furrowed. Pali wondered what he was thinking, but he didn't say any more about magic. Instead he said, "And—and—and Conju?"

Fitzroy relaxed immediately, though he did not shift position: he smiled, and the brittleness was replaced by a warmth, as if all his muscles were suddenly loose, no longer clenched. "Conju is the head of my personal household, the chief groom of the chamber," he said.

Terec smiled, but Neri had crossed her arms, her back ramrod straight, her jaw set. "And how do we know you're telling the truth? You might have ... plucked this out of our minds, for all I know."

"That has never been a skill of mine," Fitzroy murmured, seemingly unoffended by her suspicion and doubt.

Pali wondered at his equanimity. Was it real, or feigned? And if real ...

How hard had it been, for a river to learn to be a lake?

He had been unable to touch his magic all the time he was emperor, he'd said. That had never been an idea she had entertained, not even once, since she had learned that Artorin Damara had survived the Fall and revealed, in its aftermath, an unexpected gift at magic.

And if he *were* Aurelius Magnus—

She stopped, as thoughts of *Aurelius* led her to the *Aurelian Code*, and she recalled, as if from a dream, that one of the forms of torture the ancient emperor had decried was *Preventing a mage from accessing his magic*.

Aurelius Magnus had declared that unlawful. *Torture*.

There was a tingling as of magic, and a change in the light. Pali refocused on her surroundings to see that Fitzroy had tilted his head and made a gesture or two.

Did he need to make gestures? His skill and finesse with magic were so much greater than they had been, she hardly knew how to think of his work. She had admired him when they were young, thought him a fine and flashy mage then, but the casual mastery of his magic now was of an entirely different order.

The dust motes hanging in the air gathered together, sparkling, as a glowing shape coalesced out of nothing and began to shimmer into visibility.

A man, his skin the same bronze as Neri, his features sharing elements of her jaw, her eyes. He was perhaps in his fifties, slim, very well-dressed in the kind of clothes Pali had seen in Solaara: white tunic, gold-embroidered-green over-robe. He had the sleeves folded back, and in his hand held a crystal phial.

His eyes were bright, alert; he had a small smile at the corner of his mouth, a sly, amused cast to his expression. His whole posture was one of attentive interest, with the clear suggestion he was about to tell the onlooker something delightful and possibly slightly scandalous.

Pali looked hard at the illusory man, committing his features to memory, holding to Fitzroy's view of him, for he would surely become part of her life, this man whom Fitzroy held dear enough to tell two perfect strangers the deep secrets he had not yet been able to share with his own friends.

A gulped-back sob made her turn, to see that Terec was staring, face as grey as it had been when Fitzroy first asked him if he was Terec of Lund, and Neri had tears running down her face even as her hand came up in longing.

Fitzroy held the image without any apparent strain until Neri finally said, her voice thick, "You couldn't have taken that out of my mind."

"No," he said, quietly, and he and Pali sat there while the two wept.

~

Fitzroy spent the afternoon talking quietly with Terec about wild magic, and then, when Terec left, his face dazed and his eyes full of a strange relief, he focused his attention on a button he took off his coat.

Pali, for her part, spent a few minutes speaking with Neri. The woman brought her a spicy herbal tea, full of flowers Pali could not name, and after a few minutes spent sitting silently together, she said, "Do you know Conju?"

"I'm sorry," Pali replied, sorry indeed at the disappointment that passed over Neri's face. "I don't know Fitzroy from the Palace."

Neri looked at her again, and her eyes went wide as she took in Pali's robes and sword. "You're Pali Avramapul?"

"I am."

"I suppose you wouldn't have much to do with the imperial court, then."

"Not appreciably, no," Pali agreed dryly, glad Neri laughed in response. "Are you and Terec Conju's ... siblings?"

"He was—*is*—" Pali waited while that realization washed over Neri again; it was several moments before she swallowed and could continue. "Conju is my older brother. There were five of us. Terec was our neighbour, our mothers were best friends, we grew up with him and his siblings. He and Conju were best friends ... more than best friends. They were to be married, before Terec had to ... leave."

Pali hummed a sympathetic noise, not sure what she could say to that. It was too much like dealing with a homesick student, who would cry all over her. Pali only ever sat there humming sympathetically at them before offering a handkerchief, a cup of warm water, and the suggestion they go for a walk.

Somehow she was reckoned a comforting person to weep over. It was mystifying, really.

Neri had brought her own warm drink, and probably spent enough time outside, and Pali did not have more than one spare handkerchief with her. She hesitated over offering it up, but Neri produced one of her own to sniffle into.

"Terec and I call each other brother-and-sister," she went on, "in-laws, I guess, because ... we both lost everyone, we *thought* we'd lost everyone, and when we ran into each other after the Fall it was such a relief to see a familiar face."

Pali knew that quiet, raw grief. She had felt it for the loss of the Red Company, for the disappearance of Fitzroy into the Sea of Stars

—and she had seen it in her colleagues' and students' faces on Alinor, whenever the Fall was obliquely mentioned.

It was very rarely mentioned directly.

She was suddenly intensely grateful she had not asked Fitzroy what the Fall had been like for him.

"He's not what I expected," Neri said after a long silence.

"He is full of surprises," replied Pali, who did not need to see where Neri was looking to know where her thoughts had gone.

It was excruciating that she could never turn her thoughts from him for long, herself.

She made herself smile at Neri. "Could you show me around your place?" she asked. "I am curious about the life you've made here."

Neri flushed, for what reason Pali did not quite understand, so her cheeks went rosy and her freckles seemed to stand out across her nose, but she stood readily and led Pali outside, away from the building-thunderstorm of Fitzroy Angursell working magic.

CHAPTER TWENTY-EIGHT
THE BUTTON

The farm—so Neri called it, for all it was more of a village—was the result of two decades of hard work building a community and a refuge out of the magical and physical storms that had battered the region after the Fall.

"This land was never even *part* of the empire," Neri said, a little bitterly, as they stood looking at the well-weeded and bountiful vegetable garden.

There were delphiniums flowering at the back of the plots, taller than Pali and bluer than the sky. She was reminded of Elena and frowned at the prickle in her eyes.

"No," Pali agreed, recalling Fitzroy's comments as they came down the valley and scowling even more fiercely at the thought of him.

"We still felt the effects of the destruction," Neri went on, and then she smiled bracingly at Pali. "But we survived, Terec and I, and we have built a good thing here."

"Yes," Pali agreed, watching the insects work a patch of some sort of lacy white flower. Queen's lace, she thought it might be, or wild carrot. Perhaps they were the same plant. They were popular with the bugs, at any rate. There were orange and yellow pot marigolds under the delphiniums, and those were full of bees.

"I don't know what to do, knowing Conju is alive."

Pali thought back to Fitzroy hailing the post-rider as he came past the refuge in the pass between Chare and Fiellan, and though she rolled her eyes at herself for him being, once again, the answer, at least she had an answer. "You might write him a letter," she suggested. "Fitzroy is keeping in touch with his ... people, there. He'll ensure it reaches your brother."

Neri smiled suddenly, bashfully. "I would have thought of that eventually. May I—would you mind if I left you so I can write—you'll stay the night, I hope? Before you return to your journey?"

"I expect so, thank you," Pali replied, wondering how often the path was open. Some pathways between worlds only ever went one direction.

But then again—and she ground her teeth together, but it was true—

But then again, it was rare one travelled with not only a great mage, but a great mage who was the lord magus of a world.

She wrinkled her nose. And perhaps Aurelius Magnus, she mustn't forget about that.

∼

Pali found the stables, and spent most of the afternoon speaking to those who worked there, helping to muck out a few of the stalls, groom a few of the horses. She learned that Terec and Neri had indeed built the farm as a refuge, gathering in orphaned children and other lost souls, and had taught them everything they could.

One of the grooms was an older woman, older then Pali by several decades, and she remembered the Fall.

"You used to be able to see the Wall, that's what we called it," she said, in heavily accented Shaian. She was a local woman, she added, her son a professor down at the college in Tesura, and she had come to help the foreigners when they needed it, after her husband had passed on.

"A great golden curtain, it was. People said if you walked up to it it felt like glass, but I never went so near. Made my teeth ache, the feel of it."

Pali nodded and made her sympathetic humming noise, remembering her first sight of the magical border of the empire from the outside. She had been travelling with Damian and Fitzroy—

She returned her thoughts to the old groom.

"The day it fell, oh, it was the most awful noise you can imagine, like the air was screaming." She shuddered expressively. "It went on and on, and the Wall went a terrible colour, like a bruise, like the sky was bruised. We all took shelter, or most of us did, I went out with some of the folks from the town to see what happened."

Pali had been inside the walls of Arkthorpe when the Fall came, curled up in a blanket beside her sitting room fire because she had something of a cold. The Fall had felt like a spear shattering in her hand, and she had sat there, heart thundering, book fallen to the floor, dagger in hand, until the aftershocks ceased.

"The sky crumpled," the old groom said, and stared meditatively off in the direction of where a pass seemed to cut between two high mountains. "We couldn't see those mountains, yonder, before. Still can't get through, not easily, there's a forest where the mist comes up and you get well turned around."

"The Borderwood," Pali murmured.

"From the stories the stranger-folk told us, you'd know."

They were Fitzroy's stories, of course. Pali forced a smile and took her leave. She returned to the washroom, and took the opportunity to wash herself more thoroughly than earlier.

When she came out, Neri was hovering in the yard. She asked if Pali had everything she needed or wanted, her tone anxious. Pali agreed, amused by her unexpected shift to deference.

"As I was writing my letter to Conju," Neri said, "I realized you were Pali Avramapul. Or—what it meant. You were always my favourite of the Red Company," she explained shyly. "I was a cavalry officer, you see ... and you were always said to be such a great horsewoman and fighter. It was an inspiration to me."

"Even though I was on the wrong side of the law?"

Neri shrugged. "I suppose that should have mattered more to me, but I wasn't very high in the chain of command, and ... the stories were so *grand*. And of course, we thought it was all over and done with, when I was in the army. You were ... legends. Folk heroes. People in songs."

"Fitzroy," Pali said evenly, for what else could she say? "is a great poet."

She held on to that *is*, for all that she had seen no evidence that he *was* still writing poetry, bar that book of anonymous poems that broke her heart even to recall reading. She hadn't dared to ask him if he'd written them, not yet, not after she'd read that first one after meeting him in the Palace.

Neri laughed suddenly, wiping her eyes of tears that had sprung up. "Oh, as I was writing I was reminded how ... Conju *loathed* his poetry, Terec too. Terec because—well, as you heard, because he never quite forgave Fitzroy Angursell for being a wild mage inside the empire."

Pali was curious, that was all. "And your brother?"

"Conju thought it untidy. Unruly. Sometimes bloated. And far too clever by half. He used to sniff and say that he was sure it was all very well and good, but it had been banned for a reason, and anyone that full of himself—" She had started to laugh, and spluttered through the rest of her sentence, but Pali didn't care, for she was hugging to herself the idea that someone actually disliked Fitzroy's poetry for all the right reasons.

And for it to be his—the Lord Emperor's—chief attendant, the head of his domestic household—oh, what a gift!

She did not enquire too closely of herself why she was so delighted by the idea.

~

Supper was full of dishes not too dissimilar to those of Chare with which Pali was familiar, though there was a much larger emphasis on legumes than she was accustomed to, and an unfamiliar combination of herbs—dill and oregano, was it?—all served with great crusty loaves of bread and an array of delicious fresh and aged cheeses. Terec and Neri told her and Fitzroy more about their lives since the Fall, and Fitzroy told them stories about Conju.

Pali listened, and wondered if he knew that Conju disliked his poetry. It—well—it *could* have come up, presumably.

After the meal, Fitzroy presented them with the button he'd been studying all afternoon. Terec regarded it with a wary eye. "You've laid magic on that."

"I have."

It was a beautiful button, Pali considered: an inch or so across, made of jet carved with a many-pointed star inlaid with electrum. She would have been well pleased to discover it on the side of the road.

After a silence, Fitzroy said, "This is one of my buttons." He gestured at his coat, and the toggle at the bottom that no longer had a mate. "It was made on Zunidh, for the Lord of Zunidh, chosen and handled by Conju—he is not my costumier but I do recall a conversation we had about this particular design." He tapped the button with his right index finger. The electrum gleamed and glittered, not quite naturally. "I have made it a kind of ... talisman, or ... perhaps compass is the better word. It will not guide you north, but to Conju."

Terec and Neri both looked at the button, glittering and winking on the table between them.

"And he's really alive?" Terec asked, voice subdued with resurgent doubt.

If someone had told her that Fitzroy was alive, that they'd seen him, Pali would have doubted, too.

Oh gods, how she would have doubted.

"As of two weeks ago, when I left the Palace," Fitzroy said, smiling at them with a sudden brilliance, and went on with directions for how to use the button, why he had only made them one, cautions and warnings in the ways of a great and wise mage laying a quest upon another.

Pali's thoughts had seized upon *two weeks ago, when I left the Palace*, and would not move on.

Two weeks.

Two weeks ago Fitzroy had been living in that austere, luminous room, the state portrait of his imperial self on one wall, the map of his fallen Empire and the half of their travels upon the other, a jewel-bedecked nightingale in a golden cage opposite.

Two weeks ago he had still been pacing that shadowed line into the floor.

Two weeks ago he had been under the weight of those taboos, of food and touch, of custom and habit.

Two weeks ago he had still been waited on hand and foot, in the most luxurious of all possible lives.

Two weeks ago he had still been imprisoned.

Pali might have dropped her head against the table if she'd been alone, but she wasn't, and so she smiled and watched and pretended to listen to the memories Terec and Neri shared of the Cavalier Conju an Vilius, whom Fitzroy had miraculously restored to them.

∼

All the farm's guest-rooms bar one were being used, as it was somehow both planting season and harvest.

"We've got the hayloft as well," Terec said awkwardly.

"Or the floor," Neri muttered almost inaudibly. "With Conju."

Fitzroy managed to disguise any impolite response, but Pali could see that their hosts were inclined to offering him the room. Emperor or no, that was beyond irritating.

"We'd prefer a bed," she said firmly, with her best attempt at a ravishing smile. "Wouldn't you agree?"

She meant it as a jab at Fitzroy, but Neri and Terec both fell over themselves apologizing for misconstruing the situation, Neri with a fierce, inexplicable blush, and so in short order she and Fitzroy found themselves in a clean, pleasant room. With one bed.

"I hope this will suit?" Terec said, offering them a jug of water.

"Admirably, I'm sure," Fitzroy said, with one of *his* best smiles.

"Good. Good night, then," Terec said, and backed out, leaving Pali and Fitzroy to turn their best smiles at each other.

"You should have the bed," Fitzroy said, too swiftly for Pali's liking.

"I'm sure I couldn't ask your Radiancy to condescend so far as the *floor*," Pali returned.

They stared at each other. Fitzroy had magic in his eyes, but Pali was by far the more stubborn. She wouldn't let watering eyes or a quickly developing headache make her lose. She gritted her teeth and kept her smile as blinding as her headache.

He folded first, and looked at the bed. "We could share."

"We could," she agreed. She walked over to the bed and pulled off the blankets, which she set in the corner opposite the door, where there was least chance of a draught.

He gave her a narrow-eyed frown and then took the sheets and made himself a bed on the other side of the room.

They both ignored the other's attempts to get comfortable. She had the blankets: he had an affinity to fire. And the pillow.

∼

In the morning Pali woke from an unsurprisingly fitful sleep with the earliest rooster-crow, and rose gratefully. She felt stiff and sore and stupid, and blamed Fitzroy's imperial intransigence. He was pretending to still be asleep, and she scowled at his back before tiptoeing downstairs to perform her ablutions.

There was a cold meal laid out in the hall, and she gathered a boiled egg and some bread and butter for her breakfast.

Fitzroy came in, the hems of his sleeves damp from washing, and sat down a seat away from her.

"The tide has turned," he said cryptically.

Pali grunted, wishing for coffee or black tea and making do with mint, and eventually realized he meant the ebbing Border had surged back over them in the night, and that the path should now be accessible.

They took their leave, and Fitzroy their letters, and promised—Fitzroy promised—that when Terec and Neri were ready to find Conju, they would no doubt meet again.

Pali took that thought with her and added it to the rest of the questions she did not think she dared ask.

She did not want to know what he intended for the future, what image he had for what could come after his quest was completed, his reign definitively ended. What did he expect his household to *do*?

What place, she dared not ask, did he imagine for the Red Company?

~

They walked beside each other out of the farm, back up the valley. Equals, perhaps. At least in irritation.

Pali asked him only one question: "Why," she said, "did you not leave after the Fall?"

He gave her a cool, unemotional glance, every inch the emperor; his accent was once again pure court. "When one is moved from torture to house arrest, it is easy to miss, at first, that one is still imprisoned."

The day before she would have taken that as hyperbole.

He had paced a shadow into the floor of his cell.

"It was easy, at first," he said, brittle as new ice. "The dam opened, and the water rushed out in a great torrent. No need to think how to be a river, when one is a flood."

Pali glanced at him, concentrating on holding her tongue.

"I hadn't realized I would be so hard to find the old course again," he added. "I appreciate you being so clear on the matter. Your assiduousness is ... noted."

They walked the rest of the way back up the valley in silence.

~

The sandy path had slithered back into visibility, and Pali—well. She had not doubted Fitzroy's magical prowess. It was almost impossible to doubt, now. He was too obviously brilliant, too obviously powerful, too obviously *skilled*.

But she was relieved, nonetheless, that the path was there.

On the other side of the wooded copse was the ravine where they'd found the blackberries. Her broken birchbark dishes, stained purple and black, lay where they'd dropped them in their anger.

From there Pali could take the lead, guiding them back past rock formation and lightning-blasted tree to the glade where they'd left Masseo and Jullanar.

The old rule was to stay where the camp was, if it was safe, for three days. If after three days the missing party—Fitzroy, usually, but not always—had not returned, their custom was to leave a trail-sign and regroup to the nearest safehouse.

The safehouse for three weeks.

They had talked about a rule for longer waits, but a safehouse safe enough for three weeks was probably safe enough for longer, and —and they had never needed it, except the once.

The last, bitterest disappearance. Fitzroy had waited in the central, obvious place, his image on every new coin, for a rendezvous and rescue that had never come.

They reached the encampment midmorning, as best Pali could judge in the sunless light of the Borderwood. Jullanar and Masseo were sitting on piles of cushions of such unbelievable luxuriousness Pali could only imagine they had come out of Fitzroy's new bag. Whoever had prepared the Last Emperor's travelling supplies—and Pali did not think it could possibly have been Fitzroy *alone*; he would not have had the opportunity to acquire the supplies himself—had clearly felt it incumbent upon himself to ensure quality was unstinting.

Perhaps it had been *Conju*, Pali thought, as Jullanar and Masseo looked up and welcomed them back with glad cries. She smiled, hoping it was not obvious that her jaw was stiff and tight with stress.

She let Fitzroy describe how they'd been lost track of their surroundings and followed a path out into Alinor, and explain with pride and pleasure how he'd found the lost family of one of his household.

She added in comments from time to time—she did not want to be *churlish*—and wished she were as good at Fitzroy was at putting on a good front. *He* didn't seem in the least troubled. He was speaking fluently, fluidly, and his gestures were coming back.

Jullanar had made some sort of grill-bread on the fire, and they ate a simple midday meal of the unleavened bread and jam and cheese. Fitzroy was very slow about eating his food. Pali could not tell whether he disliked it or was, conversely, savouring it.

They did not have much in the way of dishes, so Pali took the handful of plates and knives to the stream to wash rather than going to all the bother of fetching and heating water. She knelt on the bank, looking at the bright water chattering over pebbles that shone like semi-precious stones under the surface. There were small fish, darting like shadows between her hands, and what seemed like a hundred different kinds of dragonfly darting around her.

When she came back to the campsite, Fitzroy was looking in his bag for something, Masseo was whittling a small piece of wood, and Jullanar had her crochet.

Pali wished she'd picked up a proper hobby. She used to spend such quiet time in camp tending to her equipment, and when that palled she'd—she frowned. What *had* she done?

At Stoneybridge she read, or went to one or other of the plays or musical performances in town—there was always something, with so many colleges in the town—or went to exercise in one of the salons.

Sometimes she sketched, but as she looked at Fitzroy, who had pulled out his harp and was carefully examining its strings, she could not bear to reveal her poor efforts.

And so she hovered, hand on her sword-hilt, knowing it did not need to be sharpened.

She could examine the threads tied around her dagger, she supposed, but she stood there, watching Fitzroy quietly tune his harp.

"You haven't done your forms for a few days," Jullanar said.

Pali looked down at her quickly, cheeks burning. She shouldn't be staring at Fitzroy, at his quiet face and his perfect posture and all the performance of himself.

"I'm sorry?"

"You look a little out-of-sorts," Jullanar said, smiling at her with nothing in her expression but gentle encouragement. "I'm sure you'll feel better if you fence for a bit."

Pali nodded jerkily, but it was good advice, and she crossed the clearing to a space a little away from them where there was enough room for one of the sword-dances.

It was a strange thing, to have a friend who knew her well enough to suggest she should practice.

CHAPTER TWENTY-NINE
PRACTICE

Pali stretched, slowly, carefully, gently. She could feel the tension in her body, and could not think why she had not thought to practice at all, these past few days.

When she'd been younger it would never have occurred to her to miss a day.

She did a handful of lunges, switching her legs halfway through, and remembered how it had not been just her, when she was younger. It had been Damian, and Faleron, and at least one of the others would join them. Jullanar and Fitzroy, most often, as Damian had first found his way into friendship by teaching them how to fight.

Pali shook out her hands, cracked her neck, and drew her great-grandmother's sword and the dagger Masseo had forged for her out of the fallen star. She frowned at the threads wound about the hilt, and after a moment set the blade aside in case it had been adversely enchanted. She did not think so—she felt no magic when she touched the dagger, or no magic beyond that created by Masseo's skill as a smith, the runes he had carved into the steel, her own blood.

She drew her second-best dagger instead, and since her mind felt empty of all decisions, turned to the same pattern she had danced at the three-way crossroads on top of the mountain.

The shēhen of the Siruyal, the Great Challenge, the dance of sword and dagger, footwork and precise gesture.

Again and again the memory of the Siruyal assailed her, its three feathers, its three wishes, its three quests.

One wish, that she might understand.

A second wish, that others might understand her.

A third wish she had never dared utter.

She finished the first routine, began again at half speed, her blood singing as her muscles warmed. Her hair in its long braid bounced against her back, flying out as she wheeled, whirled, lunged forward and recovered back, the sword calling softly to the wind, the wind answering.

Oh, had she not followed its quests?

Had she not sought glory, and knowledge, and joy?

She had never sought dzēren, to be *brimful* of that quiet, radiant, tranquil joy, at *peace*.

She performed a flurry of moves, came once again to the Great Challenge, and increased her speed, her heart catching in her throat, her attention on the way the air moved languidly around her, the magic heavy and curious, friendly; the feeling of eyes watching her.

Familiar, friendly eyes. Once this had been familiar.

She swept up again, the Great Challenge almost startling her when it came around again in the shēhen, and she knew, oh, she knew, that she had spent half her life trying and failing each attempt to follow the third quest.

∼

When she stopped she was almost quivering with exhaustion.

Three times had she faced the Great Challenge, and three times had she tumbled away, back down into the stable patterns of the shēhen, not launching herself forward into finding a new sword dance.

She was disappointed in herself, when she came to the point of sheathing her sword, her dagger, and walking her breath and heartbeat to their proper pace.

Fitzroy was playing, a song he had written long ago when he had first watched her at her shēhen; a song he had written to accompany this particular one, whose rhythms matched her steps.

She turned away from him, pretending she needed to pace out her breath, her heartbeat, let the sweat cool.

How *dare* he play that song?

How did he *remember* these songs? It was so long since they had last been together—

And she had never read anywhere that Artorin Damara was a musician. He enjoyed listening to music, all the court memoirs mentioned that. He had instituted prizes for compositions as for other arts, part of his effort at reformation and cultural strengthening.

But himself a musician?

No.

She faced the trees, wiping her face of the sweat, refusing to look at where he was playing that song whose rhythms were so familiar, were *hers*, with the tonal combinations that came out of her own clan's musical traditions, when he had sat around their tents listening to those playing the oud and zither and the small drums.

She reached the trees and turned around, measuring her pace, her breathing, eyes averted from the campsite.

Masseo had come over and was leaning up against a tree not far from her, a sack in his hand. "I set a few snares earlier," he said. "Want to come with me to check them?"

It was—it was *good*, Pali told herself fiercely, that she had friends who understood her. Who remembered how she was, and could see how she was still very much that person. No matter how she tried, she was still herself.

The rigid and heartless Pali Avramapul, whose sword and tongue were equally vicious.

Nevertheless, she followed Masseo when he pushed himself off the tree and set off towards the stream. He led her up a few hundred yards, to a slope that lifted up into the moorland. There were rabbit-signs everywhere, and a few sentinels close to their burrow entrances.

The first two snares were empty, but the third had caught a rabbit. Pali held the lines from the first snares in her hand, running her hand down the wire, coiling it neatly in her palm. Masseo disentangled the rabbit from the noose, and they retreated back down to the stream, where he began to dress it.

"Are you feeling better?" he asked after a few moments.

Pali had seated herself on a rock a few feet away, where she could dip her hands into the water. She sighed. "I suppose so."

"Did you and Fitzroy have an argument?"

She glanced at Masseo, but he was focused on his task. She looked up at the sky, the milky grey brightness that hid no sun. She had never understood where the light came from in the Borderlands.

"Yes," she said.

He concentrated on skinning the rabbit, and Pali concentrated on the feel of the water on her hand, the dragonflies patrolling the air, the pressure of a bump on the rock on her right thigh.

"I keep hurting him," she admitted. "I don't know ..."

Oh, she knew *why* ...

How to stop, perhaps.

"You saw him in his palace, didn't you?"

Pali nodded shortly. There were midges around them, not biting but getting in her eyes. She shook her head to dislodge them, to little avail.

Masseo spoke with that even, thoughtful tone Pali had always admired. He had a good voice, deeper than Fitzroy's, not quite as mellifluous but rich and resonant nonetheless.

Why did *everything* have to come back to *him*?

"Jullanar and I were talking, when you were gone, about how ... hmm, how should I put this? You seem to be struggling with Fitzroy."

Pali drew her feet up, trying to keep her laugh from coming out harsh and bitter. "I'm sorry it's so obvious. Do you ... do you not find it ... him ... hard?"

Masseo did not misunderstand her. "We were talking, Jullanar and I, how when Fitzroy came back, he came *as Fitzroy* for us. You didn't have that, did you? You saw him in his palace first."

Pali felt her words choke her, and she simply sat there, the stone hard beneath her, her wet hands icy cold.

"What was it like? What was *he* like, there?"

Masseo had argued quite convincingly for Fitzroy's potential *third* identity as Aurelius Magnus. Pali blinked back hot tears as the image of that austere study came once more into her mind's eye.

"Have you ever seen how a caged animal paces?" she said. Masseo nodded gravely even as he finished with the rabbit and washed his hands and knife in the stream. Pali swallowed. "He had worn a path in the floor of his study, Masseo."

The smith closed his eyes. "I see."

Pali unfurled herself, suddenly unable to keep still. She balanced on the rock, staring up at him. "I can't stop seeing it, thinking about it. Every time he retreats into that blasted emperor face I cannot—I can't help it. It makes me want to claw off his expression." She grimaced at the blood on the rock. "And so I do. I'm not proud of myself, Masseo. I shouldn't be doing this."

"Did you know you were hurting him?"

"How could I?" she spat back, because anger was easier than admitting she had misjudged *his* expression that badly. Masseo regarded her levelly, and she turned away, ashamed at her outburst. "He told me he thought of himself as a river that had been dammed into a lake, and he'd been unable to break through and so he'd learned how to be a lake. He was a damn fine lake," she added, the irony tasting like metal in her mouth. "I am the acknowledged expert on his reign. I never saw—"

She stopped, and had to press her palms against her eyes to stop the treacherous tears.

Masseo waited, and finally she said, with a tremulous, tenuous lightness, "He said he had burst free of the dam in a great outpouring, and that was *easy*, he didn't need to *think*, it was pure instinct to expand forth ... but now, that initial impulse is subsiding, and he has to relearn how to be a river. Not though I'm helping that any."

Masseo wrapped the dressed rabbit in some broad dock leaves he found growing near the stream, and put the carcass into his bag. He left the entrails and skin under a bush, murmuring a prayer Pali didn't listen closely to, offering the gift of a meal to whatever chose to take it.

They started walking again, slowly. Pali burned but had no words to express her emotions. All the knots loosened by her practice seemed to have seized up again. Perhaps she could simply not say anything for a while, and that would give Fitzroy the space he needed to ... reclaim himself.

"He can't pretend the lake was never there," Masseo said quietly. "It's ... shaped him."

Pali took a breath, then huffed it out. Of course he could not cast off thirty years as the hundredth and last Emperor of Astandalas.

She wished she'd seen him again first as Fitzroy.

"It's curious that he'd use that analogy," Masseo murmured thoughtfully. Pali looked at him, and he smiled slightly and continued. "One of the things that appealed to me about the Cirith religion is its way of looking at people's characters. They have a four-elemental approach—well, some schools have five, and one has seven, I think, but the one I follow has four."

"Earth, air, fire, water?" Pali asked. "Fitzroy is fire, of course."

Why was he *always* first on her lips? She scowled at the tufts of lank grass under the trees, which were some beech-like kind she didn't recognize.

"Yes, but the Cirith view is that no one is solely one element. They might incline mostly towards one, but are generally better understood as combinations of two. I'm fire and earth, as befits a smith: I like being settled, but I like a bit of danger, a bit of excitement, too." He grinned at her briefly startled look. "I used to hide that, I suppose."

She nodded. "Jullanar is earth, too, isn't she?" She thought of Jullanar's love of gardens, her soft gentleness, her yielding but stubborn nature. "And ... water?"

"Yes. I would consider you as air and earth. You are restless, light-footed, ever in motion, but you also are deeply rooted to your home, and you were able to be content, even happy, in one place, weren't you?"

"For a time, yes," Pali agreed warily. But she had been *content, even happy*, at Stoneybridge.

Most of the time. When the wind blew from the north, and the wild geese called ...

Oh, sometimes she missed the desert, and the stark challenges of life there.

(It was inconvenient that some inner voice that sounded like Jullanar in her mind pointed out that she had found those stark challenges, beautiful as they could be, boring. Dzēren, again, no doubt. She could not bear the thought of losing herself in it.)

"Fitzroy is fire and air," Masseo said. "It's hard to think of him in any other fashion. Quicksilver, restless, brilliant, always in motion ..."

"He called himself a river."

"He called himself a river dammed against his will into a lake," Masseo corrected, using her own words.

"He told Terec, the wild mage we met, that he *could not* touch his magic when he was emperor," Pali said, as they came in sight of the campsite and halted while they were still out of earshot. "He was *prevented* from even feeling it, when he was bound with the enchantments upon the figure of the emperor."

And oh, there had been so many enchantments upon the figure of the emperor. The whole empire had wheeled about him. Five worlds conquered by violence and gold and magic, held together by magic bound into the golden throne, binding the emperor into his place as the five worlds were bound under his authority.

"I don't think it's terrible that you are so alert to every time he slides back into that ... lake," Masseo said earnestly, quietly, sympathetically. "But perhaps you could try to be a little less ... relentless about it."

Masseo clasped her on her shoulder, and when she looked into his face, he gave a one-armed hug. She leaned into his touch, keeping her mind blank, refusing to think about Fitzroy never having anyone to hold him. Refusing to think of the resounding non-expression when he'd thanked her for her assiduousness.

She closed her eyes and wished, oh she wished, for someone to fight.

~

They cooked the rabbit and ate it with the last of Jullanar's grill-bread and some raspberries Jullanar and Fitzroy had found.

Fitzroy ate the raspberries with excruciating concentration, one at a time, regarding each one as if it were a ruby brought in tribute.

It was hard to imagine him looking at rubies with that much pleasure.

After they washed up, Fitzroy brought out his letter again. He frowned over the final pages, sitting there for a long time with the ink drying on his pen.

"Do you need a word?" Jullanar asked him, when he looked up at one point, eyes unfocused.

"A valediction," he replied dully. "Something ... ordinary."

"'Regards,'" Masseo suggested.

"'Your servant'," Jullanar said, and then, when Fitzroy gave her a mildly sardonic glance, grinned at him. "In a manner of speaking."

"That'll do," he said quietly, dipping his pen into his inkwell. "That'll do."

They all woke early the next morning. A wind had risen before dawn, or what passed for dawn in the Borderlands, and it brought the scent of something intriguing with it.

"Voonra is that way," Fitzroy said, turning his head into the wind, his eyes washing gold and his garments fluttering about him. He'd dressed in dark blue trews and a royal blue tunic, with his brilliant scarlet mantle wrapped casually about his shoulders and flowing out behind him.

He should have looked ridiculous. He didn't.

Pali carefully positioned herself to walk beside Jullanar, letting Masseo walk ahead with Fitzroy, her horse on a line walking quietly behind them. She asked her friend to tell her about running her bookstore. She was so engrossed in hearing about Jullanar's early adventures solving mysteries and making friends that she hardly noticed when they passed out of the brighter, thinly wooded parts of the Borderlands and entered a dark and grim forest instead.

She did notice when Fitzroy lit the tip of his staff so it glowed a fine, clear, gold, just the colour of late afternoon sunlight.

Jullanar nudged him with her elbow. "Doesn't he look *just* like a storybook wizard!" she whispered gleefully, and then, because this was Fitzroy—despite everything it was, it was—she said the same thing out loud, and made him laugh.

Pali had not managed to make him laugh, not once.

She gripped her horse's reins with one hand, the hilt of her sword with the other, and glared balefully at the dim shadows in this grim wood.

"Why don't you walk ahead, and I'll hold your horse?" Jullanar said, nudging her forward. "It'll be like old times."

She and Fitzroy had very often been the vanguard, as Damian and Pharia had taken the rear.

Pali nodded sharply, and almost didn't look at Fitzroy. But she did look, and therefore saw how some emotion flashed through his eyes, though his face was emperor-calm, before he smiled with the abstract courtesy he had presented to Domina Black of Stoneybridge before he realized who she was.

Pali smiled back, or grimaced back, and stalked forward to stand on his right, as he was holding his staff in his left hand. She could do better. She *would*.

CHAPTER THIRTY
BIRTHDAY CAKE

They passed through the strange, dim forest, warily skirting rings of ghostly night-luminous toadstools. The trees were heavily-mossed evergreens or thickly lichened trees with only a handful of dry leaves on their branches. There was no wind, but the leaves rattled like a lingering cough,

Sometimes Pali thought she could see the limbs moving, always in the corners of her vision; everything was still when she turned her head.

The grasping branches recoiled from Fitzroy's golden light.

"This was a verdant land, once," he said at one point, stopping to consider a safe path through an area where the rings overlapped like ripples from falling rain on a still pond.

It was goblin-land now, the dark and twisted edge of Faërie. Pali held her sword drawn in readiness, the weight of the blade comforting, familiar.

It was also unexpected, strange. It had been almost as long since she had last walked beside Fitzroy in the vanguard as it had been since she had walked with her sword drawn.

But though she was sure there were eyes watching them from

every tree, every stone, every one of the monstrous fungal outgrowths, nothing dared come within the circle of sunlit magic Fitzroy cast.

For all Pali's yearnings for a foe to fight, none came out to meet her blade. She almost wished—

Almost. She kept her hands out of her pockets.

～

They made no camp in that wood. They walked silently, clustered close, Pali's horse crowding at their heels. Pali steadily cased their surroundings, head moving steadily left to right, all her senses alert for danger.

Danger stood all around them, but not in the circle of light, not when they stayed upon the path.

"How do we know which path it is?" Jullanar whispered once, when Fitzroy turned his head, eyes blank gold with his magic, considering the maze of fairy circles, before stepping forth, slow and steady and entirely confident.

"Someone went before us," Fitzroy said, his voice soft and dreamy as it had been when he thought he was dreaming them into existence. "There is a thread through this maze."

Pali walked beside him, behind him, as the endless dim day wore on, the marginally darker and dimmer night, and still admired his skill and strength.

～

They were all tired when at last they came to the end of the forest.

Fitzroy was as upright as he had been on entering it, but his face was as still and serene as it had been when Pali met him in his palace, and his skin drawn drumlike across his skull, his jaw, around his eyes.

They stepped between two rough boulders, encrusted with livid yellow-orange lichen, and suddenly the air was clear and the sun was shining and the birds were singing, and a hitherto invisible thread in

Fitzroy's hand was gold and red and white and tied with a knot Pali knew.

They all breathed deeply, grateful for the clean air, clearing their lungs. Pali's horse neighed loudly.

"That is my sister's work," she said, touching the knot. A familiar warmth tingled in the pads of her fingers, familiar and dear as the soft smile in Jullanar's eyes, the scent of Fitzroy's magic, like a sudden waft of burning sandalwood.

"Arzu's?" Jullanar asked, touching the pyramidical knot. "Did she come this way?"

"It is a long way from Kaphyrn," Fitzroy murmured.

Unlike Pali or Sardeet, Arzu had never been inclined to far travelling. She had married a man of their clan, had been their mother's right hand, had taken their mother's place in her turn. *She* understood dzēren. She had been brimful of joy. Pali passed the cord through her hands, feeling the smooth silken twist of it.

"It is a long way from Kaphyrn," she said, "but I travelled so far. So did Sardeet."

Jullanar grinned at her, eyes bright, but Masseo touched her shoulder and squeezed gently, which she appreciated.

She dared not wish Fitzroy were anywhere near as tactile as he'd once been, when he might well have slung his arm over her shoulder and walked beside her for a ways, with her tucked against his tall lankiness in a way she had never admitted she missed.

～

The braided cord was tied to a brass ring set into a squared-off pillar, and wound crazily from tree to stone to shrub to wooden stake. No two supports were alike or the same height, nor in anything resembling a straight line.

"I think this must be Sardeet," Pali muttered at one point, as they were precariously balanced on a round and unstable log to cross a wide river, the cord humming taut between two trees on either side of the river, a kingfisher perched on it, his breast the blue of the jerkins Faleron had always worn, his back the russet-red of Faleron's hair.

"Why do you say that?" Fitzroy asked, walking across the log with that same serene countenance and bearing. He must be exhausted, Pali thought, smiling at him and seeing how his eyes sharpened on hers, his face coming into focus, for a bare moment that was not, quite, a responding smile of his own.

"Arzu is a weaver. She couldn't possibly countenance something as erratic as this."

Jullanar laughed and unbalanced, sending both herself and Masseo tumbling into the river.

It was noisy and swift but not deep, and though they were both more than half soaked they managed to splash to the bank without too much trouble.

They stood there a moment, the four of them, two dry and two wet, and then Jullanar started to laugh. "Oh, you must be right, this is entirely Sardeet! What on earth do you think she made the path for?"

"We're almost to the end of it," Fitzroy said, gesturing with his staff towards a gap in the woods on the far side of the river, where they could see the roofs and smoke of a village of some form. "Or at least, I expect that's where we're headed."

"You never know," Pali murmured, well aware that Sardeet's mind did not work the same as hers, but indeed, when they reached the edge of the wood, there was another squared-off stone pillar with a brass ring, to which the end of the cord was tied.

Hanging from the ring were nine scarlet ribbons fluttering in the breeze, and an arrow, chiselled deeply into the stone and chalked red, that pointed to the town.

"Most mysterious," Fitzroy said gleefully.

"It would be hard to be *more* obvious, don't you think?" Jullanar objected.

"That's the mystery," Fitzroy replied imperturbably, and after trailing his hand across the ribbons, letting them curl and twist around his fingers for a moment, he gathered his friends together with a carefully courteous glance and set off again.

∽

By the time they reached the village, Masseo and Jullanar were nearly dry. Pali eyed Fitzroy thoughtfully, but did not ask whether he'd been involved in this remarkably quick process. The sun was bright, the warm air breezy, and perhaps they had not gotten as thorough of a dowsing as Pali had initially thought.

The village was sizeable, though not so big as Jullanar's Ragnor Bella. Perhaps a hundred houses clustered together around a triangular green. The buildings were wooden, wide-windowed; their roofs curving outwards at the edges, the tiles glazed green and blue and a near-purple.

The people were typically West Voonran in appearance, their black hair straight and glossy, their faces broad, cheekbones prominent, eyes more angular than Pali's and with uncreased eyelids. They wore loose trousers and long jackets with high collars and impressive embroidery.

They clearly saw some travellers, for although the villagers looked curiously at their small group, they were not regarded with suspicion or shock.

Curiosity, though, very much so. Curiosity, and a certain ... surmise, dared Pali think, when they saw her?

She lifted her chin, glad she was wearing her proper robes, her Pali robes, and strode up beside Jullanar.

"Where do you think we go?" Jullanar murmured to her.

Pali stopped at the edge of the green to survey the surroundings. A young woman, shorter than her despite her thick wooden clogs, hesitated a few yards away and then came clacking over, eyes bright and hand up over her mouth to badly hide her smile. "The café is there," she said, pointing across the green to a building with a gaily striped awning.

Pali said, "Thank you," since there wasn't much else she could think of to say.

The young woman bowed politely and scampered back off to join a group of other young women, who all giggled and whispered to each other, eyes bright and cheeks flushed.

"Perhaps there are confections," Fitzroy said.

"I could stand a coffee," Masseo added.

So could Pali, to be honest. And if someone looked at her and immediately directed her to a café—

Her heart seemed to be thumping a quiet, gleeful, anticipatory whisper of *Sardeet Sardeet Sardeet*.

Jullanar took her arm, just the way Pali and Elena had sometimes walked in their rambles around Stoneybridge, and squeezed gently, anchoring her to this moment, this place, this company.

They walked decorously across the green. Pali looked openly around, at the laundry hung on lines strung by the houses, the roosters crowing here and there, the gardens full of vegetables and flowers, many of them familiar, many of them strange to her eyes. There were little stone sculptures everywhere, round-bellied bear-like creatures with grinning faces, and miniature stone huts, hardly bigger than her fists, clustered at the feet of trees or half-tucked under shrubs.

And everywhere there was water, ponds and fountains, rills in stone channels criss-crossing the green. Between two buildings she caught glimpse of a large wooden waterwheel, ponderously turning.

It was a prosperous, pleasant village. The people seemed relaxed, cheerful; their houses in good repair, and several shops of one sort or another, full of interesting wares attractively displayed.

And there, drawing closer, the awning striped in pink and white and fresh springlike green. Pali was reminded of the peonies Elena particularly loved, great blowsy flowers in pink and white and carmine she loved stuffing with abandon into her collection of vases.

They neared the café and stopped with one accord at the sight of its wooden sign.

In curlicued lettering, painted green and pink and white to patch the awning—to match the bunting hung across the facade of the building, and the cushions of the seats set outside under the awning—were the entirely unexpected words:

Sardeet-Savarel's Tiger Café.

Jullanar said something about *"Tigers?"* but Pali did not, could not, attend, and instead she walked forward to the door.

She was barely conscious of the others coming behind her, the crackling strength of Fitzroy, his warm body, right behind her, the other two a step back.

She opened the door, and a bell tinkled pleasantly.

There were half a dozen round tables, all painted white, their cushions striped the same green and pink. Most were filled with customers, who at a glance were eating elaborate pastries and drinking all sorts of things, chattering or reading or, one or two of them, writing. One was petting a large and oddly-shaped cat.

At the far end of the room was a glass-fronted display case full of the confections, with teetering stacks of cake stands rising up above it. On the back wall were slates, some of which listed items and prices, some of them decorated with chalk flowers and butterflies and small animals.

Pali took all those sights in, not catching details, only the blur of scents—chocolate and vanilla and cream and honey and something fruity, coffee and caramel and—oh, it was a warm and delicious fug, and a bright and cheerful place, with all that pink and green and white—

And there, behind the counter, was Sardeet.

Pali stopped halfway into the room and stared in joyous disbelief at her sister.

For her part, Sardeet smiled at the man she was serving and then beamed at Pali. She clapped her hands, as if no one had looked up at the strangers' entrance.

"Ah!" Sardeet cried happily. "I do apologize, everyone, but my sister and friends have arrived! Take your cups and plates, don't worry!" She clapped her hands again as her customers stared at her. "Don't look like that," she chided gently, and pointed at a section of her slate sign. "It clearly states that when the Red Company arrives, I'll be closing."

Pali, like everyone else, looked at the sign. In the same curlicued, bubbly lettering she recognized as Sardeet's Shaian hand, it said, *All service will be suspended when the Red Company arrive.*

"I didn't think you were *serious*," someone said blankly.

Sardeet smiled kindly at him. "I know, dear."

"What about my cake?" the man at the counter asked.

"Sayo Kivim, I'm sorry, but I've made it very clear that the special cake was yours only if Fitzroy Angursell didn't come for it—and since he's here, I'm afraid it really is for him, you know. You can have the macaron fantasy instead."

Sayo Kivim grumbled, and Pali, latching onto this familiar situation, stalked forward with her hand on her sword hilt. "Are you giving my sister any trouble?" she asked, almost daring him to.

He was not young, but younger than she, and did not seem particularly inclined towards the arts of war, but then again, you never knew. He blenched satisfactorily when he turned to look at Pali smiling at him.

"Don't be silly," Sardeet chided, coming out from behind the counter and touching her elbow. "Pali, this is Sayo Kivim, an excellent customer of mine and the local mayor. Sayo Kivim, this is my sister Pali, and these are Masseo Umrit, Jullanar of the Sea, and of course, Fitzroy Angursell."

Sayo Kivim stared at them as if it was only just now sinking in that they really *were* the Red Company of infamy and legend. Fitzroy inclined his head that way he had. Sayo Kivim bowed automatically in the face of such regal bearing.

"You wouldn't take someone's birthday cake from them, would you? Of course not," Sardeet said, reaching across the counter for one of the glass cake stands, which held a layered cake in the same colours as the café. "Here, Sayo Kivim, you may have the Macaron

Fantasy. It's delicious." She deposited the cake in his hands, making sure one grasped the plate securely and the other held the glass dome in place. She then gently pushed him out of the store, chivvying the remaining customers out as she did, and finally pulled a small wood-and-slate board, the sort children used to learn their letters in parts of Alinor, and hung it on a hook outside the door.

She then shut the door, locked it, and turned around to give them even more brilliant smiles. "Oh, give me a hug! It's so good to see you!" she cried, and swiftly embraced Masseo, Jullanar, and Pali.

Pali held on to her sister tightly. She was a comfortable, comforting bulk, plumper than Jullanar—Sardeet had always been much curvier than Pali, and was now almost as proportionately fat as Gadarved—and smelling of chocolate and sweetness.

"Oh, Sardeet," Pali whispered into her sister's hair.

Sardeet's arms tightened, and then she released her so she could smile into Pali's eyes, and Pali could only wonder at how happy, how *joyous*, Sardeet was; she felt solid, grounded, full of life.

Sardeet turned last to Fitzroy, and though she was still smiling, her face was more serious, more sad. Pali watched as he looked down at them, his face drawn, serene without the underlying joy so prominent in Sardeet.

(*He* had not found dzēren. He was not brimful of joy.)

"Oh, my dear," Sardeet said softly, "you have had a hard time of it, haven't you?" She took a few steps forward, arms extended, but stopped before she quite touched him. "May I hug you?"

He swallowed, his throat working, before he gave Masseo his walking stick and opened his arms to Sardeet. She hugged him around his chest, for though an inch or two taller than Pali she was still much shorter than he, and he ducked his face over the top of her head.

Once his hair would have flopped forward and down, his exuberant curls bouncing freely. Now his bare skull shone in the sunlight coming through the windows.

When Sardeet released him, his eyes were bright, but he did not otherwise show anything.

"It's good to see you in person," Sardeet said quietly. "You'll be happy again, Fitzroy."

"Will I?" he asked, softly, urbanely, lightly ironic.

"You look so sad in all your portraits."

Fitzroy went very still. Perhaps they all did. Certainly they all looked at Sardeet, who laughed merrily.

"Goodness, didn't you all know?" She pointed at a state portrait on the wall, where it was such a familiar element of Astandalan public buildings that Pali had not even begun to notice it as an oddity. "I've tried to learn to draw people, but I'm not very good at faces, so I thought I'd have Fitzroy's up, at least. I liked this one best."

Pali looked at the portrait, which was later than the ones she'd seen on Alinor. He was perhaps in his late fifties in it, settled into himself, serene and radiant as ever, but there was a hint of a smile, a hint of true inward peace, in the set of his shoulders and his mouth.

"That's ... quite recent," Fitzroy said. His voice was very neutral.

"Yes," Sardeet said blithely, "I have a pen pal from Zunidh. I tried to get myself arrested once, you see, when there was an ambassador here, so they'd take me up before you, but they wouldn't believe I was really Sardeet Avramapul. Too fat to be the most beautiful woman in the Nine Worlds, they said." She shook her head. "I told them they had a very limited concept of beauty but they refused to be budged. I am sorry, Fitzroy, I did try."

They all stared at her. "You have put on some weight," Pali agreed eventually.

Sardeet laughed. "Oh, just a *teensy* bit!" She bounced up and down so her stomach jiggled. "Oh, goodness, it's so much better now, so much more relaxed. It was terrible being *ogled* all the time, you know, and never being considered as worthy for anything but my outside. Not you," she added hastily when Jullanar made a noise of distress and denial, "but you must acknowledge that strangers can be most obnoxious at times."

She shrugged, and then said, "Come in, come in, let's have something to drink and eat cake for supper. Sit down, Fitzroy, and you too Masseo—oh, it's good to see you!—and Jullanar, oh, this is so lovely! I knew you'd come eventually. And for it to be *today*, well! What a splendid thing! Happy birthday, Fitzroy, by the way. I put flowers on your portrait but it's not a shrine, don't worry."

"Thank you," Fitzroy said after a long, uncertain moment, sitting down at a mostly-clear table in the middle of the room. "It's not my birthday, though." He pondered. "It's a holiday, many places."

"Oh, your *official* one is, to be sure," Sardeet agreed, setting a ceramic cake-stand in a fine, clear scarlet—the Red Company's scarlet—down in front of him. It contained what Pali supposed was a cake, or at least a confection, small golden balls of dough draped in glistening chocolate and caramel, bits of pastry cream peeking out here and there, and the whole thing gilded and studded with sugared violets.

It was a spectacular cake and Pali could see why Sayo Kivim had been disappointed not to receive it.

"I always remember you saying your birthday was going to be the fourth day before the spring equinox," Sardeet went on, bringing them plates and cloth napkins and a pitcher of water, stacks of attractive bubbled-glass cups, and finally went to busy herself behind the counter with kettles and coffee pots. "Because that was the day you met Jullanar and Damian, and the day you first named yourself. So … happy birthday, Fitzroy. It's very good to see you again."

CHAPTER THIRTY-ONE
KISSIE AND PEA

In short order, Pali and the others were given coffee and a choice of tea, which Sardeet offered with lashings of cream and more cakes, pastries, and sweet confections than Pali had probably eaten in the past decade. Looking at the array her sister had set on the table in front of them, she could not decide where to start.

"Try these first," Sardeet said, passing her a plate with tiny tartlets piled with some sort of tiny translucent berry in a luminous scarlet just the colour of a stained glass window catching the sun.

The berries were sharp, popping against the roof of her mouth, offset by a cool creamy custard and a barely-sweet pastry case.

It was, quite possibly, the best tartlet Pali had ever eaten.

Sardeet blushed when Pali told her sister this. "Oh, you're too kind! Jullanar, did you have one of the chocolate éclairs? And Masseo—oh yes, those are an invention of my own, lavender-glazed buns, they're filled with honey cream—Fitzroy, did you want a ... fork? The croquembouche is a bit sticky!"

Fitzroy was regarding the tower of caramel-draped tower of pastries with a very still and serene expression. Pali assumed he was hiding his emotions, and almost said something before she remembered Masseo asking her to be less *relentless*, and so she held her tongue and focused on the pastries.

They were an easy distraction. Out of the corner of her eye she saw Fitzroy take one of the pastries and set in the plate in front of him. He stared at the pastry while rubbing his fingers together, his face very blank. Without missing a word of her conversation Sardeet handed him a knife and a fork and a cloth napkin. He was extremely correct, albeit incredibly slow, about cutting up the sticky confection.

Sardeet happily talked about how she'd studied pastry-making in some minor city Pali had never heard of, but which had Masseo nodding eagerly and asking questions. By their ensuing conversation Pali learned that Masseo had spent the period after the parting of the company wandering around Voonra as an itinerant blacksmith.

Voonra was not a large world. No one had ever found more than its one main continent and a few offshore islands of various sizes. People who sailed off to the horizon rarely came back; or if they did it was not by sea, and they spoke of other worlds.

"I didn't come to Voonra until after the Fall," Sardeet explained. "I found myself ... hmm, where was it? Somewhere on Ysthar, far to the east of Astandalas. I got a bit lost as I was trying to get back to the Silver Forest, and ended up near the tea gardens. I spent quite a bit of time in the area, going deeper and deeper into the mountains. At some point I crossed over into the Borderlands, and was somewhere in the outer regions of Fairyland when Astandalas Fell."

They were all quiet, as everyone always fell quiet when the Fall was mentioned.

"That must have been particularly difficult for you," Sardeet said, leaning forward and staring intently at Fitzroy until he lifted his gaze from his plate to meet hers.

Pali was sitting beside her sister, across from Fitzroy. She could see how still and sombre his expression was, how shuttered his eyes. He did not say anything, but after a moment nodded gravely.

Pali thought of his earnestness when he had told Neri that he had not wished to be forsworn, that though he had had not wanted to be emperor in the least (*in the least,* Jullanar's voice in her mind whispered, though the real Jullanar was smiling painfully at Fitzroy and tracing crumbs with her finger), he had also done his best to fulfil and uphold the oaths he had sworn.

Some thought almost surfaced, something Pali had not yet dared say to herself, but before she could do more than shy away from its looming presence, Sardeet made a tsking noise and rose from her seat.

She went to a padded bench set along the wall, where one of the misshapen cats was curled up in a dumpling-like pile. She picked up the animal and brought it over to Fitzroy, who did not resist but did look vaguely startled when she deposited it on his lap.

Pali regarded the creature warily. It was about the size of a large cat, with a much more pointed snout. In shape it was more like a pangolin or perhaps an armadillo, but instead of scaly plates it had luxuriant long fur.

The colour of the fur was extraordinary, a kind of yellowy-orange with creamy white stripes. The animal's ears were pointed and alert, and its eyes were a shiny button-black. It did not appear anywhere near as surprised as Fitzroy was to find itself on his lap, for it snuffled at his sleeve, investigated the pastry on his plate, and then snuggled down with a relaxed sigh.

Fitzroy stared.

"Go on, pet him," Sardeet urged. "This is Kissie, he loves pets."

Fitzroy did not move. Sardeet kept smiling at him. She had always had the most alluring smiles: no one could help but wish to see them again.

Fitzroy could keep his face straight and calm, though his eyes were bleak, even bewildered, but he could not resist Sardeet's smiles. He lowered his hands to bury in the animal's fur. His expression was so still Pali could only see the emperor in all his portraits.

"There, Kissie will be good for you," Sardeet declared.

"What *is* Kissie?" Jullanar asked, regarding the animal with astonishment. "It looks like a furry ... armadillo?"

"He's a tiger, isn't he?" Sardeet said, and reached down beside her chair with an adorable little grunt to pick up another one of the animals. This one had fur of a more definitely orange-red shade, and the lines on its face made a kind of peregrine-falcon pattern. "This is Pea," Sardeet declared, kissing it on the nose.

"That's not a tiger," Pali objected. The one in the imperial menagerie—the one that had been injured, and which paced in its captivity—

She took a breath. Fitzroy had not eaten any of his birthday confection—cake was clearly not the right word for it—though he had a piece speared on his fork. Slowly, as Pali watched, he bent his head to look at the creature's eyes.

"Definitely not a tiger," Masseo said. "I saw one recently. Much bigger. Also magical, admittedly."

"I think they look like tigers," Sardeet declared imperturbably. "I found them after my time in the village of the blind sages. I'm not sure if they were like this originally or if they were affected somehow by the Fall, but there was just the one litter. There were four of them, but the other two adopted other friends. These ones have been excellent friends to me, haven't you?" She kissed Pea again. A creature less like a pea Pali could hardly imagine. Even on Sardeet's ample lap its bulk spread out.

"Where did the names come from?" Jullanar asked.

"Oh, this one is Aurora and the Peacock, but he prefers Pea, and Kissie is from Kissing the Moon, naturally."

None of them had anything they could immediately come up with in response to that. Pali dared not express a criticism of Sardeet's naming habits, not when Jullanar had teased her for still not naming her horse. Pali had argued that names were private, but Jullanar had merely laughed at her.

Fitzroy, who should have been the one to riff on such an opening for the rest of the evening, did not even crack a smile at their names. He bent over Kissie's fur and whispered something into the creature's ear that Pali couldn't hear.

Pea snuffled and Sardeet offered it one of the berries off Pali's remaining tartlet. "There you go," she murmured, and smiled that radiant smile at them. "Oh, it's so splendid to have you here! There, that's better, isn't it, Fitzroy?"

Fitzroy had a silver line of tears wavering in his eyes, Pali saw with a shock. She had to turn her head, vividly embarrassed for his sake.

He'd never been embarrassed about weeping, not when he was younger. He'd never seen any loss of strength in showing his vulnerabilities.

That was not a weakness the emperor had been permitted. There was something all too raw at the sight of that cool composure fracturing like this.

Something hot and hard came into Pali's throat. She was glad to discover a damp snout snuffling at her fingers, and have the opportunity to bury her own hand into Pea's fur.

It was just as soft and comforting as it looked.

"There we are," Sardeet murmured. "We're all friends here. You're safe here. You're not an object to any of us. You can find your way back to yourself."

"Can I?" he said, and this time his voice was not light and urbane, but low and rough, broken, almost inaudible.

"Yes," Sardeet said with solid certainty. Pali swallowed against the coldness in her stomach. Kissie grunted as it twisted around to lick Fitzroy's face.

Jullanar and Masseo, on either side of Fitzroy, leaned up against him, and whether it was Sardeet's words or their presence or the heavy weight of the creature on his lap, Fitzroy was able to bow his head and let the tears come.

Pali was horribly embarrassed and could only sit there, her hands in Pea's fur, knowing her words would almost certainly come out the wrong way. She'd never been very comforting.

Sardeet reached out and gathered Pali against her side, and held her there while Pali turned her own face into her sister's long, sweet-scented hair and let her own tears come.

Perhaps, the thought came, *she* didn't need to be comforting. She could turn to those who were.

∽

After they had gorged themselves on the pastries, helping Fitzroy finish his birthday cake—the balls of pastry were filled with cream and drenched in caramel, and even more delicious than the tartlets, if sweeter than was entirely to Pali's taste—Sardeet showed them around her store and her living space above it. The building was on three floors, but the upper two had been very quirkily put together, so there were odd steps and odd-shaped rooms and more corners than seemed at all practicable for the space.

It was charmingly decorated, with fabric and pottery and plants everywhere. The kitchen was painted yellow, with blue curtains, and there was a blue rug on the floor.

The bedroom was painted blue, as well, and Pali looked at the soft powdery colour with something like wonder. There had been a period—a long period—in which Sardeet had shied away from anything blue, especially anything blue to do with her living space.

She had been stolen away by the Blue Wind to be his bride, taken to the god's blue glass palace high on a mountain at the edge of the holy desert.

Pali had slain that god.

She glanced sidelong at Fitzroy, who was examining a hanging basket containing a plant that looked like jade beads on a string. He had silvery-gold glitter on his hands and brushed across his cheek and one ear. The glitter had been somehow magically generated by Kissie. Sardeet had said the tiger-cats did that, when they really liked someone. Fitzroy had tried not to show how pleased he was at being *really liked* by the creature.

Pali knew how to deal with gods, that was the problem.

∽

Pali stabled her horse next to Sardeet's three milk cows, which were tended by the neighbour. The animals were short-horned and extremely sleek, obviously groomed as well as any horse. There was a horse in the barn as well, a huge destrier such as were ridden by the Voonran court's knights, who wore plate armour.

The destrier, a strawberry roan gelding, whickered and suffered Pali to stroke her hand gently down his long roman nose. Pali gave him some fresh water before she turned her mare loose in the empty box stall opposite.

Back inside, she discovered that Sardeet had bowed to someone's blandishment and provided some savoury foods to nibble on through the evening. These took the form of cheeses, fruits, butter, several kinds of bread, and an array of cold cooked vegetable salads and spreads, all of which she arrayed on the table in the yellow kitchen.

"There," she said, and offered them wine and tea and more coffee and some sort of fermented cider, and then they piled up all Sardeet's cushions and half of Fitzroy's on the floor, and told over stories of the old days.

∼

Sardeet invited Pali to sleep with her in her bed, which was a large, comfortable mattress. She had a guest room, which after some debate Jullanar had taken, leaving Masseo and Fitzroy to make themselves comfortable with Fitzroy's camping gear.

Pali lay beside her sister, the tears standing in her eyes as she took her presence in. "You seem so happy," she whispered after Sardeet had blown out the candle-lantern and they had lain in silence for some time. "Brimful."

She heard Sardeet roll over, and felt her breath stirring her hair when she replied. "I am."

"I'm glad," Pali said, and cursed that her voice broke.

"You've been lonely," her sister said. "Even after finding them?"

They had told the stories of their reuniting, already polishing the words until they became jewels Fitzroy might set into a story, a song. Pali had not been able to describe meeting him in anything but the driest academic terms.

Fitzroy had described his surprise, his joy, and his regret that he had not been able to go immediately with her, but had had to take the time to ensure half a lifetime of work did not go to waste by his hastiness.

"It's only been ... two months," Pali said, struck by how short that was. Two months since she had found Jullanar, a month since she had discovered Fitzroy in that high tower, and left him there to pace his prison. Been persuaded to leave him there.

"You're angry," Sardeet observed. "You're all knotted in yourself."

"I'm trying, Sardeeet," Pali whispered. "I'm really struggling with ... everything."

"Everything?"

The darkness surely hid her blush. "Fitzroy," she admitted, even more quietly.

Sardeet was quiet, her breath even in the dark. One of the armadillo-cats had crawled into bed with them, and was snoring with a faint, not unpleasant whistling noise somewhere in the vicinity of Pali's feet.

"Anger is sometimes a way we hide our fear, our sorrow, and our shame," Sardeet said presently. "There is a holy mountain behind the town, where people go to think these things through. Perhaps you might go there in the morning."

"Do you think that would help?"

"It's unlikely to hurt," Sardeet replied, and even in the dark Pali could hear how she had smiled, that ravishingly beautiful smile, the one that had caused the Blue Wind to steal her away. "Good night, Pali. I'm so glad you're here."

"Good night, Sardeet," Pali replied, and rolled over, sure she would lay sleepless; but she fell into the soft, comforting embrace of the darkness almost immediately.

CHAPTER THIRTY-TWO
THE WIND-EYE

Sardeet got up well before dawn, when the town roosters were uttering their first sleepy crows.

Pali woke up when her sister rose from the bed, and stared in groggy disbelief as Sardeet hummed while she collected her clothing. The cat-thing—Pea, she presumed, but in the dim predawn it was hard to tell—watched Sardeet alertly, making the snuffling noise that was all the sound Pali had so far heard from them.

"You needn't rise now," Sardeet whispered when she saw that Pali was awake. "I've got the ovens to light and pastries to make. No sense wasting my supplies."

Pali yawned, but now that she was awake she was awake, and she felt the need to move, to act, to *do* something.

(There was not going to be anyone for her to fight here, either. She could feel the peace of the town laying over it like a thick, comforting blanket.)

"I'll make you coffee, then," Sardeet said happily. "Be quiet on the stairs, they creak rather. The privy's through the second door, and the washroom's the next one over."

She padded out, the tiger-cat jumping heavily from the bed to follow her. Pali rolled into the warm depression left by Sardeet, wondering if she could fall asleep again after all, but her head seemed to be full of a buzzing urgency.

The holy mountain would not *hurt*, she told herself. She had to change *something*.

~

Sardeet already had a fire going in her smallest oven, and by the time Pali had fully woken had made her coffee and gave her some of the previous day's leftover pastries, which was a fine breakfast by Pali's standards. She watched as Sardeet moved about her café's kitchen, lighting the stoves with practiced motions before turning to the great bowls in which she mixed flour and butter, yeast and salt, and other arcane items of the baker's art.

Pali could cook just fine on a campfire, but no one had ever been excited for it to be her turn on the cooking rotation. Sardeet hadn't been one of the great cooks of the company, either—that had been Jullanar, Gadarved, and Faleron—but she clearly would be one of them now.

"Now, Pali," Sardeet said, washing her bowls and then turning to her with a stern expression. Pali was struck how much Sardeet looked like their Auntie Rhu in that moment, and found her chin coming up mulishly.

Sardeet was not Auntie Rhu, however: she dissolved into delighted giggles instantly.

"Oh, don't look like that! I really do think you'd do well going to the mountain."

"Is it magic?" Pali asked warily.

"Oh, not any more than anywhere else. It's full of caves and tunnels and things, and that makes it holy. Holey, too, naturally." Sardeet laughed again, her whole body wobbling with her ... joy.

That was what this was, Pali realized, regarding her little sister with awe and a pang that was not quite envy. Sardeet was brimful of joy.

"How did you find such—" She stopped.

"Happiness?" Sardeet asked, and did not pretend she did not understand. "I uncovered the hard and ugly parts of myself, and studied them," she said thoughtfully. "When I stayed in the village of the blind sages, they didn't *see* me, you know. They were blind, after all. They didn't look at me and see the most beautiful woman in the Nine Worlds. They knew me, Sardeet, by what I said and what I did. And living with them, I came to understand myself that way, too."

"It can't be that simple."

On the clean wooden worktable, Sardeet laid out a bowl of butter, a bowl of flour, a cone of sugar, a jug of water, and a tiny crock of salt. She turned out a dough she must have made earlier, pillowy and with a fine dull sheen to the risen surface. She gestured at the items. "These are very simple, but that doesn't mean it's *easy* to make an excellent croissant."

Pali watched as she sprinkled flour onto the table, knocked the air out of the dough, and rolled into a long rectangle. She cut a pat of butter and set it in the middle of one end of the dough.

"I'll be doing this for a while," Sardeet said presently. "If you go out the back door and head past the stables, you'll see a white-washed house. Go along the lane to its left, and at the end you'll cross into a lane lined with hedges on one side and a stone wall on the other. Turn right and follow it till you come to the moon gate—that is, it's a round archway—and you'll be at the foot of the mountain."

"And then what? If it's not magic?"

"Follow your heart. There are caves to go inwards, and heights to surmount. Right at the peak there's a wind-eye. Some people go for the stream-valleys and look for the hidden pools and hanging valleys. I'm sure you'll find something worth the searching, if you go with an open heart and open mind. You might want to ask yourself just *why* you're so angry."

Pali opened her mouth, but had nothing to say.

Sardeet looked up at her. She had a dusting of flour on the side of her face, mirroring the white spots Pali had gained when she had fought the Scorpion-Men who guarded the tunnel between the human and divine realms, when she and Arzu had gone to rescue Sardeet from her wicked first husband.

"Be gentle with yourself," Sardeet added, smiling radiantly. "You do not need to *fight* your way to inner truth."

And with that she turned to the butter and pastry-dough, and hummed as she rolled it out once more.

∼

Pali followed her instructions, because Sardeet had clearly learned wisdom as well as joy.

The town was quiet, sleepy, in the morning. A few people were out and about—farmers on their way to tend their animals and fields for the most part, as far as she could see—but though they nodded at her, no one spoke.

It was a cool, hazy morning, grey-blue before the sun rose. Pali found the lane easily. She walked briskly for an hour or so, listening to unfamiliar birdsong.

She did not want to think why Sardeet had so immediately recognized that she was *angry*.

Pali had always been prone to strong emotions. She had learned to use them as weapons, as she had learned to use her small frame and speed as weapons when fighting. She did not have the reach or muscle mass of someone like Damian, but she was skilled and swift.

Her tongue was perhaps more swift than it was skilled, when it mattered.

She frowned as she ducked some overhanging festoons of greenery with greyish-green leaves and cup-shaped blossoms in a pale yellow-cream, lightly freckled with purple-brown. Pali stopped to breathe in the faint, ethereal scent of the blossoms: just a hint of almond and something sugary-sweet, like the lingering aromas of Sardeet's pastries in her sister's hair.

The problem was, there was no one to fight: no one but Fitzroy, who hated it; and herself.

She strode yet more briskly, more swiftly, no longer listening to the birdsong, no longer noticing the plants or small animals except in that quiet subterranean way of keeping alert for any threats.

Not that there were any threats.

The road underfoot was earth, firm on the edges, with deep muddy puddles in the ruts from cart-traffic. She strode, half-running, telling herself she was limbering her muscles for the climb ahead, but she knew, she knew, she was running from Sardeet's soft addendum.

Pali had never been gentle with herself. She had never needed to be.

The lane passed through a cluster of buildings, hardly a hamlet—there couldn't have been more than four or five houses, and one of them seemed to be given over entirely to a piggery—and dwindled down to a footpath. No one drove wagons up here, she surmised, as the path climbed up a long shallow incline. The sky was lightening ahead of her, grey-blue shifting slowly towards a bright warm white.

There was a brighter light ahead of her, formed by the end of the overhanging shrubs on either side of the lane. She slowed as she approached the end of the lane.

The moon gate, Sardeet had called it: a round archway.

Pali had imagined something like the gilded metal and stone gates that marked the places where the highways of Astandalas had crossed between worlds. They had been stitched together with immense works of magic, and had always set her teeth on edge coming near.

Fitzroy had—

She shook her head violently. No matter Fitzroy's nervous gabble or silent appreciation when they came to those gates, his wonder about the magic, his intense curiosity about the ways the Borders had been affected by the Astandalan wizards' magic, his questions about what lay behind the gates for those who walked around them rather than through—

No matter that. Her inner truth was not about Fitzroy.

(This was almost certainly a lie, Pali knew, and refused to admit. *Why* did he have such a hold on her?)

This gate was made of slate, dark purple in colour, like a deep bruise.

The stone was in jagged blocks, the short edges irregular and the long sides flat as the stone had cleaved along some sort of underlying grain. Whoever had built it had created a circular arch with no mortar or support other than the stones holding together by gravity.

Pali examined the gate for several minutes, knocked out of her inward preoccupation by its quiet, simple, magnificence.

There were tiny pincushions of moss growing between some of the stones, and wispy grasses, and a few patches of harebells with wiry stalks and pale periwinkle blossoms the shape and size of thimbles.

No mortar, no magic. Just the stones balanced so perfectly they held themselves in the curve.

Pali studied the moon gate, wondering how the artist—artists?—had made it.

Wondering, for a brief, wild moment, if *she* could learn to do such a thing.

As if that would be a useful hobby for an adventuring scholar and swordswoman, Pali scoffed to herself, immediately retreating from the image of a garden somewhere that was full of Jullanar's flowers and Fitzroy's music and her own strange, beautiful, precariously balanced stacks of stones.

She blinked back tears and made herself walk through the moon gate with her head high and her back straight.

Ahead of her the land was open and undulating. It rose up, green grass interspersed with rusty-green patches of something like heath or ling, thickets of a larger but still compact shrub with white flowers, and patches of scree, the stone a paler grey than the slate of the arch now behind her.

There were sheep, mostly white-fleeced, grazing in the distance, and a handful of some sort of deer further off.

And there was the mountain.

It rose up steeply, white stone breaking out of the turf like the battlements of a fort, full of folds and spires and strange hollows. She could hear the sound of water rushing off in the distance, and spied a few narrow valleys that probably contained streams.

High above her one crag rose a hundred or more feet above the rest. It was sculpted by the wind or rain into the shape of a tooth, curving up to a tapering point in which there was, impossibly, an opening. The sky seemed a different colour through the hole: bluer, maybe, or more brilliant.

It was not, perhaps, an enormously tall mountain, but it sat in the landscape with such presence that Pali felt it resonating with something deep within her.

She set her mind on the wind-eye in the highest peak and determinedly set forth to reach it.

∾

It was not, at first, difficult.

The sun was rising to Pali's right, which gave her a useful means by which to orient herself. She followed the sheep-trails, angling towards the nearest valley that cut into the heart of the mountain. She was already higher than the river that ran through it, and though she peeked down at attractive pools and ferny grottos, she felt no lure to explore their mysteries.

No, that wind-eye cut through the stone at the highest peak, that was what called to her.

The river-valley stopped abruptly at a cliff-face. The river disappeared into it, or rather issued out of it; the low entrance tunnel was not so low someone who was drawn that direction could not have found their way in.

Pali was not afraid of the dark and the enclosed—had she not walked for twelve days and twelve nights in the tunnel between the mortal realms and the world of the gods, fighting off the Scorpion-Men with a fist-sized lump of iron pyrite?

Did she not have the white spots all down her side, on her face and her hand, as witness of that journey?

That time she'd walked hand-in-hand with her older sister; Arzu had come out of the tunnel with her black hair entirely white.

Pali was not afraid of the dark and the enclosed. She doubted there would be anything to fight, in this mountain; not even herself.

She had brought Arzu's carpet, folded and tied about her waist, just in case.

She was tempted—

But no. Sardeet would surely think that was cheating.

Come to that, Pali felt it was cheating.

So she kilted up the skirts of her robes, tied off her sleeves, and climbed up the side of the cliff.

∼

She climbed up, saddle to low cliff, boulder field to steeply slanting hillside, until she came to the false summit of the mountain.

It was well into midmorning, and the sun was warm. She found a spring of fresh water at the base of a stone carved with a spiral form, and after drinking from her cupped hand, sat cross-legged on the grass looking up at the wind-eye.

Two or three black birds were circling the peak. Ravens, she thought, from their size, and relaxed away from a certain frisson of concern that one of them might have been a certain wild mage who had learned how to turn himself into a crow.

The false summit was a pleasant place to rest. It had a fantastic view in all directions: when she turned her back on the wind-eye, she found half of Voonra spread out before her.

That was an exaggeration, of course. Voonra was not *that* small.

Sardeet's village was a toylike cluster of buildings, blue smoke rising up in lazy spirals from its chimneys. From up here Pali could see the preponderance of streams and rivers, and counted five different mills. At least two were sawmills, with rafts of logs caught in their millponds.

Farther out were the patchwork of forests and fields that from up here did not look any different than Chare had looked when Pali had stood at the edge of the pass and looked back on her old home.

She considered that thought.

Stoneybridge *had* felt like home, for a certain value of home. She was sure of it. She had been content, even happy, there.

Content just enough, happy just enough, a voice whispered. For all her anger and frustration with herself, with Fitzroy, these past weeks with Jullanar and Masseo and Fitzroy back in her life had been so much more real.

Be gentle with yourself, Sardeet had told her. But Pali did not know how to be gentle.

She stood up, took another drink from the tiny fountain now that it had refilled itself, and studied the landscape with a ferocious concentration.

The summit sloped down to a narrow ridge, nearly knife-edged in portions where the land fell away most steeply. Then there was a jumble of stone outcroppings, and what looked like a natural stone bridge to the base of the peak proper. On that side she thought there might be a chimney slanting up at an angle to where a tongue of improbably green turf spilled out of a cirque; the crag with the wind-eye rose on its northern face.

∽

The thing was, Pali had always been physically skilled.

She had grown up riding, shooting, playing at swords and daggers with her sisters and the other children of the clan. They had run after the adults, learning to draw the short recurved bows the horse-archers used, learning to use the weapons of their people, learning to know their bodies and trust them.

When she was fourteen, she had followed a vision to the Black Mountain, where she had studied intensively with the Warriors of the Mountain.

She had left her studies four years later to rescue Sardeet from the Blue Wind, and spent the next two years carrying the bones of his six dead wives home to their peoples. By the end of that journey Pali had felt herself honed in her vocation, restless for a sword in her hand, a horse under her, the wind in her face.

She had known, slaying the Blue Wind, that she might not be granted the veils of the Warriors of the Mountain, for she had been sent out to resolve an injustice without bloodshed.

They had listened to her account of herself, and decided that while she had failed to attain the Second Veil, she would be granted the status of a Warrior of the Third Veil.

With that validation, Pali had been granted the honour of her great-grandmother's sword, with which her great-grandmother had cut down the sun, and all the freedom her wits and her weapons would grant her.

She had followed the wind until she found the Siruyal drinking at the oasis, and the great bird had granted her those three wishes.

She did not find the climb impossible.

It was hard; very hard. But she loved to work her body, which was still strong and limber. She was more careful, perhaps, than she had been as a younger woman, but she had travelled—all the Red Company had travelled—in the Divine Lands. She had drunk the mead of the Sun, the waters of the Moon, could still remember the taste of starshine on her tongue.

She walked upright, spine straight, chin up, eyes and heart and breath steady, across the knife-edge ridge, though the land fell down a hundred feet on either side of her; and when she had threaded her way through the jumble of crags, she walked even more steadily across the foot-wide natural bridge, though the wind whistled and whipped her clothes around her, and the ravens flew beneath her.

They were not crows, she snapped at herself, angry for noticing, for caring, even as the stone thrummed under her feet and the wind pressed against her with forceful, fickle blows.

When she stepped off the bridge, she spent a few minutes leaning against the solid, stable face of the mountain, and knew she needed to look at that anger.

She let go of the rock face and looked up at the chimney slanting up to bowl-shaped cirque spilling out the green fall of grass, and above it all the white eye of the wind, and promised the mountain she would do it there.

～

The final ten feet to the wind-eye itself were the hardest.

The crag was nearly sheer, the foot- and handholds minute. It had been hard to climb that steep fall of grass, and she'd needed to dig her toes into the turf, her hands into the roots, so that she did not slide back down.

It was harder to clamber out of the steep-sided cirque. There was a tiny tarn at the bottom of the cirque, hidden from below, a bright kingfisher-blue. Pali was nearly tempted to sit there, sheltered from the wind by the walls of the mountain, with the fine herbs and the harebells and some sort of cottontail grass bending and whispering around her.

She lay there for a few minutes, her robes spread out about her, her head cushioned by low-growing thyme, the scent of the herb rising up around her, perfuming her hair.

The high overcast had mostly cleared, and the sky was a fine blue, feathered here and there with clouds. Laying there, the wind murmuring in her ears, the mountain cradling her, Pali could almost imagine being gentle.

It was the sort of thing Fitzroy would take and write a poem about, and it would be a beautiful poem that said five different things to three different readers.

She sat up and looked into the tarn, which was protected enough to present a mirror-smooth surface.

She looked at herself: her copper-brown skin, the dark freckles over her nose which the sun had brought out, the white speckles down the side of her face from those sparks her fool's gold had struck from the Scorpion Men. Her thick dark eyebrows, just barely shaped; she'd always thought them an attractive arch on their own, and she liked the mole that rested at the top of her right eyebrow.

Her dark eyes, catching a few glimmers from the sun in the sky, and her lips, firm and full. She'd not bothered with the kohl this morning; it had been too early. She had wrinkles, of course, and she liked those, too, the signs of a full life.

She had never been as beautiful as Sardeet. Her nose was just that touch too long, her ears just that touch asymmetrical, her expression too severe.

A severe brow, and a caustic tongue, Elena Vane's brother Higgins had described her.

She still had a severe brow and a caustic tongue.

She could not look at herself, in that tiny pool cradled in the cirque nearly at the top of the mountain, and be content. Over the shoulder of her reflection was the crag, and its wind-eye.

She broke the surface to drink, and then she turned to the curve of the basin, and readied herself to leave its shelter and its calm.

She had never been one for serenity, for stillness, for calm reflection, after all.

It was a hard clamber to zigzag up the bowl, which curved nearly back upon itself. She could feel gravity pulling at her, and the wind buffeting her, tugging at her hair and her clothes.

But her hands were strong and her knowledge of her body's

strength true, and if she had to rest now and then with her body pressed against the grass, her nose full of thyme and tickled by harebells, she felt no shame at the fact.

There was a tiny ledge at the base of the crag proper, where the topmost rim of the cirque was padded with some sort of cushiony plant with pink-and-white flowers on wiry stalks. It was just wide enough for Pali to sit, her back to the crag and her feet dangling, as she looked down along her path.

From here the mountain looked much higher. She stared down, at the falling slopes and cliffs, at the very distant white spots of the sheep, and the black birds flying below her.

Her hand strayed to her sash, where dagger and carpet were both tucked safely.

And then, her breath caught, her heart steady, she grasped a rocky outcropping, twisted herself back to a standing position, and pressed herself to the stone for the last dozen feet to the wind-eye.

It was slow work, with the wind whispering blandishments in her ears, inducements to falling. Pali moved cautiously, attention focused on finding handholds, places for her booted toes to rest, testing each support before she gave her weight to it.

Out around a bellying curve, and then there was a place where she could wish she was another foot taller.

Short as her arms and legs might be compared to some, she was at least light in weight, all muscle beneath her robes. She had none of Sardeet's softness.

The thought came to her that she never had.

Sardeet had been stolen by the Blue Wind, ravished away by the god, taken to his blue glass aerie high on the edge of the Black Mountains, overlooking the Holy Desert. In their culture that was an honour, a gift, but though Pali had performed the correct rites and behaviours for such a splendid occurrence—for though their legends were full of divinities and magical beings, no one had seen so much as a feather of a roc in generations—she had not, in her heart, been able to reconcile the loss of her sister.

Pali stopped for a moment as the wind gusted, bringing the croaking calls of the distant ravens into her ears, and focused on a wide greeny-gray circle of lichen on the rock before her. It was a beautiful set of overlapping circles, none of them quite regular.

When she had seen Fitzroy leaning down from that high balcony, magic coruscating around him, his face and his eyes full of such brilliance she had not been able to imagine him human, she had not been able to say *yes*.

She had never been able to say yes to him. Nor had she ever been able to say *no*. And so they had danced around each other, him with ever more extravagant declarations, she with ever more elaborate prevarications, until that moment in the Silver Forest when the protections surged up and separated them and Pali, stepping towards Fitzroy to find herself abruptly on another world, had finally known the answer in her heart.

And so she had tracked him, all the way across the width of the Empire, all the way from the Silver Forest near the centre of Astandalas to that tower on its most distant edge.

And when she had reached there, and could find no sign but that he had leaped his horse right into the Sea of Stars, right off the edge of Colhélhé, she had unfurled her sister's carpet and followed after him.

Seven days and seven nights had she followed after him, until she could not bear the strangeness of that inhuman place, and she had decided to turn back.

Pali worked her jaw, and pushed aside these thoughts, for her fingers were cramping and she would not fall now.

She pushed herself up with her toes, pulled with her fingers, worked her mind and her body, and finally she found herself in the eye of the mountain.

CHAPTER THIRTY-THREE
CARPET AND CROW

The wind-eye was larger than she had guessed, though once she thought of it she knew it had to be sizeable, to be so visible all the way down at that arch at bottom of the mountain. It was perhaps twenty feet in diameter, a jagged oval at the top, water-smoothed at the base.

It was all of five feet wide. On the far side the crag fell down even more sheerly, not a dozen feet to the green bowl of a grassy cirque but several hundred feet down in a staggered series of rock-faces, all the way down to a forest that brushed up, darker green than the grass, against the northeastern flank of the mountain.

The view was unimaginably vast.

She had thought it wide from the false summit, but now she could see the other side of the mountain.

She could see the sea to the west, which she had barely remembered was there; it had been a long time since she'd last looked at a map of Voonra. She could see the heavy mass of the great Forest of Adroon in the north. She could see the double-file ranks of the mountains, curving like the curve of her sword across this quarter of the land. To the southeast there was a huge lake—the Inland Sea, she corrected herself, remembering journeys on the trading boats that plied its shores.

A speck of gold might be one of the old Astandalan gates between worlds, mirror-image to the moon gate on the mountain's other side, which did not lead between worlds but into the self.

Due north and due south were blocked by the arching stone of the wind-eye's frame. She knew that to the south would be the misty fertile lowlands, full of lakes and canals, where the Queen of Voonra had her castle.

The wind reverberated through the space. The rock hummed under her, as she sat on the stone, cross-legged at the lowest point of the circle. She shifted position a few times, adjusting the tightness of her sash, the angle of her daggers, unable to feel quite comfortable on the stone.

Sardeet had probably not meant this, but—

But Pali was not fourteen, not eighteen, not twenty-eight, not forty. She unclasped Arzu's carpet from her waist and unrolled it. It was long enough the ends draped over the edges of the wind-eye, so the wind caught the tassels.

She sat on the middle, where the faint scents rose up, and her hands could trace the patterns in the weave, the Tree of Life surrounded by the knots of love.

Be gentle with yourself, Sardeet had said.

Pali had not stopped at the intriguing pools and small cascades of the river issuing from the heart of the mountain. She had not stopped at the false summit, though the view had seemed expansive. She had not stayed in the cirque, protected from the wind, looking at that pool of cold, clear, water.

She lay down, body curving to match the curve of the stone, and listened to the wind until her thoughts grew silent and still.

∼

The Warriors of the Black Mountain believed that in order to be a great warrior—and no one who won the veils was less but great—one needed to master oneself first, and then one's weapons.

Pali could calm her thoughts before a fight. She had trained her body to move fluidly, her mind to see possibilities where others saw hopeless odds, to never give up. She had learned to be still in herself, and sought justice in herself and her duties.

She had never been able to cleave herself from her emotions. She had learned to wield them instead, weapons to her hand, no longer liabilities. She thirsted for justice; she loved righteous anger.

But anger was not only righteous.

The wind was warm on her face, drawing hairs loose from her braid to tickle her cheeks and chin. She tucked her hands behind her head, brushing the hair back, and thought about what Sardeet had said. Anger could be a mask for fear, for sorrow, for shame.

Pali had resisted that suggestion, with an immediate, furious resistance.

She had climbed up this mountain refusing to entertain it.

She stared at the pale stone of the arch, a white limestone nearly as luminous as the alabaster stone of Fitzroy's emperor-self's study.

She was a fine scholar.

When her students were looking at a pile of miscellaneous primary sources with confusion and distrust that they could ever come up with a coherent idea, let alone a compelling theory, about them, Pali told them to study the materials until a pattern started to emerge. Then they took that first inkling of a pattern, that first hasty sketch, and returned to the body of sources looking for elements that agreed or disagreed.

Slowly, very slowly, something at first delicate, later increasingly sturdy, would emerge.

The mountain hummed with the wind, steady stone and ceaselessly moving air.

What it would be, to be full of air and fire, and forced to become that still, serene figure on that golden throne, in that luminous stone room, that ethereal cage of magic and power and responsibility?

She had been able to be content, nearly happy, as a Scholar of Stoneybridge, taking up the weapons of debate and scholarship, never failing to maintain her physical prowess. Restless nomad that she was, called always by the wind, there was a part of her which was solid and steady as the earth.

A part of her that was intransigent and unyielding as the stone.

Righteous anger was a glorious thing. There had never been a lack of things to be righteously angry about.

But this ... this turmoil ... this was not righteous anger.

She acknowledged that thought, and hesitated over it. She was not accustomed to this baffled fury, this impotent rage, this misdirected *hate*.

She shied away from that word, but it was true. She *hated*—

She stopped.

What *did* she hate?

(Study the evidence, she told her students. Let the patterns emerge.)

Anger could be a mask for sorrow, for shame, for fear.

Sorrow—as soon as she formed the word in her mind, she was assaulted by grief, by the keening loneliness of those years without her sisters, without her friends, with the knowledge that she would never see Fitzroy again, or if she did he would not be *Fitzroy*, he would be some god who had returned to his divinity, riding his horse too far into the Sea of Stars for her to follow after.

She lay there, hands thrust into the soft pile of the carpet, fingers tracing out the threads that marked the knots of love and the Tree of Life, and acknowledged that sorrow.

She had grieved for Fitzroy all these years.

She had ridden this carpet, her sister Arzu's magic flying carpet, seven days and seven nights into the Sea of Stars, until she had grown too afraid to continue.

There was that second part of this anger: shame. Oh, she was ashamed, still, of giving up. She had never given up; had never turned back because of fear; had never quailed, bar that once.

A year and a day had it taken her to return, in the end, to fight her way through the strangeness and her fear, to reach safety. She had returned to the mortal realms, and done the same rituals she had done when she had heard Sardeet had been taken away, ravished away, by the Blue Wind, one of the gods of the holy desert, and lost therefore to her mortal family.

She had tried, she *had*—oh, she had *tried*—to mourn him as dead.

She lay there with her sorrow, her shame. And her fear?

There was a rustle and a scrape, a noise not the wind. Pali opened her eyes and sat up, to see that a crow had landed on the stone just past the border of the carpet, and was strutting up and down along its hemline, examining the pattern.

She scrubbed her eyes, glad she hadn't lined them with kohl this morning: she would have been malar-marked like a peregrine falcon or Sardeet's strange tiger-cats.

"Hullo," she said, voice gravelly.

The crow looked at her with a bright, intelligent eye.

Uncannily intelligent? Was that Fitzroy behind that dark window?

"Fitzroy?" she said hesitantly. The crow tilted its head, and made a querying sort of noise before hopping onto the carpet and pecking at the centre of one of the knots of love.

"Right," she murmured under her breath. "Of course you'd focus on that."

The crow shuffled around a few steps before settling down and fluffing out all its feathers. His feathers.

Pali sighed, but she could feel a smile tugging at her mouth, her heart. No matter how angry she was, Fitzroy *did* always manage to make her laugh.

"I missed you," she said, and they sat there together, the crow with the wind ruffling his feathers, her with the stone thrumming beneath her, setting her bones to sympathetic resonance.

Fear, sorrow, shame.

"I grieved you," she said. "I followed ... as far as I could ..."

But there was the shame. She flushed, but they were private up here, as private as it was possible to be. This wind was not listening; and the mountain would hold her secrets.

"I turned back," she whispered. "I was afraid. I was afraid ..." She hesitated, but she had to say it, didn't she? The crow regarded her with one bright-black eye. "I was afraid I would lose myself. I have always been afraid I would lose myself to you."

He had always seemed divine to her, a god as brilliant, as wonderful, as amazing as the Blue Wind must have seemed to Sardeet when that god stole Pali's little sister away.

Fear, sorrow, shame.

These were old stories, old worries, old griefs, old shames, old fears. There were more recent things to regret.

"I'm sorry," she said, plucking at the hanging fringe of her sash. The fibres fell over her hands, silky, smooth, blue as the sky to her left and her right. "I'm sorry I have been so ..."

She trailed off, unable to finish the sentence, watching as the crow lifted his head and turned to face her more directly.

"Formidable?" came the familiar, resonant, beautiful voice, threaded with humour and power, and Pali jumped, for he was behind her.

She was a warrior: she jumped upon her feet, dagger in hand. Startled, Fitzroy jumped too—stepped back—wavered at the edge.

She caught his elbow, steadying him.

The crow squawked and hopped a few feet away.

Pali looked at the crow and then back at him. "That's not you?"

He laughed, his teeth flashing whitely, and dropped down to sit. Not quite easily, lightly, cross-legged, but with his knees drawn up. He was dressed very simply, in a wine-red tunic and purple trews, with an open coat in matching purple cloth. It showed off his broad shoulders and still-compact waist, and from the faint clink held something in its deep pockets.

He probably did not sit cross-legged often, Pali guessed, unable to imagine that serene and glorious figure, that distant golden idol, sitting tailor-style on the floor.

"Did you think that was me?"

"No, I preferred pouring my heart out to a stranger crow," Pali retorted, unable to muster a sting. She sat down facing him, cross-legged and upright, not quite close enough to touch.

"Formidable is not quite the right word, is it?" he said, musingly, reaching out with one hand towards the crow. It let him stroke its breast with one gentle finger. Pali looked at him, and he smiled at her, about as compassionately as he had smiled at Terec when they spoke of being a wild mage under the Pax Astandalatis. "Redoubtable might be better. Formidable *and* fortified."

Pali glanced down, but could hardly deny this. "I'm sorry. I am trying," she said quietly, knowing it was not enough.

"So am I," he said.

They sat there for a few moments. Fitzroy stroked the crow, and the wind sang in the stone.

"Did you come to find me?"

He smiled lopsidedly at her. "I'd like to say yes, but honesty compels me to say no. I was flying, and went up too high. I was aiming at the top of the crag for a perch, and missed. Flying is easy," he added thoughtfully, "landing is harder."

"You've always found that," she replied, without heat. He did look windblown, exhilarated; if he'd been lighter-skinned he would have been flushed with exertion, and if he'd had hair it would have been tangled and tumbled.

"If you'd rather be alone, I'll leave you to your thoughts."

"Don't be absurd," she said. He looked sharply at her, and she said, "You need to rest—" But that was not the truth, or the whole truth, was it? She plucked at the edge of the carpet. "I'd like you to stay."

"Thank you," he replied, very gravely. He shifted position, fixing the drape of his coat, and she was struck by the incongruous curiosity of what he looked like, preening himself as a crow. He frowned and dug into his pocket, finally pulling out a somewhat squished loaf of bread.

"It was Sardeet's, fresh this morning," he said mock-mournfully. The crow beside him made an interrogative noise, eyes fixed on the bread. "Would you like some?" He glanced at her, and though his voice was light Pali could not help but recognize the peace offering for what it was.

"Please," she said, her throat dry.

He broke the bread, and handed her a piece before taking the other in his own hand. They both offered a crumb to the crow at the same time; Pali was obscurely pleased that it came to her hand first before settling down in front of Fitzroy.

"I am trying to ... sort out my anger," Pali said, pushing out the words with much less effort than she ever had anticipated.

Oh, he was easy to talk to, wasn't he?

She had heard his voice in her mind, his and Jullanar's, commenting, reassuring, remonstrating, cheering.

He turned his full attention to her, and she basked in it for a moment: that sunlit regard, that grave expression, that smile lurking in the corner of his mouth, his eyes. Oh, he was Fitzroy, wasn't he?

Fitzroy, and also Artorin Damara, and also—

Did it matter?

She held that thought there, like a handful of snow, melting even as she looked at it.

But *did* it matter if he were really Aurelius Magnus? What might that mean? Whether or not he was, he was certainly—*certainly*—Fitzroy, their Fitzroy, her Fitzroy, himself.

"After we were separated in the Silver Forest, I went back to our camp—I'd been thrown to Zunidh—northern Dair, I think it was—and I tracked you as far as I could," she said, not meaning to say it, but committed once she had begun, for she had only ever turned back for fear once, and she would not do it again. "I followed you to the Long Edge, to that tower where you said you'd lived."

"I didn't go back in," he said. "I was caught there."

"For me, coming some months behind you, all the traces I could see suggested that you'd jumped your horse off the edge of the world."

He looked down, and for a moment Pali could see with terrible clarity how much he *wished* he had done that.

She licked her lips, which felt very dry, "I had Arzu's carpet," she said, patting the weave they were seated upon, "and I sailed it seven days and seven nights into the Sea of Stars after you."

He looked at her, and she let him, though his eyes were full of both magic and a tremendous pain.

I gave up, he had shouted at her, and she had not been able to do anything but sneer hatefully in response, as if she could not understand why, how, anyone could ever give up.

"I grew afraid of how strange it became, and ... the fear overmastered me, and I ... I turned back."

The words hung there, in that unceasing, restless wind, that thrumming stone, the sky embracing them and the world far below.

He knew what those words meant to her.

"I was afraid," she repeated, "and I told myself that if you had gone that far, then you could not be human after all, and were ... not for me."

Fitzroy's hand had stilled, and the crow, making an affronted noise, nudged at his hand with its beak until he started to stroke it again.

"I was always yours," he said, lowly, as if it were a secret he had never said, rather than a declaration he had shouted to the world five times a day and twelve times on holidays.

"I was always afraid ..."

"Of me?" His eyes flashed with hurt, and horror, and Pali could only recall that recounting of the people who had committed suicide because the new emperor had said the wrong criticisms to them, of the woman Fitzroy had whispered he had burned when he touched her by accident, of Commander Omo of his household who bore those golden scars down his arms from when Fitzroy, seeking comfort in his pain, had grasped him.

"Sardeet was ravished away by a god."

"But I'm not ..." His voice trailed off. "I never was, Pali."

"I didn't know how else to make sense of how I felt when you looked at me, that first time we met. I've never ... No one else has ever ... I was ... a fish caught on a line, the hook in my heart, the line never to be broken."

He was quiet for a few moments, and then he said, subdued, "That's a very violent metaphor. I had no idea I'd hurt you so. I'm sorry."

Pali listened to the wind, felt it in the stone, humming under her hands, her palms laid flat. She felt as if her body were trying to vibrate in sympathy with its thrum, shake loose its stiffness, its rigidity, fly.

She'd always assumed he'd chosen to catch her, as the Blue Wind had chosen Sardeet.

"How did you think of it?" she asked, a question she had never asked.

He worried at his lip, and Pali was struck by how white his teeth were. "I saw you, and I felt my whole being come into focus ... as if I were a lodestone, and for the first time I had found another."

He stopped there.

Pali sat there, staring open-mouthed at him.

She had known she was important to him—had never truly been able to doubt it, though she had doubted his endless hyperbolic protestations of love, because how could she not? She was not Sardeet, stolen away by one of the gods. She was Pali, who had slain that god.

You are magnificent! We should get married!

She, the fish on the line, the falcon on the jess, the horse bridled, the animal *tamed*.

She had been sure she would lose herself to him. She had been sure that if she accepted his regard, fully opened her heart to him, she would be ravished and lost, as Sardeet had been ravished and lost.

She had not expected Sardeet to rescue her. She had not expected that he had imagined them as a pair of such ordinary, common, homely things.

She had never expected him to be afraid.

She swallowed, and her jaw was aching, her eyes burning, but she forced herself to be steady. There had been times when she had studied her materials and all her beautifully crafted theories had fallen apart because of a new piece of evidence, a missing link, a misunderstood source.

The only honest thing to do was to start over.

Before she had quite decided what to say, Fitzroy said hesitantly, "Is it such a terrible thing, to be shaped by those you love?"

She looked up at him, startled by the tentativeness in his voice.

He ducked his chin, blushing. "I've always thought it made me a better person, to be guided and influenced by you. I have spent so long isolated ... this fiction of a deity, of someone immutable, unchangeable, unable to be influenced, and ... it hurt, Pali, it hurt so much that I wasn't allowed to have *connection*. I *wanted* to touch people. I wanted to *be* touched. I wanted to change and be changed. I wanted to be *alive*. I wanted to be ..."

"You wanted to be human."

He looked at her, his eyes brilliant, his face just barely composed, his lips tight together, and nodded.

Pali wanted to hug him, to hold him; to be held by him. But they were not there yet, were they? There was still a knot in her heart, a churning turmoil.

She took several deep breaths, composing herself, and then she said: "Fitzroy, I am the Alinorel expert on your reign, and I did not *realize it was you*." She had to stop there, but he waited, for he had learned patience, that river turned to a lake, that fire doused, that free wind bound within its walls of alabaster stone. "I am so sorry. I cannot understand how I did not see it. I thought I understood so much ... and I missed *you*."

He winced, but then he smiled. It was a small smile, pained, but she could see in his eyes that he was speaking the truth. "And yet, Pali, you *do* understand me. Your questions hurt because they were so *good*—because I—because I am not a god, Pali, I am a human being, and I make mistakes."

Gods could make mistakes—

Pali amended that thought. *Her* gods could make mistakes. Fitzroy had always been fascinated by Damian's One Above and the idea of a perfectly good, perfectly transcendent deity.

She stopped, struck.

Her gods could make mistakes.

And yet she had held Fitzroy to a standard to which she did not even hold her deities?

"I make mistakes, too," she said, blankly, as some emotion, some revelation poured into her mind.

"I am afraid I have forgotten how to be Fitzroy entirely," Fitzroy said, his voice raw. "I was so afraid you wouldn't like me any more ..."

"Now that I know," she said, hearing his words but not able to answer them directly, not yet. "Now that I know, I look at all I know about your reign and I can see you *everywhere*. Every portrait, every coin, every decision, every policy—you were shouting who you were every way you could, and I didn't see it."

"I am still here," he said.

"You are," she answered, and she smiled at him. Her face felt stiff and the expression unfamiliar. "Oh, Fitzroy. I'm so sorry for hurting you."

"Pali ..."

She had grieved for a man who was right here, beside her, on the top of a mountain; who had been hidden in plain sight all the time she had thought him dead or divine or otherwise lost to her

She had been afraid, but she was still Pali, and the fact that she'd faltered once—might falter again—(oh, she had faltered again and again, each time he had asked her to marry him she had come up with a parry, a deflection, a block, pretending that she never understood anything more than a feint—).

She was ashamed of some of her actions, her words, her decisions, but she was still Pali, and she had apologized for those she could apologize for, and she could *do better*.

That thought came to her, and she looked at him, at the crow that had settled into his lap, all its feathers fluffed out as he cradled it in his hands. Against the shining black of its feathers his hands looked an incredibly deep brown rather than the true-black she so often imagined him.

"You don't have to be perfect, either," he said. "Not for me, not for Sardeet, not for Jullanar, not for anyone."

And *that* hung there, for Pali had always sought excellence and justice and had been righteously furious whenever anyone failed to be either. Whenever *she* had failed to be either.

But that was not righteousness at all, was it?

She picked at the end of her braid, the red ribbon with which she'd tied it off, scarlet as the flag the Red Company had laughingly accepted as their own when Gadarved's people had insisted they have one.

Seek dzēren, the Siruyal had said. The third quest. The one she had never finished.

"What would you wish, if you could wish for anything?" she asked Fitzroy, putting her hand into her pocket where the beans and the feather and the glass marble were jumbled together.

"Wishes are dangerous things," he said, and then he smiled at her. "And—after so long—I am once more on my way to everything I ever wanted."

Oh gods of her mother's desert. He could say that? To her? Here? *Now?*

He met her eyes gravely. "What would *you* wish for, Pali, if you could?"

Pali drew out the feather, fingers pinched around its shaft, and examined the glistening white vanes, the ink-dipped tip. Fitzroy caught his breath.

"I didn't know you had more than one of those."

"I was given three," she replied. "One I used to learn to speak and understand the languages of the first three people I met." She smiled up at him. "Not that I have ever needed Renvoonran, but your facility with Old and Antique Shaian has been appreciated at times."

He ducked his head, blushing again, and she remembered him saying that his tutor had punished him for misbehaving by making him learn dead languages and etiquette manuals.

No doubt both had served him better, in the end, than the tutor had ever expected.

"The second you wished for us to know *your* language."

"Yes." The wind was tugging at the feather, wanting her to let it go. "I've thought, often, about what my third wish could be. But you are right. Wishes are dangerous things. The possibility of a wish, now ..."

He smiled, and if it had been in other days Pali would have thought that kindling light the sign of a poem being born.

He gave her a long, very solemn look, a great mage's look. The air was crystalline with significance.

"What do you *want*, Pali?"

CHAPTER THIRTY-FOUR
THE THIRD QUEST

Pali sat there for a moment before she could speak. "I don't know."

It was a quiet admission, not—not *wrenched* out of her, unless the past month since she had encountered Fitzroy in his high tower, pacing a shadow into the stone, had done the wrenching.

Four weeks, if that. It had been no longer.

She offered the admission up, a small truth beside all his extravagant ones, and nearly held her breath waiting for the response.

She, Pali Avramapul, admitting such a thing!

(She had admitted she had turned back out of fear, had *given up*.)

Fitzroy was quiet, and then he gently set the crow in his hands down, and reached forward to take her hands in his. The crow muttered and flew off, a shadow caught in the wind, flung into the sky, choosing to fly.

His hands were warm, dry, smooth. Pali gripped back, not hard, but enough for him to know she was grateful for the touch.

"It is such a relief to hear you say that," he said, and his voice was almost too soft to be heard over the wind thrumming in the stone. "To know that *you* are uncertain ..."

"I tried so hard to mourn you, to put you aside, to say *you were gone, you were not for me, you were ...*"

"Lost."

"Apotheosized, to use Masseo's word."

Fitzroy grimaced and looked down. His hands clenched on hers. "I'm not ..."

"No," Pali said, suddenly certain: as certain as she had ever been, facing any wickedness. "You're not. You are a human being, a man, a *person*. You're Fitzroy Angursell of the Red Company, sometime Emperor of Astandalas. My dear friend. My *dear* friend."

He looked up at her through his lashes, which were beaded with diamond-drop tears, his eyes seeming a much darker amber than usual in the shadow of the stone.

She swallowed. "You are brilliant and funny, splendidly skilled as a poet, as a mage, as a statesman, as a friend. You are aggravating and impossible and I have always loved you, Fitzroy."

He swallowed and glanced down again, and he brought her hands up to his lips for a moment, kissing her knuckles.

A moment later he spluttered, and let go to wipe his mouth, and then seized her hands again to examine her fingers.

"What is it?" Pali asked, too spent to be anything other than mildly curious.

"Your hands are all dusty and dirty!"

Pali tugged her hands back and examined her fingers, which were scratched and, indeed, rather grimy. She raised her eyebrows at him. "I did climb a mountain a short while ago."

Fitzroy stared blankly at her, then leaned over so he could look down the vertical crag to the steep curve of the cirque, and below that the fall of grass and stone to the natural bridge and the valley floor far below.

"You *climbed* up?"

"How did you think I got here?"

He gave her a sardonic smiled and patted the carpet. The tassels stirred and the weave rippled as the fibres responded to the magic in his touch. Pali placed both her hands flat on the fabric, spreading out her fingers to cover two of the knots of love.

Oh, Arzu, making a flying carpet out of the knots of love and the tree of life. Pali carried her home with her, her sisters and her friends, the possibility of adventure—and, she added to herself, at the remembered image of those nine red ribbons and the tenth, the thread tied to stone and shrub and tree and stake, her *way home* too.

"I don't think I could ever have climbed up here without any assistance," Fitzroy declared, and he smiled at her, openly admiring. "What a splendid person you are, Pali Avramapul! Such a swordswoman! Such a scholar! Full of so many surprises!"

"Am I?"

"You are."

Pali considered herself—had always considered herself—to be a very decided sort of person. She did not think she was full of surprises.

Did she *want* to be full of surprises?

She thought of the great and wonderful surprise of seeing Sardeet running her own business, prosperous and happy and wise and, yes, *brimful*.

The beautifully balanced stone arch at the bottom of the mountain came to her mind, the beauty formed from balance, from opposing forces held in tension, something airy and magnificent created out of the heavy, solid, fractured stones.

Pali did not want the specifics of Sardeet's life, but perhaps she could come to want that kind of *brimful*.

She *had* come to want it, over the weeks since she had challenged the night at the crossroads. She wanted the quest to seek dzēren, to change, to grow, to discover who she might be if she were not afraid of losing herself, but instead willing to see what she could become.

Because no, it was not such a bad thing, to change and be changed by those whom you loved.

Three feathers, three wishes, three quests. She drew out the third feather again, and moved to release it.

"Don't," said Fitzroy, reaching out to stop her.

"Don't?"

He sat back, biting his lip. "Were you going to wish for something?"

"No."

His lips quirked. "I didn't think so. Don't let it go, Pali. You might yet want it."

"Not *need* it?"

"Have you ever needed it?"

She had not wished to find him, when she was seven days and seven nights out into the Sea of Stars, and neither time nor space nor her own physical existence had been quite ... *right*.

She had not wished to return in safety, when she had grown afraid of the depths above her, before her, below her, and turned back.

She had flown a year and a day back, through storms made out of laughter and tempests of fear, sustained by her stubbornness, knowing her direction only because she had a knotted thread Arzu had made for the Red Company that guided her towards them.

Each knot had contained some essence of one of her friends, some spark that reached always towards them. Pali had held the length of braided yarn in her hands, had followed the magnetic pull, until each knot unravelled in her hands, the magic spent, the direction lost.

Eight friends, and eight knots unravelled; and the ninth, the friend whose direction was the other way, had pulled nowhere but had throbbed in her hands, an anchor for her physicality, until the carpet reached that endless waterfall that was the edge of Colhélhé and the last knot fell away to ashes in her hands.

The last gift of Fitzroy Angursell, she had thought, throwing herself down on the grass below that tower, sobbing at the feel of the rough grass on her face, the spray on her naked skin, the sun hot on her shoulders.

She had released her friends as the knots had released in her hands. She had let them go, granting them the freedom from her heart's thrall, her heart freedom from their thrall.

She had known she would not follow their tracks, not as she had tried, and failed, to follow Fitzroy's. She, Pali Avramapul of the Red Company, Pali Avramapul of the Oclaresh, Paliammë-ivanar, had looked at that impossible quest to find nine beloved friends, and ... *turned away.*

She had turned away.

Even from Sardeet. Even from Jullanar. Pali had scoured her heart empty, scorched as a pot on a fire, flying alone into the Sea of Stars, and she had needed ... She had needed to heal.

She had imagined them moving on to new lives on this side of that abyss. Eight of them, and herself the ninth; and the tenth ... on the other side.

And then she had begun the long, impossible attempt to root him out of her life and her heart and her mind.

She had never, truly, believed him *lost*. Gone, yes. But not lost.

She held his gaze now, that golden sunlit gaze, as he regarded her with a steadiness and stillness that he had learned in his long exile from himself, but which was not only the resignation and hopelessness of a prisoner forgotten in his cell.

The feather was soft, silky, in her fingers, tugged lightly by the wind. She would have imagined the wind moaning and howling through this hole in the mountain, but it hummed. It hummed. The third feather; the third possible wish.

"No, I haven't," she said. "Not yet. The possibility of a wish has always been enough."

"A wish, and an adventure, and something new over the horizon."

That could have been a line from one of his poems, but it was not one Pali knew.

She could hope it was the seed of a new poem.

She set the feather back in her pocket, with the dried beans that would grow fantastic vines to a country behind a cloud if she planted them, and the marble that held no magic but which she enjoyed as an object for its own sake. A common and ordinary good, which Fitzroy had once extolled to the skies.

"Do you want to fly down?" Fitzroy asked.

Pali snorted and patted the carpet. "I had intended to."

"Oh—I meant—" He ducked his chin the way he did, and brushed his hand across his face as he grinned boyishly. For an odd moment she was reminded of Jullanar's friend Basil, telling stories of his lost cousin Kip. "I meant, I could try changing you into a crow. If you'd like."

She shook away her distraction. "And—have you ever—"

"Turned someone into a crow?"

"Turned someone *back* from whatever you turned them into."

Fitzroy coughed. "The man I turned into a table reverted after a couple of hours, none the worse for wear."

Pali waited a moment, but he merely smirked at her. She rolled her eyes. "Why did you turn him into a table? And *really,* no effects from that transformation?"

"I didn't say there were *no* effects. He certainly decided to refrain from public criticism of my viceroy."

Pali tried to control her reflexive grimace at the thought of Fitzroy's viceroy. "And why a table?"

"I had a terrible headache," he admitted, expression much more genuine. "And Cliopher has done *so much,* you know, for everyone on Zunidh—for me *personally*—and this man was simply odious. I wanted to do something terrible to him, but I ..."

"You've never been a tyrant," Pali supplied into the silence. Fitzroy looked up at her, face twisted. She reached out to him, once again took his hands in hers. "You never lost yourself."

"I came so close, Pali," he whispered.

She squeezed his hands. "I haven't spent the past fifteen years becoming the leading expert in your reign as Artorin Damara not to be able to say with *absolute confidence* that you did your best, Fitzroy. The whole project of the empire was flawed, but you *did your best.*"

"I tried."

"Yes, I know."

And she did. It was there in every policy, every attempt to clean out corruption, every award and prize for scholarship, for the arts, for exploration, for courage, for trade. He had failed, because he had been one man, without consort or concubine, confidante or friend to stand beside him, and because the empire had been rotten to its core.

He had gathered friends, confidantes, as lord magus of Zunidh, and without the weight of the empire literally torturing him daily he had been able to be so much more than simply *not a tyrant*.

"I'd like to hear more about what's happened on Zunidh since the Fall," she said, tentatively.

He leaned back and grinned at her with a sly, secretive tilt to his head. "I can lay most of my success at the feet of my viceroy."

She was better able to keep her expression, her thoughts, pleasant. There was, alas, clearly no way she was going to avoid the man's company. Fitzroy had always needed a confidant and a friend, someone he could rely on.

Pali had always needed one, too.

Or more than one, for was there not Jullanar and Sardeet as well as Fitzroy, distant Arzu as well as Damian and Masseo, Pharia and Faleron, Gadarved and Ayasha, all of them binding their lives together with friendship and shared experience and one or other sort of love.

And if Pali could like Jullanar's new friends—she could try. No. She would do better than *try*. Surely the man had *some* redeeming features beyond his apparent natural genius at statecraft.

"Sardeet told me there are excellent natural hot springs in her village," Fitzroy said, looking pensively out the wind-eye.

Pali gratefully accepted the postponement of the political conversation.

She felt ... oh, as if she was a cloth wrung out to extract the last drop of water, and now she had been laid out, carefully smoothed flat, to return to her proper shape.

She leaned back against the stone. The visiting crow, the stranger, had flown off and some point, rejoined the flock circling the crag. Fitzroy turned his head to watch them, and she watched him, enjoying the simple joy on his face, the answering, brimming joy in her heart.

He turned to meet her eyes, suddenly, and smiled as he did, and she felt that same, unexpected, physical jolt.

Two lodestones, he'd said, meeting for the first time.

She had played with lodestones, magnets, marvelled as everyone did at the invisible forces at play. Keeping them apart, bringing them together.

He was a great poet: he understood the telling phrase, the precise word, the perfect metaphor.

Two lodestones at loggerheads, until one of them turned.

It felt *good* to have turned, as if another dislocated joint had returned to its place.

Her heart might lift out of herself with its happiness, light as one of those lanterns the cloud-people had, and sail into the sky as if she were on her sister's carpet.

She glanced down, and her eye caught on the red and gold pattern, and she smiled.

"What is it?" Fitzroy asked, unworried.

Some whim caught her, some effort to choose joy, to choose that overflowing, brimful dzēren, that lantern-light, and she said: "We could race down, you and I."

It took him a moment to catch her meaning, and then his face lit slowly, shyly. "Flying?"

"Flying," she agreed, and stroked the carpet to waken its magic.

He was a crow before she had risen an inch off the stone, but with a whoop and a caw they flung themselves out into the tumult of wind circling the mountain.

CHAPTER THIRTY-FIVE
SOMETHING NEW

She chased him, the fine black crow with the golden eyes: tight against the crags, swooping down so that his feet trailed in the water of the tarn in the bowl of the cirque, tumbling him beak-over-tail as she executed a feint and a loop-de-loop right around him.

She knelt on the carpet, balanced as for a horserace, trusting Arzu's craft to hold her as Fitzroy grew bolder and less cautious. He rose in a tight spiral on some thermal wind, then as she followed close on his tail, spiralling up almost to the top of the crag above the wind-eye, he folded his wings and plummeted down the middle, cawing wildly.

Pali laughed and tipped the carpet down in a vertical fall, held against the weave by magic and the pressure of the air alone. She felt the air like a giant's hand pressed comfortingly against her breastbone, holding her safe even as the crow tried to turn out of his dive, stalled, flipped briefly upside down, and, as Pali dropped below him, casually guiding the carpet to slow, the wild cawing became a hiccough and suddenly instead of a crow there was Fitzroy plunging down, laughing so wildly he was curled around himself, long limbs folded like a falling spider, heedless.

The mountainside was rising swiftly. Pali had just a moment in which she could shake her head, amazed and aghast, as ever, with Fitzroy's ability to thrive with such insouciant joy, before she had positioned the carpet at the right angle to catch him.

The carpet folded around his weight, under the momentum of his fall. He was still laughing, and Pali could not help but laugh with him as they tumbled together into a tangle of limbs and clothes.

She caught him: but they were too close to the earth, and they hit an unexpected bump in the ground and tumbled themselves off.

They rolled down a long hill, laughing like children, until they ended up sprawled, all their limbs and clothes askew, halfway to the stone arch. High above them the wild crows circled, cawing, laughing at this human interloper, this incontinent shapeshifter, these fools.

She sat up, dizzy and exhilarated, and smiled down at Fitzroy Angursell, hundredth and last Emperor of Astandalas, as he crawled over to her.

He sighed and flopped down so his head was in her lap, as once had been his habit.

Both of them froze. He was very tense, but did not move away; she kept her hands to herself, though she longed to feel the shape of his skull, the warmth of his skin. His face was very still; his eyes were closed.

She considered, and then she asked, "Did you truly laugh hard enough to turn yourself back human?"

Fitzroy's lips twitched. He did not open his eyes. "There's a story fit for a myth!"

"It was not only our ancestors who could live them."

He was silent for a moment; when he spoke his voice had lost the urbane, gentle irony, and was almost rough-edged with wonder. "I had almost forgotten."

"So had I," Pali admitted.

He opened his eyes, and he looked up at her peering down at him. She could see the dark shapes of the circling birds reflected in his eyes.

"What's it like, being a crow?" she asked.

"Almost too easy." He did not look away. "I am nearly afraid of how easy it is."

"I'm sure," Pali said with measured gravity, "that we shall discover the consequences at some point or another."

The ground felt solid, secure, after the thrumming wind-eye, the carpet. She could feel Fitzroy's torso moving with his breath against her legs, wonderfully alive.

"Would you mind," she said, trying to be as careful and as matter-of-fact as Sardeet had been when she had asked him if she could hug him, "if I touched your head?"

He closed his eyes, and exhaled very slowly before whispering on the inhale. "Please."

Pali stroked his forehead, sweeping her hand up as if she would catch the twists of hair that had always flopped over his eyes. His skin was very smooth, warm, a little damp from perspiration. He was breathing in a measured rhythm, to a count, she was sure, of seven. She watched his eyelids fluttering, the line of silver tears beading on his eyelashes.

His skull was almost infinitesimally downy, like the ruddy cheek of a sun-warmed peach. Pali traced the gentle indentations of his temple, the arc of his crown, and then, feeling the tremble he had not yet been able to articulate, lifted her hands away from his skin.

"Your hair is starting to grow out," she said.

His face relaxed and he twisted around to sit up. "Is it! You're not simply saying that?"

"I would not."

He laughed. "No, I suppose you wouldn't." He leaned back, one hand catching the flap of his coat, and he stopped with his hand on something in the pocket. "I think," he added, drawing out a bottle, "that this may call for some sort of a celebration."

"A splendid idea," Pali agreed, watching as he frowned at the bottle. "Would you like me to open that?"

"I forgot a knife."

That was a frankly inconceivable thought, but then again Pali had not spent the past however-many-years being waited on hand and foot. She reached into her inside pocket for her utilitarian knife, and was surprised to find the small book of poems there as well.

"Did you bring poetry?" Fitzroy said, leaning forward eagerly. "I—may I look at it?"

"It's yours," Pali replied, exchanging the book for the bottle. While she fussed with the cork, Fitzroy weighed the little book in his hands.

"What a pleasing size this volume is! Hmm ... *The Correspondence of Love and the Soul* ... I'm sure I should remember if this were mine, Pali. When did I loan it to you?"

Pali popped the cork and stared at him with the dagger in one hand, cork still impaled on it, bottle wafting forth a worryingly vinegary scent in her other. "Did you not write it?"

"Not under that title." Visibly curious, he flipped open the book to the first of the ninety-nine sonnets. He went very still, nearly ashen, and after swallowing, he said, in a much more subdued voice, "Ah. Yes. Those are mine."

"I thought so," Pali said, as sympathetically as she could.

Fitzroy drew himself up, arms around his knees; he let the book fall to the grass beside him. "I don't understand how they came to be published. I ... I wrote them in the middle of my reign as emperor ... it was the only poetry I managed." He poked at the book with one finger. "I never finished the hundredth ... I set it aside and ... let myself be busy with other things. I found them, the manuscript of poems, years afterwards—just before the Fall. I read them and it was ... it was so hard, Pali, to be reminded ..."

The poems were of prisons and freedom, memory and forgetfulness, light and shadow and stone. Birds flew and the poet paced, grounded, dissolving sometimes into light, sometimes into shadow, but never free.

"I was so angry—" He stopped, and smiled crookedly at her, and she knew he'd spoken with Sardeet this morning as well, by the words that followed. "So sorrowful. So afraid. So very ashamed."

Pali slowly set the bottle down so she could work the cork off the point of her dagger.

"I could not face them, my poems, what they meant, what they showed, what I had become ... I climbed up on the table—the window in my study, the one that wasn't barred, was too high to reach otherwise—and I threw them out the window. I regretted it, of course, five minutes later, but by then it was too late." He looked wonderingly down at the book. "I've thought about them, from time to time, my lost, last poems. Wondered whether they were as good as I remember them being, as ... painful."

"Painful, yes," Pali said, as gently as she could, "for those of us who know and love you. Beautiful, for anyone. There is such pain and such hope in those poems, Fitzroy."

"I tried," he said, almost as neutrally as his emperor-voice.

Pali remembered Jemis's enthusiasm as he talked about the still centre of light, of hope, of peace, that welled out of those poems. He had spent most of an hour, as they walked together to Dart Hall, telling her about them.

It had been hard for her to see the dzēren in those poems of imprisonment and loss, when she read them first. But that had, perhaps, been her eyes, not the poet's craft.

"You threw them out the window, and by fate or wild magic they fell down in front of a passing Alinorel lady, who gathered them together and accidentally took them home with her when she returned to Alinor the next day. She always wondered if she'd missed a sheet, that they finished at ninety-nine."

"No. I couldn't write the last. It felt ... oh, it was superstitious of me."

Fitzroy was a great and wild mage. Pali would have listened to his *superstitions* over almost anyone else's logic.

"She went home, and thereby survived the Fall, though things were tumultuous enough she did not do anything with the anonymous poems she had found for many years. When she did eventually read them, she realized their great value, and saw them published."

"Is that all in the introduction?"

"I never read introductions," Pali declared loftily. "Jemis Greenwing, Jullanar's bookseller-assistant, told me about it."

"Ah yes, the dragon-slaying viscount! What a gallant young man." Fitzroy laughed, a somewhat relieved, not-quite-hysterical laugh, which concluded with a cough.

Pali offered him the wine. He took a healthy slug and nearly spat it out again.

She took the bottle back and took a much smaller sip, before making a face. "It's not bad vinegar."

"Thank goodness you think so," Fitzroy said, "I was beginning to worry my palate had atrophied entirely."

Pali wiped her mouth. "You have shown some ... interesting ..."

"Have I been that obvious?" He grimaced. "Of course I have. There were so many food taboos, Pali ... and even with the things that weren't forbidden, I grew so ... I just let my household decide, for the most part, what they wanted to give me. Sardeet putting that spread before us was almost the first free *choice* of food I've had since ... since ..."

"The old days."

"Yes."

Pali swallowed, irritated by the faint aftertaste of vinegar, and said, "There will be many choices for you in future, Fitzroy."

"All the choices."

She knew he meant this hyperbolically, and did not protest with logical limitations.

Fitzroy sighed extravagantly. "I am entirely worn-out with all this ... what did Jullanar call it? Healthful conversation?—I wonder whom *she* talks out her emotions with, don't you? It certainly didn't seem to be her ex-husband."

Pali smirked, delighted at knowing the answer. "Her friends Basil and Sara. They're innkeepers in the Woods Noirell—do you remember the Bee at the—Fitzroy?"

He sat right up, only to stare down at her, and then he actually put his hand on her arm.

"Did you say Basil? Basil Mdang?"

"I think it was White ..."

"That'd be his wife's name, of course—they're a matrilineal society." He flopped back, gazing intently at her. "If only I'd known! Basil's Kip's cousin, Pali!"

"Yes, I know," she said, puzzled. "How do *you* know that?"

Fitzroy laughed till the tears started. "Truly a cousin for every occasion! Oh, Pali, the things I have heard about Kip's cousin Basil!"

"But who is Kip? He was supposed to have died—"

Basil's cousin Kip. The one who had taken one look at a portrait of Fitzroy, of the emperor Artorin Damara, and declared that their fates were entwined. The one who had wanted to reform the government.

Pali groaned, and gently shoved him out of her lap. "He's your lord chancellor, isn't he."

"My viceroy," Fitzroy replied as he sat up, his eyes bright, amused. "You met him when he was Lord Chancellor, yes."

For a moment Pali could only inveigh against the unfairness of fate in her heart.

But she was trying to be better, wasn't she?

"You have a nickname for him."

"It's his family nickname," Fitzroy replied, almost bashfully. "He gave me permission to use it."

Pali heard what he did not say: that this Kip, Basil's cousin Kip—that bureaucrat-of-bureaucrats, his brilliant jailer—had claimed him as *family*.

"He's given me so much, Pali. He kept me sane."

Pali glanced at him, and was struck by how open his face was, how human, how *real*.

She took a deep breath. But he *was* the great poet, great with words. "How would you parse dzēren, Fitzroy?"

He closed his eyes again, face going his emperor's-countenance. Such a hard-won serenity for when he was thinking, feeling, doubting, loving. Pali watched him thinking, and found it in herself to admire that serene countenance, that steadiness and strength. He had blazed brightly before: but he had not had such a *weight* to him.

Then he smiled, and Pali was once more in that strange rural tavern, with her fate leaning down from the balcony, his eyes meeting hers and his voice ringing through the silent room.

"What a splendid word," he said, his smile almost as ravishing as Sardeet's. "A slow dawning, is it?" He murmured it to himself, the vowels rich and strange on his tongue. "It's this, isn't it?" he went on, and his eyes were glimmering with satisfaction and wonder.

Pali caught her breath.

"This moment: this gradual filling-up of the world with light, in the time before the sun quite rises. A tide turning, rising, filling the barren strands. A cup brimming with wine. Dzēren. What a perfect word for this moment."

He hesitated, and then gave her an almost tentative look. He didn't say anything, and she realized he was silently asking her to make the next step.

She didn't like that she was sitting down, and stood up. He shifted position, and she held out her hand to aid him to rise.

"Thank you," he said gravely when she had released him.

She looked at him, straight in the golden eyes, lambent as the dawn.

"I would like," she said as softly, as clearly, as plainly as she had ever said anything, "to learn who you are now, Fitzroy Angursell, sometimes emperor of Astandalas."

His voice was low, husky, raw. "I would like to know who you are now, Paliammë-ivanar Avramapul, sometime professor of Stoneybridge."

"I want to be your friend."

"I want to be yours," he said, even more lowly, huskily, rawly.

She reached out, and found his hand reaching towards hers. He hesitated, and she waited until he was ready to touch her, skin to skin.

"I'm not certain," she said, for she had never been certain, "of anything ... more."

His hand gripped hers, not too tightly, but clasped with intention, deliberation, choice. She was very aware of the long length of him standing before her, her indigo robes brushing against his purple trews, the heat radiating through the layers of cloth.

"I'm not certain," he said finally, "that I am currently capable of anything *more*, myself."

Pali let out her breath, relieved, and knew she was blushing, and was glad that he was taller than she, looking over her head. He was always so confident, so supremely certain of himself—

No. He too was raw, bruised, uncertain, unready for anything more than the beginning over again of something ... new.

She stepped back, and looked up at him. "What did you mean, that first time you said we should get married?"

He held himself terrifically still, and then he smiled, a small, rueful, gentle smile. She had never thought of him as being *kind*; but he could be. He was.

"Two lodestones meeting for the first time," he said. "You were so magnificent, and so mysterious. I wanted to spend the rest of my life with you, to learn who you were beneath those robes, behind that sword, when you smiled." He paused, and bit his lip, and then offered her an even smaller, shyer smile. "I still do."

She swallowed, her heart thundering, but she had known the truth then, and parried it, and she would deflect no longer. "So do I."

She might not have added anything further, except that she knew the ways of epics, of myths, of legends in the making, and she knew that if she would not wish for it with the third feather, then she must submit to the terms of the quest. She hesitated, but the next step of this one was ... *Be generous* ... and she could do that. She would.

Therefore she said: "Will you tell me about your viceroy?"

Fitzroy spluttered a laugh. "Really? You'd like to hear about Kip? I didn't think you, ah ..."

"I despise him," she said resolutely, looking straight at him. "I have sworn vengeance upon him for the hurt he has done one of *mine*. If you want both of us in your life, as I presume you do—"

"If I—yes. I do."

There was a sparkle in his eyes. Pali presumed it wasn't the prelude to him turning her into an item of furniture. She fixed him with her sternest, most redoubtably scholarly mien.

"You'll have to convince me he's worth it."

"Ah," he said, lips twitching. "A challenge for us to share."

When the quest was true the path had always unfurled before her, one step at a time. She knew the tracks of what she was looking for, now, even if she still did not know what awaited her at the end.

She shrugged, elaborately nonchalant, grinning. "I was given understand that you needed a new hobby."

~

They managed to walk back to Sardeet's village in perfect amity. It was pleasant, as a change.

To be honest, Pali was only able to do this because she was imagining the look on Jullanar's face when they arrived back, together, having talked through their emotions and successfully come out the other side.

Fitzroy was humming, but that could have meant anything.

They spent a few minutes wandering over the hillsides, never far from each other, looking for the flying carpet, and then after Pali had carefully shaken it out and folded it back into its small, compact shape, they walked shoulder-to shoulder, looking forward, together.

"Kip hums *Aurora*," he said as they passed under the stone archway.

"Does he," said Pali.

"All the time."

Jullanar was going to be *so* proud of her for not saying anything.

The best thing, Pali reflected, was that Basil had *undoubtedly* told Jullanar all sorts of embarrassing stories about his cousin Kip.

It was only prudent to take what weapons one was offered, after all.

They turned onto the track that led to the tiny hamlet, which still seemed deserted but for the smell of something good cooking in one of the houses. Pali's stomach rumbled, and Fitzroy laughed. "Sardeet has turned into a most excellent cook, hasn't she?"

They talked about their favourites so far of Sardeet's pastries, and Pali felt a warm glow of pride in her sister and the life she had made for herself.

(And if she also reflected that it was good that Sardeet was her *younger* sister, and therefore did not have nearly so many embarrassing stories of Pali as, say, Arzu might, well, that too was only prudent.)

At Sardeet's café Fitzroy gave Pali a sly, conspiratorial grin and then turned sternly, even imperiously, to Jullanar. "Jullanar!"

"Fitzroy!" Jullanar cried back, unfazed. She was sitting at a table with her crochet, but did not appear to be working hard, for one of the tiger-cats was lying on her lap with its paws in the air, snoring loudly.

"How could you not have immediately informed me that you are acquainted with Basil el Mdang sayo White?"

Jullanar's eyebrows raised up. She had smudges of a silvery-purple glitter in her hair, which amused Pali more than it probably should have. "I'm impressed you can say 'Mdang' properly."

"I've been well instructed."

"Which cousin—*oh*," she said, her smile widening. "You know Kip, don't you? Basil said that in his letters—"

"He received them? And didn't reply?—" Fitzroy turned sharply to Sardeet, who was sorting papers behind her counter. "Sardeet, may I have my letter back, please? I must inform Kip that his cousin Basil is alive."

"I'm sorry," Sardeet replied placidly, "but I sent it. You sounded as if you thought the other letters were quite urgent, and I had one for my penpal all ready to go."

"If I write another—"

"Well, of course, you *may*," Sardeet said, coming around the counter with her papers. "But I won't be able to send it for a fortnight. Perhaps two." She smiled fondly at the dumpling-creature snoring in Jullanar's lap, and gestured at the other one, which was similarly asleep on a chair in the window. "Kissie and Pea are *all* tuckered out, poor things, sending *four* letters to Zunidh and receiving one back!"

Pali wondered if she wanted to know how Sardeet was able to send letters to another world by the agency or assistance of two magical armadillos, but before she could ask Jullanar interrupted. "Sardeet's been reading out her letter, telling me all the gossip from your palace, Fitzroy."

"Oh?" Pali asked obediently, sitting down next to Jullanar and stroking the so-called tiger. Kissie, she thought. She added, in a pretend whisper, "You should be proud of us, Jullanar, we talked about our emotions."

Jullanar bit back a giggle as Fitzroy huffed and sat down across from them. "We spoke of many things," Fitzroy declared. "Where's Masseo? He'll be pleased too."

"He's gone to visit the local smith," Jullanar replied, and then gave them both a bright, genuine smile. "I *am* very proud of you, well done!"

Fitzroy sniffed magisterially, but he had a happy glint in his eyes. "What's this gossip, then?" he asked Sardeet, stealing one of the tartlets off Jullanar's plate. "Let me guess: They are all professing to be prostrate with grief at my absence, but in reality are doing just fine with my viceroy at the helm. Someone is in a tizzy because one of Kip's reforms is marginally impinging on their untaxable income. Someone else is campaigning on behalf of, oh, sea turtles. And the

Nijani police service has held another strike." He grinned, as at some private joke.

Pali looked at Jullanar, who whispered, "Sea turtles?" And then they giggled quietly together until Fitzroy and Sardeet both frowned at them. Pali didn't care, because she was with Jullanar and Sardeet and she had a new quest to follow and Fitzroy, well, he was Fitzroy.

"I have heard a great deal about sea turtles," he said, pretending to be wearied of the subject. "And the rest? How perspicacious and well-connected *is* your penpal? Are they in the Palace? How did you meet them?"

Sardeet sighed, then smiled at him. "We've never met in person, alas. Soon, I hope, now that we're travelling—especially with *you* in the company."

Serendipity and wild magic, of course.

Pali could not pretend it didn't tend to make things more interesting, travelling with a wild mage.

"You're too kind," Fitzroy replied. "Please, go on. You've never met in person ..."

Sardeet blushed, and Pali made a mental note to ask her about this penpal later on, in a quiet moment, when a bit of sororal teasing was called for.

"After I failed to get myself arrested, I wrote to the embassy explaining the situation—that you were really Fitzroy Angursell and it was imperative I be taken up before you—and someone wrote back, and the letter was so kind and funny and interesting I continued the correspondence." Sardeet chuckled. "At first we had to go the usual route, with the traders, but then I found that Kissie and Pea could activate this pair of stone pendants I found once and create a small portal between them, just big and stable enough to send a letter through to Zunidh."

Fitzroy regarded her with amazement. "You are incredible, Sardeet."

She flapped her hand at him. "Thank you, dear. Do you want to know the rest of the gossip?"

"Oh yes," he said, settling down with another of the tarts. "What could possibly top that?"

"Let's see," Sardeet said, glancing down at her letter and skimming for a moment before she said, "Oh! Apparently your viceroy has made you Poet Laureate."

Pali got up and briskly prevented Fitzroy from choking to death on his tartlet.

"There," she said, sitting back down, this time beside him. "Remember this, Fitzroy: *he* made you choke, and I saved you." She nodded firmly, as he started to laugh, and turned back to her sister. "Do go on, Sardeet. We're going to need *all* the details."

AUTHOR'S NOTE

The Redoubtable Pali Avramapul is the second book of The Red Company Reformed series, after *The Return of Fitzroy Angursell*. Look for the next book in 2023.

In the meantime, the adventures of Fitzroy's splendid viceroy, Basil's Cousin Kip, are to be found in *The Hands of the Emperor* and its forthcoming sequel, *At the Feet of the Sun* (autumn 2022).

And if you haven't been introduced to the younger Pali and her sisters Sardeet and Arzu, the first two Sisters Avramapul books (*The Bride of the Blue Wind* and *The Warrior of the Third Veil*) are available, with the third, *The Weaver of the Middle Desert*, forthcoming later 2022.

Further details of all my books are available on my website, www.victoriagoddard.ca.

Printed in the USA
CPSIA information can be obtained
at www.ICGtesting.com
LVHW070623180923
758461LV00001B/97

9 781988 908571